...ses!

ONE KISS . . .

Sighing gently, she laid her head back down on his chest. She could feel the steady thumping of his heart beneath her cheek. "The villagefolk say that when you ride out in the middle of the night, there is a hump on your back. They say you are a terrible monster; no one would dare to fâce you in the dark. They say you put people in chains, in the dungeon, and torture them until they scream for mercy . . ."

"And what do you think?" He lifted a strand of her ebony hair and pressed it to his lips.

"I think you might do those things. But very slowly . . . not fast, as rumor has it. Slow, slow torture . . ."

His lips brushed her cheek. "How would you like your torture, Juel . . . swiftly or slowly?"

Lifting herself, she splayed her cool hands upon his broad chest and looked deeply into his brown eyes. She could not find her voice to answer him. Then he was touching her, kissing her fingertips, then her lips, gently at first.

"Sweet Jesus," he murmured, "you are beautiful. So soft. So warm. So tantalizing."

Misty tendrils of desire swirled about her like sensuous fog. Her head was back and he was kissing her throat. Her arms went around him, pulling him closer. "Slowly, please," she murmured as her lips found his . . .

SONYA T. PELTON

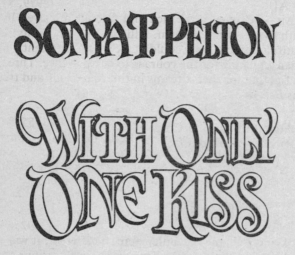

WITH ONLY ONE KISS

ZEBRA BOOKS
KENSINGTON PUBLISHING CORP.

ZEBRA BOOKS

are published by

Kensington Publishing Corp.
475 Park Avenue South
New York, NY 10016

First Printing: December 1992

Printed in the United States of America

Part One

With Only One Kiss

The Story

The flames from the fireplace shone in their eyes and they were as bright as Juel's . . .

"Once upon a time there was a maiden who sat upon a hill, on a log, reading a story. A dragon intruded and breathed a long flame that knocked her off the log. She was stunned. But her armor was made so well that the dragon's fire could not penetrate the links."

"And?"

Juel Reynaude smiled down at the children on the floor and held up a slender finger. "There wasn't a chink in her armor."

"What about the dragon?" one of the orphan children wanted to know. Another asked, "What was she *reading?*"

"Wait," Juel said, her greenish-hazel eyes moving slowly along the curve of children below her. "I'm not finished. This was a scary dragon who loved a lady. A spell had been cast on a man, turning him into a dragon and he couldn't be turned back into a real man until she kissed him. This would also turn her into a princess."

7

The children giggled shyly and Juel went on. "Then she had to get close enough, despite his heat, to lay a kiss on his scaly and scary face. In his spell he did not know her and breathed fire on her. But the intricate pieces of her armor were made of small parts carefully fitted and riveted together. Her armor pressed lightly upon her body and the metal joints moved freely. She almost forgot she wore it until she felt a crossbow's arrow strike her. But this her armor turned easily aside."

"What about a lance?" one of the older boys asked.

"A lance glanced harmlessly off her cuirasses because the plates were joined like expensive glass and a dagger could not even pierce and enter."

Eyes, so big, so bright, looked up at her. "What happened then?"

The moment was tense and Juel leaned forward, elbows on her knees. "She got near enough to that flaming dragon and planted a kiss on his face."

Seven voices sang out, "And?"

The young woman smiled and her lips were a mysterious curve of sweetness as she said: "We shall have to see . . ."

Prologue

A church not far from Sutherland Castle
1395

"England was thrown into a panic by the news: the enemy, the French, were riding over the country, slaying, burning, destroying. Joined by a group of Spaniards, they landed at Rye opposite Boulogne and subjected it to three days of savagery—looting, burning, killing men, women, and children and carrying off girls to the ships. It was a deliberate emulation of the English savagery inflicted on the smaller towns and villages of northern France . . ."

After reading the ancient words, in the passion of Our Lord as told in the book of Matthew, the holy man folded his hands on the book and rested his head on them. Before him, the candle burned with a bright little flame, still and straight. He rested immobile. His head was still on his hands until the candle guttered out, just about the time the first shimmer of dawn came slanting down through the window high up in the wall. He knew what must come.

9

But first the people would come. There was no time to warn them or hide them. And the bell which usually sounded the alarm had been taken down for repairs. Dear God, he knew it would be Scardon this time. Father Luke Grande had come late in the night to inform him of the pillagers coming ever near.

At first the people came blissfully unaware to the parish church, from manor, and wattle and daub houses.

They felt it all at once, the way the air stands silent preceding a violent storm.

"Mummy?"

"Hush, son." Julia Sutherland patted Orion's dark, silky head. "Oh . . . listen . . . listen . . ." She said a prayer he could not hear . . .

A humming sound such as swarming bees might make arose from the gathering in the churchyard. Suddenly it stopped as the war-horses galloped into sight. There came an intense silence, so complete that the people could hear every creak and jingle, every thud of hooves over the soft earth of the open field.

A cat sneaked out of the church portal, and the boy with the deep-brown eyes and dark, silken hair watched it as long as he could and craned his neck to do so. He did not feel the presence of death all about him as the adults did. He kept his eyes on the cat, carefully watching each move as the gray fuzzball crept belly down out of the church.

The boy, Orion, giggled. The cat's back was covered with bits of straw and its whiskered mouth twitched as it watched its prey. A surprised sigh left the boy as he sighted the scurrying mouse and his eyes widened as the cat pounced. "Mummy . . . look!"

Their blades glinted brilliantly when catching the light and Orion's head jerked this way and that with the curiosity of a small boy. He turned to his mother, then to his father. Their faces looked strange, gray with horror and fear. He pumped her hand, but she only stared straight ahead. At the horses coming . . . and the blades held aloft.

Julia was suddenly not so still. She grabbed her son's hand and tugged her husband's sleeve.

"Inside," she yelled. "Everyone inside. They have come to kill. We must pray. Hurry!"

John Scardon, along with his band of rugged and rowdy drunken knights, had plunged into their usual frenzy of pillage and murder and rape.

"Come!" Scardon ordered his men. "There might be a boy I might like."

The wayward knights frowned but followed their conquering master who would obtain anything by force no matter what anyone thought of his evil deeds. He had violated women and some girls. But a *boy?*

"They have moved inside the chapel," Scardon hissed. "Gone the back way, some of them to escape. You. And you. Go!"

Hooves of the great war-horses clattered up the stone steps and then entered the dimness of the church, Scardon looking like the devil himself. His eyes slanted into his skull as he looked about. "You, there . . ." He gestured as he saw the boy. "Outside where I can get a better look."

Scardon watched them move slowly.

Inside the chapel a richly dressed man stood and

11

crossed himself, holding his wife and son behind him while praying these baseborn pillaging knights would not harm his family.

"No! You must not!"

Colin Sutherland's wife Julia was a bold woman. When she saw the villagers being slain, falling left and right like discarded puppets and dolls, she stepped out of the chapel ready to battle the first ravaging knight she came upon.

Scardon spoke. "Ah. A fine lad."

The four-year-old boy broke from his father's hold and tore after his mother. Frightened and confused, his little legs pumped fast. He had to help her, somehow. His mind told him this was not the usual church service. Something was wrong . . . the bad men were going to hurt Mummy!

"Son!" Colin Sutherland ran after the boy. "Come back . . . son!"

A sword was raised aloft again and promptly sliced through the back of Colin's neck.

"Son!"

This was the last Colin breathed, for he was slain before he could reach his wife and son. Cut down, lying in a pool of blood, the lad's father stared with sightless eyes at his son, who stood looking down with horror awash on his sweet boy-face.

Now Orion felt the presence of death all about him and it seeped through his bones like a cutting gray wind off a winter sea. His face was as white as a meadow flower and he gulped a quick breath.

A bloodied blade was raised to Julia and her head would have been severed had not a man on a black destrier stayed his knight's hand.

"No! Leave her. And the boy." Scardon whirled his wild-eyed mount. "Take her." His voice was lower as he reached for the boy.

"What say you?" asked his man-at-arms. "Take the boy and the woman?"

Scardon looked the devil himself. An ugly man possessing a hooked nose in a skinny face, Scardon was a lean, mean individual with upward-slanting black eyes. And his man knew Scardon was not to be defied in anything. Otherwise it could go bad for him; he could be killed, too.

"Yes, both, you idiot." Scardon reached for Orion and the dismounted man handed him up. Scardon looked down at the handsome boy with the glistening brown eyes. "He will be my son," he proclaimed. He'd always wanted a son, yet—even though he tried—he'd not been able to get a woman to take his seed.

The knight Hadwin took the woman onto his own horse, grateful that she had come quietly. He was an evil-looking man with a scar that ran from his forehead down to his cheek and he had one stone-white, sightless eye. But there was a fire in Julia. Her willingness to obey was none other than her wish that she not be parted from her son. She knew her own obstinate folly had brought them to this pass when she had faced the villains down.

Julia hung her head. Her flowing spice-brown hair mantled the dejected stoop of her shoulders. Her soft ivory hands lifted to adjust her hood and she hid her shame in the soft folds of the heavy brocade cape trimmed with green velvet. The horrible man named Scardon must be obeyed. She watched the wind ruffle her son's dark hair and caress his smooth cheeks. Obey.

Whatever the cost, Julia knew this.

"Your name," Scardon snapped at the woman. "Now!"

Chin high, she answered, "Julia Sutherland."

"I am Baron John Scardon," he said with devilish pride.

She was not glad to meet him; she said nothing.

"From where do you come?"

Julia swallowed her grief as she tore her staring eyes from her dead husband and looked past the evil man's face. "My home—Sutherland Castle."

Scardon stroked his chin. "Good. I've need of a new stronghold in this area." He turned to his men. "We go there." To Julia, he said, "Tell us the way." His eyes glittered dangerously. "And don't lie," he warned her, dragging his gaze sharply to the boy.

Julia gasped softly. In times of acknowledged peace, they'd sent all their hired knights home; Sutherland stood unprotected and open to this robber baron.

"We will take Sutherland Castle before nightfall." Scardon's eyes fell over Julia with shining lust.

In the horror-filled moments of his father's death, the boy Orion had forgotten everything, his memory blotted out in a single swipe. All Orion knew was that this nice man had protected him and now held him gently. Neither did Orion give a care that the robber baron stroked his cheek now and then.

The boy did not see the dread in his mother's eyes as she cursed the bloody bastards. And she prayed, very hard, all the way to Sutherland Castle.

Chapter One

East Sussex, England
1415

How could she have gotten lost? So utterly lost.
She had been in this forest so many times before.

Two nights alone in the dark. The March nights were chilly and damp, even beneath the fronds and the ferns. Spongy moss served as Juel's pillow and night creatures sang lullabyes to her, silvery and lyrical.

Sinking into the forest again, the sun was a huge red ball. Resting now, she wriggled her toes that were sore from so much walking. The wood shoes fastened to her feet by cloth straps had begun to hurt. And her blue homespun gown of swanskin—a soft woolen tunic made in four sections with side seams and a seam center front and back—was snagged and torn at the hem. She carried an old book.

Juel's face pressed on the warm bark of a tree trunk while she rested for a time before finding a place for the night. If she moved the slightest out of the sun's rays

15

she could feel the chill of the earth coming on, seeping into her bones that had not warmed fully from the previous night.

At times she couldn't see the sun at all, only the red glow invading, coloring her surroundings. Her heavy hair swirled about her like a dark mantle of rich satin, tangled now from being uncombed. Her eyes were weary in their search for a flickering gleam which would take her back to the world outside this wooded prison.

I'll not sleep yet, Juel told herself, *but keep on till the moon is high.*

She walked again, a lone figure in the wood. Now the moon shone fitfully among the fluffy clouds seen intermittently, and she guided herself by its uncertain gleams, pausing occasionally in deep phantom shade to wait for more light.

She clutched the cloth sack for berry hunting to her waist and walked, each step hurting her feet more than the last. She'd been hunting wild whimberries two days before, and she still carried the sack, to store food when coming upon it and to hold her book. But there were only a few whimberries and cloudberries and edible herbs left; by morning she'd have to find more food. If she could find a stream she might even be able to catch trout.

Juel came to a spot where she could rest for the night. It looked comfortable with all the leaves and moss, a slight depression in the earth where she could lie down and cover herself with fronds and ferns. Placing her berry bag at the foot of a tall larch tree, she slumped to the spongy forest floor and looked around. With so much moss in the area, there could be water nearby, she told herself. She'd find out in the morning. She hadn't had a drink since yesterday morning when she had drained her receptacle of the last drop.

Too weary even to eat the berries, Juel closed her eyes, wishing she was back at the little house in the clearing where she lived with her father. Her brother was away on a pilgrimage just now; otherwise he'd have found her by now.

A tear squeezed out of her eye. Jay was always going away on long journeys. He was searching for something, but no one knew just what, not even Jay.

Juel stared up at the cloud-capped trees. There were birches, larches, oaks, elms in this forest. She had been there hundreds of times, had never gotten lost, but this time had gone farther from home than ever in her search for the whimberries, or cloudberries, she loved so much. To make pies, the whimberries were the best. But she'd best not think of pie just now . . .

A huge swallowtail butterfly swooped down, alarming Juel for the brief moment she thought it was a big bird. Her brother had pinned one down one time and measured the wing span of that particular butterfly, coming to four inches; a giant of a butterfly.

She missed her brother Jay who was older than her by four years. She herself was nearing twenty. Jay had taught her much about life. As villein to Orion Sutherland, her father, Peter, had been too busy. Some said Orion was King Henry's secret agent and that he did not like to be linked with the Scardon name. But what did she really know of him? She had never met Orion Sutherland, but there were rumors that he was a dark individual with grim facial cast, he was a hunchback, born a bastard with an evil spirit. He roamed foul-tempered, through the dungeons of the tower, or The Keep as it was called in Sussex. And on top of everything else there was supposed to be a ghost, a dragon, or a ghoul that followed him about.

Bah! Dragons in the tower? She didn't believe it.

Juel shivered and bemoaned her situation. *I am so cut off from the world. Alone. I've been alone, but never this isolated from the circle of hearth and family.*

I am hungry, too. I could eat a whole pig.

Cold, getting cold. All I have is leaves and ferns.

She thought of her father. Kind-hearted and gentle Peter Reynaude. A woodcutter and rich peasant. He'd worked harder than the rest, so he would have more wealth. But to the nobles the family was still peasants. Villeins. They weren't free. They owed heavy labor service to their lord, Orion Sutherland, were subject to his manorial court, bound to the land, and subject to certain feudal dues.

Her mother had died several years ago. No one had known what had ailed her, and the doctor had arrived too late to save her. Papa said he saw Dalenna's spirit depart and float into a stream of wondrous light which drew her upward. To heaven, Peter Reynaude had said. Now she was gone and they missed her very much.

They lived in a one-story, wood-framed house with thatched roof and plaster walls of clay, stone, and pebbles. It even had tiny windows, walled chimneys, a stone floor outside in back for enjoying their weedy little garden. She wasn't much for gardening; she'd rather read bound manuscripts, books, or work on

18

ledgers under the elms out back and make up stories for the orphans.

Dragons were her favorite subjects. Though only fairy tales, images she often got while daydreaming, they still delighted the children and herself as well.

Juel popped a few berries into her mouth. After she had swallowed them, she found she was hungrier than ever. *Think,* she instructed herself. *Keep your mind off food and a soft bed of duck and goose feathers.*

Home. Their home contained a trestle table with benches, two other plain tables, featherbeds, chests of good oak, cupboards, wardrobes, iron and tin cooking pots, clay bowls and jugs, homemade baskets, wooden buckets and washtubs. All this in addition to farming tools. Compared to their neighbors, her family was rich, but the lord of the manor could come and take all of it for taxes or whatever, all of it, anytime he pleased. So what good was it? she wondered. When you die, someone else gets it. You couldn't take it with you to heaven.

Even so, Peter had even acquired a few vessels of copper, glass, and silver. They employed ten field hands, six woodcutters, and Peter had given Juel a dowry of a hefty bag of gold, plus a fur-trimmed mantle and fur bedcover, and had hoarded money to send his son to a university. Regularly, they ate pork and fowl roasted on a spit. Peter also had access to eggs, cheese, onions and garlic, peas, beans, salt fish, and lard. And she grew some leafy vegetables in her own kitchen garden, cooked fruits in juice or dried them for winter, baked rye bread, and collected honey.

Neither slave nor entirely free, Peter belonged to the

estate of Baron Sutherland. He was under obligation to pay rent or work (in his case, as woodcutter) for use of the land. In turn, he could enjoy the right of protection and justice.

As villein, Peter also was obligated to provide a constant supply of firewood and care for the stables and kennels. The spinning, weaving, laundering, and other crafts for the manor, or keep, were done by women. Juel had never been called to The Keep, nor had Sutherland come to their home. Someday, Juel knew, she might be called to perform these women's duties, especially should Orion Sutherland wed.

Knight. Orion Sutherland. Baron Herstmonceux. Lord.

What did one call such a man? How would you even know how to address him? She hoped she'd never meet him face-to-face and have to do these women's things. She worked for her family, not some bad-tempered hunchback who crept about in the shadows like a fire-breathing dragon who ate people for his dinner.

It was growing darker and she wished to be back in her cozy little home with a book and her cats following her about and keeping her company on lonely nights.

Oh, how did I ever get myself lost! Will I ever come out of this woody green forest alive? Dead, she would never know what it would be like to have—? To be—? What was she trying to ask herself? What more could she want? She had a wonderful brother and father. She was free to worship God. She had food. Clothes. Pets. Friends, though they were mostly children. There were so many things to see and do in a day. Discoveries to be made. Flowers to smell. Babies being born. Couples holding hands . . . There, that was it! She'd never held hands with a man—as lovers do. Her hand had been grasped and she'd been kissed when not wanting to be kissed, touched when not wanting to be touched.

"Someday you'll wed," Peter had said. "You're too comely to end up an old woman alone with just your cats and your housework. You're a smart girl. Hear me, Juel, and hear me well: You won't marry a poor man. He'll be rich as the baron himself and not so hard to look at, either. He'll fill his eyes with your pretty face and hear your pleasant voice. You will marry and give me grandsons."

Pretty? Juel had thought. Oh, no, she could not be called pretty. Her eyes were the color of garden weeds. Her hair was too dark and too thick. Though she'd never seen herself in a looking glass, just the pond, she knew her nose was too long, her legs too skinny, her breasts too small, her buttocks too round, her ears like seashells . . . She could go on and on. Her father had just been kind, that's all.

Who would want her? Juel shrugged against the tree and plucked the petals from a yellow woodflower. The answer was, No one. Just as her answer would be to a man: I want no one. I have all. There is no need for more.

She didn't need babies. She had the orphans. They needed her.

Juel inhaled the woodland flowers. She felt like she'd become a tree or a plant herself. Like in a fairy story. But she was only a simple maiden who loved to read and tell stories.

Young girls, and boys, were usually married at the

age of fourteen or soon after. In cases of the highborn, it was frequently legally arranged in childhood, even infancy. Twenty now, Juel was well past the age of marriageability.

One of Jay's friends had described the perfect woman to her brother. He said she possessed a sweet pink mouth, hazel eyes, dainty brow, round chin, camellia throat, firm high breasts, well-made thighs and legs—and was intelligent and resourceful.

"Morgan said she is a luscious damsel." Jay had looked at her with his handsome grin. "You, sister, he speaks of you."

And Juel had gawked at Jay. "What do you say? Me?" She laughed and struck the wall with an open hand, thinking this most funny.

"We'll see one day. You won't laugh, then" was all Jay had added. He'd walked away and left her frowning, talking to herself. "He could not have meant it. No. My brother makes jest with me again." That was that. Until the next day.

Juel had laughed when she encountered the fellow with the big, bold eyes. Not merely words this time, words he knew Jay would reveal to her, Morgan had gone one further, putting a hand where it should not have been put, and so he had gotten his arm broken by her angry brother Jay. She had not liked Morgan touching her. Not only because his actions were uncalled for, but he had touched a secret part of her deep down inside. A part that did not belong to Morgan Macnair.

Little of life was hidden from the unmarried girl, noble or otherwise. Behind a woodshed where she had been gathering wild-duck eggs, Juel had overheard her brother speaking to the bold redhead of Herstmonceux. "Tell me true, Lily, is there hair between your legs?" Lily had replied most saucily, "None at all, Jay Reynaude, Rascal of Herstmonceux." Jay came back with, "I believe you, Lily, since grass does not grow on well-beaten paths." And Juel had tiptoed away, biting her lip to keep from giggling out loud. They did not call her brother Jay Lover or Manstaff for nothing.

Jay always said with roguish laughter that women were, "deceivers, changeable, quarrelsome bitches, petulant, two-faced, lewd, shameless," and with another laugh had added, "Although not necessarily all of these at once." Her brother had come home from the university with high-sounding words. And he had become very grown up, quite the handsome devil even though his nose was "still sharp as a knife and his eyes still pierced your soul," as the flirting females said.

Being unmarried, Juel had been denounced by a priest of the severest order for being too occupied with orphans and books, being overindustrious, and too earthbound to give due thought to divine things. He had said she should either marry or become a nun!

Bah!

Juel frowned now in her little sanctuary in the woods and punched her pillow of moss. Bloody men, she snorted. She did think of divine things and was a lover of God. That silly priest was wrong. Celibacy and virginity were perfect and preferred states because they allowed total love of God. But what of romance? Juel wondered about that at times when she had flights of fantasy and into her vision would come a big,

23

handsome knight. He would smile down at her and she would get goosepimples all over.

In *Roman de la Rose,* the bible of love, the Lover wins his Rose in an unabashed description of opening the bud, spreading the petals, and spilling a little seed just in the center and—*Oh, my God!*—"searching the calyx to its inmost depths."

Juel blushed in the dark.

The clerical conception of women held that beauty in them was false and artful, that it disguised untruth and physical wantonness. "Wheresoever Beauty shows upon the face," warned the priests, "there lurks much filth beneath the skin."

Well, no one could call Juel Reynaude one of those women! She was half French. But certainly not wanton nor dirty.

To hold back her fears of the dark, deep night coming, Juel kept up her train of thoughts, hoping they would induce her to fall into deep slumber. That way, it would be morning when next she opened her eyes.

Quickly, sleep, come quickly, she thought. *I am afraid to be alone, not knowing what will sneak up on me in the dark.* She was deeper into the woods now and felt even more helpless than the last two nights she'd spent there. The darkness of a house was different and she was used to getting around in their simple dwelling in the dark. True, the noble lords, the rich, could prolong time by torchlight and candles. For others, night was as dark as nature intended.

She prayed there were no ghouls, ghosts, sorcerers, or demons in these woods. Fairies did not frighten her much, though they could touch and manipulate humans. Fairies or angels could take you to heaven, but demons, with shrouds of black for bodies, and glowing red eyes, could gather round and violently escort a departed soul into the shadows of hell. This was where the people who caused others harm went. To hell.

As Juel was falling asleep, she wondered if the dark, bad-tempered Orion Sutherland would go to hell. She knew she would never see him there—ever—because she planned on going to heaven!

Chapter Two

"Wench Dawn! More!"

Pacing the chamber and tossing things about, Orion shouted for more drink. But no one came. Not even the kitchenmaid Dawn. He had been ranting and raving for hours and everyone had hastened from his path.

Everyone was hiding from him. Terrified, they cringed and fled. That was all right. He would get more himself.

Crunching the heels of his boots over broken shards of pottery and glass—expensive glass—he ran shaking fingers through his hair, raking the limp, unkempt strands back over his shoulders. It was useless, for when he slumped forward over a table, slapping his hands on top, his long dark hair covered the handsome features of his face once again. His clothes hung loosely on his tall frame, and he smelled of sour wine.

Who cared? No one saw him.

"I am cursed!" he shouted and gnashed his teeth. His eyes were devil black and his soul felt the same. There was a name for his pain. It would come to him soon.

Was it a man's name? A woman's?

His laugh was coarse, his words foul. Perhaps it was both man and woman. He had never received good from either one. Rajahr and Shadow, they were the only ones that counted in his life. His faithful servant and his beloved pet.

Orion could hear the woodland creatures off in the distance as night settled in. His heart was heavy as he reached for the half-empty vessel of wine and tossed the red liquid down his throat. As he looked up, his eyes were full of the past. There was no peace, no beauty of life in his world. It was dark and ugly, full of demons that haunted him.

He sighed and looked around with empty eyes.

Now he had gone and chased off the only ones that mattered: Rajahr and Shadow. They would not be returning this night. He was alone, as usual, when he imbibed overmuch.

Alone. He wanted it that way. He was drunk. He wanted it that way, too. The king. King Henry. He would continue to ride for him at night, spy for him.

He was married. By God, married! Wed to the bitch by proxy. What was she to be like? Would she run from him, too? Was there ever to be anyone who would tame the savage beast in him?

Orion laughed, a deep, resounding sound in the huge chamber, and he answered this himself: No.

He would always feel alone in his dark soul.

Orion slept. He was dreaming of a young woman with heavy hair that swirled about her like a mantle of dark, rich silk . . . no . . . satin. She was lost. As lost as

28

he was, day and night.

Orion looked at her in his dream. She was truly lost, locked in her wooden prison. Aye. Bars of woods encircled her, kept her frightened and alone. She was alone, aye, but never as alone as he was, even surrounded by castlefolk all the day.

He kept watching her in his dream. He followed her. The moon shone fitfully as she clutched a sack of cloth. Whimberries and books came to his sleeping mind.

Now he could see a little house in a clearing. She was searching for her home and could not find it. He had almost reached her when a giant swallowtail butterfly swooping down snatched her up. He heard her voice as the butterfly took her away.

"Dragon!"

He looked up, seeing her dark hair swirling in the purple mist. "I am not a dragon!" he shouted back to her in a voice filled with anger and torment.

Her voice was drifting away fast. "Then . . . who are youuuu . . . ?"

"I am . . ." Orion murmured restlessly. "I am . . . lost."

She did not answer.

Not far away, in the woods, Juel spoke to herself: *Thoughts, more thoughts. What should I think of next? Thoughts keep me company. But they must be deep thoughts, otherwise my mind will stray to the dark closing in.*

Deschamps, the poet, spouted nonsense when he spoke about women in the *Miroir de Mariage,* where marriage is depicted as a painful slavery of suffering, sorrow, and jealousy—*My God!*—for the husband!

Husband. Juel had decided when she turned thirteen that she didn't want one. She needn't marry, Papa said, not until she was ready.

An owl hooted in a tree nearby, *Who? Who?* And Juel's nerves gave a little leap. "Well, sir owl, no one. No man, that's who!" She punched her moss again. "Humph!"

Men were dragons, except for Papa. Peter Reynaude had not wed again after the death of her dear mother. And her brother Jay swore he'd never take a lady to wife, either. So she would not take a husband. As plain as that. No man could force her, she thought, and flexed a muscle beneath her head. Just let him try!

Obedient to a man other than Papa? Never!

A manual of conduct composed by a man of Paris for his fifteen-year-old wife stated, "She should obey her husband's commandments and act according to his pleasure rather than her own . . . *because* His pleasure should come before hers. She should not be arrogant or answer back or contradict him in public. It is the command of God that women should be subject to men . . . and by good obedience a wise woman gains her husband's love and at the end hath what she would of him."

Hath what she would of him. Like what?

The wife's duty was to earn her husband's love and gain peace in marriage by constant attention, good care, submission, docility, patience, and . . . absolutely no nagging. Whew! Rolled into one? "No man can be better bewitched than by giving him what pleaseth him."

Who said *that?* Which of the poets or demanding

noble husbands? Juel shrugged. She didn't remember. *And why am I going over all this? I'm not about to marry or become obedient to any man . . .* she paused, as if in torment. *Then why can't I get all this nonsense out of my mind?*

Pleaseth. Pleaseth him.

Juel turned to her back and looked up at the few twinkling stars she could see. She bent her arms beneath her head. What then, she wondered, pleaseth a man? Papa and Jay were pleased by a good hearty meal laid out on the table; clean dry clothes; swept floors and fresh rushes laid down upon them; beds made neatly; kitchen cleaned, and so on. She had only Papa to please now, since Jay was off fortune hunting in the cog he'd sailed away upon. He'd been gone a year now.

Juel had once worked for a merchant, started when she was fifteen and ended only a few months ago when his new wife said she could not come there to work anymore. Her husband was home now and they could do without Juel. She had managed the merchant's household, his town house, and his business when he was absent. In addition, she supervised sewing, weaving, marketing, directed servants, kept accounts, and even plied some skills in medicine and surgery. Then she would go home to work some more.

She wished she could have half the books the merchant had owned. After returning from university, Jay had taught her how to read in his free time, when he was not getting his fill of the town wenches. Jay was considered handsome, even though his cat-green, lecherous eyes scared a few women away.

Juel had had anything but a leisurely life, yet she still found time to tell stories to her beloved little friends,

31

the orphans. And, much as she enjoyed the company of others, she frequently went to some uninhabited place of beauty and rest: a quiet woodland glade or a lonely churchyard if possible. If she could go to neither, she would go to her room and shut herself away from the world and turn her thoughts inward. Or toward heaven.

Juel thought of her father now. He would not miss her, for he was away to The Keep to cut wood for the wicked Orion, Baron Herstmonceux. Peter had been gone two weeks and would not return till the middle of April, two more weeks away yet.

Would the baron ever call her to come? She hoped not. She did not know the way there; nor had she ever seen either The Keep and its crumbled walls or the manor house of his estate.

The Keep. Such a mysterious place. For a mysterious man. Frightening stories abounded. The place loomed in her night visions. She had had a nightmare that a dragon dwelled there, one that would devour her should she draw near. The baron!

Juel shivered but not from cold. She prayed she was not near The Keep now. Then again, if she *was* near it, she would find her father. He would help her to get back home.

In the morning she would try again to find the way. She had to head toward the sun, did she not? But every time she tried, it seemed she went in circles, had even arrived yesterday in the same place she had started from.

Toward the sun. Follow the sun. Someone had once told her if she ever got lost to study flowers. Tulips, phlox, sweet William, coral bells, and canterbury bells.

When shaded, these turn their heads toward the greatest source of illumination, Jay had told her. The daisylike leopard's bane which flowers in the springtime is a true sun-follower. From sunrise to sunset the leopard's bane flower turns toward the sun. She also had read in the merchant's manuscripts that moss would be found on the north side of trees.

Would that I had some more books, she thought now, books like those the merchant kept in his big library. She loved books, the many bound manuscripts a person could read in one's spare time.

The merchant had also given her hot, spiced wine and she had learned how to prepare it. Hippocras was what it was called. He could afford wine. In her father's house they drank beer, ale, and cider. She liked the cider, but not beer and ale much. She had many times mashed malt for beer and could not stand the smell it gave off.

Now more lonely than ever, Juel looked up at the moon, gazing and hoping to grow drowsy. The creatures of the forest seemed to be settling down . . . but not so herself. All her senses felt alert. She might try walking at night, by the moon. She had once read that the moon can give direction and be an effective guide, though by itself it gave no light, she knew, shining only by the reflection of the light of the sun and other heavenly bodies.

If only the birds and animals could talk, they might tell her how to find her way. Ah! In the early morning the eastern sky would be brighter, and this could give her a sense of east and west. She would try it. What did she have to lose?

The stars passed overhead as Juel blinked and

watched. She blinked drowsily and then her eyes flew open at the sound of scurrying in the leaves. And then all was still again, but only for a time. The stars! With a little imagination you could see designs of people, animals, birds, fish. Capella, Canopus, and Sirices, among other stars, were brilliantly white; and Arcturus, Procyon and Pollux, yellowish . . . Orion?

Orion rises, on its side, due east, irrespective of the observer's position, and reaches its highest point in the heavens over the Equator. It sets due west . . . seven hours after Orion has passed overhead the Southern Cross will be seen to the south in its highest position . . .

Orion. Orion. I love stars. Orion, mythological hunter, handsomest of his race. In Greek and Roman mythology, a hunter whom Diana loved but accidentally killed, he was then placed in the heavens by Diana as a constellation . . . how romantically tragic this. Wait a moment.

Orion!

Juel sat up. That was the name of the Baron Herstmonceux. He was their keeper. She laughed softly. And he lived at The Keep. Not actually *lived* there, in the old stone tower, with its crumbled ruins and rumored to be haunted. Peter said the baron lived in a fine manor. She wondered if he had a scar somewhere on his body. Rumormongers told he was not Scardon kin at all, but a Sutherland; and that he'd lost his mind when just a boy of four or five. Some said he'd lost his parents in a raid while they'd been in church praying. There'd been a massive shock to his system. Poor boy . . . if true.

Juel lay back down, plumping her moss. Orion. She

34

liked the name. Was he truly a dragon of a man? Was it true that he had a hunched back? Did he eat spiders for dinner?

Her dragons, in the stories she told the children, were not all that terrible. Some of them could turn out to be good fellows—of a sort.

Listen to me. My thoughts are rambling. She yawned . . . she was getting tired. At last. Her lashes fluttered and closed over her eyes.

Juel dreamed of flying dragons. She was sound asleep now. But in her dreams she was wide-awake and walking through a strange land. Dragons flew in and out of her dreamscape. She was alone again. The fog was beginning to stir and there was a slight breeze, just enough to roll the fog into thick swirls which drifted through tall grasses like clouds. She walked effortlessly and felt filmy, heavenly, her body astir on air. Or so it seemed.

If someone were to touch her, she was certain the person's hand would pass right through her body and a hand *did* reach out to her just then, and it did just what she felt it would. Passed right through her, as if she were a puffy cloud. And it was a man's hand.

Juel screamed and came instantly awake, her arm shielding her eyes. From what? she wondered. A fire-breathing dragon? No. It felt gentle and warm, like the soft, soothing rays of early-morning sun. She indulged herself in the warmth for a few moments before moving to sit up, her arm falling to the mossy earth. *So, I am alive then?* She thought she must be, since she felt the ground, her aching head, and her cramped muscles.

Her eyes opened and she looked around. A squirrel was busy in the layered carpet of the forest floor. And over there a noisy little blue bird flew from branch to branch. The woodland was awakening and Juel smiled, because the sun was slanting into the piney glade where she had spent the night, unharmed, still alive and well. There were no dragons, friendly or otherwise.

She had made it through another night.

He slept naked.

Rising from his curtained bed, Orion Sutherland donned linen drawers, walked across the room, and peered into the steel mirror. He ran tanned fingers through mussed hair and shook his head, slowly, somewhat painfully.

As he gave a groan, the sound rumbled up from deep within his wide chest.

Clutching the wooden frame which held the basin of cold water, he stood bent for a time, his torso bare. The morning sun slanted in the window to burnish the hairs of his huge, muscled chest. He lifted his head at a sound behind him.

"You spent a sleepless night, but look no worse for wear," said Rajahr as he laid out the long-sleeved tunic and a second tunic of green; sleeveless and lambskin lined. He took a closer look at Orion, noted the red-rimmed eyes, and cocked his head. "Well, perhaps—"

Orion gave a soft snort. "Please, Rajahr. Do not remind me of last night." He donned the clothes, slipped on long hose attached to a belt with a metal buckle. He sat to pull on low boots, then hung his head and sighed deeply. It would be nice to stay abed and not have to dress at all for the day, he thought. But he could not linger abed and had no desire to spend the day

36

alone in his chambers. It was too lonely, even with Shadow for company.

Orion's clothes were not decorated with tassels or feathers, nor adorned with any jewels such as the garments of most other lords. For festive occasions he might wear a silk belt with gold thread, a colorful surcoat, and gold rings with bright stones. But he hardly ever attended any festivities, nor did he entertain anyone but the king and his men.

Orion Sutherland was sometimes called a loner. He surrounded himself with his knights, Rajahr, and his pet monkey, Shadow. He saw King Henry V occasionally. Orion had only come to know the king personally in the last five years, and at that first meeting Henry had been prince. The man had never come to The Keep when John Scardon was in residence. Orion had sought audience with him and told him of his problem. The inheritance of property by the correct bloodlines was an extremely serious matter, part of the whole social order. Their meeting had involved the hauling forth of ancient genealogical rolls, and Henry was still having the Sutherland documents pored over by experts.

Just how much of the Sutherland estate John Scardon owned was unclear. Henry had come to believe there was an unsolved mystery here.

"Where is Shadow?" Orion asked Rajahr.

Rajahr cleared his throat. "I think you frightened him with your drinking last night. He was curled in a ball sleeping on the window seat in the hall." Rajahr clucked. "Poor Shadow."

"He usually sleeps in my room." Orion stood and closed his eyes for a moment. He'd never drink that much again, he swore to himself.

Rajahr read Orion's thoughts. "And you will do it again. Like a dog returns to his vomit."

Orion shuddered. "Do you know where Shadow is or do you not?"

Straightening the bed, Rajahr spoke over his shoulder. "Dawn, the kitchenmaid, was serving him bits of banana and honeyed crust a short time ago. Shadow looked most sad."

"Devil be damned!" Orion flung a goblet from the binge of the night before across the room. The loud clatter as it struck the wall sent his hands slamming over his ears. "Damn again! You needn't remind me who the kitchenmaid is. The little bitch, I told her Shadow must not eat honey; it will upset his system."

"He already soiled that new expensive carpet, on your new expensive oak floors in the—"

"Enough!" A sound like thunder filled the chamber. Orion's voice. "I'll throttle that bitch and feed her carcass to the hogs."

"Your language is foul. As usual." Rajahr adjusted the green-and gold bandeau circling his head; the tails hung down next to his straight gray-black hair in back. "Dawn is not what you say. She sings badly, but is most lovely, her looks befitting a princess. You frightened her last night, you know. You almost took her to your—"

Orion held up his hand and cut the air with it.

"I know. Enough!" Rajahr shouted, folding his arms across his lean chest and grinning when Orion clapped his hands to his ears again.

"You taunt me."

"Yes. You need censure."

Tormented by the demons of the morning after, Orion slumped into a huge red velvet-upholstered chair, big enough to hold his huge frame. Squinting one eye, he peered at Rajahr. He sometimes wondered why he put up with the servant. Huh. Servant? Rajahr was more like his keeper. The wise little Indian had been at The Keep for as long as he could remember. Orion could not recall the time before he turned five years old. It was all a blur, his early childhood. Rajahr had always been there when he was growing up to ease his uncontrollable fears and soothe his black temper.

Rajahr looked at Orion's dark head from behind. He held the goblet that reeked of wine the young man had tossed and wondered what would become of Orion. Now that Scardon was gone these eight years and presumed dead, Orion, being the man's "ward," had taken over as Lord Baron Herstmonceux.

Rajahr had been in John Scardon's service when Scardon brought the boy Orion to this keep. Scardon had sent for Rajahr, who had just come off a ship from India and was looking for a place to settle. Rajahr had long wanted to visit southern England. When he came, he had not meant to stay so long. The dark-haired boy had become his reason for remaining. Rajahr loved Orion like his own son. He had no children of his own, no woman. He was in service to his lord, wholly dedicated to making Orion become well someday. So far he'd failed. Orion was a raging, tormented man who would kill an enemy at the drop of a . . . goblet.

Perhaps when Ranice, the woman Orion had wed by proxy, arrived, Orion would become whole and sane. Rajahr prayed this would happen, but one never knew with Orion Sutherland. He might drive the woman away, tearing her hair out by the roots as she went. Many women had fled from Orion's rages of anger.

King Henry did not see Orion as a madman, but then Orion was always on his best behavior when the king came to check on "matters"; he and Orion would talk long into the night. Rajahr was not dumb. He knew what was going on when Orion became a dark figure that rode out at night alone. And he also knew how to keep secrets, especially where Orion and the king were concerned.

There were other secrets surrounding The Keep. Rajahr knew them all. All but one: about the tower room in the old keep. That was a mystery, and one that must be kept a mystery at all costs. Otherwise, Scardon had warned, Orion's life would end if he went there. "Only Lydia may go back and forth to The Keep," Scardon had instructed. Orion had a great fear of the place, had been taught at an early age he must not go within. He had walked around staring up at the tall stone structure and kept his distance. It was as if a curse waited there for him. One day his curiosity might get the best of him; intoxicated by drink, he would be done in by the curse. But Rajahr was always on guard and had Orion's own knights watching. Just in case.

John Scardon was mean and nasty-tempered, and Orion had taken on the man's traits. There was no virtue in Scardon. He was all bad; there was no help for him. Scardon had taken the boy for long walks in the woods and taught him all the darkness that dwelt within him. Rajahr could not undo what Scardon had indoctrinated into the lad's mind. Rajahr hoped and prayed and watched, looking for the good in Orion. He knew there was a soft-place in Orion's heart. He was kind to birds and animals. They came to him. People were a different story. They did not approach as easily and trod cautiously within his reach.

As Orion went down to breakfast with his knights, Rajahr heard the wind blow as he passed the mullioned window and stopped to stare out the many-paned glass. Expensive glass; all the old windows and walls of the manor's fourth floor had been refurbished. Recently, many of the windowpanes had been broken and had to be replaced. It was well known among the castle folk that Orion was foul-tempered and destructive during his bouts with the bottle.

Rajahr was looking from the manor out to the crumbled ruins surrounding The Keep. The graceful bridges that had spanned from tower to tower had deteriorated. The manor had been built over the ruins of the old castle and there were secret passages that went down into the bowels of the old keep. Only the high, round tower remained of that fortification, its window slits staring down onto the courtyard, housing dark secrets one only dared guess about.

The small man hastened to his tasks.

Chapter Three

Dawn Peyton wiped her fingers on her old, bleached apron to free them of flour dust and turned to the heavy work table in the kitchen. She was baking rissoles, crescent-shaped pastries made of rye flour and stuffed with minced veal cooked in oil. They were Lord Orion's favorite.

Great iron cauldrons hung over the fire on a hook and chain that could be raised and lowered to regulate the temperature. Alice, another kitchen maid, was lifting boiled meat out of the pot with an iron meat hook, a long fork with a wooden handle and prongs attached to the side. She stirred the soup with a long-handled slotted spoon, the end of her sleeve trailing in the broth.

Alice was humming, very pleased with herself because she had a new lover. She had her mind elsewhere, not on her work, dreaming of cat-green eyes and a lean, strongly muscled body. She was preoccupied with her fantasy and didn't hear Dawn speak until the younger woman came to stand before her.

"Alice!" Dawn's voice became louder, stern. "Alice, you must not wear hanging sleeves. You know this." Alice only stared at her and blinked. "How many times have I told you your sleeves slop into the broth when you wait on tables." Dawn stared at the elegant scalloped sleeves with their shiny colored red lining. "Another fancy dress! Where did you get this one? I have not seen it before."

Dawn's eyes lowered and she frowned. Alice's generous breasts jiggled beneath the silk material and she caught Dawn staring there. Alice smiled to herself like a contented cat. She had Dawn here. Alice liked to flaunt her curves before the younger woman, who was flat-chested and hipless. Still, all the handsomest and strongest of Orion's knights sought Dawn out for conversation. Hah! That was because that was all they could get from the sexless little orphan. True, Dawn had long, heavy yellow hair, a winning smile, an angelic face, and . . . that was enough!

Alice stared defiantly into Dawn's nut-brown eyes. She put a hand to her hip and stared down the smaller woman. Or *girl,* she couldn't tell how old Dawn really was. No one knew, because Dawn was an orphan found on a merchant's doorstep when she was only a babe. Looking at her flat chest, her unlined face, Alice guessed Dawn was not more than sixteen. Still, she had looked the same way for the last several years, so she could be twenty for all anyone knew. But Alice had wrinkles near her eyes and mouth; Dawn did not.

"The dress?" Dawn persisted. She was only trying to help Alice stay out of trouble, though Alice never believed this.

That hand was still cocked on Alice's hip. "Wouldn't you just like to know."

"Not really," said Dawn, flipping her fat yellow braid back over her shoulder to keep the ends from touching any of the food.

Rajahr was adamant: the kitchen must be kept clean, foodstuffs handled scrupulously, with care. Clothing must be clean, sleeves kept short while working in the kitchen. The knights overran the rest of the manor, especially the great hall, monopolizing space and making a mess of things. Away from warfare, crusades and training, Orion cared nothing for disciplining his big knights, and Rajahr didn't dare. These were very big knights.

Dawn went on. "You must have gotten a new lover. And that is no business of mine. But this I have to say, to warn you, as many times before: you are a servant, and of the common folk. It is dangerous to imitate your betters. You might have to stand before Lord Orion and you know his temper." She smiled as a visible shudder ran through Alice.

"And?" Alice snipped.

"And Rajahr severely disapproves your flaunting of any gifts from a lover. One can barely tell servant from master when you dress this way."

"Humph. There is not lady of the manor here one can call 'mistress.' Only the lord himself and he hardly dresses better than his knights or the common folk." Alice waved a pastry in the air. "Someone has to brighten this place with a little color. Look at you, girlie, dressed in drabs of brown and green. You look like a little church mouse."

Alice showed her defiance by biting down on a strawberry-filled pastry, yet she shuddered when Dawn gave her a stern look of disapproval. So, she shouldn't eat until her work was done. What did she care? She was on top of the world; she did have a new lover.

"Lord Orion does occasionally have nobles and their ladies come here," Dawn argued softly. "You have to remember, too, Alice, that Lord Orion has been married by proxy and that the Lady Ranice will soon come here. Then let us see you wear the cloth of your betters!"

Dawn kept working, pounding meat and mixing it with bread crumbs, stock, and eggs. This she would poach, producing a delicious quenelle. Lord Orion loved these dumplings. He had many favorite foods, in fact. He loved to eat and drink. But he drank too much. Maybe Lady Ranice would change all that. Dawn liked Lord Orion, even if he did get angry at her and come into the kitchen yelling, and throwing things about, even very sharp utensils. She'd had to duck many times, along with the head cook who often forgot to order mustard. He would catch hell then, mustard was a favorite ingredient among Orion and his knights; it was used by the gallon.

Alice stared at Dawn's quick-moving hands. Besides hardworking, the younger, smaller woman was so efficient, orderly, and methodical that it made Alice sick. She felt deep emotions of jealousy and rivalry. How could Dawn's hands still appear so soft and pretty after all the work she did? Dawn even took on the workload of others so they'd have free time in the village. Still, who did Dawn think she was, always ordering everyone about? She told Cook what to do and could even charm that nasty little Indian Rajahr into seeing things her way. Hah! Dawn made work seem like child's play, like *fun.*

Fun! Alice snorted under her breath. *I'd rather sport in the hayloft with a lusty lean-hipped male—like Jay Reynaude.* Now, there was a man. Too bad she'd never noticed him in Herstmonceux before; of course, he'd been away on a sailing ship.

Alice quickly shot a look at Dawn and her eyes darkened with fear. She'd have to keep Jay away from Dawn; upon seeing the yellow-haired maiden, all her lovers had first sought Dawn out. And when their entreaties failed—which they always did—the gallant wooers came to find Alice.

"I say again—" Alice tossed over her shoulder— "Someone has to brighten up this place."

"Yes," Dawn agreed. "But not you."

Alice did not heed the warning in Dawn's voice. Later that day Rajahr brought Alice before Orion, and it was a sorry day for Alice. Orion's dark mood was made even blacker by the disagreeable symptoms he suffered from his drinking binge. Added to that, Shadow had not come near him all day. The spider monkey was acting true to his name, hiding somewhere and, Rajahr had thought, no doubt afraid of his master repeating his behavior of the night before.

From his slumped position in his great chair, Orion frowned up at the kitchen maid. One long, tanned finger was pressed to his temple, his head inclined to the side, as if the appendage was holding his aching skull up.

Alice blinked and Orion spoke.

"Magnificence in clothes is considered a privilege of nobles, Alice, and those persons should be identifiable by modes of dress forbidden to others."

Alice gawked dumbly. The words were slamming about in her brain. What did he say? She had not understood a word he'd said.

Rajahr had nodded in emphasis to Orion's words. The room suddenly grew still and he looked at the servant as she opened her mouth to speak, but all that came out was a muffled "Huh?"

The manservant leaned to Alice and clarified what Lord Orion had just said, using plainer language. By the time Rajahr straightened, Orion was looking impatient, his brown, bloodshot eyes straying to the mullioned panes of glass. A strange, faraway look entered his eyes, and for a moment his rigid features softened. He looked the handsome young man of twenty-five again, not the usual frowning, angry human that he was every day of his miserable life.

Rajahr caught his lord's look and was instantly concerned. "What is it?" he asked Orion. "Are you feeling worse? If you are, I shall fetch some—"

"No." He waved his hand. "It was nothing . . ." he said but stopped there. There *had* been something, a misty vision of . . . a person. A female. Ranice, perhaps? He had not yet met his wife but had heard she was very beautiful. He was suddenly eager for her arrival at The Keep.

Features no longer soft, Orion forced his attention back to the woman Rajahr had brought before him. He had been informed of Alice's wanton behavior, but this did not concern him overly much; it was her defiance in

48

dressing in rich clothing which irked him.

"How far must your defiance go before I see no other way but to have you punished?" Orion asked her.

Alice stared and blinked at Orion, feeling as if she'd swoon anytime now. He terrified her. He excited her . . . so much she was afraid she'd become a silly fool and fall at his feet. Rajahr usually dealt with her himself. And never, not since she'd bedded with a particular knight of Orion's, had Rajahr brought her before the lord himself. She had had dreams of him, and always when she was with another man she'd imagine it was Orion himself. She almost smiled now because she felt smug and happy. Jay Reynaude had made her feel like a real woman and there had been no pretending Jay was Orion.

Alice knew Orion was awaiting her answer. She wanted to shout, to let him know what others thought of him. He was crazed in the head, nasty, evil-tempered, and a drunkard, too, who crept around at night with that monkey on his back. The castle folk said he rode out at night and the villagefolk had seen him mounted on his dark destrier and entering the woods. Where he went no one knew because no one dared to follow him.

"Alice?"

"Yes, m'lord. I will not wear the fancy clothes of my betters, the clothes I get from my aunt in the village : . ." She paused. "As gifts."

Orion and Rajahr exchanged a look. "Gifts," Orion said. "How did you come by this last one?" he said of the expensive gown she was wearing.

Alice decided swiftly she would tell the truth this

49

time. "I got this one—" she fingered the silky sleeves—
"from Jay of Herstmonceux."

"Jay who?" Rajahr asked the now-nervous kitchen
maid.

"Uh . . . Reynaude."

"Reynaude, Reynaude," said Orion thoughtfully.
"Ah—the woodcutter's son."

"Mmm—yes," Alice said dreamily. "Peter Reynaude
has a daughter, too."

Orion's full, dark eyebrows lifted. "I had no idea."
He pushed himself from the massive chair. "How old?"

Alice frowned, trying to recall. They had talked of
many things in that hour in the hayloft. Jay had told
her he had been away, sailing on a cog, but was now
back to stay. He was looking for his sister. He knew his
father was working right there at the castle. He had left
the hayloft, saying he had to return to their house on
the other side of the big forest to see if Juel was at
home.

"Juel!" blurted Alice.

"What?" Orion frowned, stared at the woman as if
she were an ugly bug he might squash. "I ask you the
age of Peter Reynaude's daughter and all you can think
of is jewels? Woman, you are defiant! I should have you
whipped for your insolence."

Orion took a step toward the cowering kitchen maid
and Rajahr immediately restrained the large hand that
would have clamped on Alice's shoulder. "Wait,"
Rajahr said. "See what she has to say."

"J-Juel," Alice said, cringing back. "Juel, the girl.
Juel Reynaude."

That strange look crossed Orion's features, and

again a vision came to him, of a young woman—dark-haired, delicate, fair-skinned, slim.

Orion whirled to face Rajahr. "Have this Juel Reynaude brought to me. I must see her."

Alice blinked and, shrinking back against the wall, she asked herself what she had done. She should not have mentioned Jay's sister, for he'd told her Juel had led a sheltered life, and was special to them; they did not want her being forced to work at the castle. Juel had never been farther away from home than the village and had only worked for a merchant because that was what she wanted to do. She did not wish to come to The Keep. Alice could understand the girl's fear. Orion's reputation ranged far and wide. He had the disposition of a fire-breathing monster, a dragon no less!

"Ah, m'lord . . ." Alice began, then stopped abruptly when he turned a withering look on her.

"Speak," Orion said, ready to dismiss her since his mind was now on other matters.

"Juel Reynaude is not at home. She . . . she's away just now." Alice hoped this excuse would work, that Lord Orion would not press the issue, that he would let it drop. But this was not to be.

"Well," Orion said. "We shall just have to find her then."

With that, Alice was dismissed.

When Orion was alone he thought about the small house that the woodcutter Peter occupied when he was working for him. He was in need of a permanent woodcutter and carpenter. The man Peter had both a son and a daughter. He could use them, too. Especially the girl. He wondered about her now. Juel Reynaude. Why did that name seem familiar to him?

Again came that vision of a dark-haired, dainty woman. She was slim and hadn't much in the way of curves, as he'd heard Ranice possessed. Then again, he'd not been daydreaming of his wife, Ranice. No. It was this Juel Reynaude he had had a vision of, she of the winsome face and charming manner. But why her? And why did he think of her as so fetching a female? He had thought he might be able to love his wife and then the thought had followed that love didn't exist, not the passionate variety between man and woman.

Yet love was the most powerful emotion known to man; its intensity was sung and expressed by poets. But it existed only in songs and words. He had never known love but for his pet, Shadow. He felt devotion for Rajahr, or was it the other way around? He didn't know. He'd believed courtly love was merely focused on another man's wife. An illicit affair could have no other design but love alone. Love was considered inappropriate to marriage.

So Scardon had taught him, and he had believed this. This, and so much more. He would be unfaithful to his wife, he knew. And she would be unfaithful, too. He could do without any of the romance. All they needed were heirs, as Scardon had said.

Unbidden, the thought came to mind of why he needed a wife at all. But he was married now and must make the best of it. The king had said a French wife could aid in his "activities." Young Harry had needed a loyal male stationed in southern England for his campaign; a secret agent, no less. But a *woman* to aid him? Foolishness.

He wondered what Ranice would be like . . . and also this Juel Reynaude he had sent his men after. Especially her, Juel, the woman of his visions. Or was it hallucinations?

He rose from his chair. He needed a drink.

In the halls, Rajahr watched Orion walk away from his apartment. He knew where Orion went. The Indian shook his head in compassion. Orion was as deeply lonely and emotionally twisted as a person could be.

Chapter Four

The magnificent forest covered thousands of acres of primeval wild cherry and pine, willow, alder and quivering aspen, ash and elm, oak and birch. The home of deer, wild boar, wolves, heron, and every kind of bird, it was a paradise for the hunt.

But Juel had seen no hunters.

Sunlight filtered in here and there. The mist was fragile as spider's webbing and it stirred beneath Juel's shoes. Her green dress-tunic felt damp, soft. Dew on plants hung like strings of jewels in the sifting sunlight. It was early morning and silence reigned but for little chirps of birds and the lamentation of mourning doves.

She felt the doves' lonesome call in her spirit. She felt lonely for so many reasons, not only because she was lost and in the forest alone. She missed her mother, who was dead but not gone from her thoughts and her heart. She sorely missed having her to share lovely thoughts and times with—walking in the woods together, picking berries, sharing the delight in the singing of the birds, the sunshine and the shadow. Sewing, cooking, cleaning the house. She missed having her mother Dalenna work beside her or in the next room making beds.

She must not think more of Dalenna now, else she'd begin to cry and then she'd soon be sobbing. That would never do.

"No, never," Juel said aloud, just to hear her voice. Did anyone hear her? Probably not. How could they; she was isolated from the human race.

Suddenly the trees seemed to part for her as she slowly walked. Juel gulped and found herself staring ahead at the most incredible sight.

Ten more steps. Then she whirled in a circle. Ahead of her the fog clawed at the foot of the tower, creeping, as if on dragons' paws. Yet, outside that towering structure, in the clear pureness of dawn, the castle—or what was left of it and the crumbling walls—was gray and rose, like the huge manor house, the whole structure standing tall on high ground and commanding a river crossing.

Two more steps . . . three. Wobbly-kneed like a new-born fawn, she was. Scared, wondering what she'd find.

In moments she had come out of the forest!

The Keep. It must be, Juel told herself. This was where her father worked. The moat was dried up, spanned by a drawbridge and encircled by a chemise, the inner, walled enclosure of the castle.

Was everyone still abed? Juel wondered. Where were the lord and lady, the falcons and the hunting dogs, the servants, horses, pigs, and poultry?

Ah. Juel felt satisfied when she could see the archers

56

and knights as she walked through the gatehouse. *All right, Juel, you feel fine and brave, just a little hungry and weak, but what of the guards when they see you? What will the knights of The Keep do?*

"Halt there!" came the cry from above, and then the scampering of feet down the stairs.

"Greetings," said Juel brightly to the rotund guard. "I am Juel Reynaude of Herstmonceux. My father is the carpenter and woodcutter here. His name is Peter—"

Wait a minute!

Juel whirled about. The trees! So many trees had been cut down, their stumps protruding from the green turf and making the outer grounds appear gloomy and forsaken. Such a waste!

Sadly Juel turned back to the frowning guard. "Why are they cutting down all these beautiful trees?"

"What business is it of yours, girlie?" Riley's watery blue eyes squinted, looking her up and down. Then he softened, for she clearly posed no threat, and she did look to be suffering from hunger and fatigue; he'd seen that look on returning knights before. "Juel of Herstmonceux, who are you here to see?" he asked gently.

"My father, sir. He works here."

"You have come from afar?"

"Oh, yes," Juel sighed. "Very far. From the other side of the great forest."

"You will have to see the overseer of the manor. He is there just now; his name is Rajahr." He allowed her to enter and when she walked by after thanking him, Riley called to her, "You can't miss him, Juel Reynaude. He's a little fellow, dark and exotic-looking."

57

Juel nodded, but what she did not see was the circle of knights that had been gesturing to Riley—the gatekeeper saw them now—and those knights watched her every inch of the way as she walked to the manor house.

The knights were making certain she did not leave before Lord Orion had seen her and spoken with her. Her description had been given to them and they had been setting out to search for her. The mesnie head, Ruark, had just come out to behold her, too, and now that he'd looked upon the winsome face of the dark-haired, otherworldly young woman he knew what it might be Lord Orion was wanting her for. And it wasn't to work!

The light on her was only sunlight, and yet she seemed to glow, with a face and long, shimmering hair that could only be a dream. Was he awake, he wondered?

Yes, Ruark thought as he watched her approach the manor house, her cheeks flushed pink, her slim back held straight, Orion had something special in mind for this one.

Just what, remained to be seen.

Chapter Five

Her eyes were too big and they were an odd shade of green mixed with gray. Her hair was not the right shade of brown. Truth be known, it was too dark; almost black.

This was the way Juel had seen herself in the quiet azure pool behind her house in the wooded glade, and she wondered now how those here would see her. Her confidence was dwindling rapidly as she put her hand to the solid oak door. She swallowed and squared her shoulders.

Just then her stomach growled like a ferocious and hungry beast. She blanched.

Rajahr opened the door to this sound coming from the lovely, round-eyed girl standing there. He blinked, wondering how this dainty creature had produced such a growling vibration, and he looked behind her to see if there was a large pet accompanying her.

"Did you say something?" Rajahr asked the girl—or woman—he couldn't tell if she was a youth or a maid in her twenties. She was dressed like a peasant, that much

59

he could tell. And her clothes looked like they'd been slept in.

"Not yet," Juel answered. She quivered as she stared into the fierce dark eyes and heard him say, "What do you want? Why are you here?"

"I am . . ." Juel began to sway and she was seeing spots before her eyes. "I think I am going to . . . to f-faint!"

And she did.

Against his better judgment, Rajahr reached out to break her fall, caught her in his arms before her head could strike the doorjamb. He held her while her head rolled on her neck, her arms and legs limp as a ragdoll's.

Rajahr tried to drag her inside. "You sure are heavy for a little lady." Lady? What was he saying. She was a mere peasant, a rustic bumpkin in rags. She was weighty and muscled for her size, Rajahr thought as he managed to get her into a chamber where there was a cushioned bench.

Voices came and went for Juel, and shadows blurred together. Juel breathed in the scent of man, little comforted by it. "What will you do?" Juel heard someone ask, and she thought it might be the voice of the dark, exotic little man. His voice drifted in and out of her unconsciousness. "She is as white as a bone," he said with concern. *Was* it concern?

Then she heard another voice say, "Hunger and fatigue." His voice was very nice, making her think dreamily of deep, dark velvet. Something was wrong with the other voice, though, and she felt the person belonging to it was troubled deep down inside. Or maybe her weary mind was making this up in a dream?

No, she was coming to, and she felt warm, so warm.

When Juel opened her eyes she beheld a bright fire burning in front of her. And was she lying on a long, soft cushion?

A shadow moved just behind her and suddenly Juel remembered hearing tales about a man who had a hump on his back and lived in or near The Keep. Stories also abounded that the ancient fortress whispered of awesome supernatural things, of dark magic, that the lord of this place was disreputable, repulsive, and hot-blooded. Now the shadow moved to the front of her and she could almost imagine there was an ugly hump moving on his back.

Juel wanted to scream, but the sound would not emerge, and her throat felt dry, dry as a . . . bone. With a hand to her mouth Juel bit back a cry, and tears came hotly to her eyes. Then they were let loose and began to course down her cheeks.

She could not understand it. Why was she crying? She was not that afraid. Or was she?

"I must be," she said in a whisper.

"You must be what?" asked the deep, wonderful voice that seemed to come from heaven. That troubled voice.

Juel gasped, as all of a sudden she was looking into a pair of brown eyes. Strange, they were cold *brown* eyes; she had only seen cold *blue* eyes. She didn't know brown eyes could turn so frigid. Unfeeling, heartless, and hostile, she could almost feel rather than see the void within his black soul.

She looked at him more closely. His was a handsome face, what she could see of it, with dark hair pulled back and bound at the nape with a leather thong. The

61

rest of his body was in shadow and it struck her that much time had passed and it must be close to noontide. A dark noon, erasing the sunlight and bringing blue-violet shade, as if an eclipse had blackened the day.

She flinched as a cool hand stretched out to rest upon her hand—the very one she'd placed on her mouth to stifle the scream. "Oh," Juel murmured. "I feel light-headed." Suddenly the cool, dark hand withdrew and she could no longer make out the larger shape of man.

She tried to sit up, but the small, dark man appeared to hold a hand to her shoulder, to keep her from rising. Then he was gone, as if he had melted into the dimness like a mystical phantom.

The dark-velvet voice belonging to the bigger man said, "You have nothing to fear. Rest, and I will speak to you. Just lie there. Let me talk to you."

She blinked up at the man half in shadow, half in firelight. Talk to her? What did he want to know? Who was this man and what did he want from her? Perhaps she had done something wrong by coming here uninvited. Juel swallowed hard, the lump dry in her throat.

Her stomach growled and Juel blanched whiter than bone. "I am very hungry," she said, feeling embarrassed. "I am sorry."

The deep voice grunted, "Apologize for your need for food?" The head shook and the dark eyes lowered to her hands folded over her stomach. "You need not." He shifted. "There is food being prepared and you will eat soon." Again he shifted, unaware he was making Juel nervous. "Now, I must ask you some questions. Are you strong enough for that?"

"I—I think so," Juel murmured, not looking up. She was looking across the room and noticing she was in a plain, oak-walled chamber with leaf-green tapestries and dark wooden beams overhead. Heavy weapons crisscrossed one wall, several sets of them in various sizes and shapes.

With curious eyes, Rajahr watched Orion. He had never seen the lord act in so pleasant a way, since the young man was rarely good-natured unless it had to do with animals that were not of the cat family. This was very interesting, watching his fierce lord loom above the young woman lying so quietly on the cushioned bench. Orion was often cruel and insensitive with women, especially if they were loose and immoral. But this woman did not seem such a person.

"Rajahr," Orion said. "Go now and find Dawn, see that she prepares the food and brings it here."

Rajahr's eyes, usually small and slanted, grew large and round. "You wish to be left alone with—?"

"Yes," Orion cut him off. "And have a servant prepare a warm bath."

"A . . . warm . . . bath?" Rajahr wondered if he'd heard correctly.

"That is what I said: a warm bath." Orion raised one dark eyebrow. "You know what that is, do you not?"

With that, Rajahr said no more and hurried off to do Orion's bidding. He wondered what his young master could be up to. "Prob'ly no good," he muttered to himself.

Orion turned back to the young woman lying so quietly and noticed that one hand was clutching a pelt of red fox that draped over the back of the cushioned bench. She looked quiet and tense. As her eyes closed, he noticed her thick, dark lashes, so long they brushed the tops of her delicate pale-pink cheeks. She had the smallest waist he had ever seen, and great swirling masses of walnut-brown hair, looking black in the shade of her throat and so long and thick that the ends went to her waist and curled about it like a heavy silken sash. Her eyes seemed a greenish-hazel, and big. Lying down, she seemed very small-breasted.

One long, slim forearm lay across her brow as if she were warding off the rays of strong sunlight, and Orion spoke as if to a child. "Why have you come here?" He paused for only a second. "And who are you?" he half whispered.

She looked out from the crook of her arm and saw that he had bent down beside the bench she was lying upon. "May I get up, please?"

"Of course." He moved back a little. "Why didn't you ask before?"

"Because I did not want to before. But now I would like to sit up, if you do not mind."

"Please do." One corner of Orion's mouth turned up in a wry smile. He watched her as she came up slowly, then shifted until her feet were planted on the floor. She weaved a little and he reached out a hand to steady her. "You are still weak. Are you sure you can manage to stay in a sitting position without swooning again?"

"Yes, I think so." She blinked and looked up, getting her first really good look at him. He was rugged and dark, tall and handsome, and when she glanced down she noted how large and brown his hands were. Looking up again, she found herself staring into mysterious brown eyes with lashes as long and thick as a woman's. "I—I am fine," she stuttered.

64

She couldn't look away from him and his long, bladelike nose, high cheekbones, strong chin, and dark hair that swept back from his forehead. She was held mesmerized by the deep shadows in his features and the full, firm mouth that somehow appeared dangerous to her. She noticed something else: the greenish pallor along the planes of his face, as if he'd been sick recently. There was a twist of sadness, too, a definite melancholy.

"How are you?" she found herself blurting.

Orion stared at the lovely face. "I?" he said.

"Yes. Have you been ill recently?" As soon as the words were out, Juel felt as if she shouldn't have asked the question. For all his outward calm, this was a threatening man she was dealing with.

"Why would you think that I have been ill?" he asked, a muscle twitching in his cheek as he waited for her answer. "I believe I'll forget you asked that question. *I* ask the questions here. Now, who are you and why have you come?"

Tearing her eyes from him, she began to explain. "I am Juel Reynaude and have come here because I was lost in the great woods." She was going to ask why all those trees were being cut down, then decided she'd best not. "I spent last night in the woods, and the two before that."

Before she could go on, he cut in, "Your father, he is Peter Reynaude."

"Yes, that is correct."

His next question was uttered in a low voice. "Where has he been hiding you all this time?"

Juel felt a shiver run through her. "Peter has not been hiding me." She wet her lips that had suddenly gone dry. "I have been out in the open for all the world to see. Does that sound like someone has been hiding me?"

A strange look crossed his handsome face and she thought she could read some melancholy pensiveness in his eyes. Yes, she decided, something was ailing this man.

This man! He must be . . . Oh, God!

Her voice quavered and then she cleared her throat. "You are Orion Sutherland, baron of Herstmonceux, lord of this castle?"

His eyes were dark and intense. "I am not sure who I am." He saw the surprise light up her eyes to yellow-green. "I was raised by a man named John Scardon. As for the Sutherland, I am not sure about that, either. I *am* Lord Orion and, yes, I *am* lord of this castle . . . what is left of it."

Juel's features softened. "You do not know me and yet you shared that with me. Have you done this before, Lord Orion?"

He was suddenly uneasy and stood from his bent position to go to a deep cushioned chair, the likes of which Juel had never seen before, not even in the merchant's house where she'd worked. The chair was ugly, the carving like evil claws, a satyr's chair.

Though he was slumped lazily in that massive piece of furniture, Lord Orion managed to look like a ruggedly elegant prince of yesteryear. He was big and handsome, making her heart thump wildly in her chest as she stared down at his fingers resting negligently along the carved beasts' arms.

Watching her silently, he sat there and then finally spoke. "You have been playing cat-and-mouse with me, Juel Reynaude."

His voice was like deep velvet. The whole man was like dark velvet and forceful steel. It was a strange way to think of a man. *Had* she been playing this game with him of which he spoke?

"What do you mean?" was all she could think of to say.

"You are still hiding from the world, Juel Reynaude. It appears your family has been keeping you from us. Had Scardon known of your existence he would have sent for you long ago. You should have been working here at the castle." Now this princess in rags had him calling it a castle. "I should say, the manor, a lesser form of the castle hall which we call . . . or Scardon calls . . . The Keep."

Orion hated the name Keep; someday he would rename it Sutherland Castle, what it had been rumored to have been called yesteryear. He didn't know for sure about that. He knew nothing for sure when it came to the past. Nothing but Scardon's dark magic and the demons placed in his own soul.

She looked him straight in the eyes. "If Scardon had sent for me five years ago I would only have been fifteen."

He said to her, "So you are twenty now."

"Yes." She looked away; then back. "Almost."

His dark, intense eyes bored into hers. "That would have been a perfect age to start. But now that you have found your way here, you must stay."

"To work, I presume." She waited for his slow nod. "Lord and tenant rarely meet face-to-face. The manor's affairs are usually left to the steward or bailiff. This I know. How is it that you are speaking to me, a mere villager?"

"You are a rare one, Juel Reynaude." Running a long finger along his cheekbone, he looked at her with curled lips, almost a smirk. "I find you matching me almost question for question. How is it that you can speak to me, Lord Orion, like this?"

For a moment Juel felt some apprehension, but it was gone instantly upon seeing the look that crossed his dark features. His expression had turned to one of pain and she watched as he clutched his hand over his middle, bending over as if he were hurting there.

"Are you unwell?" she asked, pressing her hand over her throat.

She became alarmed. His heart? But he was too young to be afflicted by an illness that usually did away with the elderly. What a sad waste to see this handsome young lord placed in an early grave.

He moaned. Now she was even more alarmed.

"Perhaps it was something you ate?"

In one movement, he was up and out of the chair. His hand was no longer clutching his middle and he was coming toward her. She looked up as he stood before her and she felt the fascinating power, the captivating danger of him. His eyes were dark and his features looked strained.

"How is it that I knew you were coming to me?" he asked.

"You knew I was . . . What do you mean? I was not coming to you, I was lost in the woods, that is how I came to be here. My father works here and I thought I'd be safe. Now I believe I was wrong. I think I should leave—"

A long finger touched her face and Orion felt her

recoil from him at the same time he saw the flicker of fear in her eyes. "You are safe, Juel Reynaude. For now." Two fingers touched her hot, flushed cheek. "Truth to tell, I was just sending my knights out to look for you. You must not leave here, Juel, not until I find out what it is you are doing to me."

She blanched. "I?"

"Yes, you. Are you a witch? I don't understand these feelings. Have you cast a spell on me?"

"My lord!" She pulled away from his touch and tried to back away, but she came up against the bench. Witches were burned at the stake! "I am not a witch and have not cast any such spells. I do not even know any witches and I am not doing anything to you. I don't even *know* you. We are perfect strangers."

"Not anymore, Juel. We have shared, as you said yourself." He stepped closer and Juel realized he was a good head taller than she. "We can share more."

She bit her lower lip and felt her knees knocking together. "Oh. Like what?"

He bit out a curse and she shrank back, saying "Oh" again, and then once more.

"You needn't sound so breathless, Juel, I am not a dragon. I'll not eat you." He did not see her surprise as he turned at a knock on the heavy door. "Ah, the afternoon repast."

Oh, that was all they were going to share. A meal!

She breathed easier as a dainty young woman with fair hair entered the room with a huge tray which she balanced on her hip.

"Put it there on the table," Orion said to the maid. "Then you may leave us, Dawn."

The maid glanced Juel's way, gave a gentle and

kindly smile, then went out. Juel thought she had never seen such a lovely, fair-haired girl—or woman, she couldn't tell how old she really was. Perhaps near to her own age.

When Orion pulled the cloth from the huge platter Juel gasped. She had never seen so much food. The odors of various foods wafted to her, smelling delicious. The afternoon repast? she thought. No wonder this young lord had clutched his middle. He must eat like a pig!

Orion selected a leg of some kind of fowl and began to eat, tearing the pale meat off with straight white teeth. When she had not moved to take some for herself, he stopped chewing to look at her.

"I thought you were starving?" he said, flicking the corner of his mouth with his tongue.

She licked her lips, hearing her stomach growl like a wild dog. She sat back down onto the bench daintily. "You go ahead. I can wait." She fought off a wave of dizziness and nausea. She was so hungry and tired.

"You must eat," he insisted, piling food on a trencher and handing it to her. "You are too thin."

She thrust it back at him. "No, thank you. I will eat when you have finished and have left the room."

"Who said that I was leaving?"

"You must have things to do." She watched as he placed the trencher of food back onto the side table. Her eyes never left the succulent ribs oozing their dark-brown juice or the plump portion of fowl, pork, beef or the various crisp vegetables, including one of her favorites—lettuce. And slices of apple! "Don't you have some knights to train?" Her eyes drifted to the last course, arranged neatly in a circle about the main dish:

cheese, nuts, more sliced fruits, and spiced wine.

"My knights and men-at-arms are trained already," he said, selecting a hunk of golden cheese.

She felt tears sting her eyes. "How about conferences with stewards or bailiffs?"

"Done, this morning early." He chewed the cheese and washed it down with a gulp of wine.

"Your wife," Juel tried. "Does she not attend Mass in the chapel with you?"

Orion went very still, then said, "My wife has not arrived yet, and I never attend Mass."

For some reason Juel's heart sank when he said that, about the wife. "Has she been away long?" She was so weary and hungry that she could not think straight.

"Very long." He stared at her over the rim of his goblet. "We have not met yet."

Juel blinked. "Not . . . met?"

"We were married by proxy. Her name is Ranice."

Her shoulders slumped and she felt defeated for some reason. "Oh, of course, I'd forgotten about that." When he stared across the table with a frown, she went on. "Villagers do gossip, you know. They talk about Lord Orion and The Keep as often as they sweep floors or prepare soup." She gave a tight laugh. "And they make soup often."

"Soup. I have not had soup in years." He looked down at his lap, then up again. "You will make it for me soon."

"Oh, no," she told him and smoothed her homespun skirt. "I must get back home. My father Peter will return there soon. I have much to do before he arrives. There's the dry-salting of meat and I have to soak sheets and towels in ashes and soda—"

71

"You can do all that here. You will not lack for work, Juel Reynaude." His eyes narrowed as they stared straight into hers. "You will be kept very busy, count on that."

"Oh, no—"

"Oh, yes." Wiping his hands on a wet towel, then a dry one, he turned to leave. "I'll put you in charge of the pantry, the breadery, to start."

"But—" Juel waved an arm as he stood in the middle of the room, one hand resting upon his hip. Her gaze that had rested there snapped up to meet his dark stare. "I have to keep my father's accounts and—"

"You can read and write?" He stared at her hard, with renewed interest.

"Yes . . ." Her voice drifted away. What had she done?

"My steward has been, well, let's just say that some stewards are true, but many more are false."

"Steward? But that means an apprenticeship, and the course takes from six months to a year."

"You are well informed and intelligent, Juel, I am seeing that more and more. But you still have much to learn. I am going to look into your past, the village records."

Juel gasped. "You are going to check on me?"

"I will. Or else you can tell me all about yourself and how it is that you have learned so much being a mere villager's daughter."

With that, and sporting arrogance in every step, he walked from the chamber, shutting the huge door behind him. Juel snatched a leg of mutton from the tray and tossed the greasy limb at the door. She sat down hard on the bench, clenching her knees together.

She cried at the door, "That man is a dragon! He is not only cruel, he is also a slavedriver. A lecher they say! I'll not stay here and be seduced by him! Once I find father I shall leave. Yes, that is what I will do. Leave quickly."

Oh, damn, Juel thought, using one of Jay's favorite swear words. Jay! If only he would return to find her, then she could quit this place. He would help her.

She glanced at her surroundings, feeling the gloom of the strange masculine chamber. *I cannot stay here,* she told herself. *And why not?* something in her asked right back.

"Because," she said in a half whisper, "I am afraid of him. There is something about Lord Orion that makes me want to run back into the woods and hide." That hot look in his eyes . . . he would not be gentle.

Hide? Orion had asked about that, why her father had been keeping her from everyone at The Keep. If the castle folk knew of her, why had she not been brought to The Keep to work; he must be wondering that, and she was too.

And why did it seem that Orion and she had met before? That was stranger than anything else she'd learned here today.

Chapter Six

The manor house was an informal group of buildings all constructed of timber and stone. These comprised the hall, chapel, kitchen, and farm buildings, all of which were contained within a defensive wall and ditch. The ground-floor hall was flanked by towers and further defended by a moated enclosure, now dried up and useless. There were private living apartments on the third and fourth floor and service rooms at opposite ends of the great hall, which was on the second floor. The manor enclosed an irregular courtyard, with battlements, gatehouse, and secret exits outside the broken ramparts.

The castle tower, an old fortification built in the eleventh century, stood alone, apart from the manor house, surrounded by a crumbled and broken wall and steeped in whispers of mystery. No one went to the round tower but Lydia Mari. She went there early in the misty dawn and late at night. She had perceived much and she hid many secrets.

Lydia Mari Flanders had married at age fifteen, and

ten years later became widowed. She had wept long after her husband was buried. In the village of Herstmonceux, she found herself alone with two children. Without relatives and with few resources, she had come to work for John Scardon; not long after, both her daughter and her son died within a few years of each other, the more cause for tears.

She was often caught weeping in the pantry, or in the chapel, though she always dried her tears when the castle folk found her. She had acquired the nickname Teary Mari, for her eyes were always misted and sad. Lydia, as Orion called her from a distance, not caring for the other name, loved the ragamuffins and the strays, the children without parents.

Orion kept his distance from the plump, moon-faced woman. She went to the round tower, where he never dared venture. He knew there was an aura surrounding Lydia and he didn't wish to come near her. He had his superstitions.

At the moment, Lydia was going one way, Orion the other, and their eyes never met. She would like to talk to him but realized his fear of her—or of *where she went*. There was talk, Lydia had heard, that a new female had joined the household yesterday. Lydia had not yet met her but Dawn had told her she was lovely and that Rajahr had put her up for the night in the small chamber where the tablewear and candlesticks and linens were kept.

Odd, Lydia had thought, that the new maid was off by herself, in a room of her own, away from the other maids. But thinking no more about it, Lydia made her way to the dark old tower with her tray of food.

Orion was weaving in and out of piles of brick and stacks of wood, looking for the carpenter, Peter Reynaude. The man had not been at the carpenter's cottage.

The manor house had been built in stages, an irregular and incompatibly fashioned mélange of roofs and timbered walls. The gardens were in shambles. With the new use of bricks and terra cotta and black walnut, Orion knew he could produce more elaborate buildings and apartments.

Orion already employed twenty stonemasons, and some two hundred other craftsmen, such as woodcarvers, painters, lead and iron workers, roofers, and carpenters. He planned to keep Peter Reynaude on as long as he could, thereby keeping his daughter Juel as well.

Wood, yes, he had to keep the fires blazing in the manor, since he hated the darkness and days like this one, which was gloomy and threatened rain. The clouds overhead looked like dark and purple bruises to Orion. Yesterday, when Juel Reynaude had come, the sun had shone. Where was it today, he wondered, feeling cross, and he frowned darkly when he came upon Peter Reynaude, who was carving an intricate design along a length of the softer woods. Orion tipped his dark head to look down.

"You must be the master carpenter."

Peter Reynaude, a handsome man in his early fifties, looked up to see Orion Sutherland frowning down at him where he sat cross-legged on the ground. Wiping his hands free of woodshavings, Peter stood to extend a hand in welcome, when he realized one should never do this unless the lord first wished to be charitable. But Peter was always friendly and sincere and expected this in return from others, even his betters.

Orion watched the handsome older man scrub his hand on his homespun shirt, then drop it to his side; there had been no handshake. "I am Peter Reynaude of Herstmonceux." He grinned widely, not able to help himself beneath such a serious face as this young man's. "You must be Lord Orion Sutherland."

"Just Orion. You may drop the Sutherland." He knew the man was puzzled, but he had no care one way or the other what others thought. "We will talk," he said, indicating the braced stack of logs in an overhang of recent construction. "I believe it is going to rain."

"I think you're right," said Peter, holding out his hand as he felt the first drops. "We'll sit here, where it's clean, if that's all right with you."

Orion only nodded, indicating that Peter could be seated. After the older man was settled on a stack of fresh wood, Orion did the same, on another stack.

Usually the seneschal, or steward, or reeve, came to see Peter if something needed to be done, and he wondered why Lord Orion had come himself instead of the manorial overseer. It must be important, what Orion himself had to speak to him about, Peter thought.

"Your daughter has joined us."

Peter looked up, puzzled. "My daughter?" He only had the one. "Juel?" He was at once alarmed. "My son. Something has not happened to him?"

Peter would have come to his feet, but Orion lifted his hand. "No. It is not about your son, although I have heard Alice, one of the maids, mention him. It seems she is dallying with him."

"Ah," said Peter. "That is my son, Jay. Excuse me, my lord, but he always sports with the maids. He is a very healthy rascal." When Orion did not smile, Peter cleared his throat. "So, my daughter is here." He frowned. "Why has she come?"

"It seems she got herself lost in the great woods, picking berries, and found her way here."

Again, Peter would have stood. "Is she . . . well?"

"Sit down," Orion said. "She is fine. But I would like her to stay and work here at the manor. Do you find that agreeable?"

Peter blinked. He was asking? It was highly unusual for the lord to ask this of a commoner, and Peter wondered what else was on the man's mind. "She can do many things" was all Peter said, already resigned to the fact Juel would be working here. What the lord of the manor said was law.

"I find that to be the case," Orion said. "We had some words yesterday. You have a feisty daughter with a mind of her own." *Also, she is lovely,* he did not add. "It is settled then. Juel will work here and when you leave she must remain."

Peter's heart sank. Not to have Juel at home where he could look out for her welfare and safety? This, Peter did not care for. Juel was a virgin still and he had often feared that some young man would ravish her. Now she would be here at The Keep with this man, Lord Orion, who was rumored to be bad-tempered, ungodly, and the corrupter of young maids. No, he would not like leaving her behind.

Peter looked down at the ground. "If you say Juel

79

must stay, there's nothing I can do to change your mind. I have no voice here." He was only a villein.

"That is correct," Orion said.

The lord of the manor held discretionary power over the majority of villagers, the land-holding villeins. Orion could seize Peter's holdings. He could increase his rents and services at will. Unless a tenant failed to perform his services, the villein remained in possession of his holding and could pass it on to his heir, in this case Jay, his son. And the stubborn or rebellious were threatened with fines.

"Juel is now ours." Orion looked away, then back at the man. "Mine. She belongs to the manor."

My God, the man is heartless, Peter thought as he watched the tall, dark man walk away. *Why did he even come to tell me this?* Peter was asking himself when the woman named Lydia stopped by, as she had the day before, to give him a loaf of dark rye bread that was left over from her trip to the round tower.

Peter looked down. The bread loaf was three feet long, and crusty. He could feel and hear his stomach rumble.

"I appreciate it, Lydia. I'll share it with a few of the carpenters at our evening meal." He stared into her sad blue eyes that seemed to water perpetually. "My daughter's here."

"Ah, so it's your daughter who has come to The Keep. I hear she is very lovely and has a strong will. I wonder why is she kept alone? And what did Lord Orion want with you?"

Peter blanched. "She's kept in a room of her own?" He saw Lydia nod. "Yes, why *would* Sutherland keep her away from the other maids?" he wondered with fear in his voice.

He saw she had no answer for that.

"Sutherland?" Lydia said, her eyes curious. "Why would you call him that? He's hardly ever called by that name. No one dares."

Peter felt a shiver along his spine. "Can you tell me why not?"

Lydia chewed her lower lip that had a tiny purple mole on it. "I cannot say; I have been sworn not to. Scardon might return. If he heard that I had spoken of Orion's past, I would be killed instantly. And Orion, he's a shadowy, mysterious man no one can get close to. He goes out riding the moors with a monkey on his back, in the dark of the moon, and locks himself away in his apartments during the evenings he's not out, with fires blazing away."

Peter's gaze went to the dark structure she'd just come from. "Why do you go to the round tower in the morning and at night?" he asked abruptly. "Why do you bring fresh linens and toweling, then bring the soiled ones out? We've seen you empty chamber pots. Who is in there?"

Now Lydia *really* looked alarmed. "I go to feed and care for the guard posted there" was all she offered.

Peter laughed at that. "Why is there a guard when no one lives there? And," he shook his head, ready to burst into laughter, "why would a guard have need of fresh linen, delicate food, and chamber pots?"

"I must go now."

Peter watched Lydia go, and now he knew the rumors circulating around the old castle were in fact truth: the round tower was inhabited. But by who? A male? A female? Maybe some of the food fed the guard, he decided, but, my God, not all.

He thought back to something Lydia had said, that Lord Orion rode out at night with a monkey on his back? Peter thought this over with a deep chuckle. He sobered and frowned.

Now Peter was really worried for his daughter. He would stop his work for the day. Jay! He suddenly realized the manor lord said Alice had dallied with him. Jay was back!

His next thought was to find his son, and but a little while later he was on his way to the village. He would bring Jay back with him and tell the overseer Haymo that Jay was going to work for him. In reality, he was going to have his son do some spying to see how Juel was faring and keep her safe and sound.

If anyone could find out what was going on here, it was Jay. And it was plain that Juel needed protecting, for Peter himself had to get back to their home in time for spring planting. His only wish now was that he could go back and spend more time with her. Time was fleetfooted. She was growing into an adult. He smiled; Juel was a bookworm just like her mother and . . . He would not think of that other man now. It would make him sad and feel guilty that he'd not . . . that her mother had been with that . . . that Juel was . . . *No, don't think it.*

It was time to be happy again! Peter told himself.

Peter Reynaude shook his head. Orion? With a monkey on his back? Ha!

Chapter Seven

The afternoon had turned misty and dusky following the morning rain and Juel could hear the sad, cooing call of turtledoves in the aviary as she walked along the crumbled stone wall, her dark hair swinging about her shoulders.

She had seen most of the castle grounds and Rajahr had introduced her to the people. She especially liked Dawn, with her exquisite beauty and quiet manner. The expression in Dawn's eyes had seemed to ask for friendship. Juel knew they were going to be good friends even though Juel was not planning on staying long.

She was determined to leave here as soon as her father's work was completed for the season.

Juel had been warned that she must never go to the round tower. A muscle quivering at his jaw, his dark eyes serious, Rajahr had told her that even Orion himself never set foot there.

"Why?" she had asked. "Is it haunted?"

Rajahr backed away and blinked rapidly at her.

"You must go to work now, to bake bread. Go and see Dawn in the kitchen. She will tell you what you must do."

Juel stopped him. "Where is my father? I wish to see him."

"He has gone to the village and will not be back until late this night."

"I thought you said I should ask Lydia what must be done?" she called to him, as he was walking quickly away.

"Forget Lydia. She is busy elsewhere. Go and find Dawn, as I have ordered you to do!"

"Humph," Juel snorted.

The wind whipped color into Juel's cheeks as she walked through the castle courtyard, hearing the smith working at the forge on horseshoes that clanked with resonance. Servants emptied chamber pots and basins and were bringing in rushes for the freshly swept floors in the kitchen. Everything was alive with sight and sound and smell. Many smells, Juel thought, wrinkling her nose and thinking it never smelled like this at home.

The smell of garlic and onions was bitingly strong when Juel stepped into the kitchen, where great iron cauldrons hung over the fire on a hook and heavy chain. Juel looked around for Dawn. When she spotted her at the end of a row of tables, cutting up a whole chicken, Dawn smiled and wiped her hands on her apron.

Here was a girl she could trust, Juel thought.

Juel headed Dawn's way, keeping her gaze on the twinkling nut-brown eyes and accidentally bumping into a table where one of the kitchen maids was stuffing pastries with berries.

Alice had not met Juel yet. She was humming as usual, once again daydreaming of cat-green eyes and Jay Reynaude's lean and muscled body. "Hey!" Alice yelled when she glanced up, seeing who had dared to bump her table. "What'dya think you're doing, you clumsy little tart!"

"I am very sorry," Juel said. "I was looking for Dawn and did not notice your table."

Alice's hands clamped onto the curves of her ample hips. She loved tormenting new maids, and this was surely a new one, by the looks of her in her drab peasant garb, Alice thought. "So, you did not see my table, hmm?" she said as she came around the table and put her face in Juel's.

Juel leaned back, sizing her up. "That is what I said."

Dawn smiled to herself. If only Alice knew who this young woman was, she would be lifting Juel's hands and kissing her fingers one by one and telling her what a beautiful and witty sister Jay had.

"You're a smart and mouthy one, aren't you?" Alice shot back at the new girl. "I'd watch out if I were you, with that mouth, else you're going to get just what you're asking for around here."

"Oh?" Juel crossed her arms on her chest. "Just what am I asking for?" Juel's eyes had turned summer-green, flecked with bits of yellow lightning, in her answering flare of temper.

Alice stepped back and frowned. "Well now, just who in Hades do you think you might be? The queen of—"

"That's enough," Dawn said, flipping back her fat yellow braid. "Alice, get back to work. Juel, follow me and I will show you what to do before Rajahr or Lydia comes in. Cook Cimmerian is easy on us, but not the other two!"

"Cimmerian?" Juel said, weaving in and out of tables right behind Dawn, looking back once more at Alice. "Who is she?"

"He. And he is as dark as a Nubian slave. But he is kind, you will see. He likes everyone."

"Even that one?" Juel whispered as she glimpsed Alice over her shoulder hacking furiously with a butcher knife.

"Well . . ." Dawn said, and left her words unfinished. "Come. I will show you the foods that need to be prepared. Would you like to do bread or vegetables?"

"Bread," Juel told her. "That is what Rajahr said."

"Oh," Dawn said flippantly. "Rajahr does not know everything about the kitchen. He just likes to think he does." Dawn screwed up her pretty face. "Truth be told, both need to be done because I have so much other work. I am way behind. Do you think you can manage both?"

"Of course. I've done more for my father and brother than just cut up vegetables and bake bread!"

Dawn gave her a slow and secretive look before she spoke. "Dear Juel, you do not yet know Orion and his strange eating habits. If you fail to prepare something just the way he likes it . . . Off with your head!"

"What?" Juel said, clamping a hand over her heart. Then she laughed when Dawn grinned at her surprise. "Are you serious?"

"He yells a lot and throws things around," Dawn said, showing Juel where the flour was kept. "He can be quite frightening at times."

Juel sighed and shrugged. "I'll just have to measure up."

"That's the right spirit!" Dawn said, handing Juel a measuring vessel.

As soon as Dawn led Juel into the pantry Alice smirked and began making her devious plans. Her own hair was as dark as the new girl's and she pulled out a few now, hiding them in her apron pocket. One thing Orion hated worse than burnt bread was finding hairs in his food. It made him a ranting, raving maniac!

That haughty new maid was in for a big surprise, come mealtime!

Chapter Eight

"Send her to me!" Orion thundered as he tossed the dish of vegetables across the room. Shadow scurried away, and as soon as Rajahr opened the door for him, the monkey was gone.

"You scared him again with your shouting," Rajahr said, starting to pick up the mess. Then he stopped, his eyes wide, as Orion pulled another dark hair from between his teeth. "The new girl is not only arrogant, she is stupid. She will need to cover all her hair from now on."

Orion frowned darkly. "She will have to do more than that. I believe I will send her to work in the stables." His eyes narrowed into cold brown slits as he drank heavily from his cup of wine. "It might be that she has done this on purpose. Do you think that is possible, Rajahr?" He cupped his fingers over the arms of the chair.

With a shiver of revulsion, Rajahr pulled another long dark hair out of the pile of vegetables. "This might not have happened if you had taken your meal with the knights in the hall." He grinned. "One of them might have gotten the hairs instead."

"Not very humorous, Rajahr. I asked you, do you think she did this as a jest?" His voice dropped with an edge of disbelief so that it didn't sound like a question. And he did not wait for an answer. "I believe she dislikes me. Why do you think that is?"

Clearing his throat, Rajahr paused and then said, "There are many here that are terrified of you, Orion. Look at Shadow."

The younger man stood so quickly and violently that his wine spilled on the fine plush carpet at his feet. "I want this woman to like me." He retrieved his cup and shook out the last drops, then wiped it with the table linen. "I do not wish for her to hate me."

With a platter of vegetables in hand, Rajahr blinked at Orion. "Why do you wish that?"

"If she dislikes me so much, what will my wife think of me when she arrives?"

Now Rajahr thought he understood. "You want Ranice to love you upon first sight, is that it?"

"Of course," Orion said, a touch of wonder in his voice. "If my wife does not love me, how are we going to make children together?"

"Children?" Rajahr almost choked. "You wish for children?" He waited for Orion to nod, and he did. "I did not know you cared for children. The orphans—"

"I know," Orion cut in, pouring himself another vessel of wine from which he drank deeply. "I do not seem to care for them." He looked suddenly miserable, and Rajahr wanted to caress his head as he'd done when Orion was a small boy. "I do care, but I cannot touch them. They are not mine."

Rajahr shrugged. "The orphans belong to no one."

"I know that."

"And you think you must not show tenderness toward another human being. This is because you were not shown any by the man Scardon who took you in after your parents died, the one who called himself your father." He sniffed, watching Orion wipe his mouth with the heel of his hand. "I nurtured you myself, Orion, and I loved you as if—"

"Please, no maudlin tears now, Rajahr," Orion groaned. "You know I can't stand it when you wax sentimental."

The small, thin man shook his head and sighed, picking up pieces of carelessly scattered clothing as he walked. "I will get the new maid for you." He turned at the door to look back at Orion. "What will you do to her for letting some hair fall in your food? Take her like a child over your knee? Or will you bellow and roar like a lion? Or—"

"Rajahr?"

The servant watched Orion pour another three fingers of wine. Rajahr flinched, thinking, *Oh, no, not a repeat of the other night.* He steeled his shoulders.

"Yes?" Rajahr said.

"Bring Juel Reynaude to me now."

She stood outside the heavy chamber door, waiting for Rajahr to walk away. After several moments, Rajahr moved toward the oak staircase; and still he did not go completely away. He made motions for her to

91

knock and enter.

And Juel did not move to knock, either. She had not cared for the way in which he had summoned her. "You must come with me now. Leave the work. Someone wants to see you," he had said, frowning at the quizzical Alice. "Back to work, meddlesome woman!" he snapped at Alice.

"Who wants to see me?" Juel had asked Rajahr. "Tell me or I will not move from this spot." Juel had crossed her arms over her chest and Alice's eyes had widened.

"Him! He wants to see you, girlie. You must hold your tongue and come with me. Now!" he had almost shouted.

"Him!" she had snorted, following Rajahr. "Him must means His Royal Highness."

"No," Rajahr said. "Orion is not the king. Only King Henry is called that. And you will see him when he comes here one day."

Juel had lagged behind. "The king comes here?" Her eyes were wide and hazel-green. "When will that be?"

"Soon. You will see him then. For now, you must keep your mind on what Orion tells you. He is angry, so be careful what you say with that whiplash tongue of yours."

She had never come this way; up and up they went to the fourth-floor apartments. Juel had never gone so high in a house; not even the merchant's domicile had been this lofty. The stairs were of dark oak and broad, the landings with tall leaded panes of glass. Up close she noticed that the stained glass had bubbles captured in the panes, and she wondered briefly if glass would ever be made so that one would be able to see through it clearly.

On the third floor, Juel could see an open door at the end of the long hall, where there was a spinning wheel, and behind that another window, this one mullioned. No one was in the room, no one that she could see anyway.

Now she was on the fourth floor. And Rajahr was still waiting for her to knock and disappear inside. When she did, she received the call to enter. Rajahr was satisfied when at last he saw the door close.

Juel stood just inside the door. The apartment was huge and messy and took up the entire fourth floor, she could see. The furnishings were masculine, the floors oak with colorful squares of Oriental carpeting, and the bed was massive with deep-green hangings. Great tapestries featured hunting scenes in rich colors, with forests so high they touched the clouds of silken thread.

One tapestry caught Juel's eye, and she walked over to stand beneath it. It was a depiction of the Garden of Eden. Looking at it, she could almost hear the birds' songs, the rustling of bright forest leaves, the rippling of streams over jeweled rocks, could almost smell the wildflowers. Her eyes shifted to the next tapestry.

A deep male voice sounded behind her and Juel jumped. "No sickness, death, decay, or sorrow enters there in Paradise," he said. "The flowers are all white with golden centers and the grass is like velvet, a place of spectacular color and a thousand scents which never fade and have healing qualities."

Juel was breathless when she turned to see Orion standing there, so close she could feel his breath. "That was beautiful, what you just said." She turned to look up at the Paradise tapestry again. "How do evil souls make their way to the next world, do you suppose?"

"I'm not sure. They must be good while on earth, I would think, in order to enter Paradise," he said in a tight voice. "Man cannot know why all things are as they are."

"They are as God pleases," she answered. She stopped then and turned, realizing he smelled of drink. "You are befuddled?"

His gaze came to rest on her questioning eyes. "Not intoxicated by drink. No."

Juel decided he wasn't telling the whole truth, or else he did realize that he was indeed half drunk.

What had he meant then? Her sweeping lashes lifted and her hazel-green eyes filled with confusion. She was bewildered at his words. "You sent for me. What is it that you wanted?"

Orion, a war of emotions raging within him, could not remember at the moment why he *had* sent for her. Again, he felt there was some bond between them, and it was even stronger now as he looked at her lazily through half-closed lids.

Orion felt a tug on his well-guarded heart. He stared at the ebony ribbons of hair plastered to her temples and cheeks, aware that she had toiled in the heat of the kitchen fires. He felt his own body sweat and his heart pound strongly as he lifted his eyes to the ceiling and its dark, heavy timbers. His gaze drifted downward again, fell to her small breasts, one corner of his mouth pulling into a tight smile.

Reaching out, he lifted a strand of her hair from her

chest. "How did this beautiful hair of yours get in my food?"

The smoldering flame she saw in his eyes gave her a strong jolt. Young men in the village had looked at her this way, but never with this man's intensity. She felt a curious pulling at her heart, then her mouth dropped. Hair? Did he say hair?

"My hair was in your food?" Her breath caught in her throat and she felt alarm within her. "I am so sorry. You did not choke, did you?"

"Almost." He continued to play with the curl that lay over her shoulder. "Such soft, radiant hair. It smells of lavender and roses."

"I washed it just this morning. It takes a long time to wash and dry b-because it's so long and heavy."

"I believe it."

He was so big and so close, Juel thought, feeling the heat of his legs coiling about hers. Awkwardly, she cleared her throat. "You are not angry, are you?" If he was angry, she wondered what he would do. And she asked him, "Will you punish me?"

"Yes." His voice was deep and rumbled in his chest as he stepped closer, breathing deeply and gazing straight into her eyes with his depthless ones. "I am going to punish you right now . . . with a kiss."

"Oh." Juel moved back a step. "You would know that would frighten me, with my b-being a virgin and all."

His dark head tilted. "I had no idea." He studied her thoroughly for a moment and saw her blink rapidly. "Think, Juel, I can hardly take your maidenhood with a kiss."

"Oh," she said with a blush. "Of course, that would be q-quite impossible, w-wouldn't it?"

"Quite." He watched her cheeks become reddish. Most maids turned pink when flushed. "You turn red when you're embarrassed."

Juel's hands flew to her cheeks. "I didn't know!"

He caught her hands and held them to his throat. "And you stammer."

"I—I do?" She gasped then when he brushed his lips across her knuckles. "My God, what are you doing? I—I think I better g-go! Th—this is not right, what you are doing!"

He peered into her eyes. "It is right, if I say it is."

Juel heaved a shuddering sigh. "You have had too much drink and are very befuddled, my lord."

He grasped her hand and held it tight. "My name is Orion. Say it. Not 'my lord.' I hate that. You see, Juel, no royal blood flows in my veins. Only fire. Say Orion."

"O-O-Orion. Please, you must let me go now." She stared down at her hand which was held within his. She looked up again. "There is f-fire in you?"

"At the moment, yes. And it is not because of the blazing hearthfire in this chamber," he said softly.

"I intended to ask you about that," she said, trying to switch to a safer subject. "Why is the manor house kept so hot? Why are there so many blazing fires? You cut down far too many trees, it's such a waste . . . O-Orion."

"You need not concern yourself over the cutting down of the trees. As for the many blazing fires, I like them. It is gloomy in the manor without them and it

96

chases away dark spirits."

She gave a soft exclamation and said, "I do not believe that!"

While Juel's mouth was still open a little from her words, Orion snatched her close and pressed his lips to hers. His arms wrapped around her like a band of steel, while her hands hung at her sides, her entire body rigid in shock at the hard-yet-soft press of his lips. Her head reeled and her limbs began to tremble, her mind screaming, *This could not be happening!*

"My God!" Orion said, lifting his mouth from hers and shoving her back so hard she came up against the wall. "You are a witch!" He turned on his heel, away from her. "You'll not cast your spell upon me, sorceress. Get out!" Orion thundered, swiping her soul-stirring taste from his mouth.

"What?" Juel looked at him from dazed eyes.

He was pouring himself another cup of strong brew, not looking at her, inhaling and exhaling like a fire-breathing dragon.

"You are cruel and horrible, just like they say. I believe every word I've heard about you now, that you are—"

"Be gone, witch, else I'll have you burned at the stake."

"I am going," Juel said. "Just remember, Sir Dragon, you kissed me, not the other way around." She swiped at her mouth with the back of her hand and spat his taste from her lips. "Do you call that a kiss?" she taunted. "I have been kissed better by a frog with two heads!"

Orion did not turn to look at her as he growled over

his shoulder, "Tomorrow you will work with the men. You will carry rocks to the quarry, pull weeds in the garden, and then you will shovel dung from the stables. And at mealtime you will bring me my supper . . . without hairs in it!"

A mischievous grin broke out on Juel's face as she closed the heavy portal behind her. "From shoveling dung to the kitchen, hmm? No, my lord Orion, you will not get hairs in your food this time. No, a few careless hairs in your food are much too good for you." She giggled softly as she descended the narrow stairs. "I promise to make your meal very tasty indeed this time!"

Chapter Nine

Juel had slaved with the men, hauling rocks to the quarry until her arms felt as if they would fall off. The men had been happy with her presence and when she had sung them some courtly and bawdy tunes, they had been so delighted, they made certain her piles grew smaller and that the rocks she carried to the quarry consisted of the smallest ones. When she had shoveled the dung, delighted to spend time stroking the beautiful horses that whinnied and rubbed velvety noses across her shoulders, she had found her tasks lightened there, too, for the stableboys helped her out and laughed when she sang one of Jay's favorite drinking tunes.

Juel had met more of the castlefolk, and Lydia even brought her light fare and drinks of fruit water. Everyone had talked to her, and though she had made some friends, she was certain she had made an enemy of Alice. When Juel had gone to the kitchen to return some dishes and speak with Dawn, Alice had given her an ugly, hateful smirk.

Juel made her way to the garden now, rubbing the

small of her back. She was happy with the way the day had gone so far. She had met so very many people that she likened the manor to a small hamlet, a community of kindly and cheerful people.

It seemed that Dawn Peyton knew everyone and was received jovially by all. Everyone liked her and Juel could understand why.

She would not spoil her day by thinking of that dragon Orion who spent so much time indoors, locked in his chambers, or housed in a private room off the great hall with his knights. He had no care whether her arms fell off from heavy labor or that she dropped dead from exhaustion! He watched her from an upper window, she knew, for she had often made out his taunting face at the east side of the house where she had worked on the crumbling wall with the men below.

"Does Orion ever come out of the house for fresh air?" Juel had whispered to Dawn when the lovely maid brought her and the workers some refreshment.

Dawn had leaned closer and poured Juel some fruit water. "He goes out mostly at night and doesn't return until the small hours of the morning. He rides that black demon of a horse. If you were in the stables, you know exactly which one I speak of."

"Oh, yes, I do. He is very beautiful and he kept rolling those huge eyes at me. Though I did not go near him, I heard one of the men call him Angel and thought it a strange name for a dark horse."

"Orion is a strange person, Juel. And it is funny what you said about the horse. His full name is Dark Angel." Dawn shuddered. "There is something dark and frightening about the man, too. Even though I like Orion he gives me shivers up my spine. He seems to be made of stone and I wonder if he feels any emotion at all."

Juel thought for a moment as she stared at the pile of rocks and stones, recalling the man's kiss and the anger that followed. Now she could believe that the kiss had made him feel emotion he hadn't liked feeling. But how? How had he felt? A tug at his heart, as she had felt?

Now, on her way to the weedy gardens out back, Juel slipped into the kitchen and, seeing that Alice was nowhere to be found, walked quickly up to Dawn who was just heading into the huge larder.

Dawn whirled with a container of mustard when she heard Juel's voice, almost dropping it. "You half scared me to death."

"Dawn . . ." Juel began quickly, looking over her shoulder. "What does desire feel like?"

The dainty young woman blinked and swallowed hard. "You are asking me?" Dawn's voice was low, her face filled with wide-eyed innocence.

Juel nodded. "I should have known. You know about as much as I do when it comes to passion and lovemaking."

"Well," Dawn said. "I don't know about that. I mean—" She cast a quick look about the pantry and kitchen—"I've seen the act of coupling."

"Seen it?" Juel gasped. "How did that happen? Oh, your parents."

"No, not my parents. I have never known a mother or father. I was left in the village on a doorstep." She shrugged nonchalantly when she saw Juel's look. "It does not bother me, not as it does some of the other orphans who had been abandoned. I am happy with my life. I know I will meet a wonderful man some day and we will be very happy. He will want a boy and a girl just as I do. A little cottage with a stream out back and—"

"I have the same wishes you do," Juel interrupted excitedly. "Exactly, down to the cottage and the boy and girl. Maybe even twins." She looked away, staring sightlessly at a row of pickled fruits. "It seems I will never find the right man. I am already near twenty."

Dawn looked melancholy for a moment. "I don't know how old I am." She sighed. "No one knows."

"How sad," Juel said, forgetting what she had come to Dawn with in the first place.

"Not really," Dawn said with a whimsical grin. "Truly, I *am* happy. In fact, I am so happy right now that I wonder what is going to happen next. I feel that something wonderful is about to take place."

"Hmm, maybe you are going to meet that particular individual very soon."

Dawn looked dubious. "Here? At The Keep?" She chortled and wrinkled her nose. "That would be a miracle for sure!"

Now Juel remembered what she'd come for. "You said you have witnessed the act of coupling?"

"Yes," Dawn said shyly. "It was by misadventure that I came upon Alice doing, you know . . ." Dawn shrugged. "That. Young men have come seeking for me to lie with them." She went no further.

"And what happened?" she asked Dawn. "To the ones who did, I mean."

"They went away with black eyes." She flexed her arm, and a muscle of unexpected brawny contour became visible. "See, I can take care of myself. I'll not

102

let some lusty oaf steal my maidenhead." Her voice became defensive. "A very strong knight from outside performing castle-guard duty tried to force me once. He almost did the evil deed, had not Shadow jumped on his back, and scared the gigantic knight half to death so that he ran away and never returned. He hurt me. His manstaff was as large as a battering ram. It was only because of Shadow that he did not hurt me all the way!"

"Who is this Shadow?" Juel wanted to know. It was a strange name for a person to have.

"You'll see" was all Dawn said, whirling with her braid flying behind as she went back to work.

On her way to the garden in the inner courtyard, Juel turned right, walked outside where the wild overgrown shrubbery and weedy underbrush hugged the manor too closely, and came to a sudden halt. Someone was immediately behind her!

She was about to scream when the hand clamped over her mouth, from behind. Warm breath was on her neck, making her think of a gigantic cat.

"Not happy to see me, sister?"

The deep male voice cooed and purred. She could almost see the twinkle of mischief in the cat-green eyes.

"Jay!" Juel cried when he slipped his hand away from her face. "Oh, Jay, Jay! Where have you been?" She gave a tiny, high-pitched squeal of joy and surprise. Her smile was a merry one.

His own face grinned with a zest for life, with glowing health, showing her the handsomest smile in all of England!

Then he lifted her and swung her about high in the air, shouting that she was the most beautiful wench he'd ever come across, that he loved her utterly and endlessly! . . . all this while a pair of darkly disturbed eyes watched from the upper story chapel window.

Orion rushed from the chapel to his apartments, walking over to the heavy portal and wrenching it open. He bellowed for someone to come to him and then swore when Shadow, who was slouched outside the door, peeling a banana, glanced up with round hazelnut eyes, heard the bellow and shrieked.

Ruark, the closest servant, on the third floor, came hurrying up the broad oak stairs, saw Shadow scurrying down the passageway the other way, and said to Orion, "One of these days, m'lord, your pet is going to find another human to love."

"That will be a most sad day, I'm sure," Orion humphed. "Now, I want you to check on a new arrival for me, find out how he managed to get inside. I've never seen him." Ruark moved to go and do as bidden. "And Ruark, send the new maid Juel to the kitchens."

"What!?" Ruark said, astonished. "She has not weeded the gardens yet."

"I don't care about the gardens! See that she goes directly to the kitchen and prepares my food."

"It's not yet time for the evening meal."

"Ruark, I don't care that it is not time to eat. I am hungry and I wish to see the new maid, Juel. We have some unfinished business."

With that, while Ruark still lingered, Orion pulled the hangings back over the mullioned window, making the room dark but for the blazing fire in his chamber. "I know, Ruark, it is not your responsibility. You have your job as head of the mesnie, the military personnel. Go back to the men below and see that Rajahr gives Juel Reynaude the message. And Ruark . . . See who the intruder is?"

"I will do that, m'lord—"

"Please, don't call me that. You know how I hate to be considered proud and lofty when I am not."

Ruark smiled and backed out, with the kissing exit of India, such as Rajahr did when he wished for Orion to share some good mirth.

Orion did not smile this time. His thoughts were on Juel and the handsome young man, again seeing them embracing and sharing endearments. He wasted no time on jealousy. Hatred, yes, because all he really wanted to do while staring at the gardens below was murder the stranger in cold blood!

Chapter Ten

Juel had been too weary to follow through with her scheme of sending a plate of vegetables surrounded by stable dung stirred into tasty bits of meat to Orion. Besides, it just was not in her to do such an evil thing, no matter how tempting the idea had been at the time. She could see Alice doing such a mean thing . . . like placing hairs in food on purpose just to get back at . . .

"Hairs! Alice!" she almost shouted, then looked around to see if anyone had heard her.

Of course, why hadn't she thought of it before? Alice's hair was the same deep shade as her own and Alice would be thrilled to pieces if she made Orion rumble and yell at someone other than herself. Revenge was just not in Juel, however, and she thought that God took care of fools who did folks harm by playing bad jests or trifling with their emotions. And strong ones they had been, too, if a few hairs in his food could make Orion so amorous!

Now he had sent for her again and she wondered what he had in mind for her this time. She planned to ask him about her father, since she had not seen him working with the other carpenters and woodcutters. One thing made her happy; her brother Jay was here. He had told her that Peter had come looking for him in the village, but Jay did not know why he had not returned to The Keep. Their father had said he had some things to see to; Juel was nervous about why it took him so long.

Juel knocked on Orion's chamber door, balancing the food tray on her hip. Beneath the covered platter lay meat with dumplings, peas, onions and saffron for flavoring, honey, oranges, butter, spiced wine, and a crusty loaf of bread she had baked just that afternoon herself. Since she had not eaten but a few crusts of bread and fruit water, the delicious odors were making her stomach rumble.

"Enter!" a deep voice called out. "And be quick about it."

The tray was getting very heavy and when Juel reached for the handle, something scurried behind her, startling her so that the tray went flying, the food scattered all about the floor, and an orange was sent rolling toward the stairs.

When the door was wrenched wide, Juel stood there with her mouth agape, while Orion glared at all the food scattered about the floor, the orange going bump-bump-bump down the stairs.

His hands were cocked on his lean hips, the material of his dark-green hose stretched tight against them, as well as clinging to his thighs. Juel stared down, then up to his black velvet eyes, her lashes fluttering rapidly.

"I'm sorry," Juel said. "Something startled me. Did you not see it?"

Orion couldn't believe it. Another meal ruined! At this rate, he was going to have to go hungry else have someone other than this distracted hoyden prepare his food and bring it to him.

"I saw nothing," he snapped, then added in a lower, huskier tone, "Liar."

Curse his bloodthirsty heart! "Believe me or not, there was something . . . like a shadow th-that—" Why was he staring at her? What had she said? Was he going to punish her again? With another kiss?

"Ah! I understand now." He did not apologize for his surliness. "It was only Shadow." He stepped aside to allow her to enter the room. "Come in. I must speak with you."

Is that all? she wondered. Then, as she walked into the dark chamber with the blazing fire and the many gorgeous tapestries and heavy pieces of furniture, she came up short, and turned to face him.

"What or who is this shadow?" she asked him, realizing her stomach was clenched tight.

Orion stared. He couldn't do less, for she was intoxicating him once again, far more than any strong drink ever could. "It is only—" He'd been about to tell her, then decided to let her find out for herself. "You will see one day."

"Dawn Peyton told me the same," she said. "Why is this shadow such a mystery?"

Orion shrugged lazily, smiling as if bored. "This whole castle keep is a labyrinth of mysteries, some solved, some not so. If you can solve the riddle of The Keep, you can win the prize, Juel Reynaude. I'll decorate you myself with the escutcheon, the medal of honor and glory for a job well done." He ended with a smirk, reaching for the wine jug.

"Your words are filled with ridicule." Juel tossed her head. "Do you enjoy tormenting people and making them wonder just what you mean? Is it because you yourself are so miserable and your own soul so filled with hostility and conflict?"

"Would you like to experience lovemaking with the devil?"

Juel almost gasped. He meant himself, she knew. "N-no, of course not," she said.

"Well then, cease your driveling defiance, else you'll find yourself beneath an eager thrust. It has been a long while since I've made love with a woman."

Juel could not help what came out next. "You call it *making love,* what you most likely do with a woman?" A soft exhalation followed. "I doubt it. 'Twould be more like *making hate* I'd dare say. And how could any woman want to couple with you?"

She was shaking so hard, it was like standing with a fierce wind whipping at her back, blowing clear through and tearing at her soul.

"Juel, you dare too much with that vixen's tongue of yours!"

She tossed her head, making her dark hair swirl in a black aura about her shoulders. "How good it must feel to vent your wrath on poor kitchen maids."

Orion grinned. The animation of her features was enchanting, and he knew that one day soon he would have her panting and writhing beneath him.

"Come here," he growled deep in his throat.

"No!"

She backed away and he lunged foward, catching her around the waist. She struggled and squealed like a frightened piglet, even tried kicking him in the shins. Her hair swirled about her body wildly, tumbling carelessly down her back. Her eyes sparkled with mischief when she took in the bulge beneath his dark-green hose.

Then her knee came up, but her heavy skirts kept the blow from contacting his crotch.

"Damn you, wench!"

"I am not a wench!"

"A damnable wench, you are!"

She yelled right back, "Not!"

He pulled her with him to the carpet and her body stiffened in shock, her breath caught in her lungs. Panic rioted within her. What would he do now? She looked up at him, her brow creased with worry.

"Witch," he said, his eyes smoldering with fire. "I'd sooner make love to you here on the floor than in that bed."

"Love?" she spat. "You know nothing of the emotion!"

True, he had no thoughts of love, yet never before had he felt this strength of desire for a woman. The gnawing pain of lust overwhelmed him, his manhood throbbing as heat gathered in his loins.

"Oh!" Her outcry was brief because she knew what he was going to do and she needed to put up defenses, not waste breath appealing for him to release her.

"Don't worry," he said, running a finger across her lower lip. "All I want to do is make you squirm. You are most lovely when vulnerable."

"You are evil!" she hissed into his mocking face.

He moved atop her, lifted, lowered, and his body came against hers hard and heavy. The hard bulge of him pressed into her. Juel felt a fiery knot building inside, well below her waist and between her thighs. It continued to flutter then, wildly uncontrollable, hot and moist and wonderfully frightening.

He lowered his hand to cup the curve of her bottom and she cried out. He fondled her boldly, and smiled wickedly into her face.

She began to struggle, squirming beneath him. There was no help for it. He was stronger than she by far. And didn't she want this? Truly want him to touch her in secret places? No! She struggled, again futilely.

"Is that the best you can do?" he chuckled. "Why don't you faint from my touch?"

Her brows drew together in an angry frown. "I never faint." Her gaze settled on his mouth. She would have forgotten her name if asked for it right now. He was breaking her down and she knew she must get away. "Let me up!"

"As you say."

"What—?" She was suddenly moving very fast.

He pulled her up to stand with him with such force that she reeled on her feet. She stood there dizzily trying to gain her balance. With a springy bounce, she moved away from him, then gazed into his hot eyes as he came to stand in front of her. "I have work to do. I will go now."

"You won't get far," he said, leaning over her, his eyes cold.

When she began to walk away, he reached out, swinging her around to face him.

In one swift movement, he had encircled her in his arms and her armor of resistance vacillated and tottered precariously. She was going to melt, she just

112

knew it. *I must get away,* she thought, *because if he kisses me again with that beautiful mouth* . . . She leaned back, then realized her mistake in another moment.

He reached up to touch her breast and she slapped his hand away. "One day, Juel, one day," he vowed.

She said nothing. It was a tug of war.

Looking down into her eyes deeply while hugging her fiercely, he cursed her and brusquely said, "Let's see who wins this time, witch!"

She grinned into his face. "What happened to 'wench'?"

"You try my patience!"

She laughed this time.

His reaction was swift and violent.

Chapter Eleven

He was hugging her, close to crushing her!

She felt as though she were in the clenching grip of an iron maiden. She should have fled while she had the chance, instead of letting him get a hold of her.

She dared to chastise him. "You are unforgivably rough and ill-mannered, Lord Orion!"

He did not smile at her words, only stared down into her beguiling face.

When his mouth came down hard, Juel squirmed and tried nipping at his lip, but he slipped out easily from the bite and kissed her more thoroughly. Now, curiosity and a fascinating appeal held Juel in its grip. Pulling his mouth from hers for a moment, he gazed deeply into her misted eyes and forgot the terrible emptiness he carried with him from childhood.

He groaned deeply from within. Then, catching her face in his big hands, he reclaimed her lips, crushing her to him again.

His kisses were far more persuasive than she cared to admit, an odd mixture of pleasure and pain. Outside it was raining again, making the mullioned panes of glass sparkle like jewels. But Juel neither saw nor heard any of this. She was feeling her first taste of desire.

She was burning him with the soft swells of her little breasts and long, boyishly slim legs and hips, her arms that were creeping up his nape, her touch searing into his soul. It had begun the day before, to last forever, he knew, with that first kiss. Never had he been speared through to the heart with one kiss.

A bittersweet wrenching in his chest, Orion snatched his lips from Juel's and stared down at her; he wished he'd never known the name of Juel Reynaude. She had ensnared him in something he had no use for, indeed dared not have.

"Go away, Juel Reynaude."

Juel licked her passion-bruised mouth. "Again?"

"Yes. Again. Next time I will not be tempted by your empty, toilsome charms."

Empty? Toilsome? Hah! Now she knew *he* was the liar. "You felt what I did, Sir Dragon. I know you did. We shared something special and you are afraid to admit it. These kisses of today and the ones that came before cannot be pushed aside as something as trivial as you are implying."

He had backed away, but now he started for her again. "Would you like to make it *really* something special? Kisses are nothing compared to what we could share. Yes, I feel the passion. It is lust; nothing more significant. I could have you and send you away, and you would be forgotten more quickly than the batting of an eyelash."

"Let's walk outside."

"What?" Orion stared at her, his mouth curled on

116

one side. It was raining outside and he hated rain.

"I want to see you in daylight. No," she said, when he moved to open the window hangings. "Outside, where I can really look at you and see if there's any color in your eyes other than black."

He snorted. "You mean my *soul,* don't you?"

She almost smiled, thinking he was not as dark and frightening as he would lead others to believe. "Please. Come outside with me. We will walk. The air is fresh and smells of the earth and trees."

Orion felt a tug at his heart and wondered at the strength of emotion. When he trained with his knights he usually did so far on the other side of the stables, to put distance from him and the round tower. He could go to war, even to France, away from England, but he did not like walking anywhere near the round tower. It irked him when he had to go somewhere on the castle grounds and feel that tower scowling down on him like some hideous monster. He didn't like feeling vulnerable.

Juel tipped her head. "Why won't you tell me what you are thinking? Won't you allow anyone into your thoughts?"

She had felt his pain when they had kissed and had hurt inside, as if sharing his misery. What had happened to him in his life? she wondered and was about to ask when the door was pounded upon as if by a battering ram.

Orion was almost glad for the intrusion but nonetheless growled the word "Enter" in his surliest voice. Juel's back was turned. She felt she could not face anyone, else they'd see how flushed and excited she was. She wondered if people could read desire on the

117

face of another? If so, she knew hers would be red and fiery, just like she felt in certain secret places.

"You must come, there is a band of outlaws sacking the village. Ruark is already calling the knights together and readying their weapons."

The voice was so deep and wonderful that Juel knew she had to turn and look, red face and all. When she finally turned she was not prepared for the angelic face her eyes encountered. The voice did not fit the man's features. He was blond-haired and beautiful, and when his soft blue eyes met hers, he smiled as if the sun had come into the room.

Howell Armstrong, Orion's best knight, thought he had just looked upon the loveliest creature on God's earth. She was dainty, hazel-eyed, with great masses of coiling dark hair. He was instantly in love and knew he would follow her to the ends of the earth if she but said the words.

"Who is she?" the blond knight murmured. He had been away and just returned, so he did not know she was merely a servant from the village.

Orion's eyes narrowed into slits of onyx. "Juel Reynaude."

Howell was waiting for introductions but Orion offered none. "We will go," Orion said, walking over to a coffer and slamming doors to a wardrobe. He pulled out a heavy sword that made Juel gasp.

"I am Howell Armstrong, and I am at your service, my lady."

"Not at the moment, you are not," Orion grumbled. Then he saw Howell's besotted expression as he continued to gaze at Juel. "We have something important to do, if you recall." Orion looked at Juel.

"She is the new maid at The Keep."

"Maid!" Howell shouted. "How can this be—?"

Just then Duncan, another knight, came barging in, shoving a cussing, dark-haired man in front of him. Orion glared at the young man, the same one who had been embracing and speaking endearments to Juel in the garden.

Orion wanted to strangle the handsome man, but first sarcastically asked, "And just who are you?"

A roguish grin split the newcomer's face. "I am Jay, Peter Reynaude's son. I have come in place of my father who has taken ill and cannot leave the village." Jay heard Juel gasp, but sent her a conspiratorial look and nodded. "Yes, Juel, he is ill."

With a severe frown, Orion looked from one to the other, finally making out the resemblance. "Ah," he said with a near groan. "You are Juel's brother. You are a carpenter and a woodcutter and are skilled enough to fill in for your father?"

"That's correct. And I'm ready to start right away."

"Good." As Orion lifted the heavy sword, Jay took a backward step. "Do not worry. It's not for you. There's trouble in the village and we're shorthanded, what with so many knights away."

"I'll come with you," Jay said, flexing his sword arm. "I'll fill in as auxiliary knight. One more is better th—"

"You can fight?" Orion asked, already brushing past the men and going out into the hall.

After Jay had sent Juel a reassuring look he followed Orion. "I can," he answered him. "I've even trained with King Henry's men."

Juel giggled softly. Trained with the king's men? She didn't know about that. Jay, ever the charming

119

fabricator, had gotten himself into more trouble, always thinking he was a knight in shining armor and could fight with the best of them, as he'd boasted.

She sighed as she watched them go, then turned to the window and walked across the room to push back the hangings. Rain was falling softly and Juel prayed her brother would be safe as he rode out with the other men. She hoped they would give him a gentle mount because Jay did not like horses.

Now, besides warring with the conflicting emotions of attraction and desire, Juel was worried about her father. Was he really ill, or was this something Jay and Peter had devised together, to have Jay take their father's place? But why, she wondered, why in the world would she need a protector?

Juel sighed and left the chamber. When was Jay going to find another woman to protect? And when he did, who was going to protect her?

Her eyes twinkled with the secrets that only a woman's heart could understand as she made her way down the broad oak staircase. A furry black-and-white cat bounded from a room on the third floor. Juel gasped as it curled itself about her legs.

She reached down to pick up the friendly cat that was purring contentedly. "So," Juel said, stroking the silky fur. "You must be the shadow everyone speaks of, hmm? I can see why, since you are more black than white and you sneaked up on me quite suddenly again. Well, let's go the kitchen and get you a saucer of milk, Shadow. I think you will enjoy that."

The cat purred and rubbed his face against Juel's shoulder, happy to be cradled in the gentle human's arms. One of the servants in the great hall saw Axel, the cat, in the new maid's arms. Axel was loved by all the castlefolk—all but Orion, who hated cats with a passion.

"Here you are, Shadow, here's some milk."

As Juel placed the saucer on the floor, the cat began to lick the milk at once. Just as Alice, nearby, smirked at what the new maid had called the cat, Axel's fur bristled and the real Shadow rushed into the kitchen, snatched up a piece of fruit, blinked at Juel twice, screeched and hurried away.

"What was that?" Juel had her hand over her heart.

"That," Alice snickered, "is a spider monkey. Don't you know anything?"

Juel huffed through her nose and began to walk away. "I've never seen one. But I know one thing. It must be a relative of yours!"

Chapter Twelve

They thundered out of the courtyard, Orion on his black war-horse, the knights riding close behind with Jay Reynaude. Like the trees in the forest, they were clothed in green and brown. They wore no armor, only shields and bows and arrows and sword. They galloped fast in their light garments to the village of Herst, crossing the Brighton-Hastings Road.

It did not take long to ride through the great forest mounted on their war-horses, the same great forest Juel had lost herself in. Orion's men knew it better than he himself, for they went out more often to hunt.

Orion's small-shield, worn on his forearm, was stamped with the mythological hunter from which his name was derived. When they drew close, having come quietly through the forest, they slowed and crept through the trees, coming onto the wall. Orion viewed the village through the tall hedges and brush. They intended to surprise the pilferers.

"Do you see anything?" Howell asked as he reined in close to Orion. Jay was on the other side of Howell.

"Not yet," Orion answered the fair-haired knight in a low voice as he backed his black horse from the hedge.

They waited for what seemed like hours, when actually it was only a matter of strained and tense minutes.

While they sat their war-horses, shifting softly, Orion remembered his times with King Henry. The young king and he got along famously. Henry had released and restored a young earl of March to his noble position. Henry had also elevated a young man to earldom. His friendships extended beyond the royal family. The coalition and safeguarding of his court created new privileges, such as naming his brother John Duke of Bedford. Henry had gained great power and many changes had been made and still were being made.

While Jay was studying Orion's profile, the accomplished knight thought of the time Henry's men had trained him to become a warrior. He had been known as an auxiliary knight of non-noble descent, mainly because Henry had rewarded him for his excellence in the field of battle. Previously, only one of knightly parentage could become a knight. However, King Henry thought differently. He believed John Scardon had been hiding something and said as much, that Scardon was a devious and dangerous man. Henry also elevated Orion to Baron of Herstmonceux, since Scardon had not yet returned and was thought to be dead. Henry also believed the inheritance of property by the correct bloodlines was an extremely serious matter, and he was still involved in hauling forth ancient genealogical rolls to prove that Orion Sutherland was true heir of The Keep, which Henry had believed was Sutherland Castle.

"We ride!" Orion growled like thunder in the hills when he heard a woman scream and a child cry out. "Into the gates, right on the other side!"

Bursting forth from the trees, they jumped thickets and thundered between the wooden gates which had been crashed open earlier by the band of pillagers.

In these moments of battle Orion's blood pounded through his veins wild and hard. He knew no fear of anything now. He heard the woman crying and the boy trying to comfort her, and he veered to the right where the clustered houses of the village began.

"Mama, you're going to be all right!" Geoffrey Johns shouted and pulled at her limp arm which lay on the rush-covered floor full of blood. "You are, aren't you, mama?"

"Come away, boy," Orion said, coming down off his war-horse to kneel where the woman lay. He checked her pulse and found there was none. He stared at the boy's shocked and frightened eyes, seeing all over again himself at that age. This boy could possibly be a little older, but what did it matter, his mother had just died, murdered in cold blood by strangers. "You must come with me. You can help her no longer."

Geoffrey Johns stared at his mother for a long moment, then accepted the hand that reached down for him. "I can't go and leave her! Look! The fire is coming this way. Mama will burn!"

"Boy . . ." Orion said firmly. "You have to leave her. There is no way to put out the fires. You must come." He felt the painful twist in his gut; he was remembering the time when he'd had to leave his own mother and father.

125

Remembering! How was this possible?! He thought he had pushed it all back far in his mind, never to be taken out and looked at. But now it was all happening again, as if it were yesterday. He saw Scardon lead him away, saying it was going to be all right, that Scardon was there to help him. But was that the case? Or was John Scardon one of the murderers of his parents?

"I don't want to leave her. Oh, please, help me! The fire's coming." The boy looked up into Orion's tormented eyes as he twisted before him on the horse. "Are you sad, too? Did you know my mama?"

"No, I did not know her. I can see that she is . . . was very pretty. Boy, you must not think about it now. She is gone to a better place." Did he just say that? He could not believe he was talking about paradise to a little boy, being so tender to someone.

"You must mean heaven. Mama talked about it a lot. Is she really going there now?" He groaned. "But I want to go with her."

"Ah, I believe I will not allow that, boy."

"My name is Geoffrey Johns. Who are you?"

"I am Orion, baron of this village."

Geoffrey gulped as he rode smoothly in front of Orion as he checked out the village, seeing his men help the villagers who had been hurt, robbed, or the women raped. "I heard you are a bad and evil man, that you hurt people. Are you going to hurt me?"

Orion's heart leapt and his throat contracted. "No, I am not going to hurt you, Geoffrey Johns. This happened to me when I was a little boy, too."

"It did?" Geoffrey twisted around to look into Orion's eyes. "Did a nice man take you away, too? Did you lose your mother?"

"I lost more than my mother, lad." *I lost my life.*

They were creeping through the fog that lay thickly about the boles of the oaks and elms. There were fifty or sixty men, far outnumbering Orion's men. And they were already having their fun with a pretty little redhead when they heard the horses in the forest.

"They're coming!" a man with a scar hissed, slicing his hand in the air for silence. "Leave off the maid and get us behind that thick stand of trees."

Autumn Meaux scurried into the bushes as soon as the men who had been about to ravish her let her be. Her long mass of red hair was tangled, her white blouse dirty, her skirts torn and soiled—but her virginity was yet intact. She could thank God for that at least.

These men were evil, Autumn thought; they had killed her parents when they had all been visiting relatives in the English town of Brighton. She and her sisters had traveled to this village in hopes of escaping the madmen, but they had been there waiting. Autumn had no idea what had happened to her sisters. They had always been together, all their life, four girls born at a single birth.

Autumn hugged herself, keeping her knees in front of her chest and her head low. Now there were more of them coming. The men were sunk low in the bushes and behind the trees, waiting.

She prayed that these new men would not hurt her. Where were the others of her blood? What had happened to them? Oh, she was so afraid for her sisters! And for herself, she could only pray.

127

Chapter Thirteen

"Get ready, men! They come!"

Hadwin was an evil-looking man. He had a scar running from his forehead down to his cheek and an eye that was stone-white, without sight. He was in command of the band of renegades that had sacked the village now that their leader was not with them.

They waited in the shadows to ambush their pursuers and Hadwin thought they should remain silent and hidden, if they were outnumbered. But he didn't think that was the case. If it was the grown lad from The Keep who came, Hadwin knew the strong and skillful knight Orion—whom King Henry favored—would ride with fewer than Scardon's own.

But Scardon was not with Hadwin and his men.

Autumn now ran from the trees, straight for the pursuers, thinking it could be no worse for her with them. Since the pillagers were in hiding and lay in wait, it was the more likely choice.

129

As she ran into a clearing, her red hair tangled to her waist, Orion and his men reined their horses up. She stood frightened and shivering and managed to spout out the words, "They wait for you! Please . . . help me!"

"We can't take you now." A crooked smile of encouragement came to Orion's face as he saw her alarm, then he shifted and handed the boy down to her. "Keep him safe as you can." In an instant, Orion took in the expensive cloth of her torn red dress. "We will deal with those who have hurt you, mademoiselle."

Orion and his men spurred their horses and wielded their swords above their heads, charging into battle, not knowing or caring who the evil men were, only knowing they were ahead of them, waiting to ambush them.

Orion saw them first, as he was in the front, charging with reckless abandon into the center of the sackers who burst from the trees. They were outnumbered, Orion and his men, by thirty or more. With his shield of the hunter in the starheavens stamped on his steel, Orion wielded his sword, cutting one down and then another. And yet another head went rolling . . .

From his hiding place, Hadwin fell back in dread and dismay, seeing no fear in his formidable foe. It mattered not how many men he had; this would be a battle he would lose. He swore, knowing he must get away and report this to Scardon, who was seeking diversion in France, and let the man take it from there. Scardon would not like losing so many men.

Orion's men fought with ferocity, scattering Hadwin's own in fear. Some fought valiantly but died in an agony of spilled guts and blood, some with split skulls and severed limbs. Off their horses and onto the ground, Orion's men rushed into the battle, killing and maiming as they went, scattering their foe to the four winds.

From his hidden vantage point Hadwin drew his bow and let the arrow fly, striking his prey.

"Ouff." Orion wrenched with pain as the arrow sliced through his thigh and stuck in the bone of his leg. But he had felt worse pain before, and as he looked down, the blood trickled from his leg as the shaft of the arrow protruded. He reached down and, grabbing the shaft, yanked it from his leg, ripping the flesh of a gaping red wound.

The blood flowed and the pain was intense, but he fought on with the courage of a lion. Orion's men now routed the sackers who were left, but they ran and hid in the woods. Howell Armstrong saw Orion go down to one knee and called for his men to halt the chase.

"Orion is wounded!" he announced.

Orion staggered to gain his footing but could not. He had lost too much blood. Jay Reynaude, swiftly at his side, took a cloth and placed it over the wound. Wrapping it tightly to staunch the flow of blood, he stood back. Orion smiled weakly up at him.

"We must get him back to the castle," Howell said. "One of you men see to the boy and the girl and bring them along." He looked at the girl and saw that she was pretty and noticed, as had Orion, that by the looks of her red gown she was one of some wealth.

Ruark looked down at Orion who was staring up in pain. "A fine battle," Orion said with a grimace, as everything grew black and the forest swam in twisted shadows before his eyes.

Then he knew no more.

Juel was in the hall with Dawn and Alice when Orion was carried in by Duncan and Howell. An hour before, the overseer Haymo had brought word that Orion had been wounded, and that it would take some time to bring him out of the forest. And there were others with them. All the maids looked at the small boy and the tall girl coming in with Ruark, and Alice stared at the fine dress the redheaded girl wore, thinking it a tragedy that such beautiful clothing had been torn and soiled.

"Where is the physician?" Howell snapped, disliking the greed in Alice's eyes. He knew her well. They'd once been lovers, but not anymore.

Dawn stepped forward. "He is not here. I have already looked for him and have been told he went to Brighton last night to care for a relative. I have sent to Herstmonceux for another."

Ruark followed close behind. "You might as well forget him. He has his hands full in the village with what has just occurred there. Many of the villagefolk have been hurt and burned."

"Send for him anyway," Duncan Kingsly snapped, and everyone gaped at the young knight while Dawn went in search of Rajahr.

"But that is impossible," Howell said as they rested Orion on the cushioned bench before making the climb up the broad oak stairs. "He is needed there." Howell looked at Juel Reynaude and his heart wrenched, seeing her concern and wishing it were for him instead of Orion.

"I will care for him," Juel said, brushing past Alice who had stepped in front of her to stare at Autumn's red gown with its pale rose-patterned tunic and sash.

"You?" Alice gawked at the maid. "What can you do?"

Just then Jay stepped into the hall. "She can do more than a physician," he announced. "Being a woodcutter's daughter, she has seen and tended hundreds of cuts from axes and serious wounds from kicked-back trees. He has a serious wound." He turned to Orion's men. "You can trust her."

As soon as Jay came into the hall everything else had ceased to exist for Alice. Her lover was here! She filled her eyes with him, his cat-hazel eyes, his strong and lean physique, and recalled all the exciting things they had done in the hayloft.

"Jay!" Alice cried, starting to come around the long table when something in his eyes made her halt.

"Alice," Jay said. "How are you?"

All she could do was blink in stupefaction.

Juel was getting impatient. "Don't stand around, men," she ordered. "Bring Orion upstairs and put him on the bed."

"Yes, you would be wise to do as she says," Jay put in, seeing that Orion's most trusted men were watching them closely. "He may die from that wound if it festers. It has already been a long while since he was wounded."

"Upstairs!" Juel shouted. She turned to her brother and told him what things she needed, then she turned to the knights as they lifted Orion. "How is it that none of you men know how to tend a wound?" she questioned. "What sort of knights are you? You haven't even torn his hose away and washed the wound." There was so much blood!

Duncan and Howell blushed and looked confused, but Ruark was not feeling the same discomfiture and puzzlement. "Who are you to say what must be done?" Ruark said tersely as they climbed the staircase. "You are nothing more than a working maid."

"She is more," Orion mumbled, his eyelids fluttering. "You . . . will . . . see for yours—" His head lolled against Duncan's arms—"sselvess—"

"What did he say?" Ruark looked at the knights, but they continued to carry Orion as Juel followed alongside. "More? She is more? What does he mean?"

Duncan and Howell did not look at the military leader as they carried Orion through the solar and into the upstairs bedroom. Just then Rajahr came into the chamber wringing his hands. Shadow jumped onto the bed and began to bounce up and down, but Rajahr shooed him away. Shadow leapt onto a massive chair with huge, carved arms and sank down, his long limbs stretched wide. He appeared to be very nervous, his beady brown eyes passing back and forth, blinking. Juel paid him no mind.

"We must bleed him," Rajahr said, looking down at Orion as several maids entered and added more wood to the already blazing fires.

"What?!"

Everyone stopped what they were doing to gawk at Rajahr.

"Ah, Rajahr," murmured Howell. "Why don't you just pray, hmm?"

Rajahr looked very affronted, feeling the insult like a slap in the face. He looked down at Orion lying on the bed and held back the purple-and-gold bed hangings, feeling as helpless as the monkey.

Juel took charge again. "We must move on and not tarry. Cease the disputes and the bickering. It does Orion no good." She told the maids that the room was too hot and ordered the men to remove Orion's clothing immediately. "Cover him with a sheet when you have him undressed."

The huge blond giant Howell stared at Juel, feeling the line of red creep up his throat. He swallowed hard. "With you in here?" He did not think he could disrobe a man and have this dainty beauty look on. Things could happen to his own body he might have trouble controlling. When she batted not a lash as he stared, he asked, "Are you sure?"

"Of course," Juel said, turning to the maids, then talking to Howell over her shoulder as she took up a knife one of them had fetched from the fire. She turned back to them as she tested the blade's edge. "Not sharp enough," she announced.

All four men stepped up to the bed, making a human wall as they stood together almost touching hands. Ruark was the first to speak. "You'll not touch Orion with that, little lady." He reached out to take the knife from her when Orion spoke from the bed.

They all turned, seeing his eyes flicker, hearing him mumble, "Enough of the grumblings. Let her do it." Then his head rolled and his eyes fluttered shut.

"I've had enough of this madness," Duncan said. "I am going to find a physician at once."

"Yes, go," Juel said. "One less to be moaning about his lord and his safety. He's safe enough. Now," she said, facing Howell. "Do you have a sharper blade than this?"

"I—I think so." Howell reached down to pull an eighteen-inch dagger from its sheath. "Will this do, m'lady?"

Saying nothing, she took the weapon, tested its edge while the three remaining men looked on agape, and then handed it to Lydia, who had come into the room after hearing about Orion's wound, to hold in the fire until it glowed.

"I know about these things," Lydia told them, her back turned to the room. "I can help."

"Why did someone not say so?" Ruark demanded. He looked to Rajahr and Howell, who only shrugged.

Juel looked at the men, at Lydia. "Why is it all so secret? Most of you know Orion is afraid of Lydia. They avoid each other like the plague. She goes to the round tower and Orion is aware of this. I have come to realize there is a mystery there."

Everyone seemed to get busy all of a sudden and the chamber grew terribly hushed. The men had Orion undressed in minutes. When Juel pulled back the sheet exposing his muscular body, everyone heard her soft gasp, it was so quiet in the room. She gulped, feeling his raw masculinity reaching out to her. My Lord, she did not know a man could be so huge! He was big all over; even his great calves bulged with muscle. And his toes, too.

Juel sighed, followed by a little whimper. Shielding her eyes from Orion's most vulnerable parts, she said to the man closest to the bed, "Turn him onto his side. I can get at the wound better." When Howell, with a red face, did as ordered, Juel bent to him and flung out a hand for the knife. Lydia handed it to her and Juel brought it to the wound. The sound of burning flesh

filled the space as Juel seared the wound closed.
"Ohhhhh . . ."

One of the maids fainted dead away and Juel ordered Howell to see to her, to take her away. He did as she bid and removed the maid from the chamber, carrying her outside the portal where Jay had been waiting to help if he could. He had just returned from caring for the horses, as Ruark had asked him to do, after he had gotten the linens and other items Juel had requested be brought to this room.

Back inside the chamber, Juel finished up with her ministrations and handed the dagger back to Howell when he returned. Juel stared down, then up again. "Where is the deformity on his back?" she asked, wiping her hands on a white linen cloth. "The villagers say he has one."

"D-deformity?" Howell said. "I know of none such." He would have grinned, were the circumstance not so serious.

"Come now," Juel said, looking him straight in the eyes. "You must know of what I speak?"

Lydia spoke up, coming over to Juel. "They must leave now. Orion is restless. There is too much conversation here."

"Yes," Juel said. "You must all go now." Ruark blinked at her coolness and aplomb. "You, too, Ruark."

"I stay here," Rajahr said, with arms crossed over his chest. "With my master." Shadow spilled from the chair and came to stand with Rajahr, blinking up at the woman and looking suddenly very calm. "Shadow remains also."

Juel looked around the chamber. "Shadow? I do not

see the cat."

"This is **Shadow**," **Rajahr** said with a lofty expression. The **monkey** made a face, then shook his chin from side to side. "He is a spider monkey. I brought him from India. He is Orion's pet."

Juel's hand pressed to her forehead as she looked up at the heavy-beamed ceiling. "Shadow . . ." she laughed. "The monkey! The kitchen cat is . . . ?"

"That would be Axel," Lydia offered. "My cat . . . who is everyone's cat. He loves the whole castle, Axel does." The graying bun on top of Lydia's head quivered as she shook her apron out, then made to leave the room.

"Lydia . . ." Juel said. "Wait. I want you to stay . . . to talk." When the woman paused, Juel said softly, "Please. We have so much to talk about."

"Like what?" Lydia asked Juel as the men started out the door. She was nervous, fiddling with her apron, her eyes anywhere but on Juel Reynaude.

When they were alone, Juel dropped the salvo. "Like the hump that is on Orion's back. I've no idea how large it is supposed to be. I've only heard rumors of a hunchback who rides beneath the moon. The villagefolk say it's Orion Sutherland who rides out and has this horrible bump. This deformity."

Juel looked over to the bed but could see nothing suggesting a deformity. Orion seemed perfect. She'd like to stare at him all day, but that would be improper.

Lydia's eyes drifted to Shadow and the monkey's eyes went back and forth between the humans. It grew quiet, very tense.

Lydia pretended ignorance. "What did you ask me about again?"

"I *said,* where is the hump?" Juel knew Lydia was not ignorant. "He is supposed to have a hump. I've . . ." Juel sighed tiredly. "I'm not going to repeat myself." *Maybe the hump only comes out at night, like the moon.* Juel almost giggled aloud at the absurdity of Orion turning suddenly into a hunchback.

Suddenly, Shadow squatted low in the middle of the floor, on the thick Persian carpet. He crossed his very long and skinny spidery arms and wrapped them around his head, and then on top of it. Only one eye peeked out. It did not blink.

The sight was humorous, but Juel did not laugh. Someone around this manor had to know something. She waited for Lydia to speak.

The monkey blinked, once, and shook his jowls.

Chapter Fourteen

"It is you!" Lydia cried. "You are the one!"

To Juel's amazement, Lydia turned and fled from the chamber. Then, even more astonishing, the monkey rose and performed a flip in the air, chattered incomprehensibly in Juel's face, and then he, too, fled the chamber, his arms flung high overhead.

Though at a loss as to why Lydia and Shadow had fled suddenly, Juel was captivated and delighted by Shadow's frolicking play. But what of Lydia? Why had she been so afraid of discussing Orion with her? And what had she meant by her words: 'It is you. You are the one'?

Ah, Juel thought, it is only the mystery surrounding this place. Things were becoming interesting. She didn't know if she wanted to escape The Keep, not when—

"Water . . ."

A moan from the bed brought Juel quickly to Orion's side. Reaching for the dipper to get him a drink of cool water, Juel was surprised yet again when a hand suddenly clamped on her wrist. She looked down to see Orion's hand sliding over her fingertips, then resting there with a gentle yet powerful grip. She dropped the dipper with a clatter.

Feeling his stirring touch, Juel swallowed hard and stood very still. This was nice, merely standing here with him holding her hand, his eyes closed while she could study him without flickers of apprehension coursing through her.

She studied him, feature by feature, taking in the virile and clean-cut cast of his reposed expression. He was so handsome, with his bladelike nose, the aristocratic curve of his lips, the thick, straight slash of dark eyebrows, lean and strong cheekbones, powerful chin with a cleft in the center of it. His hair was lit by the fire and it shone a near bluish-purple hue where the shadows kissed the long strands.

Juel was thoroughly engrossed in her study of the man, perusing every inch of the body covered by the thin sheet. She could make out each bulge of muscle and sinew, a man of brawn and mighty force, endowed with a knight's physical fitness . . . yet was he really in good health? She wondered at the greenish pallor he sometimes had, the amount of intoxicating spirits he consumed, and the fact that he was almost a recluse. But surely not celibate? When then, she thought, did he take his pleasure of women? He'd only toyed with her. While waiting for his wife?

Wife. That one little word made Juel feel melancholy, but she had no idea why it should so affect her. He was a married man and she had no right looking at him the way she had been doing.

And it was just then she found her eyes resting on

that most intimate part of him, the part that told he was more man than most. But what would she know of man's secret and intimate shape? Well, she thought, there was the tight hose men wore . . . there was no help for it since it was the fashion of the times. One could usually tell how well endowed . . .

Juel sighed dreamily and raised her eyes to find him watching her. She gasped, yanking her hand from his light grip, and straightened back from the bed, realizing with horror that she'd been steadily bending over him, like a willow in a strong north wind seeking asylum in the warm earth.

His eyes caught and held hers. "Please," he said in an otherworldly voice. "Do what you were doing. Continue."

His gaze lowered as did his voice, and Juel could not hear what he was mumbling. His eyes drifted shut and then fluttered open again.

Softly she said, "I was not doing anything, m'lord."

"Ah . . . but you were. You were moving closer to me. I need you here. Put your mouth on me . . ."

Juel jumped back. "What?" He must be delirious. "I will send for someone; perhaps the physician has come by now." She turned to go. "I will see."

"No."

His voice was soft, but his grip was strong, very strong. It did not feel right, in fact it was in the wrong place, Juel thought as she turned to look at what was keeping her from moving to the door. She heard his groan of pain at the same time she saw his leg wrapped about her hips.

She felt herself moving and gaped downward as his leg was pulled back to the bed—with her still wrapped

143

within his bent knee. "Oh, you must not!" she cried. "You will hurt yourself. Let go or you will cause yourself more pain."

That most vital part of him was what caused Orion the most distress at the moment. True, his thigh ached abominably where the arrow had been and he'd lost a lot of blood. Everything was vague and muddy to him, all but the soft little woman with the firm legs in his bed. She was very real and she felt so good and exciting to him.

He found himself wanting her. To carry her to him. To make her his bride. Ranice? It must be, his wife had finally come to him, and now he could have her. So long, he thought fuzzily, so long since he'd buried himself within a soft woman. Was he up to it?

"Why not," Orion said in a slow voice.

Juel had no idea what she'd gotten herself into; all her thoughts were of Orion and the pain he must be causing himself by keeping her imprisoned there. And what had he said? "Why not?"

"Leave go, m'lord. You are hurting yourself." Not to mention what was happening to her own body!

"You must not struggle so," he said, his eyes rolling and blinking as he fought to keep them open.

"I am not struggling," she said. Or had she been? She could not even remember that, a short time past, since all she knew at the moment was feeling—a lot of tender and sensitive feeling, making her raw and on fire all over, from the top of her head to her toes.

Her toes! Easily, without confinement, she wriggled them. When had she taken her shoes off? She tossed a glance back over her buttocks and saw her shoes on the floor. How had they come off? Of course, now she remembered. She had removed them because her feet had hurt, still sore as they were from her days of walking in the woods and her assignment of carrying rocks to the quarry.

Juel did not like having any part of her body touching another human. It made her think of the forbidden, she realized. Feet were . . . feet. Bare feet in bed, to her thinking, were too intimate, alluding to lovemaking. And the back of her knees. Or the small of her back. But feet, ah! Almost more intimate than having someone touch a part of . . . her breast.

Her breast! Yes, he was touching the underside of one of her breasts!

"Orion . . . you must not." Her voice carried little strength; was in fact, almost a squeak.

She realized then that their position had caused her to think he had his hand beneath her breast. He had, but she didn't think he had put it there. It had rested there when she had been dwelling on the masses of quivering sensations in her body. And his pain, she thought . . . he must be in so much pain. She shifted so that his hand fell away from her rib cage and was shocked to find that it had fallen to her belly. She shifted again and was mortified and flustered when his hand fell again, this time to a part of her that was *positively* forbidden!

"Orion, please, you must wake up." She bent over, her hair tumbling over one shoulder and onto his smiling face. "Come now, take your leg off me . . . that is, if it does not hurt too much. Here, I'll help." She heard his groan of pain when she tried to lift his leg. "I'm sorry. We must not be found like this. What will the castlefolk think?" She knew he could not answer, so

145

intense was his daze.

Orion squinted one eye over Juel as she surveyed their position, looking first from under her arm, then along her backside, then with her face resting on his chest. He noticed she was wearing a simple gown of olive-green, and this bodice scooped lower, like one of the gowns Dawn wore. She must have borrowed it, he thought fuzzily.

Juel sighed with delight. "Hmm, you have a very nice chest, so very powerful and wide. I could rest my head here the whole evening long."

"Your hair, it tickles," Orion said, then shut his eyes quickly when she lifted her face to look at him.

"Are you delirious, m'lord?" Juel giggled softly. "If you are, then you can hardly answer me, can you?" She sighed, running a fingertip along his rib cage, daring not to venture up over the hard, muscled hill with the brown nipple standing taut. "Oh," she murmured wickedly. "I like you this way."

And I like you this way also, Juel Reynaude, Orion was thinking. So, it was she, he finally came to realize, when but a few moments ago he'd emerged from the murky domain of half-insensibility. The pulse points in his body were going mad, now that he was coming more awake. It had all been like a dream, her being in bed with him. He had been about to toss her out, when he became aware that he himself had dragged her there. It was not Ranice, his beloved, as his befogged brain had been telling him.

And Juel was not stupid. "Hmm, where is your hump, m'lord?"

"What?" Orion's eyes flew open to meet her misty green orbs. He read the impish humor there. "So, when

146

did you realize that I had come to? And what is this of a hump?"

Laying her head back down on his chest, she said, "The villagefolk say when you ride out in the midst of night there is a hump on your back and they all say you are a terrible monster no one would care to face in the dark. They say you put people in chains in the dungeon and swiftly torture them until they scream for mercy."

"And what do you think?"

"Mmm, I think you might do that, but very slooooooowly, not as fast as rumor has it."

He played with a lock of raven hair. "How would you like your torture, Juel, swiftly or slooooooowly?"

Lifting herself, she splayed her cool hands upon his chest and looked deep into his dark-brown eyes. "You have tortured me enough already, m'lord. I would like to get up now. There is much to do. The physician will come to look in on you soon."

"First—a kiss."

She blinked. "Oh, no," she said. "I recall what came to pass as a result of the last kisses we sh-shared."

"You stammer again." His eyes narrowed. "Do you not feel my desire, Juel. Feel it and know that I want you beneath me, that I would make love to you for as long as possible. Can you imagine that?"

"I can't imagine it." She pushed away from his chest. "And neither can you, if you have any sense. You've been wounded. A serious wound. A short time ago you knew not what you did. You pulled me into this bed with your leg hooked about my hips. What were you dreaming, m'lord?"

He looked her straight in the eyes. "That you were my wife, Ranice, finally let go from her father and come to me."

"Release me now!"

"What's the matter? Jealous, are you?" He chuckled and saw that he infuriated her further. He grimaced as he tightened his leghold on her hips.

"You are cruel. I say let me go now. I wish not to lie with you a moment longer!"

"Cruel?" He sneered when she turned to frown at him. "Why should I be cruel to a woman who's about to become my mistress?" He took in her shocked expression and went on heartlessly. "Yes, I believe that's what I'll have you be. My mistress. Ranice will not mind, she'll have her own lovers, too. I believe my "beloved" has not her virtue yet intact." He shrugged. "I don't care what she is. I'll only require heirs from her loins."

"Never!" Juel hissed. "I'll never submit to you now!"

"Ah. So you thought about it before, did you?"

"No," she lied in a small voice.

He looked down into her gaping bodice. "You are not as flat as you appear when standing up. In fact, your breasts are quite nice, like soft doves or small hills." His hand slid down along her slender leg, then between it. "A mound like velvet, too."

"No!" Juel gasped when he cupped her womanhood. Her skirts had been wrinkled between them; now they were hiked up to her waist as he had expeditiously placed the hem there. His hand returned, this time to further explore.

She moistened her lips with her tongue and her eyes grew huge as they looked into his while he plied his fingers to the soft, moist cleft. He bent her like a willow twig, ripped her bodice with his teeth, flinging his head back like a mad dog, then put his mouth to the little rise of breast.

Juel could only gasp and pant with pleasure, feeling that most secret part of her begin to throb and beat as if a tiny little heart had grown there. She cried out as he also put his mouth to the tip of her breast and suckled. Heat rose in her body as he became emboldened with his feathery kissing touch and sliding caresses.

"Now, Juel, touch me, now."

Juel was so on fire that she heeded his command, sliding her hand down his slim hip and taking hold of . . . oh . . . so big! "I must not," she cried, and wrenched away. "You are married and have not even been with your lady wife yet! We must not!"

"Oh, but we must," said a feminine voice from behind.

Juel gasped and reached for the hem of her skirts to cover herself.

Orion pulled back his hand and lifted his head. He groaned in misery and pain as Juel wrenched about.

They both looked up then and gaped, for there stood the most exquisitely dressed and most attractive fair-haired woman Juel had ever seen in her life. And with the fullest and most perfect bosom!

With a dangerous frown, Orion clipped to the woman, "Who are you?" He lay back and clenched his teeth.

"Your wife, Ranice," she sneered.

"You lie. My wife has dark hair. You are not she."

Juel slid slowly out from between Orion's leg as he lifted it ever so carefully, beads of sweat as huge as thumbnails dotting his brow. She got down as far on the bed as she could, the bedhangings covering her shame and embarrassment. And her torn bodice!

His wife! Juel blanched as she listened to them argue back and forth.

Ranice humphed. "My father, Richard de Monteforte, lied, not I. He did say you preferred dark-haired women, but—" she heaved a mock-weary sigh and glared at Juel with the dark hair—"I was all there was. My sister of the raven hair ran away with a mere stableboy. The king said to wed you to me, by proxy, when Clytie de Monteforte defied father's orders. The name of your wife would have been Clytie instead of Ranice. Father, in his cups, failed to mention the color of my hair. What else could poor father do? He had only me left."

"I . . . see." Orion winced in pain, his brow creasing. His eyes sought and found Juel beneath the covers and his frown ironed out as they exchanged soft looks. "Well, my lady, your father can have you back," he said to Ranice, then fell back with eyes closed to the pain— and the beautiful, conniving woman.

"I'm afraid not, my handsome dragon of a man."

Juel gasped softly at her boldness.

"What matters the hair color? Dark hair on a woman is dull anyway . . . blond is the color of princesses."

Juel gasped again and peeped up at the comely woman from amid the purple-and-gold hangings that draped her like a royal veil. "Why are you afraid you cannot return to your father? Will he beat you? I've heard of such—"

Ranice's hands plopped onto her generous hips. "Be still, wench—and begone with you!"

As Juel emerged and stood, Ranice laughed with the haughtiness of one who'd grown up with an abundance of wealth. She wanted more castles and more land, but her father could not get them for her; he was all worn out and wanted peace. She wore beautiful, richly colored gowns and the one she was wearing now was unusual, Juel thought. The gown's full, rustling skirt was patterned with damselflies, silver ones, flitting about a black background with green leaves embroidered on bodice and hem, and the sleeves were purple, like Ranice's deep soulless eyes.

"My lord," she snickered, looking at the man in the bed. "Why do you dally with such a skinny wench as this one?" She sashayed about the chamber, delighting to discover that it was so large. However, she would have to do something about the ugly tapestries, she thought. And the massive, unfeminine furniture. She would discuss it with him now, oblivious to the fact that he had been so recently wounded.

Ranice turned to the bed. "My lord Orion?" she began, then gaped and said, "Well!"

He was snoring! When she looked about the chamber, she also discovered that the skinny maid had disappeared.

Later, as Orion still lay sleeping, Ranice came suddenly to her feet. She'd stared at the handsome knight long enough, wondering when he'd awake. He had not done so. Not once. So, let him sleep. He would need it, since she was not going to let him rest very much once he mended!

Ranice looked back at the handsome male again. She had him by the pellets . . . hmm, and big ones too, they must be.

Her deep-red mouth twisted. If he wanted dark hair, then dark hair she would have. Dyes were easy to mix, she'd done it before while dallying with a count who already had a blond wife and wanted a change.

Ranice sashayed about the room, her skirts a loud rustle in the quiet. She had to plan her next move, and she continued to scheme as she walked about.

She stopped beneath a tapestry; her eyes saw without seeing. Her thoughts were deep on her next move. True, her father had helped her lie in order to wed her to a baron. Piers de Monteforte was not in his right mind most of the time, so he'd been easy to manipulate. He had been half insane when his beloved Clytie had disappeared all those years ago.

Ranice snickered. She'd changed her plans to use her sister's name . . . too complicated. True, Clytie was the dark-haired one . . . *Was*.

Ranice suddenly felt as if she had choked on something. She visualized, huge hazel-green eyes looking at her with defiance. That skinny wench . . . she was just like Clytie. Her sister . . . the image of that one.

Could it be? Ranice felt faint. She sat down hard in Orion's favorite chair. No . . . she could not be Clytie. She'd had Clytie taken to a nunnery in northern France. Or could she be—? *Mon Dieu,* no, impossible.

Clytie and her cousin Elizabeth looked like twins, at least they had when they'd been small. This girl could not be Elizabeth, since she still lived with her poor parents in the woods somewhere. Her mother had had a rich lover and she'd been very beautiful what with her long dark hair and smoldering eyes.

Ranice smirked. Elizabeth was an heiress now, but she had no idea of it, poor thing. Her father, Guy

Hunter, had passed away, leaving Elizabeth wealthy, with lands and holdings. Too bad there was no one to claim it now. She had already checked on that. Not even her father could lay claim to it; because Piers de Monteforte was half mad the king disallowed any inheritance. The dead baronet had no other children; he'd only had the two bastards. She had no idea if the other was girl or boy.

Ranice yawned, feeling bored. Her eyes flickered and flared.

When she had seen that Clytie and Elizabeth were like twins, Ranice felt she'd gone crazy. She'd had to eliminate Clytie, else she, Ranice, would have gotten nothing but crumbs. There wasn't enough to go around. And murder was too ugly. Maybe Clytie was dead then.

She tapped her chin, then coiled a lock of blond hair around her index finger. The cousin, Elizabeth, she had another name . . . a middle one. Ranice shrugged, unable to recall it, for it had been so long ago.

Ranice shot to her feet. She would think no more on this.

Yawning, she went to see why her trunks and chests were taking so long to arrive. She had brought her coffin, too. It was made of lead, beautiful, heavy, like the mummy chests of ancient Egypt. And it was shaped to the form of her very own beautiful body. She patted her hair as she passed a polished mirror and was extremely pleased at her reflection.

Now, to see about her things.

She never traveled without bringing the beautiful coffin along. It was her favorite piece of art.

Chapter Fifteen

The morning was spent in routine tasks. In the castle courtyard the grooms swept out the stables, fed the horses, while the smith worked in the forge on wagon fittings, horseshoes, and nails. Horses nickered and porcine grunts and cows' moos were heard from the stables and pens. Guards stirred atop what remained of the castle's battlements. Peasants and tradesmen and stonemasons milled about discussing the work to be done. Domestic servants bustled about. The laundress soaked sheets, towels, and tablecloths in a wooden trough which contained a solution of caustic soda and wood ashes. She pounded the sheets, rinsed them, and hung them to dry in the cool March air. The smell of sweet clothes hanging on the line drifted to the two young women from the area outside between kitchen and larder. The laundress disappeared back inside the castle.

Juel and Dawn were working in the kitchen garden, weeding out old onions and garlic plants, peas and beans, and the common weeds themselves. The new girl named Autumn, rescued from the pillagers' ravishing, had worked with them willingly, and then Lydia had come to fetch her inside. Autumn was already weary, since she was not used to so much heavy work. The knights were still searching for her sisters, but they were proving hard to find, and Autumn feared they might be dead.

The morning sky was cloudy and gray, the cool wind whipping at Juel's wool shift of forest green with its olive-green tunic. Dawn wore an orange-and-brown shift with rust-colored smock over it. Juel's outer garment had a slash in the short, belted tunic; Dawn's smock a deep, wide pocket in front. They had dressed that morning while it was still dark. As Juel had come with only the clothes on her back, Dawn had lent her fresh smocks, tunics, and shifts. The two girls were the same size and height, so there was no altering of hems or bodices needed. They had braided each other's hair before going out into the brisk morning.

Peter had not yet returned to The Keep, and Juel had searched for Jay, finally locating him eating with the knights in the hall. He had told her he had gone to the village to see their father, and learned he had escaped injury in the raid but was still recuperating at the home of an old friend. Peter had an ailment that wouldn't let him keep his food down, and had told Jay not to bring Juel to see him until he was better. Jay told her he had laughed, saying he might be to The Keep before she knew it.

Jay had also been to their house at the other side of the great forest and had asked a neighbor to see to the animals. Juel was satisfied with the news, but she still wished to return home soon to check on things herself.

She missed her cats, Owl and Flaxen and Hemmingway.

Juel lifted the hem of her green wool shift, stepping over a pile of dead brown weeds. "What do you suppose Lydia meant yesterday when she said to me: 'You are the one'?" She straightened to look at Dawn.

Though Dawn was wearing an old shift and smock, she still looked lovely, and despite the lack of sunshine, her hair was shining like palest gold. She wore a thoughtful look now as the two girls paused together in the gray day.

"Maybe Lydia believes you are an angel come to save us all from doom when the devil Scardon returns." She shrugged. "If there is such a man." A laugh followed. "Or ghost."

Juel continued to probe the mysteries of The Keep. "Why do the villagefolk call Orion by the name Scardon, Baron Herstmonceux? It was told he did not care to be called by that name and—" she shrugged. "Not Sutherland, either. Who is he really? Just Orion, the legendary hunter in the sky?"

"I have no idea, Juel. To me, Orion is in fact Lord of The Keep and Scardon a phantom of the night, as some others here also believe. Some say he really lived here and he was a dark, evil man, a substitute father to Orion. Some simple souls say they felt the suffocating evil lurking all about them. I was too young to remember. They say Scardon twisted his ward's nature to satisfy his greedy desire to possess and control the poor lad's mind and heart."

"Had the king no idea Scardon was doing this?"

"Rumor says John Scardon was deeply dishonorable to the older king, Henry's father. Henry himself

157

was busy in the affairs of the king's council, wrestling with the difficult problems of royal finance and foreign policy." Dawn smiled as she thought of her young king. "Henry was supposed to have been a madcap prince who indulged in adventurous and illegal exploits with a pack of his rascally friends. Orion was supposed to have been one of those friends. He got away from Scardon and went in search of the young Prince Henry. Scardon left not long after and has not returned since. But Orion has been back for five years or so."

Juel smiled. "Even hardworking princes relax at times, and it doesn't surprise me that those relaxations take a rowdy form, especially among the young fighting men. Even my wonderful brother Jay has been rowdy most of his life. And as for Orion, he must have been quite the lady's man and the drinker among the prince's crowd."

Dawn's voice lowered. "Rumormongers say Orion is not John Scardon's kin at all, but a Sutherland, and that he lost his mind when just a lad of four or five when he saw his parents killed. All he knew when he came here was of dragons and demons. And from Scardon he learned how to be very amoral and ill-tempered."

"Dragons are not all bad. I will tell you some good stories one day."

"Stories?" Dawn said.

"Yes. I make up stories to tell the orphans of the village."

"There are many orphans here." Dawn smiled shyly. "I am one of them."

Now another had joined The Keep. It seemed Autumn Meaux had lost her entire family in the last several months, and she couldn't be more than thirteen or fourteen, Juel was thinking.

"What about this ghost I hear talk of?" Juel wanted to know as she piled the weeds into a cart near by.

Dawn was right behind her and rested her arm on the cart. "There's supposed to be one in the round tower. But who knows for certain."

"I have heard so many stories," Juel said with a snort. "I could put them into a book, if that were possible, but women do not write the stories; only men do that. I can only express them by the telling. As for the stories I've heard, some of them are fearsome. They say Orion is a dark man with grim facial cast. They call him a fearsome dragon."

Dawn nodded. "At times he is that."

"He is a hunchback." Juel waited now.

"What?" Dawn laughed. "He looks normal of bones, build, and flesh to me. A dark man with a brow like a thunderstorm at times, but still handsome and easy to look at." She widened her soft brown eyes and blinked. "Sometimes one would rather not look his way, though."

"He is a devastatingly handsome man with an evil spirit and his temper is foul," Juel proclaimed.

"That does bear repeating, does it not?"

Juel said, "Yes!" then thought for a moment. "Maybe he is not all that evil, not really."

"Are we gossiping too much?" Dawn wanted to know, with an impish grin.

"Of course. But who cares. Tell me what else you know. I am gathering all this to write a story in my mind of Orion, the beautiful but nasty dragon."

"That evil spirit comes from the bad influence of his foster father, who he is said to never talk about. Orion

159

does not remember his real father, nor his mother."

Juel picked up a limp weed and looked at it, then her gaze went to the round tower as she remembered more. "He roams through the dungeons of the tower, with demons trailing behind."

Dawn shook her head, stirring long, thick braids of palest yellow. For a moment Juel stared at Dawn's hair, noting that it was the same color as the hair of Orion's wife, Ranice de Monteforte. Or was she Sutherland now, Juel wondered briefly.

Dawn picked up a lovage plant, long dead and dried, then looked at Juel. "Orion never goes to the round tower. This is the only thing in his life he fears, I am told."

"I have heard something about that. And now, there is supposed to be a devil or a ghost or ghoul that follows Orion about. I think I can figure that out: Scardon is the nasty devil they all talk about. But Scardon is gone and his evil still lurks about, as you said. A ghost can be an aura of such a bad person."

Dawn frowned. "That would mean Scardon is dead and his ghost has returned."

"Yes." Then, almost as if to herself she announced, "I would like to go to the round tower."

A gasp escaped Dawn's lips as she looked about to see if anyone had heard Juel. Someone indeed had, and Alice Becker came over to lean into Juel's face. "You go there, wench Joelle, and you'll get your tits cut off," she sneered. "There's a nasty guard there that'll do it, too. I know him." Alice tossed her head as if proud of her naughty reputation. "Yardley's a big one and he's watching over something there that's a secret. Myself, I think it's treasure that that nasty old Scardon's gonna

160

come back for one day."

"What do you know of him?" Juel quickly asked before Alice could walk away.

"Well now," she sneered. "Wouldn't you just like to know."

Juel looked at the mean, lowborn maid. "Of course. Why else would I have asked."

Alice put her off with her lofty airs. "I'm going to meet someone. I have an assignation."

"My," said Dawn. "Now you use big words. Before long you will be called on the carpet for that, too."

"Who is she to meet?" Juel asked Dawn, curious as to the identity of Alice's lover.

"Alice can't hear so well at times, or she doesn't listen is better," was all Dawn offered. "She calls you Joelle and still doesn't know that you are Jay Reynaude's sister. *That* is her lover. She goes to meet him."

"She *what?*"

Juel made to start after Alice and was caught up short when Dawn touched her arm. "No. You must not. Let Alice find trouble for herself. And she will. She always does."

"And Jay will give her plenty," Juel said. Her eyes fell on Dawn's bright hair. "How is it that you know my brother Jay?" If he ever saw Dawn, he'd fall for her at first sight, Juel was thinking.

"I don't," Dawn said over her shoulder as she headed for the kitchen. "I have only heard about him from others, and one day Alice boasted of his name and what a perfect lover he is." Dawn stopped walking. A thrill of anticipation had touched her spine and she wondered at its source. She ducked her head at the rose arbor and turned back to Juel. "The world is full of

161

lovers. I believe fidelity is a treasure in a human being. If you have this, you have the world in that one person who prizes loyalty and faithfulness above all. And two of this mind, all the better. Then they can forever be faithful to each other. This is what I would like in a man. Constancy and devotion, and friendship second."

Wisps of dark hair tickled Juel's cheeks and she brushed them back with a dirty hand. "A man is not going to find this in Alice Becker." Juel did not smile as she thought of her brother and that woman. "My brother Jay has had many women; none were affairs of consequence and he flaunts his virility as carelessly as Alice does her lack of virtue."

Dawn just stared at Juel, beginning to wonder about her brother Jay. Dawn liked his name, but she thought, *a name is just a name.*

Of a sudden Juel said, "My brother is here."

Dawn turned red. "Staying here at The Keep, now?"

"He works here, as a carpenter and woodcutter."

"Hmm," Dawn said, beginning to walk again while Juel followed her inside. "I'll be sure to keep out of his way!"

"You need not go that far. Just watch out for him." Juel saw Dawn's shoulders lift in a shrug. "He's clever and knows how to lift the skirts."

"Well, mine are made of strong stuff and my chemises are of iron. Let him try to get through that. No man has yet who has tried."

Juel laughed. "Iron-clad skirts won't stop Jay."

They stood in the kitchen washing their hands and giggling, stealing some deliciously oozing sweets from the cook's board. With cherry juice from the tart rolling down her chin, Dawn said, "Want to make a

162

wager on that?"

They laughed together.

All day long Jay and Dawn's paths crisscrossed, but they never came face-to-face, managing only just to miss each other. He would come into the kitchen after she had just walked out. She would go into the court-yard after he had just gone to speak with a fellow carpenter. He had no idea she existed. And Dawn could not keep Juel's phantom brother from her mind. She couldn't go looking for a man just because she wondered what he looked like. After a time she was so busy that Jay Reynaude was cleared from her thoughts at last.

On her way to Orion's apartments, Juel picked up his smallclothes, undertunic, and hose from the laundress. She was again his maid for the afternoon. She wondered if he had asked for her himself or if Rajahr had ordered her to come. Ruark had told her to go to him, and that was all he said before walking back out to the area where the knights were training.

On the second-floor landing Juel glanced out the window, the round tower in her line of vision. She kept moving up the staircase. Phantoms in the tower? Bah again, she thought. There was probably no mystery here at all and it was only in the minds of the people of The Keep. They had to have something to divert them-selves with, for no outside entertainment seemed to be provided for them.

"That will most likely change, now that Orion's wife is here," Juel was saying to herself as she came up the last flight of stairs, smoothing her hand lovingly over the soft dove gray of Orion's hose atop the pile of clothes.

Juel came to a sudden halt. What she saw in the hall before Orion's door caused her heart to turn. There, on the floor, sat Shadow, looking sad and neglected. His head was down low and he was picking at his toes as if he hadn't a friend in the world.

"Ohh," Juel murmured, setting the bundle of clothes down as she rushed to Shadow's side. "No one to play with? Where are the castle cats?" She laughed as Shadow shook his head in a dismissing gesture. "Don't like them, hmm? Or don't they like you, poor boy?"

Shadow came slowly to his feet and looked up at her, his brow wrinkled and eyes huge and unhappy. He looked so sad that Juel wanted to cry, and she leaned down to put out her arms. Shadow didn't blink once before he went into them. A tear slid slowly down Juel's cheek as the monkey rested his head on her chest, hugged her, and made a sound she had never heard before.

Or was it, Juel wondered, only a sigh of contentment.

Chapter Sixteen

A nightmarish sound ripped through the gloomy stillness of the afternoon.

In the hall, Shadow leapt from Juel's arms, sped down the stairs, and disappeared from sight. Juel stood alone, shaking from head to toe while she stared at the portal and realized that the sound straight from hell, had come from the other side of the door.

She stood there, a mass of quivering flesh, and wondered why no one came running, why no one else had heard the horrible and tormented cry.

Not wasting another second, she went inside. There across the room, in the dimness of the huge bed, sat Orion in a jumble of sheets. Sweat was pouring from his face. He stared at her, studying her intently for a moment. Then he spoke.

"It was a nightmare." A half-smile crossed his face. "Lucifer's teeth, I'm hungry," he exclaimed.

Juel released the breath she'd been holding. He was all right. As she came closer to the bed, he watched her closely. "You had a nightmare?" She laughed lightly.

"You must have dreamed of food—that could hardly be called a nightmare."

His eyes darkened. "The dream was not of food." All of a sudden his expression was closed as he lay back down. "Where is my dark, comely wife? Or did I only dream that she came?"

Juel stood over the bed, pulling her drifting thoughts together. "Ranice is here." She grinned. "But she is fair-headed, not dark."

"Yes." He blinked and frowned. "So she is. Where is the bitch?"

She stood motionless at his bedside. "I have not seen her since last night. She was in your room when I left."

"She said she would stay." He moved with a groan. "She said something about clothes. We must talk, she and I."

Swiveling on her heel and with a look of disappointment, Juel said, "I will go and find her."

Walking into the other rooms of the apartment, Juel looked this way and that, then checked the solar and the chapel; she even checked the oriel, the projecting room, with its bay window, on the upper floor. She returned, shrugging. "She's not in the apartments. I will go downstairs and see if she is there."

"Wait!"

Juel turned at the heavy portal, looking at him as he threw his legs over the side of the bed, groaned deep with pain, and clenched the mattress. "Oh, you should not get up yet." She rushed over to him and gasped when she saw how wet his hair was. "You are ill. The sweat pours from you. You must lie down else your wound will open."

Orion glared into her concerned face. "I care not for

a little wound."

"It is not little!" As she placed a hand on his shoulder, he wrenched away from her touch. "You have a very big hole in your thigh . . ." She colored. "I cared for it myself and seared it closed."

"You?" He stared up at her. "What can you, a mere wench, know of such things?"

Her shoulders stiffened. "Do not call me a wench, as your lady wife did. I am Juel Reynaude, daughter of Peter of Herstmonceux. I am not without intelligence. I can read and write and cipher as well as the next man."

He breathed deeply of her lavender scent. "You are not a man." He grabbed and held her hand tightly. "You are a young woman, but still a wench. Better yet, a mere chick who fell from the nest." He thrust her hand away. "Fetch me something to eat. And to drink, something strong."

She bobbed a curtsy and simpered sarcastically, "As ye wish, me lord. I'll get it for ye so ye can get yerself good and befuddled." She bounced once again, wearing a comehither Alice look.

He broke into a smile. "Feisty bitch, aren't you. I should take you over my knee and give you a good whipping for your insolence."

She backed away, then spun toward the door. "I'll get you your food and drink."

"You don't like the idea of spankings?" he called to her before she slipped out.

"Dragon, that's what he is!"

"I heard that!" he yelled as she slammed the door.

When Juel returned with a gigantic bowl of soup and a jug of strong wine, she found Orion had fallen asleep.

She stood over him with the tray, determined to let the soup slip, "by accident," of course. She sighed, then sat down with a resigned shrug. She could not do it. As she watched him sleep, a feeling of tenderness came over her. He was so handsome that her breath caught in her throat. Her pulse quickened at the image of them lying together. Doing what? Kissing and touching? Or more than that? Lovers came inside of each other, Dawn had said. The man's huge organ slid inside the woman's sheath and gave her much pleasure. And pain the first time, there was much of that, she had also said. But maybe it would not hurt so much, not if the man was careful. She had no idea how it could be managed. He was so big and thick, she knew; she had felt him close and her wild imagination had done some measuring.

Juel was growing warm and drowsy. It was so dark in the room. She opened the window hangings to see if that would help keep her awake, but she was soon blinking, watching him, dreaming of what could have been if she was a beautiful princess from a faraway land . . . if she had not been of low birth, but someone with gentle highborn blood. Orion had the blood of barons . . . or did he? Just who and what was he?

Afternoon sunlight was streaming into the apartment when Orion awoke to find Juel asleep in the chair she had pulled up alongside his bed. His eyes shifted to take in the tray of soup and wine she had brought to him. He looked at her again, sound asleep in the hard chair. She was dressed in a soft green shift, the tunic over it of an olive drab. Her black hair was braided, the ends falling over her breast that was rising and falling softly with each sleeping breath. She was like a princess, he thought, and even though she was dressed

168

in the coarse clothes of a working maid, she appeared lovely, cool, clean, her skin smooth and flawless. He realized he wanted her.

Orion groaned as he looked Juel over seductively. Where was his wife Ranice? Damn his wound, he needed a woman, and needed one soon.

When his head began to ache, he realized what was causing him discomfort. Sunlight was pouring into the chamber, coming from every window in the apartment, He blinked, hating the fresh, clean light.

"Who opened the window hangings?" he roared, sitting up in bed, damning the stinging ache in his wound.

Juel came awake instantly. "It was I, my lord. Did I do wrong?" she asked, blinking away the sleep. How long had she been sleeping? "Oh, I'm sorry, I was so very tired. Garden work always wears me out. I should have stayed awake for you."

Orion growled, reaching for the wine and a goblet to pour it in. He drank deeply, then poured more, while Juel stared in surprise at the amount he consumed so swiftly. Then more. And yet more.

He was devouring it! she thought with horror. "You will become ill if you keep that up," she said, rising from the chair and grasping the back of it as if she'd tear it asunder.

Rajahr swept in like a dark little breeze and, seeing what Orion was doing, rushed over to snatch up the heavy jug. "She is right, master. You will become ill and you will also become crazed if you drink so much on an empty stomach."

While Orion glared at Rajahr's back as he went to pour the wine out in the slop bucket, Juel walked over and placed her hand on his arm, stopping him from pouring out another drop. "No, Rajahr. Leave it be, let him have it." Her eyes stared into Rajahr's and she could feel he saw the wisdom of her words. Her voice lowered so that only Rajahr could hear. "He will learn a lesson sooner or later."

Rajahr blinked into the maid's eyes as she looked at Orion still quaffing the drink as if he were dying of thirst. "He will never learn if he has not learned by now. You do not know how he loves his drink and you have not seen how horrible he can become. He might murder a person one of these days. He has torn this place apart in his drunken rages."

"I will watch him," Juel said softly. "I know how to care for inebriates. My father's brother used to be one."

"Yes?" Rajahr lifted a thin eyebrow. "And where is this uncle of yours now?"

"He is dead."

"How?"

She licked her lips and frowned. "He rode a horse standing on his head and crashed into a huge limb of a tree."

Rajahr was horrified. "That is not humorous. Though it could be in a puppet show."

"But life is not a puppet show and we should take care to save some humans from themselves," Juel said.

Rajahr looked weary. "I have tried. What can you, a mere maid, do?"

She frowned at that but said, "I will do what I can."

The little man looked grave. "You might not live to see his day of abstinence."

"I will take the chance."

Just then Orion roared like a fire-breathing dragon

170

from the bed. "More! Bring me more!"

Before Rajahr turned to put away the clothes Juel had left outside, he said to her, "You are braver than most."

Juel picked up the wine jug, clutching it in both hands. "So I've been told."

Much later in the day Orion was roaming about his apartment, going into the bright solar, then turning around to go through the chapel. He was bored with the soreness of his wound. He stopped in the oriel, wondering what to do next, and finally returned to his dim chambers.

Ranice, dressed in a cinnabar gown with wide, low neckline and a leather belt articulated with jeweled metal placques worn at hip level, her hair done splendidly in an upsweep, sashayed into the apartments and curled herself like a cat in the huge, wide armchair.

She had made her complexion pale, had painted her face with water paints, and added white and pale-pink powder. She would have had herself bled but couldn't locate the physician. Only women of ill repute used carmine for the lips to excess; she used it, but sparingly. It was *à la mode,* with the ladies to pluck the eyebrows to a thin line, also to remove the hair on the forehead and temples and the nape; Ranice removed it on other intimate parts of her body also. Returning Crusaders had brought back Oriental perfumes and Ranice had plenty to go around, but she selfishly kept it all to herself.

When Orion came in and saw his lady wife, he

171

attacked without preamble. He cared not if she wasn't truly his wife.

Ranice was not bored any longer and loved every minute of their wedding consummation, as Orion flung her onto the bed and began to rip her clothes from her body. Her fancy metal corset lay on the floor, along with the beautiful gown and jeweled belt. She lay panting when he had her naked and looked up at him with lust and excitement shining in her eyes.

"I thought you suffered a bad wound, my lord husband. Are you not in pain?" She smelled the strong liquor on his breath.

Ranice laughed deeply when he removed his clothes in a flash and tossed them all about the bedchamber. "Well, are you or not?" she asked.

For answer, Orion fell on the bed, centered over her, and entered her without any preparatory lovemaking. He drove his big body into her lustily and she lifted perfectly as he met with her and wrenched back. Her groans and moans and cries filled the air.

"Ah, Juel, Juel, Juel," he cried in his inebriated state when his pinnacle was reached.

But something was missing and Orion was soon disheartened. "Ah, Juel," he murmured in a sodden voice. And again, "Juel."

And Ranice, in her sweet death, heard only that her lusty husband called her a jewel. What more perfect endearment could any woman hope for?

Chapter Seventeen

"Oh! Did you hear what happened last night?"

Alice Becker was gossiping with another maid in the kitchen as they made oatcakes to break the fast. The tall hatchet-faced maid with brown stringy hair looked at Alice, her eyes round with anticipation as she waited to hear the latest castle gossip.

"Tell me, Ali, tell me," Freyda whined, reaching for a spice box on a kitchen shelf.

"Well . . ." Alice said as she moved closer to the skinny maid, though her voice did not lower. "Seems that wife of m'lord's, Rauline—"

"No, no," said Freyda. "Her name's *Ranice,* not Rauline. You never get names straight." She almost giggled, reminded of the name Alice used to call her by when she'd first come from Brighton: Fleta! "Go on, go on, Ali, let's hear the juicy tidbit."

"Hush up and let me speak," Alice snapped. "Now, seems that Ranice and M'lord Orion got together real quick."

Freyda's eyes were huge. "They did it already?"

"Of course, dimwit, what d'ya think I meant, not they held hands together in the garderobe?"

A high-pitched giggle burst from Freyda as she added spice to the oatcake flour. "Oh, and I thought m'lord had a thing for that pretty maid Juel."

"Juel?" Alice said, a hard look coming into her eyes. "You mean *Joelle,* don't you?"

"No," Freyda said with a shrug. "I mean Juel. Juel Reynaude, the one you always snap at," she giggled. "And if looks could do her in on the spot, you—"

"Jesu," Alice gasped as if choking. "You mean she's Jay Reynaude's sister?" Her voice rose to a croak.

"Jay?" Freyda's brows rose and she looked dumbfounded. "Who's Jay?"

"Never mind," Alice groaned. "You say her name's Juel Reynaude. Are you sure about that, Freyda?"

"Of course. Don't you ever listen to names?"

Alice's eyes scurried to and fro. "What do I do now?" she asked herself. "Jay won't like it if he finds out I've mistreated his lovely sister."

"Oh, now she's lovely?" She nudged Alice in the ribs. "Forget about Juel Reynaude for now. Maybe you can do her a favor someday and then you'll be on the good side of her. This Jay will never know about your nastiness then." She cast a glance about, then munched a warm oatcake. "Tell me the gossip, forget the other."

Alice looked at Freyda. "You're right. I'll think of something to smooth things over with Juel Reynaude."

"You could start by helping Juel out with her romance with m'lord."

"Eh? What say you?"

Freyda grinned, exposing a missing front tooth.

"One of the servants was about to clean the upper floors where the carpenters made a mess putting in that new window when she just happened to overhear m'lord and Juel Reynaude in his bedchamber. Seems they were having a tussle of sorts."

Alice looked at Freyda hard. "In his bed?"

"In his bed. With his wound and all."

"So . . ." Alice said with a knowing look. "Orion has taken himself a mistress—and right before his lady wife arrived."

A giggle erupted. "Or maybe just a hasty toss of an afternoon."

"I don't think so," Alice said. "Juel's got that look of a sly vixen who's out to get what she wants. I respect her now. I'm like that too; I go after what I want. No other woman's going to stand in my way. I'd rip her head off if she looked cross-eyed at Jay Reynaude. Jay's sister Juel is all right. She's a tough one, she is."

"'Course you'd say that now, Ali. You want to be her friend all of a sudden. And maybe you and Fat Will can help by getting Ranice out of his apartments when Juel goes up there to nurse him."

"And how could my brother and I do that?" Alice wanted to know.

"Oh, 'tis sure you'll think of a way else you can't be Ali Becker!"

Juel walked to the window to push back the window hangings, her arms high above her head. The morning light shone through her black hair, rippling and hanging to her waist. The white linen belted smock

175

revealed the curves of her body. Orion sat up as he watched her turn in profile, the rays of morning coming through her hair, her bodice, like a sensuous light catching the shape of her small, perfect breasts . . . breasts he'd never fully touched.

She was captured in mist and sunlight. Orion felt desire as if a summer storm passed through him wreaking havoc with his senses. She stoked a fire within and he had no idea what he was going to do about it now that his lusty wife had arrived. He could do nothing, for his head was a mass of aching hurt and his thigh pained him and yet he knew he must get up. There were things that must be done; he had serious work to do.

Juel knew he was looking at her with a warm golden glow in his deep-brown eyes. She did not have to see to know. She could feel it.

"You should not," Juel said as she turned to face him, realizing that her body was responding to his open gaze.

"Should not?" he asked, one eyebrow raised up.

Juel felt herself color and went to smooth the covers of his bed at the corners. "You should not drink so much. It grows worse. My uncle perished from drink. An accident." She did not tell him that he'd been riding a horse on his head and struck the limb of a tree.

Orion surprised her by rising from the bed, wearing hose, another surprise, for men usually slept naked. He walked right out of the chamber into the garderobe. She closed her ears so she'd not hear him relieving himself and when he returned, he asked for his clothes to be set out. After he began to dress, she slipped out of the room. In the adjoining chamber she found some clothes belonging to a woman. She brought them closer and sniffed. Perfume, the Oriental kind like the merchant's wife had worn. She sniffed again and grimaced, finding another unusual odor, one that she didn't like, for it reminded her of nothing she'd ever smelled before. It made her shiver all over.

She dropped the clothing where she'd found it and, stepping over the cinnabar gown and homely metal corset, she walked into the oriel and found more clothing strewn about. Again, a woman's clothing. Fine, expensive garments, such as a lady wore.

Juel stood blinking the moisture from her eyes. *What did you expect?* she chastised herself. *He is married now and it is no concern of yours what his lady wife does and how messy she might be.*

She found more untidiness and, in fact, there was clutter all over the apartments. Apple cores. Chicken bones. Hardened cakes. Spilled wine. And when she lifted a hunk of bread, then dropped it onto a small eating table, it crashed with the sound of a heavy rock falling on wood.

"This is terrible," Juel said with a cluck of her tongue. "Such untidiness, next to ungodly."

Someone came to stand right behind her. She heard a hiss before the voice spoke and wondered if the female had a snake with her, wrapped around her neck. Juel turned and looked Ranice full in the face, a face that was powdered to pink-and-white perfection. Wait . . . was that a tiny mole at the corner of Ranice's left nostril that had not been completely covered? Why, yes, it surely was, Juel thought.

177

"Servant, were you speaking of m'lord and me?" Ranice asked, blinking darkly kohled eyes. Not waiting for a reply, she turned her back to sashay about the small oriel room, where one—or two—could watch the revolutions of the stars and moon at night. But she and her husband had not watched the night sky, for he had passed out shortly after they had lain naked and dined here. "Are you m'lord's mistress? Is that why you are always here in his apartments?" Ranice hissed as she whirled to face Juel.

Juel shrank back, not from fear, but from the strong smell of garlic and onions. "You must have taken breakfast already?"

"I never eat such food for my morning meal. Eggs and pork make me terribly ill." She continued about the tiny room, knocking things over as she moved around. "I have had pickled fish, my favorite."

Juel backed away until she was bumping her backside against the old window seat. The window had been left carelessly open often in the past and the wood had rotted around it. The carpenters had been working in this room, but had ceased all work when Orion was wounded.

"I am bored," was all Ranice said, and Juel gave a brief frown. "I despise work and m'lord has laid the law down this morning early. We had a breathless time in the bed last night, but it is over now that he has sobered. He is a lover like a gigolo I once knew . . . not personally—my friend's lover at court." She watched the servant closely for her reaction.

"I would not know about any of that. I've never been to court, or anywhere, for that matter," Juel said, stepping on some dried food and kicking it aside. "This is surely and truly a mess. I am going to find someone to clean it up."

She began to walk the short distance across the wide oak floors when her back stiffened at the loud screech.

"You!" Ranice's eyes flashed. "Clean it up, girl!"

Juel looked at the beautifully gowned woman as if she had been slapped. "I?" She shook her head. "I do not clean out pigstys."

"Hold your tongue, insolent wench! You must be punished!"

Juel's gaze reluctantly returned to the pile of fine clothes. "Go ahead, tell me what it must be. I am waiting. What can you do to me?"

Just then, Orion's big frame filled the opening. "The maid does not need to be punished. She works in the kitchen." He looked at Juel. "Go now and send another to clean up this room." He looked around. "And the other rooms." He saw that the sun was shining. "I am going outside to work with my knights. Ranice, busy yourself with embroidery and other domestic projects." Looking his wife straight in the eye, he ended, "Leave Juel to herself. She does well on her own."

"She—*what?*"

Juel did not wait to hear any more of Ranice's spouting tirades, and Orion dismissed her with a look as she walked toward him. Orion said nothing more to his wife, but also took his leave, going to his coffer before making his way down the stairs.

Ranice stood alone, kicking the litter away much the same as the disrespectful and brazen servant had done.

She whirled about then. The servant, she thought.

Hmm. What was her name? Her eyes narrowed dangerously as she recalled the consummation of her marriage that had ended all too soon. What had her beautiful husband called her at the height of passion?

It had been something like . . . emerald . . . ruby . . . amethyst. No, no, no, it was like the whole of them, all together.

Ah. So it was *jewel,* was it. The same as the impertinent servant's name.

No, it could not be, Ranice thought viciously. Orion Sutherland would not prefer that skinny dark-haired maid over her. Impossible. Then Ranice laughed. And it was an ugly, chilling sound that resounded in the chamber.

She had nothing to worry about. She had brought to Orion Sutherland a marriage portion and received in return a bridal gift amounting to a third of her husband's estate, including lands which would all become hers on his death. Even without the formalities at the church door, a third of his lands were legally hers by proxy. She knew the rumor that Orion Sutherland had become John Scardon's heir, and if it so happened Orion came by another heir, and that one was slow to turn it over to her, she could bring an action in the royal courts to secure her portion. Of course, she knew that once married, a woman was under the rod of her husband. She could not gainsay him even if he sold land which she had inherited, could not plead in court without him, or make a will without his consent.

She peered at her painted and powdered face in the polished steel mirror, then gazed out the bay window at all the work being done to restore the castle. Again, she shifted to the mirror and smiled wickedly. *He is your husband, Ranice. You've made sure of that, and nothing can ever change it.* Not ever. All was hers, forever.

Suddenly she was lonely and went to look upon her gorgeous Egyptian coffin in the storeroom below-stairs.

Chapter Eighteen

Juel walked across the rough stone floor in her bedchamber, her leather slippers making a scuffling sound on the bare floor as she went to the old chest to put away some clothes she'd washed that day.

She had been moved to another part of the manor and had no idea who had ordered that she do so. Rajahr had just said that she must change rooms—not share one with Dawn, but have her own. Her new quarters were below the chapel, in one of the smaller compartments.

She missed sharing a room with Dawn, though most nights they'd been too tired after a full day's work and would retire without conversation or food.

Earlier that day she had gone to visit her father in the village of Herstmonceux. He was feeling better and had smiled when she stepped into the low-ceilinged, dirt-floored room. A smiling woman had waited hand and foot on her father. *Something is brewing here,* Juel thought, and it was not verjuice or spiced cider.

When she had left the little house, she found Orion's

knights Duncan and Guy waiting for her to escort her back to the keep. The time with her father had been happy; everything was running smoothly at their house at the edge of the woods, her cats were fat and sassy, and a neighbor was seeing to the spring planting. There was no time to wonder about Orion's order that she be escorted straight back to the Keep by the armed knights!

Juel had not seen Orion the whole day. She had sent a message to him through Rajahr, and her request to visit her father had been carried out immediately. The day had been rewarding, even though she had not seen her brother and he had not learned of her visit to Peter. She had not seen Jay for three whole days, not since the day she had encountered Ranice in the little oriel chamber.

She had discovered that Alice Becker had a brother named Fat Will who was as big and as strong as an ox. He had seemed pleasant enough as he carried a heavy wooden bucket indoors for her. And Alice, another surprise, had been friendly and smiling for the first time since Juel had come to the castle. She had even told her about the room Juel was being moved to that night, and about the old part of the castle—all but for the round tower, which she made no mention of. Fat Will was ready to assist with the heavy loads of wash when it had been her turn to help with the laundry. Yet there had been something in Fat Will's sharp and shrewd reddish-brown eyes she had not liked.

Juel dressed in a long linen nightgown, which fell to the floor in thick folds. It was one of Dawn's favorites. She made herself many clothes in her spare time, she had told Juel, and laughed that there wasn't much of that! But she had been sewing since she was a little girl and altered her clothes, adding more hemline and doing special things to the bodices of her shifts and tunics that made them look very different.

The borrowed nightgown had a scattering of embroidered gillyflowers and butterflies across the bodice. Just wearing it made Juel feel young and carefree and something she had never felt in her life: beautiful.

It was only the soft, pretty nightgown, Juel told herself, because she was far from beautiful, or even comely.

Sitting in the middle of the pallet with her legs gracefully out to the side, resting on one hip and one palm, Juel imagined she was a princess and this her exquisite lady's chamber. Her eyes gazed at the flickering flame of the fat candle. Soon, she was lounging on her side. She could tell there was a draft in the room, because the candle's flame bent softly this way, then that. It was like a sensuous dance of fire.

She continued to stare and grew drowsy. Since she had not braided her hair, when she lay down it spread across the pallet and onto the floor. Yawning, she removed her slippers with one foot, then the other.

Soon she was asleep, and when she awoke, the candle had almost guttered out. The tiny flame sent eerie shadows across the stone walls and she could tell by the pool of wax that she had been sleeping for quite some time.

"Come, Juel . . ."

Almost hypnotically, Juel rose from the pallet, walked to the door, and slipped outside into the passageway, looking this way and that. What had awakened her? she wondered drowsily.

There was a flight of stone steps to the right, she knew, for she had used them just that day. Another stairway rose at the other end of the passageway, but she had never gone that way. At the back of this section of the manor there was an old stone turret that had not been altered when the manor had been built. It was part of the old castle and the stairs went up into a turret room, which Alice had mentioned just that day. No one went there much, since it was used for storage. Called an attic room, Alice had said.

Juel went that way now, being drawn by some mysterious force that she seemed to have no control over. She had to see, to know why she must go there. Maybe all of Alice's talk had stuck in her mind. Even Fat Will had mentioned something, as if his look dared her to go there.

"This way, Juel, aye, come along now."

Her nightgown flowed around her like a luminous cloud of white in the dark as she walked, her eyes dimly seeing her way by the moonlit arrow slits in the ancient stone walls.

This deep, dank part of the manor was like a maze, as if some deranged mind had mapped out the plans hundreds of years back.

Cautiously she paused at the top of the stairs, and then walked down another passageway, a short one with two tall doors along it. She paused at one of the doors, shook her head, and passed it by. Now she went round and round, up the spiral staircase. She paused at yet another landing where a steep flight of stairs led upward. A door startled her just at the top, where there was soft light of the moon beneath the door.

"This is it. Come in now, Juel."

She found herself glancing uneasily over her shoulder and yet her blood soared at the thought of entering. She turned back to stare at the portal and reached out. She tightened her hand on the cold handle of the door. What was it? She had heard it again. Like a whisper against her neck.

She turned, but no one was there and she gasped as she looked up, startled again to see a dark shape above her. It was only an iron holder for candles. There was no candle, however, and only a little light coming from the arrow slit and beneath the door.

When she entered at last, she bit her lower lip and stole a look around the attic room. Her hands twisted nervously in the folds of the gown as she allowed her eyes to adjust to the strange, flickering light. Her breath caught as the light flashed again, before she saw it was coming from the tiny window in the round wall directly across from her.

She walked to the window, sucking in another breath as she broke through huge cobwebs. Clearing them away from her head, Juel looked out from the narrow slit. The intermittent luminous radiance lit the midnight sky—in the east, north, south, here, there—and she could feel the clammy heat steal into the attic turret. Looking down into the tangled gardens, she saw a shadow moving slowly closer. She couldn't tell what it was just yet. It just kept coming, closer, closer. A mounted knight?

Suddenly, Juel made out a hunched-back figure on a great black phantom of a horse. Far down, and right below her!

Spinning about, Juel raced back toward the door,

but before she reached it, she crashed into something soft. And hard. She looked down and her breath jammed in her throat so that she could hardly breathe. She looked up, then down again. She stared around the great square of white and gold, suspended on chains from the inverted ceiling. A bed! What was a—?

Then she heard the great latch being secured. Her hazel-green eyes blinked wide. Someone had locked her in!

Juel was wide-awake now and terrified. She was also shocked and confused. More so than she'd ever been in her entire life!

Fat Will lumbered back down the spiral stairs, his soft, broken-down shoes slapping on the stones as he went. His green hose sagged and his great belly led him everywhere, hanging way out in front of him. Long strands of yellow-brown hair were plastered to his forehead and his balding dome. He was already huffing from mild exertions.

It was the middle of the night, in the darkest hours, and he had accomplished what his sister had set him to do. He had locked Juel Reynaude in the attic room. Before he'd done this, he'd overheard some gossip. Orion Sutherland had had a visitor a few days back. All he'd gotten from what Alice had whispered in snatches of words to Freyda was: the lost heiress . . . Baron Hunter's daughter Elizabeth . . . he left his inheritance to her . . . lands and a small castle. Fat Will had whistled softly at the twist of strange happenings at this keep.

As he met the dark, lean shape coming toward him

he knew a multitude of frightening apprehensions. "You have come," Fat Will almost stammered as the commanding figure approached. "Alice said you would. Everything has been readied, even the bed."

Fat Will felt his face grow hot with a silly blush as the tall man stared at him in the arrow slit of moonlight rushing in.

"Who knows of this?" asked the deep-voiced phantom.

"No one," said Fat Will.

A black eyebrow rose as the lean young man said, "Except?"

"Uh, just my sister and—and Lydia. She used her powers to get Juel to come here," Fat Will ended with a confused smirk.

"She has used nothing. I have called Juel Reynaude here. She comes because I call."

"Then my sister lies. I thought so," Fat Will said. When he heard a foul curse issue from the man's mouth, he wondered if he had gone too far.

"Say no more," ordered the deep voice. Then, "Go now, and tell no one what you know."

Fat Will gulped. He forgot to clear the cob-webs . . . the damn cobwebs!

"Go, I say."

Fat Will was gone in a flash and the tall, lean man chuckled at Will's haste for one so big and wide. The handsome phantom was in a good mood and the ride through the forest to The Keep had accomplished wonders.

Now there was only one thing left to do.

Chapter Nineteen

Juel swallowed hard.

It was dark in the attic room now that the tawny midnight moon had gone behind the clouds and stayed there. The night was deep, dark, starless and moonless as she waited in the middle of the bed, huddled there.

She knew someone was coming.

Would it be the phantom rider she had seen below? The one who had locked her in? The figure on the horse could not have gotten up here so fast to do this to her? Any why would he? Why would anybody?

She swallowed again, her throat dry and scratchy. Could it be she was to be used in some ancient mysterious ritual? Since she had come here she had always thought Lydia to be an odd one, but would she do this to her? Was there a sharp-clawed dragon being kept in the round tower, fed morning and night by Lydia?

Putting her hands to her cheeks, Juel shook her head at the night-fantasy, trying to think of one good reason anyone would wish to harm her. She dropped her hands as a new thought struck terror in her.

Torture! She looked about the dark, eerie room wildly searching for devices that could be used to torture her. It was too dark to see into the shadows; she could hardly make out her hand in front of her face, come to that.

Then she relaxed a little. Dungeons, that's where humans were tortured, at least that is what she'd heard from Jay's friends. The lads had put their heads together and laughed when she had been horrified at their discussion of castle torture and descriptions of the wails of torment and agony in stretching devices, the screams of suffering and pain from burns and skin-peeling . . . and the caskets of nails with people inside them.

Her stomach began to roll as she stared at the great chains surrounding her. She couldn't stand much pain. Even a small cut, with little blood, turned her inside out. Even her "time" made her worry that she might lose too much blood in those days of the month.

Just as tears were beginning to mist her eyes, a disembodied voice startled her. Black fright swept through her as the hair on her nape prickled. What had he said? Who was he? The black phantom? Frantically she looked for a hump, but it was too dark to even make out his features, much less a deformity.

"Wh-who are you?" Juel asked in a voice like an owl's.

A warm, deep chuckle came across to her and she thought, *at least the phantom has a sense of humor.*

"I am here for you," he said, dropping the hood of his cloak.

She swallowed. "I thought as m-much. You are taking me to the dungeons to torture me." Now she was angry. "Who p-put you up to this? Lydia?"

He laughed softly. "Lydia?"

"Yes, Lydia." She gulped, hoping the ancient dragon was not hungry. "Where is the dragon kept?"

"Dragon?" He laughed again, a puzzled sound. "Ah. You are full of fantasies, aren't you. No, Juel Reynaude, I am not taking you anywhere. There are no dragons. You are going to spend the night here with me. We are going to make a child."

"A . . . a . . . a what?!"

Juel never moved so fast as she scurried back and bumped her head on one of the thick chains that suspended the bed from the ceiling. The great bed swayed and she whirled as she came to her knees to clutch two of the iron loops. She held onto them like a lifeline to one drowning in deep water.

He moved closer and she shrieked, then again as his legs bumped the bed. "Do not, I say do not come any closer. I will scream very loud and Orion will c-come!"

"He will anyway."

Blinking with bafflement, she said, "If you know that, then why are you here?"

"Sweeting, do not be afraid of what I must do."

Her eyes opened wider as he began to peel off his cloak and then, as she watched his dark shadow slowly move, he dropped the garment to the floor. It disappeared into the darkness and was followed by the sound of something hard thudding on stone—like some sort of weapon he released from around his hips.

Somewhere in her mind she knew this night was

going to change her forever. "You are not going to hurt me, I p-pray. I cannot s-stand much p-pain."

He said nothing to that, and Juel moaned. She spoke with quiet but desperate firmness. "I won't let you, you know." Her damp hands slipped on the chain and she felt her buttocks sliding on the satiny bedcloth. If she just kept moving stealthily, maybe she could drop off the bed slowly and hide under it.

His voice came from the dark. "There is nowhere you can hide, and if you do run, I will catch you. This night is mine and yours."

"No."

When he spoke again, his voice was tender, almost a caress in the night. "Come here, Juel. Make it easy and come to me."

"Make it easy?" She leaped from the bed and screeched when a cobweb fell across her face. "Never!" she cried, bumping against one object, then another. "Come near me and I'll scratch out your eyes!"

Now the voice was seductive, warm, inviting. "I want you, Juel, and I mean to have you this night."

His voice was getting to her, with its deepness and authority and warmth. "For o-only one night? Then you will leave me alone?"

"I cannot promise that."

"P-promise!"

"Do you come willing then?"

"W-willing, yes."

"I promise then. Only one night," he lied.

He was moving closer, slowly ever closer. She could see his huge, dark shape looming. "Tell me one thing," she asked.

194

"Yes. One thing before we love."

She licked her lips. "By what name are you called?"

Silence.

It stretched out.

"You have lied!" Juel made a run for the door, praying he had come in that way and left it unlocked. She bumped into a sharp-cornered object, cried out from the pain in her shin, then started for the door again.

He just stood there. "You are going to hurt yourself, Juel. Like a wild bird captured in a dark box."

"'Tis nothing compared with what you would do to me, phantom!" She crashed into another object, a rickety chair this time. Taking hold of a knobby spindle, she spun and she tripped, flying over the torn cushion and landing with a great *whoof*.

Now he stood over her, looking down and shaking his head. Her humiliation knew no end as Juel looked up, up the dark plum-tight shape of his hose. Down here, on the floor staring upward, all she could make out was his lower half. Standing up, all she had seen was his upper half. She had seen no hump.

It had grown even darker and the smell of rain was creeping in the arrow slits as a hand reached down to pull her up.

Surprisingly, she rose with all the gracefulness of a swan, him pulling her slowly and with gentle hands. A quiver of almost pleasant apprehension passed through her limbs as he held her hand, brought it up to cup his face in a loving caress. Then he moved her fingers to his lips and Juel thought she would swoon.

He was touching her! The phantom, or ghost, was

195

kissing her fingertips!

Her head was rolling, her body swaying with some strange weakness that suddenly overtook her.

"Sweet Jesus," he murmured, "you are beautiful. So soft. So warm. So tantalizing."

He was shaking, too, Juel soon realized, as misty tendrils of desire swirled about her like sensuous fog. Her head was back and he was kissing her throat, and when he pulled her closer, to lay her face against his shoulder, she found her voice faint as she spoke.

"Who are you? What are you doing to me?" She opened her mouth and let her tongue slide across his flesh stretching taut across his collarbone, not even aware or caring that he was shirtless. She only knew he tasted so very good. This was no ghost!

In a deep and virile voice, he spoke. "I am your lover, sweeting, and I am making love to you."

They sank to the floor then, each too weak to make it to the bed as they shivered and groaned, kissing each other and touching, caressing, kneading flesh. When his hand cupped the underside of her breast, fire swept through her. Juel emerged from the heavy mist of desire and looked down to see where they were, what they were doing. Together.

She shrieked as her bare legs pressed into the cold stone floor. He had lifted her skirts!

"Oh! I am loath to do this! It's not right. We are not wed!" She closed her eyes tight. "Who are you to do this to me, to think you can just take—" This was no dream!

"Hush!"

With a harsh whisper in her ear, he scooped her from

the floor and carried her to the bed as she screamed, bit, clawed, and kicked, slicing the air with her feet.

She looked down and saw that her feet were bare. If he touched her feet, just dared to, she would squeeze through that slit and jump to the ground below. No one touched her feet!

Protesting strongly, with a few of Jay's choice curse words thrown in, Juel felt the swaying bed catch hold of her backside as he went down with her. The huge bed moved gently now, rocking as in a gentle breeze, when her dark lover laid his hip beside hers, then slowly lowered to cover her belly.

He still had on his tight hose as he moved in a sensual rhythm as old as the world itself. She had ceased her struggles and a pleasure such as she'd never known ground into her, over and through her skirts, bold, hot, hard. She felt the hardening pressure of his manhood and felt the hot pulse inside herself answering his desire.

Next, he was kissing her, finding her lips as surely as an arrow found its mark. The impact was startling, and new impressions exploded in her brain, then her senses, as his firm and slightly moist lips moved across hers. She moaned, beginning to arch her own hips just a little bit. At the same moment she could feel the shape of his lips and the bulge of his manhood. They seemed as one, moved as one . . . and then his tongue entered her mouth!

And now Juel understood how the act of love was accomplished. She was ecstatic, for this movement of his tongue did not hurt one single bit and it actually felt good, deliciously so. Or was she only thinking like a foolish virgin that pain would be absent when he . . . when he . . . ?

"Juel." He lifted his head. "What are you doing?"

She sighed, bumping her nose against his chin. "Wondering."

His voice was a velvet murmur. "About what?"

Nervously, she bit her lip. "How it will feel when you come into me."

He sighed with a deep, manly shiver. "Why don't we find out now?"

Chapter Twenty

"I have changed my mind!"

As soon as she had spied an opening, Juel slipped out, rolled over, scrambled on all fours to the edge of the swaying bed, and tumbled off . . . only to land hard on her buttocks.

Looking up, even in darkness she thought she could detect a smile on the phantom's face. "Come back up here," the hard voice said.

She bit her lip to still the shudder his iciness caused in her. "No," she said in a tiny voice.

He lay on his stomach, looking down at her lovely shadowy form. "What?" he said with a brittle snap to his voice.

"I said No." She began to inch across the floor. "I've done a foolish thing coming here. You really must go now."

"As you wish. I'll not force you into anything."

Juel gasped as she saw him reach into the dark somewhere and pull out a snowy cambric undertunic.

She could make that out even in the gloom, since she'd washed hundreds of them since coming here. But the rest of his body lay in blackness, his face a soft gray blur. He was pulling something else on, she could tell by his movements, no doubt the chausses of soft wool she'd felt close to her when he'd first pressed near her. His body . . . feeling so warm and hard next to hers, his shoulder-length hair she'd felt brushing . . . She suppressed a shiver of desire and put down the urge to feel his kiss again.

As she moved slowly to her feet, she came halfway up to see his fuzzy form go across the blur of window. When she straightened, he was gone, vanished from the room!

"No, you can't be gone." She looked around frantically. "Not that soon. No, do not leave me here." She walked about, bumping into things, hard things, soft, woody, metal. Then, rushing over to the door, she found it locked and a feeling of dismay washed over her. "Please, help me out of here. I cannot stay in here . . . not alone."

She stood as still as stone, wondering where he had gone, how he had disappeared like that. Carefully, she walked about, feeling her way, but there was no opening that she could feel. If only she had a candle, and the means to light it.

A flash of loneliness stabbed at her heart.

Sinking to the edge of the bed, Juel began to cry, her shoulders lifting and falling with the weight of her sobs. She had been alone in the forest. Alone when her father and Jay were gone to do their work. Yes, she had had her cats, her neighbors, her housework. But what she had wanted most was a mother. Jay and Peter had their sweethearts. She had no one to hold. Not that way. Why had she never thought of holding a man before she came here?

"I want you back," Juel whispered into the dark. "Come back, please, I need you." She sniffed, louder than the whisper of her voice. "You felt so good in my arms and . . . and I do n-not care if you are a ph-phantom or not."

"You do not care?"

He was back in the room!

She whirled this way and that, hopping about on the great swaying bed. "Where are you? How did you get back inside?"

He stepped back. "I'd not stay if—"

"Do stay. Do!"

"You want me to?" He came toward the bed, looking down at her, aware she was smiling happily through her tears.

"Please."

It was more a sigh than a word this happy man heard.

"You do not trick me, just to find a means to escape?"

For answer, her arms reached out for him to come to her. She waited, but he did not hold her. Not yet. When he came to the bed, he wore nothing but his ungartered chausses.

She drew in a breath, held it for a moment, then released it. "When you were here but moments ago, you had your hose on. Now you wear braies. How did you—?"

"Men can move very fast while in battle and I have learned to dress and undress just as quickly when blood is sticking to me, sweeting."

"Have you been hurt many times?"

"Yes."

"Why were you in battle? Are you a knight of King Henry's then?" Perhaps he was a spy for the king. "When were you last—?"

"You ask too many questions. Come and kiss me."

When she just sat there, trying to see him in the blackness, his hands slipped up her arms, bringing her down closer. The jolt of his knee coming to rest against the mound of her private self made her gasp into his mouth as his lips covered hers. He kissed her this way until she was breathless and panting, the pit of her stomach in a wild swirl. His kiss grew deeper, his knee bolder.

"Kiss me, Juel. Kiss me back."

There was something familiar about his voice, yet she had no care as to what it was. She gave her best attempt in giving him a kiss, threading her fingers through his hair, pressing her lips to his. Then she felt his throbbing member brush her. When he yanked her closer and their kisses became heated, Juel felt an emotion so wild, so wonderful, she knew it could only be . . . What? She couldn't know just yet; this was so new.

"I want you," she cried with elation between breaths. She touched him, gasping. "Oh, yes—I do want you!"

He groaned against her chin as his mouth sucked her there; he lifted his head. "I know, I know, sweeting. And I've wanted you since—"

202

He stopped and she felt him grow cold.

"What is it?" she cried, with no desire to back out of his embrace. "Please, you must not leave me again!"

"Not just yet I won't." He pulled her close to his heart, threading her slender hand with his. "We will love now. And love again."

Carefully and with much tenderness, he pushed her back onto the bed and slipped the nightgown over her head. She wore a chemise, too, and he was surprised at that, for most women went naked beneath night-clothes.

"Now, love, do not be afraid when I touch you."

"Touch me," she begged breathlessly. "Touch me anywhere you want. Please, now!"

"Ah," he murmured victoriously. "You are a treasure, Juel Reynaude."

When his hand came up and covered her small breast, he drew the firm flesh together and cupped the little beauty and brought his mouth down to suckle it. Juel bucked upward and met the bulge of his manhood coming to meet her. He shifted for a moment, returned, and was as naked as she.

"Oh . . ." she gasped. "I feel like swooning." Kissing his chest, Juel was wishing she could look fully into his eyes. "Are you handsome?" she asked in between breaths.

"Like a prince," he said against her belly as he swirled his tongue in her navel.

She was a mass of quivering sensation by the time he reached the apex of her thighs. There, as she writhed against his hand brushing lightly, he kissed her, drew back as she moaned, then entered her core with his long, hard finger.

Juel bucked up and delighted in the gentle pressure. But she had no reason to cry out. She looked down at his dark head, felt his long hair that was like black pearl brushing her thighs. "That feels strange, what you are doing?"

He smiled. "You are a maiden. You feel fresh and new."

"It does not hurt." She fell back to the bed as her moisture began and he spread it all around her pale-pink petals. She feared pain, but she wanted him badly, that she knew for sure now.

He kissed her lips and touched her gently, sweetly, draining all her doubts and fears. "Oh, oh, that feels good, so much b-better." This was a dream come true.

Swiftly he rose over her, lowered his head to kiss her once. "Do that in my mouth, Juel. Stumble over your words and I will kiss you into trusting me forever and ever."

She needn't have had him ask that of her, since she did it naturally. "I-I—want you and I think I'm . . . Oh, yes!"

In one forward motion, he had entered her and the pressure was great. She bucked up, brought him deeper, bit his shoulder, tasting blood, and then he slowed, letting her sheath discover and clasp the hugeness of him. He took his time, realizing she was tight as a tiny bottle.

A curious tension was within her as he worked himself in and out; now the mild discomfort ceased and she felt . . .

He soon met his satisfaction, tossing his head and

shouting to the rafters. Gratification came hard for her, since this was her first time.

Juel knew it was over. She had sensed the change and had grown tense. "No," she cried softly against his chest. "Not yet."

"What is it, beloved?" He kissed the spot where her heart pounded beneath her heaving breast.

She blushed in the dark. "You are finished."

"Not forever, love." He kissed her throat and chuckled deeply. "I'm almost ready for you once again."

True to his word, and before she could scarce catch her breath, he was moving inside her again. Passion radiated from the soft core of her body. This time, when his thrusts came faster, deeper, harder, swaying the bed in a rhythm that would have mortified her had she stood back and observed, she met him, moving naturally, and knew the moment of ecstasy was near at hand. Hearts pounded together in joy.

Then it burst over her, a climax so great that her lover spilled his seed at the same blissful moment. From such a perfect union, a child must come, he was thinking as he hugged her close and whispered endearments into her hair.

The deed was done. And just to make entirely sure, he was thinking as he smiled with intoxicated joy, he was going to love her night after night, day after day until he met his mark and she had his child inside her.

"I have fallen deeply for you," she told him, laying her flushed cheek against his chest. "Whoever you are, I adore you." Tears gathered in her eyes.

"And I you," he said, and whispered more endearments, bringing her hand to his lips to kiss her palm. "We are very good together, lovely Eliz—" His voice carried away into "Juel."

She sighed and slept deeply, while the moon made one last appearance low in the sky. The room was bathed in silvery moonbeam when he pulled her nightgown over her head, lifted her, crept out the door with her sleeping soundly in his arms. He made the twists and turns with the ease of one who knew the manor and placed the sleeping beauty in the middle of her pallet.

Blowing a last kiss gallantly from his fingers, the phantom slipped out of the chamber and did not even stiffen when something leapt onto his back and he walked the passageways, his shadow that of a wretched hunchback.

When Juel awoke in the morning she relived in her mind the strange, wild, wonderful dream she'd had. As she looked down, her eyes flew open and she screamed when she saw the blood on Dawn's white nightgown.

Her face burned then and she knew it had not been a dream after all.

Everything was real. All too frighteningly real.

Later in the day Juel took a big leather pouch to the river with her. The water was cool when she tested it, and she stripped down, walked into the lapping waves, and washed off. When that was done she dressed quickly, found a flat rock, dug in her pack, and pulled out some bread and cheese. After a quick lunch she lay on the rock for a nap, the sun warming her, drying her long hair. The events of the night before came to her in a thrillingly sensuous dream; she shivered and awoke. She felt strangely wonderful. She braided the length of dark hair, took up her pouch, and hurried back to the castle and her work.

Chapter Twenty-One

The king was coming.

The old castle was in a flurry of activity as the manor was swept and polished from top to bottom, inside and out. The castle's own pond had long been dried up. The fishermen had gone to the nearby river and some went to the sea and brought back mackerel, mullet, ray, shole, shad, salmon, and trout, for the king and his men liked to eat fish.

Sugar, an imported luxury, was brought out of the kitchen, a special kind made with violets and roses.

"He will be hungry as soon as he comes, and will sup with Orion and his men," the black cook Cimmerian told the kitchen maids, as if they hadn't heard it many times before.

In the hall, servants were spreading the best cloths and setting up the trestle tables with silver spoons, steel knives, dishes for salt, silver cups, and shallow silver-rimmed wooden bowls called mazers.

Juel, Dawn, and Alice were kept busy as bees, and Rajahr flitted about as if he held the honor of queen bee. Even Autumn Meaux was working, cutting great chunks of cheese, and she found this kept her mind off worrying about her sisters and what had become of them. Geoffrey Johns, the orphan from Herstmonceux had found a place at The Keep, and loved staying in the roomy loft with Arne, the aviarist who kept the birds— the turtledoves and nightingales. Geoffrey's freckled face beamed every time he saw Juel, as she moved from kitchen to hall, setting a trencher at each place.

Ruark had gone to the nearest big town to look for harpers and minstrels. The king loved spinning songs, dawn songs, debates, political satires, love songs.

Juel was just coming along the short hall from outside the larder door when she saw Orion step into the garden, calling happily out to surprised folks, "The sun is shining. A fine day!"

He stopped when he saw her.

She had not seen him in days, was told he had spent some time with his wife and had been riding for exercise. She had been puzzled when told he often went on these midnight rides on his black destrier. She had wondered if his wife went with him, but did not wonder too often, for her mind and heart was filled with the glorious night she'd spent with the phantom.

She had thought of nothing else for two days now.

Orion was dressed in fine clothes for the occasion. She wondered at this, for she had heard that he hardly bothered with clothes that were decorated with embroidery, nor crimson, nor gold rings with stones.

He wore all those this day. And he looked happy!

He was so handsome that Juel's heart skipped a beat and she blushed with awareness at the burgundy linen hose that covered his muscular thighs and calves like a second skin. His tunic was of crimson-and-white stripes, with embroidery of gold thread, his surcoat a deeper cinnamon red; and a cloak, pinned on the shoulder, was lined with silk and was bordered. His boots were nut brown, matching his wide silk sash. On the middle finger of his left hand shone a heavy gold ring with a stone that looked like a sapphire.

He was like a prince. But suddenly he did not appear so happy. It seemed as if he'd just remembered something.

His cool voice broke into her reverie. "I would have a word with you, Juel Reynaude."

She broke into a deep curtsy, then blushed when he found her gaze resting on his tight linen hose. For a moment, she stared at his long, lean form. Then her eyes flew upward and she thought she detected a flicker of amusement in his intense eyes.

She swallowed with difficulty and found her voice. "Here, m'lord?"

Gesturing with his beringed hand, he said in a serious voice, "Not here. Come with me, into the withdrawing room."

A wave of apprehension went through her as she followed him. Was he going to tell her that she would not be allowed to visit her father on the morrow? Or, worse, would he inform her that she must stay at The Keep and never return home?

She had no idea how bad his news would prove to be.

"Please," he said, gesturing to a cushioned bench. "Sit there."

Please?

Alarm swept through her.

At the bench, Juel did not sit but whirled to face

Orion. "My father." She blinked with fear in her eyes. "He is well?"

Orion only nodded. He hated what he was about to say. "But your home. My knights returned from their inspections. It has been burned to the ground."

Panic welled in her throat. "My . . . h-home?" She threw her arms wide. "B-but how?"

"The same band of pillagers that sacked the village of Herstmonceux." He saw her eyes clouded with tears. "I am sorry."

"I wish to see my father."

"Tomorrow."

"You are right. The king is more important." Her voice faded to a hushed silence.

He saw her tight lips, the tears held barely in check. "I did not say that, nor did I imply that in any way," he told her as gently as he could.

She looked up into his face. Everything was gone—her home, her beloved cats, all her simple possessions. Oh how she wanted someone to hold her!

Orion seemed to hesitate, then he walked to the door and looked at her askance. "You need not work any more today, if you would rather go to your chamber and be alone. I will send Dawn to you after the king and his men have supped."

"No!"

"What?" Orion said with raised eyebrows.

She blinked, feeling lightheaded. "I mean, I must work to keep my mind off my loss."

"You are wise to keep busy, Juel." He nodded. "As you wish then."

She looked around the chamber at the heavy furnishings and great tapestries, appointments that had been polished, cloths that had been carefully brushed free of dust. Still, there was the usual clutter everywhere. "Will I live here now?" she wondered, with an outrageously huge tear bulging and sparkling in one corner of her eye.

His deep-brown eyes bore into her. "Yes."

"But I wish to live with my father and brother. As it used to be."

"The day you came through that forest was the beginning of a new life, Juel."

Juel stared at a tapestry with its border of lilies, roses, and heliotropes, the only trace of softness in the huge, beam-ceilinged chamber. "We can always rebuild it."

"You will remain at The Keep. This is your home now."

"No," she sniffed mutinously. "I do not wish to remain here."

His look was sharp as he took in the old clothes she was wearing. "You have been happy of late, have you not?"

"True." She took a swipe at a damp eye, then wrung her hands in her apron. "But now I must be with those I love."

His dark eyebrows rose. "You are not here with one you love?"

Her eyes flew to his curious gaze. "My brother is here, it is so."

On a final note, he said, "And your father also will come from Herstmonceux as soon as he is well."

He was about to leave her when she began to cry softly, overwhelmed by her loss. "It will not be the same. *Nothing* will ever be as it was."

His back stiffened and he momentarily looked at a loss as to what he should say. "It will be better," he finally said.

Surprise lifted her eyes. "How can you predict that?"

As he continued to search her face over his shoulder, Juel dropped her gaze. She felt her cheeks color. Heat stole over her and the palms of her hands felt moist.

She was ashamed of what she had done with a mere stranger—allowed him to enter her most secret self—a stranger who had answered her admission of love but had not come to her for two nights. He existed, true, but where was he now? She had wanted him with her last night and he had not come to her. Perhaps he never would again. It was a liaison for one night only, much as painted ladies at castle courts were wont to have. This was not her preference. She had never wanted a man in the first place, never been persuaded or moved by a young man's entreaties. What had happened with the stranger, she could not say.

"Trust me."

He walked out then and her mind refused to register the significance of those two tiny words.

Trust me.

Would she? Better yet, *could* she?

Chapter Twenty-Two

At first it was just a thick plume of dust on a distant hillside with a show of red and gold, and then the fairly large group disappeared below into the mist-shrouded trees . . . Now they neared The Keep.

Bright bannerets floated in the breeze as King Henry and his knights and retainers rode past the guardhouse into the old courtyard with a jingling of harness and the creaking of fine leather. Henry himself was dressed in a form-fitting velvet doublet and fine hose. He looked young and blond and strong, giving off a dashing masculinity. He rode atop a beautiful white horse that pranced and arched his neck, shining mane flowing about him. The king himself wore his thick fair hair in long wavelets to his shoulders.

Henry came down off his horse in easy, languorous movements. His squire had dismounted before him to rush over to take his mount by the bridle. The young king's long, strong legs carried him at an easy gait as he walked the short distance into the manor.

Geoffrey Johns looked up at the king, an expression

of awe on his freckled face. When the king smiled at him, Geoffrey was filled with joy. He ran to tell the other youngsters of the king's actions, and they all stood oohing and ahhing over the strong handsome knights who had come with the king.

The long trestle tables had been set up and the king and his most important knights sat with him on a raised dais of wood at the upper end of the smoky hall. Henry occupied a massive chair, with Orion beside him, while everyone else sat on benches. All the tables were covered with clean white cloths and the wine was free-flowing.

There was much talk and laughter as the maids flitted about, the knights stopping to pat a plump backside now and then as they passed through the crowd of knights.

The great fireplace blazed.

Ranice entered in a beautiful mauve brocade gown, her hair fashioned into bright ringlets of perfection. All chatter ceased, for she was the only lady in attendance.

She bowed before the king and he took her hand.

"So," Henry said with a beaming smile. "You have come at last to be with your husband." He kissed the hand he held. "You look lovely, as usual, Lady Ranice."

"And you are more handsome than ever, Your Majesty," Ranice gushed, graciously sweeping up her skirts on one side while taking a seat beside Orion when the king waved her to a chair.

Juel was serving them at the moment and heard what the king had said to Ranice, and her answer to him.

Orion lifted his gaze to see Juel pause in pouring some wine into the king's goblet. Henry, too, gazed at the lovely serving girl and a look passed between him and Orion.

Orion cleared his throat. "She is lovely, true," he said, and Henry's gaze shrewdly flicked back to Juel.

Henry sipped his wine and watched Juel move on. Then he put his full attention back on Ranice. "How fares your beloved father?" he asked of Piers de Monteforte, watching Ranice closely.

"He is sometimes better," Ranice said, clutching her goblet and feeling a moment of panic as she wondered if the king was going to mention the mixup. "He has not been healthy since Clytie . . . ah, disappeared."

Again the king's eyes found Juel as she paused at the end of the long trestle table to pour his knight a draft of wine. His meticulous eye absorbed all details. Still watching the lovely serving girl, he said, "Orion, didn't you say you preferred a dark-haired woman for your lady wife? Was this not as it should've been?" His startling blue eyes twinkled as he heard Ranice's soft gasp.

"I did," Orion answered. He looked to Ranice then. "Why did you come in Clytie's place? You said your sister ran away, not disappeared. Now that the king is here, please clarify. You said the king wished us wed."

Ranice was trembling, and all eyes were trained on her, awaiting her answer. Though she was rarely embarrassed, she was so now. "Your Majesty," she said, breathless and with her hand pressed to her chest. "We have consummated our vows."

The clatter of a wine pitcher was heard in the silence that reigned over the great hall. Henry did not look her way, for he knew who it was who had dropped the pitcher. He kept his gaze on Ranice as she sent a piercing look down the table to where the top of Juel Reynaude's dark head was visible above the edge of the table.

She was cleaning up the mess as best she could.

"Let me help." The fair-headed Duncan Kingsley bent to pick up some pieces and help her pile them on the platter Alice had rushed over to place in Juel's trembling hands.

Looking up into Duncan's eyes, seeing the love that shone there, Juel knew a moment of joy as she thought this man might be her phantom. He was tall. He was strongly muscled. He was—

Suddenly the sweet moment between Juel and the knight was shattered as Orion shot to his feet.

"Leave her. She is—"

"Orion . . ." the king said, rising from the table, "let us have a word together." He gestured to a serving maid to come over. "Bring us our meal in the withdrawing room. We will sup there." To Ranice, he said, "Lady, the musicians have arrived—you may entertain my men."

Ranice was left gasping for air, but just then she caught sight of Jay Reynaude entering the hall. Now she would not feel so alone. He was a wonderful lover, which he had proven just the night before, had not known any qualms of conscience in taking a willing lady to his loft. Her eyes beckoned the tall, dark-haired Jay to come sit beside her—and the look was not lost on the king as he left the hall with Orion Sutherland.

Orion, too, shot a last glance over his shoulder. He was looking to see if Duncan would follow Juel into the kitchens. But the knight caught his lord's harsh look and, casting one more longing look at Juel's swishing green skirt as she left the hall, he sat back down—

Most reluctantly.

Juel heard the music coming from the hall and she walked out of the hot kitchen and made her way into the "screens passage," where she paused at the partition. Above the screens rose the musicians' gallery overlooking the hall.

Doorways led to two rooms with a passageway between them that comprised the service area. A pantry, for bread, stood on one side; a buttery, for serving beverages, on the other. They were both equipped with strong shelves and benches on which food brought from the kitchen could be arranged for serving.

Listening to the music and feeling in a fanciful mood, Juel walked humming softly to herself to the third small door opening between buttery and pantry on a flight of stairs leading to the passage between the two halls.

She heard voices and backed to flatten herself beneath the stairs. A man and a woman were talking in hushed tones—she wondered who they could be. Looking up obliquely, she saw the rich brocade swish of— Ranice's skirts!

Who was the man she was meeting in secret?

The man's legs were lost in the swirl of mauve, and all she could make out were the toes of his black boots. Now she was really curious, thinking he ought to be ashamed of himself—whoever he was.

"You will meet me again this evening?"

A deep sigh. "If you want."

Too low to make out distinctly.

Juel had a feeling that the man was almost reluctant to have another clandestine meeting with Ranice. Disgust washed over Juel. Who would do this to Orion? Who would dare? She frowned. One who obviously had the idea that Ranice and Orion were not that fond of each other, no doubt.

Juel felt her face heat up as the sounds of kissing and murmuring became obvious. The two of them were not fully observable from her position beneath the stairs, but she had a feeling they must be fondling. Could it be—?

Suddenly she felt faint and alarmed. Surely this could not be her phantom? Moving a little to the right, she tried to see between the broad wooden stairs. A sound from her must have startled them, for they broke apart and she could hear the soft rustle of skirts as Ranice quickly took her leave . . . but not before whispering some hasty word of parting.

Juel waited, wanting to make sure there was no one up there before she moved from her hiding place. When she heard nothing—not even the soft thud fall beside her—she moved cautiously out and into the open.

"Aha!"

She was grasped from behind, found herself held fast by a strong pair of arms encircling her waist. Squeezing her eyes tight, Juel could feel the warm breath—no doubt of cooling ardor—on her nape.

Please God, she prayed, *don't let this be the midnight phantom.* If it were he, she knew her heart would be broken in two and she'd never be whole again.

But how was she to tell for certain, since she had not made out his features clearly in the attic darkness?

Her nerves tensed immediately as he turned her around and, as she opened her eyes—just a little—to peer up at him, their cries of amazement issued forth at the same time.

"Juel!"

"Jay!"

She stared at her brother in disgust. "How *could* you?"

Dropping his arms to his sides, Jay hid a sheepish look. Heaving a deep sigh, he tried to lay a hand on her flushed cheek, but she slapped it away.

"Juel, please try to understand." His darkly handsome face smirked softly. "Yet how could you. You are a woman."

"A woman, yes." She glared at him with overbright eyes. "And that makes me less able to understand the rutting ways of a man? Huh!" she snorted daintily. "You are my brother, but still I daresay—you disgust me."

He laughed, full and masculine. "The lady was willing. Juel, understand that Ranice approached me. She touched me."

"How?"

Devilish green eyes narrowed in humor. "Very boldly."

Juel bit her lower lip, then said, "She did?" But she was frowning a second later. "That did not give you rightful claim to answer her lust. She is Orion's lady wife!"

Jay shrugged with a deliberately casual movement. "Lord Orion has his own sweetheart, a woman he goes

221

to see at night. Alice and Fat Will were speaking openly about . . . well, actually I overheard their conversation. It seems that Orion has fallen deeply in love with one other than his wife. He kissed her once and was lost."

Juel's face clouded with uneasiness. "What does this 'sweetheart' of his look like? And what is her name?"

"They did not say. And no one knows if she is comely or shapely."

"Humph! Just like a man, to make mention of her figure."

Juel had never seen her brother look so hard, as he did now. "We were discussing Ranice. You must know the lady is a whore. She gives her favors freely. Most women do."

He saw the shocked look on her face.

Chastised by her silence, he went on. "I did not say *all* women, dear sister." The tension eased as he chuckled. "You'd think that some are clutched by iron maidens. Very few of those, however."

Just then, as Juel was thinking of Dawn's words having to do with iron skirts, she heard soft footsteps coming along the passageway and grasped her brother's arm before he could step back and hide.

He stared at the fingers biting into his arm. "Stay," she said. "I know who comes."

Jay looked around wildly. "How could you know?" He wondered if his sister was about to betray him and hand him over to a guard who would lock him up for dallying with Orion's lady wife.

"I know her step."

Each studying the other's expressions for a reaction, they listened to the light step that drew nearer. Just then the sweetest angel-voice called along the passage-way.

"Hoo-hoo, Juel, have you come this way?" Her laugh was like the tinkle of silver bells. "The knights grow rowdy and drunken. Come and help. No need to hide, they have forgotten your embarrassing moment with the broken pottery."

Dawn daintily lifted her skirts as she descended and came to a sudden halt.

"I—"

Dawn was held captive.

She was staring into the most extraordinary green eyes, flecked and ringed with gold.

Chapter Twenty-Three

Jay's breath caught at the back of his throat as he said, "Who are you?"

Dawn could hardly lift her voice above a whisper as she finally found her tongue.

"I am Dawn." For a moment she forgot her last name. "Peyton," she added.

"Dawn," he murmured, lifting her hand and holding it gently. "Aye, like soft morning sun, and eyes, ah, like velvet pussywillows."

Juel rolled her eyes heavenward, then leaned close to whisper in Dawn's ear. "Caution, my friend. You have just met my cunning brother Jay."

Jay's vexation was evident, but he smoothed it over with his endearing charm. "Sister, don't you have work to do? Why don't you go and serve the rowdy knights, I'm certain they miss your comely presence."

Breaking from the firm, warm hold, Dawn called after Juel, "I will come with you."

"Wait!" Jay was right behind them. Dawn kept walking and he hurried to keep up with her light and lively steps. "Why have we not met before?" he said, his eyes soft.

Keeping her back stiff, Dawn made all the twists and turns while the persistent young man skipped alongside. "Perhaps you were too busy looking elsewhere—"

She had no idea what to call him and could not risk calling him Jay, since she had no desire to be familiar with such a knave. She decided to say his last name.

"—Reynaude. Please," she beseeched. "Let me pass."

Jay was holding this fair-haired treasure captive as he planted his hands on either side of the stone wall. Dawn's hands came up but would not touch. His chest was near. His legs were planted wide apart. His breath was coming fast and he was staring at her in a most frightening way.

Soft brown eyes met the green darkness of his. "I am not moved by your virile charms, and I need warn you, I am totally aware of your infamous lechery, Jay Reynaude. So far, I have managed to escape your clutches. You must look elsewhere for a lover, since I am happy with my life and do not need a man complicating matters for me. You have Alice Becker and several others to warm your loft, or wherever it is you bed down. So, please, let me go to my work."

"My, my!" Jay clucked his tongue. "You are full of piss and wind, aren't you."

"Oooh! Step back and let me pass."

"No, lovely maid."

Dawn was both aggravated and excited. "No?"

He stared into her eyes boldly as, in a flash, her knee came up to wound him in a sensitive place. But Jay was swift and caught her leg, wrapped in her skirts, and held it in the crook of his arm.

"Let go, scoundrel!" She all but hopped on one foot.

Still holding her leg high, Jay stepped closer and she felt him press her against the wall. No one had ever gotten this close to her because Dawn had always sent them limping away, damning her in a high voice riddled with pain. There had only been one who'd near ravished her. She had come away from that with an invisible suit of armor, prepared to battle those who tried dishonoring her.

Dawn was about to defend herself anew, when he splayed himself closer yet and breathed in her ear. "My God, but you are soft and lovely."

"I am not soft—but firm from a life of hard work. How dare you!"

Her leg was still aloft and was beginning to strain and pull. She could feel his hard body against her and with horror realized her own body was starting to respond to his slightest movements and shiftings.

Then he held her chin and kissed her full on the mouth.

"No . . . no . . . no," Dawn whimpered, feeling something happening inside her.

"Sweet Jesus," Jay said, his breath coming hard and fast. "What is this feeling I've never known." He pressed his forehead lightly to hers. "It is not familiar."

At last, Dawn felt her leg being lowered to the floor, and when she skipped back to gain her balance, Jay grasped her gently and pulled her to his chest. He hugged her fiercely and bent his head to snuggle his face into her throat.

Dawn had never known security in her life, but she was feeling it now in Jay Reynaude's arms. She had been her own shield and protection against harm, since she was an orphan and had been so for what seemed forever.

Jay lowered his arms and stepped back. "You must forgive me. It is just that I have never known anyone quite like you."

"And you still do not know me, Jay Reynaude!"

With that, Dawn whirled and fled down the passageway, her heart thrumming with the pulse of the music coming from the musicians' gallery. She gulped hard, hot tears threatening to spill.

Before meeting Juel's brother, she had been happy, and now she was positively miserable.

She ran not only from Jay Reynaude but from herself as well. She did not trust these freshly awakened emotions. He was just too tempting and intriguing. It was true that she was unable to give herself completely to any man—and especially not to one as indiscriminate with the women.

Then why was her body aching for another touch from him?

Jay stood alone in the cold stone passageway, wishing the beautiful vision would return. He shook his dark head and slumped against the wall like a defeated warrior. Or, like a lovesick fool!

He walked along the passageway and felt more alone than ever before. Ranice! He came to a sudden halt, slapping his hand to his forehead. If Dawn Peyton got wind of his assignation with Orion's lady wife then . . . ah then she would never speak to him again.

Humph! he thought. *She hardly speaks to me now—*

and no wonder. He was a thousand times a fool. Dawn Peyton was more a lady than Ranice could ever be. Beside Ranice, Dawn shone like a jewel against a heap of rubbish—

Juel! Ah! His sister would know what to do, for Juel and Dawn were cut of the same cloth.

He went racing along the passageway, skidding around corners, bumping into great round barrels, shouting to the tomblike ceilings, "Dear God—I am in love! *In love!*"

The king stayed on for three more days and during that time he was often closeted with Orion in the withdrawing room. He spoke of his motives for invading France:

"The territories promised by the treaty of Brétigny are commercially important to the English, since the Bordeaux wine customs alone constitute a major source of income for the English Crown. In addition, the prosecution of foreign war minimizes the chances of domestic revolt by nobles who would necessarily take the field with the king. The inheritance of property by the correct bloodlines is an extremely serious matter, for it is part of the whole social organization; and the settlement of property disputes involves, as you know, Orion, the hauling forth of ancient genealogical rolls."

Orion only nodded, sipping his drink.

"I have discovered something more you should know," he said to Orion. "As for legitimate bloodlines, I believe that Scardon took this keep from the Sutherlands. You must realize that he will someday return to fight for it. He will try to take back what he originally coveted and needed at that time—a stronghold for his plundering and defense."

Orion sat quiet and brooding. He was thinking that Henry's character was by no means wholly admirable. Hard and domineering, he was intolerant of opposition and could be quite ruthless and cruel in pursuit of whatever he wished to go after. Yet, many French writers admired him as a brave, loyal, and upright man, an honorable fighter, and a commanding personality in whom there was little of the mean and paltry.

"What say you to this?" Henry asked Orion. "Are you Sutherland or not, hmm?"

Orion sat up straighter and then, after several moments of thought, he leaned to one side and clasped his hands together. "Perhaps" was all he said.

"Dear God." Henry frowned and waved a hand in the air. "Perhaps? Is this all you can say? We have searched the rolls."

"Where is my name in them?"

Henry sighed. "We have not found your name." Then he blurted, "Who is Julia?"

"You mean Juel." He paused, then said, "Juel Reynaude."

"No. Julia."

"No more suspense, Your Majesty. Who is—or *was* she?"

"Is. Your mother. Julia Sutherland."

Orion shot to his feet. "Where is she?"

Silence reigned—

Then Henry finally said, "Now that—that one mystery you must figure for yourself, Orion. I cannot aid you in this."

230

"A mystery. How must I solve it?"

The king stood to look out the window to the garden, with the old path leading to the round tower. He kept his back to Orion as he stared out.

"Courage," the king said.

"Courage?" Orion almost laughed at that. "To do what?"

Henry turned. "To allow one to lead you through your fear."

"My . . . fear."

"Aye."

Like ghosts of yesterday, the mists climbed about huge trees and clung to low bracken as a lone rider sat at the edge of the forest atop a black horse. Alone in the silence of night, Orion was recalling what the king had told him before his leavetaking; about Ranice and her lies.

Dark Angel shifted beneath him as Orion stared at the soft orange sickle moon. His wife had deceived him and he must think of a way to put her from him. Divorce, Henry had said it was called. He must have a good reason to send her back to her father. King Henry said he might have reason enough already since Ranice had lied about her sister Clytie, her half sister to be exact. The king had never seen her and he knew of no one else who had, either. Ranice pretended Clytie was still around and everyone seemed to go along with her.

Clytie had disappeared when she was very young, a mere child of five. Almost the same age as when he'd been parted from his parents. They had been killed, or so he had thought. Now the king was telling him his

231

mother Julia might have survived. If he thought very hard, sometimes he could envision a lovely woman with spice-brown hair and a charming smile. She had flitted in and out of his dreams and had been in some of his nightmares, too, where he fought to save her.

Where was she? He had almost become angry with Henry for not telling him. In fact, he wondered if the king himself really knew. Henry would not hide this from him, and no doubt he was just speculating as to Julia's true whereabouts.

He returned to thoughts of what he should do with his wife. He'd wanted to wed the dark-haired Clytie, thinking all the time her name was Ranice when, in truth, Ranice had turned out to be fair-haired and Clytie the dark one.

His brow grew dark. He had wed a dark-haired woman and that's what he'd expected and wanted! Not some silly yellow-haired twit!

Ranice and Clytie, the king had informed him had different mothers, and hence the contrary shades of hair color.

What had happened to the child Clytie? He felt he should make a visit to Monteforte Castle and question the old man Piers. He wanted the woman he was supposed to have wed by proxy; why in God's name had Ranice fabricated the story in the first place? Why even mention a sister when there was none? She had a *half* sister, but Ranice herself must have been a young girl when Clytie was lost. *Kidnapped* was more like it. Perhaps Ranice was not in her right mind after having lost her sister. It must have been a bad shock for her.

He would try to find this Clytie. Someone might have an idea where she had disappeared to years ago, and the king said if he could find Clytie, then he could be released from matrimony to Ranice de Monteforte, could send her back to her father. Ranice had said the king himself gave his blessings for their union, when, in truth, the king had never done such a thing. He had mentioned it, but at a time when there'd been such a commotion in the hall when Juel had accidentally spilled something, and the matter had been dropped. Ranice had lied from the first. He would have to confront her with these lies.

On his back Shadow chattered in his ear and bounced, eager to get back to The Keep for a midnight repast: the delicious banana Dawn had waiting for him.

Orion's thoughts were as deep as the sea as they rode back. He had a wife he didn't care a whit for and he knew she was dallying with some of the men in the manor. He was intrigued now and wanted to find Clytie; somehow it was very important. Furthermore, his mother was alive, and if his guess was correct, she was not that far away from him.

But what was he going to do about Juel Reynaude? Or, he should say *Elizabeth,* the deceased Baron Hunter's lost daughter. A messenger had come bearing a letter from Guy Hunter's barrister, addressed to him. Baron Hunter had liked books and wrote his own letters and journal; the barrister had discovered them, along with the important papers.

And if Juel was already pregnant, then what? He knew she had inherited lands and the Hunter Castle; he had wanted to get his hands on them. And now? He wanted her to have his child; she was very special to him and even now he wanted her back in his arms.

The woman herself mattered more than her new wealth. She had made him feel he was worth something. It overwhelmed him that she had given herself so freely and tenderly, that she loved him and had trusted him, that she was brave enough to assert herself in everything she did.

Did she know he was her midnight lover? If she found out, would she still love him? Should he tell her she was an heiress? He might lose her then, even were she with his child. She might go to her own castle forever. But Juel was honest and loved him, wasn't she, didn't she? He should be as honest as she was, but could he?

Orion pondered this as he neared The Keep. He turned his horse toward the river, dismounted, and shed his clothes. Shadow sat on the horse and watched as Orion jumped into the water and bathed, needing the coldness that struck him like needles of ice. He dressed quickly, mounted, and shook despite the warmth of his woolen doublet covering his chest and the heavy hose on his legs. Shadow snuggled closer to keep him warm.

Orion neared The Keep again and looked up at the round tower; it seemed to have glaring little eyes that watched his every move. It was a place he had never been inside because of Scardon's warning never to go there else he'd die. He needed a drink, there was so much pressure on his mind.

Satan's horns! What if John Scardon should return and try to usurp what was his birthright? He really *was* in need of some wine!

Chapter Twenty-Four

Not only were Orion's knights searching for Autumn Meaux's sisters, but now they also looked for Clytie de Monteforte, who had been kidnapped years ago.

Ranice had not been told what was taking place and Orion had sent her from his apartments weeping more than once. Her questions drove him mad! He could not trust the woman. She might undo all the plans he had made with the king. She might even be a spy!

He was not ready to begin questioning her himself. He wanted to see what happened first, for if Ranice was as deceitful as she seemed, then he would not take a chance of having her warn someone on the outside that a search was on for Clytie. It was in his mind that Ranice had something to do with young Clytie's disappearance years ago; the yellow-haired woman was not as young as she would lead others to believe.

The auxiliary knights who had been called into service to look for the four young women who were missing returned to the keep weeks later to report their bad luck in finding both the Meaux sisters and Clytie de Monteforte. No one had heard of the young women or seen anyone resembling the descriptions Autumn had given Ruark. As for Clytie, they had no idea what she looked like, since she had disappeared as a child. Ranice had at last angrily revealed this about her sister, but she could not be trusted in anything and he wouldn't press her with any more questions. The king had left him with the words: "Orion, you will do what you must do. For England."

Ranice whirled in the passageway when she spotted Juel going the other way. "Hold! You, Juel Reynaude! I would speak with you."

Juel waited for the woman to come to her; she would not simper before Orion's lady wife or be ordered about by her. Jay's clandestine meetings with Ranice seemed to have ended and he was spending more time in the kitchen, or else he walked about the round tower tapping his chin for hours. Try as he might, Dawn would not speak to him nor even acknowledge his presence.

Now Juel faced Ranice. "You wished to see me about something?" She looked the older, painted woman straight in the eye and did not flinch.

Ranice *did* flinch, however. She had begun to wonder what it was about this sly little maid that caused her to have sleepless nights. She came right out with the one question uppermost in her mind. "Are you dallying with my husband?"

Juel's mouth dropped. "Of course not. Why would you think that?" She stared up at the tall, cone-shaped, steeple head-dress Ranice was wearing, this one of brocade; the style always reminded Juel of a dunce's cap. "Why?" she asked again when Ranice seemed to consider something for a moment.

"He has not come to my bed, and do not forget when first I arrived that I found you and him in that big bed of his."

"It is true you did." *Things have changed since the night of the phantom,* she wanted to blurt. "That meant nothing. Orion was half delirious from loss of blood."

"Oh, of course," Ranice said, eyeing Juel up and down, taking note of the simple gown of woven green wool called *perse.* "As I said, he has not come to my bed. In fact, he . . . we have not been together since the first time. The consummation of our marriage."

Juel pressed her lips together, then said, "That is too bad." *You must not be lonely for lack of other bed partners,* she wanted to remind Ranice. "I am afraid I cannot help you in this, since I have no idea where he spends his leisure time."

Ranice snickered in Juel's face. "I hear that you have made several visits to the attic room in the older section of the manor."

Juel blanched. She thought no one knew of her nightly visits. "There is nothing to worry about. I meet no one." It was true, for her beloved phantom had not come to her again. She had not felt the tug in the night as she had the first time. Still, she went there, compelled by her own inner urgings. "Do you hear me?" she asked Ranice. "What do you stare at?"

"You," Ranice said, with a blink. "There is something about you that bothers me."

Juel shrugged. "I don't know what it can be." She flicked her gaze over the gown of rich material called *chamarre,* heavily decorated, then flicked up to study Ranice's eyes. "You tell me."

"I feel close to you." Ranice looked Juel up and down with narrowed dark eyes. "You make me remember someone I hated very much. Long ago."

"That makes no sense." Juel thought over the words. "You hate me, yet you feel close to me." She had a hard time understanding women like Ranice and Alice Becker, who were full of hate and jealousy. "You confuse me more often than not," she told Ranice.

"You think yourself very clever, Juel Reynaude." Ranice smirked, about to walk away. "So does your brother."

"Oh?" Juel wasn't going to let Ranice escape so suddenly. "What has Jay to do with anything?" she asked, happy that her brother had dropped this slut like a hot oatcake.

"I only said he was clever."

"How so?" Juel tilted her head.

"Why must you ask so many questions?"

Juel shrugged and looked at Ranice with defiance. "I am curious to know why my brother interests you."

Flippantly, Ranice said, "Doesn't he interest all women? There's a castleful of them panting after him. I would like to know what is so wonderful about him?"

Just then Juel caught Ranice's face growing red. "You must know," Juel told Ranice.

"What?" Even redder.

"Why don't you ask Jay himself?"

"I might do that." Ranice patted the perfectly arranged curls on her head. It was time to test Juel's mettle, she thought nastily. "Now. I have some work for you. First, you will clean my apartment. Then, you will launder my undergarments and mend my chemises and then make my favorite chicken pie and cherry tarts—"

"Wait." Juel held a hand up. "I am not your personal maid. I take orders from Rajahr, no one else. And I do not cook every day."

"I am the lady of this manor house and run it as I see fit."

There was some truth in that, Juel conceded. Yet, "You must speak with Rajahr first."

"Why, you feisty little bitch. I should have you flogged." Ranice sashayed about Juel. "Your hair— why is it so dull? Don't you ever wash it? And your clothes, they are frumpy. You are too skinny. Don't you ever eat? A man could find nothing but bones to take hold of on you."

Ranice laughed at Juel's sudden frown and knew she had hit a sore spot. She attacked with even greater venom. "Your ears are odd, too. You must cover them with more hair pulled forward. And how about your skinny arms and this and that and . . . that . . . and what about . . . ?"

As Ranice went on and on, finding fault with Juel's looks and personality, Juel's hands seemed to follow the woman's each hurtful remark. Resting on her hair. Then her clothes. Fluttering over her slender arms . . . her ears. Ranice went on and on. By the time she finished her cutting tirade, Juel's confidence had been drained to the dregs.

In soft leather slippers that had begun to feel like iron boots, Juel dragged herself through the day, Ranice's cruel words ringing in her ears as she cleaned and cleared the woman's three filthy, messy rooms, mended clothes, and performed many more difficult tasks Ranice thought up as she went along. She had even made the chicken pie and cherry tarts Ranice ordered, along with crusty bread, freshly churned butter, and fruits cut up and arranged on a platter so that they resembled a royal flower garden.

That evening, as Juel readied herself for bed, she thought she could not even lift her grooming brush to her head she was so tired. She did not even think of the phantom.

Finally she fell asleep, flung across her bed, in total dark—after the shaking sobs had finally been reduced to little trickles and then dried tears on her cheeks.

Never had she been so alone and so unhappy!

He came to her again that night when she was just awakening from a dream; a dream about him. Now he was here in the flesh.

"You have been weeping," he said as he maneuvered himself slowly onto the bed next to her. "What is it?"

"How can you tell I have been sad? That was long ago when I wept. My tears have dried."

"I can feel your sadness, even in the dark."

The nearness of him gave her comfort. "Why have you stayed away so long?"

"I have no answer. Just know that I am here and that I want you." His fingers stroked back her hair.

"Why do you come to me like this?" She tried to see him in the dark of the little chamber. "I want you to tell me who you are."

He sighed from deep within. "If you knew then you

might hate me. You would send me from you, I believe."

"Are you such a dragon that I would faint if I looked upon you in the light of day?" When she received no answer, she went on. "Are you fair or are you dark?"

He traced his fingertip across her mouth. "Only women are called fair."

"You do not answer me. Why?" Her thoughts spun. "What do you want of me? You said that we would make a child. Is this what you still want?" He did not answer. "You are afraid. I can feel your fear."

"Only know that I must love you. We have to be together, and you know that. You have waited for me to come to you again."

Her feelings for him were intensifying. "It is true. But you know this cannot last. It is unreal, our coming together in the dark. I want to see you by day, to know that you are real, not just part of my dream. You are searching for something. Or *someone*. I can feel it."

"You are right there, sweeting. I have been searching all my life. With you," he said, caressing one slim arm, "I find part of that search has ended. Now there are two people I wish to find."

Juel rolled from the bed and walked slowly to the corner of the room. She heard his questioning voice but kept her back turned. "I have to go into the hall. You must know why."

"I do now," he answered, reclining on the bed. "Don't be long. I will miss you."

As Juel slipped out, she glanced back over her shoulder. She could see his outline vaguely as he lay looking up at the dark beams of the ceiling. The door closed softly. She heard his deep sigh.

When she returned, she was carrying a torch!

The chamber lit up instantly, flooding light over the bed where he had been reclining. He was up in a flash, facing her. By the time he lunged forward to snatch the torch from her it was too late!

She had already seen his face.

"Orion!" Juel said, the shock of it having made her voice faint as a whisper. Her mouth dropped open and she swallowed hard. "It is you."

To her further surprise, he showed no reaction.

He stood holding the torch with her, his fingers folded over hers. They stared into each other's eyes and a simultaneous shiver of intimacy bolted through their bodies and minds. Orion nodded.

"You are very clever, Juel Reynaude. You have found me out," he said clearly, rather than in the deep whispers he had been using with her in the dark.

She looked up at him, then into his eyes again. "We have to talk."

Much later, after midnight, they were seated on the bed together, the torch in a holder at the corner of the chamber. He had paced the confines for what seemed like hours while she sat cross-legged in the middle of the bed, waiting for him to come to her and speak his heart.

"Why?" she said now, facing him, her nerves tingling from his closeness, knowing who he was at last.

Though edged with steel, his voice was like velvet. "Where shall I begin?" He stared at her like a lost child.

She smiled. "At the beginning." One shoulder lifted in a shrug. "Where else."

"Oh, that would be going too far and there are some things better left secret."

"You are too secret, Orion. We all need someone to speak our hearts with." She looked at him tenderly, wanting to know this man she had fallen in love with.

He reached out and toyed with a length of dark hair. "Who do you talk to when you need someone, my love?"

"Don't laugh at me." When he shook his head, his eyes serious, she said, "I used to talk to my cats, since Father and Jay were so busy. There were neighbors, true, and I knew I could have made friends with some. But I just couldn't find someone I could be close to. Until I came here. Then I met Dawn and we learned we could share our secrets. We are very good friends now." She smiled. "We talk about everything."

"Oh?" He was jealous over this. "Do you discuss men? Does Dawn have many lovers?"

"Dawn?" Juel laughed. "She has never taken a lover and there is no one she is interested in. My brother follows her about and looks at her from shadowy corners like a lovesick calf. I've never seen him like this."

"Why doesn't he take her then?"

Juel gasped softly. "You men are all alike. Do you think women are as lusty as men?"

His eyes twinkled. "Alice Becker? Ranice de Monteforte?"

She nodded, staring into her lap. "You are right there, I give you that." Then her head came up. "Your wife? You . . . you know about—?"

"Of course," he laughed. "Your brother Jay has bedded her, too."

"Oh," Juel groaned. "She worked me half to death yesterday. I still feel the aches from bending over to clean and clear her apartments. She just moved in them not less than a week ago and I have never seen such a pigsty."

"Why do you think I made her leave?" He saw her look away and lifted her chin to meet his eyes. "I have not been to bed with her since our first time together. I was . . . let's just say, very inebriated."

"What are you going to do about that? You cannot go on imbibing in such excess. You will destroy yourself, Orion. Why do you do it?"

"Ah," he said. "Now we are back to me."

"Yes. I wish to hear about you. What is it that troubles you so?" When he turned toward the wall, as if looking for help there, she pressed on. "I want to know, Orion. Why are you hurting so?"

"I have given a name to my pain. It is . . . Scardon."

She licked her lips. "Ah. The devil who haunts you even in his absence. Who is this man and what has he done to you?"

Orion pulled a breath from deep within and took her hand to hold it tight. "He stole everything from me that I loved. He killed my father and took me away. And do you want to know what is so insane about the whole thing?"

"Yes. Tell me."

"It is not the person I speak of. It is this place," he said as he swept his hand higher and higher in big circles. "Sweet Jesus, he brought me to my own parents' home. This is not Scardon's Keep, it is Sutherland Castle. Or what is left of it. It used to be a grand fortification."

She touched his arm. "It will be again. You are rebuilding it. Sutherland is going to be beautiful again, Orion." She came up to her knees, facing him. "You can even put in a moat again. Would that not be grand? Like the castles of old."

"Aye." His eyes shone from her contagious excitement. "A moat." Then his face fell and he looked unhappy again. "I must find my mother." He raked his fingers through his hair. "She is alive. King Henry has said so."

"Wonderful!" Juel cried. "Your mother, alive. How I wish that were so with my own mother. She died when I was but a girl."

He cupped her chin, gazing into her eyes. "You still are like a young girl. Do you know that? You are twenty years?" He took in her nod. "I know not my own age."

"Hmm. Rajahr would know. I would think you are twenty and five or six."

"Do you?"

"Aye," she said with a laugh, then quickly sobered. "You are looking for something else, too?"

Now Orion sighed even deeper. He looked at her. He nodded. "My real wife."

She blinked. "Your . . . real wife?"

"Ranice is not the one I married. I was informed that a dark-haired woman would come to me. Where is she?"

"Ah. You are still thinking of that dark-haired woman. Does she even exist?"

Orion stared into her torchlit eyes. "Why do you ask that?" He took her hand again and she stared down at his fingers. He had been outside more of late; his skin was darker from the sun. "What do you know?" he asked her.

"Just a feeling that Ranice came to you by deception. I also believe there is no sister to speak of."

"But there is." He saw her face fall. "King Henry said there is a Clytie de Monteforte. *She's* my lady wife. I want to know what happened. Clytie was taken away when a child of five. She has not been seen since, though Ranice pretends she is still around. This might be her way of keeping her mind from dwelling on her own scheme to have her sister removed from Monteforte Castle."

Juel tore her gaze away and prepared to leave the bed where they had been sitting for hours into the night talking and holding hands. And sharing. Was that not what love was all about? Sharing?

He watched her as she whirled to face him, her hair shining on the side where the light from the torch illuminated it. "Can't you think, Orion? Ranice would have been too young to have done such a thing, to have her own sister sent from her."

Orion's eyebrow rose, then quickly fell. "Ranice is older than you think. She uses artifice to keep her face looking younger. Her body shows signs that she is much older than the twenty and nine she claims."

"What will you do with Ranice?" She would not look at him now. "Will you send her from you and search the rest of your life for your true beloved?"

Orion came off the bed and put his hand on her shoulder as she faced away. "I'd marry you if I could. But you are a mere villager. No highborn blood flows in you, Juel," he lied. "Though one would believe it does, for you are so very beautiful, intelligent, and

246

charming. You have healed me in many ways. I want you with me. I never will allow you to leave. And you don't have a place to go now anyway. Your home has been burned to the ground. Your father can rebuild it, but he has been ill of late, you know."

She sniffed. "He is getting better every day. This is what Jay says when he returns from Herstmonceux and he goes there twice a week." Again she sniffed and yanked away from his touch. "Now that you find yourself truly a Sutherland, you are haughty and arrogant. A mere village girl is not good enough for you."

Gritting his teeth, he whirled her about to face him. "You are *too* good for me, Juel, 'tis true. You do not understand . . . I must hold this ancient fortress from the likes of John Scardon, the devil who raised me. I have to have an heir of highborn blood."

She tossed her chin up. "Why in God's name, then, would you want to lie with me and produce a bastard? This was your intent when you played the mysterious phantom, you recall, and just why do you ride out with that monkey on your back and search things out in the night, I must know?" Her eyes glittered. "Ah. You spy for King Henry against the French. It is true, isn't it? This is why you were closeted with him for hours while he remained longer than necessary in a . . . mere baron's keep."

"Ah, so you are paying me in kind. You are precious, Juel. A mere baron and a mere village wench. That is a story to tell. I already have word that you tell the orphans the story of the dragon and the lady. Will you tell it to me sometime?"

"I will not." She pouted, breaking away from his

tender touch. "You have your highborn ladies to entertain you, m'lord. What more do you . . . Orion, I believe I understand why it is you want this French wife, Clytie de Monteforte. This would make it easier for you to spy on the French. If the people in the pubs knew this, they would be more eager to give you the information you want. And I have knowledge that Henry relies on the anarchy in France and his arrangements with the Duke of Burgundy. He hopes by military successes to unite the English behind the House of Lancaster."

Orion gaped. "You know too much, Juel Reynaude. Maybe I need to be cautious of you. Did you really find yourself lost in the woods, or were you sent by the French? One of the brigand companies?"

"That is absurd. That would be your Scardon."

"You speak too highly to be a mere village—" He was cut off when she slapped his hand away. "All right. I will not call you . . . wench again."

"I hate it when you call me that!" She clapped her hands over her ears. "I am not a wench. I am not a spy. And I certainly am not going to have your bastard child!"

She went to sit on a hard bench in the corner, drawing her legs up to her chest. "Go away. I want to be alone. Go find your Clytie or your Ranice. Why won't Ranice do? You need not find Clytie for what you must do against the French." She tossed her head. "*I* am French, on my father's side. My mother, I have no idea what she was."

Laughing, he came to stand in front of her. "You are rambling, my love."

"Hush up! Clytie is your love. Not I. Remember, you

said who I am. But never, never call me a spy. I am neutral, as my father and Jay."

"Ah—Jay. And just what is your brother up to? He walks about the round tower as if there is something there he must discover. He has been questioning the knights and I was informed, by my secret source, that he even questioned Henry's knights when they were in their cups. I have learned your brother never has more than one or two drinks. Very cautious, wouldn't you say?"

"Humph! My brother Jay has never played the drunken fool—as some others I know do." She looked up and narrowed her eyes. "Are *you* really the drunken fool you let the castlefolk think you are? You did not seem to drink to excess when the king was here."

"Juel . . ." he said slowly. "I believe you are using your mind overly much. A woman's mind. Why do you not find other interests. Like sewing and embroidery."

"I do all that. And more." She held up her hands for him to see. "I work them to the bone. I hardly have a free moment to myself."

He caught her hand and brought it to his mouth. His lips kissed it. "You are free now." He pulled her up and carried her back to the bed. "We will make the most of that."

"I do not love you anymore," she hissed into his ear.

He chuckled. "Of course you do. We will love forevermore. You are my Juel, my first love."

"Aye. And Clytie will be the second."

"Hush up." He sank to the bed with her. "First is always best."

He raked his fingers through her midnight hair, the

tresses undulating in soft waves to her waist, hair like the richest silk holding a soft perfume all its own. He took his time in love play, slowly awakening her as he slipped his hand beneath her nightgown to cup a small, round breast. He wanted her as never before and his breath quickened at the feel of her velvety skin and her nipples hardened beneath his fingertips.

Feeling helpless and awash with sensation, Juel felt delicious tremors racing through her like wildfire, and the wine of stormy desire flowed in her veins.

As the king's phantom spoke love words into her ear, her hair, the earthy deepness of his male voice seemed to vibrate down into her quivering loins.

Breathing deeply against her moist lips, he said, "Ahh, Juel, my precious treasure, my beloved."

"You do love me?" She choked back a tear. "Really and truly love me?"

"I need you" was all he said.

The moon stole unwaveringly out from the lavender clouds down through the small arrow-slit window. His eyes flashed as he lifted his dark head, and Juel caught her breath at the brilliancy of them.

Caressing her soft cheek, he turned his hand and brushed his knuckles along her chin. His next words thrilled her soul.

"I love you more than life and you are the light in my darkest day. I did not know it at the beginning, but now I know I have loved you since first we met."

She waited for him to say more, but he only groaned as if with despair. He moved slowly against her with his iron length and she gasped at the sensation. He held fast and looked deeply into her eyes.

"What is it?" she asked.

"Nothing. Just hold me. You heal me when you are close."

"You are ill?"

"Without you, aye."

In truth, he was dizzy-drunk with desire.

Her heart pounded savagely as his hard lips twisted across hers. As if by magic, the nightgown disappeared. It slipped easily over her head and then his mouth was back, plundering her soul. Now he went lower, parting her legs and the soft curls there, breathing in the sweet fragrance of her femininity. He employed his tongue to deepen his kiss. He plied her in a slow, rhythmic pattern. The undulating motions drove her mad with pleasure and soon he brought her to a blissful peak of release.

In a while he rose and went away to the garderobe. "Now, my love," he said when he returned. "I am ready for you. I will make you shout with pleasure."

"Just try," she said with a throaty laugh.

"We will see."

His lips sealed with hers, his tongue like an ablution of pure delight in the interiors of her mouth, her face, her ears, then down to her breasts. Her heart even felt it in her chest. Two hearts and bodies came together in love's ancient melody. He placed himself into her hand momentarily and she felt the huge, velvety member as he lowered his dark-green chausses and linen braies.

He took off all then. His clothes followed hers onto the chamber floor. The torch was burning low, a more intimate light to shed over the lovers' nest. She could see his huge organ throbbing with need, even larger now that she had fondled it briefly.

His name was torn from her honey-sweet lips and her thighs tightened and throbbed as he pushed them apart and entered her hard and fast. He kissed her and she kissed him back, once, quickly, full of passion. He was fully inside her and she held her breath, arched back and forth in wonderful abandonment, in sweet flashes of ecstasy. Their bodies gleamed in the pale fire of the torch.

Her eyes were deep, deep green, and tears were streaming down her cheeks as she cried in a shrill whimper, "Orion!"

"I told you . . . I would make . . . you shout," he said gruffly.

The moon spun in with misty silver streamers and bathed the rumpled bed in its paleness as the lovers clutched and strained and whispered pledges of undying love. His face pressed into the curve of her shoulder as he hugged her hard.

They peaked and rested.

Soon enough they became each other's willing slave and coupled again. Loving and loving until nothing else mattered—only that the gift of love was flowing into her.

Part Two

Her Most Shining Armor

Chapter Twenty-Five

"Oh, thank you for having them found. Thank you! Thank you!"

Juel sat in the middle of the floor in the little oriel room surrounded by her cats, Owl, Flaxen, and Hemmingway. Just then, another crawled from the cloth sack and bounded into her lap. She cried in surprise, "And, pretty puss, just who are you?"

Orion hated cats. He stood back in the arched frame enjoying the sight of Juel looking so happy with her furry pets, her green eyes glinting with gold. He chuckled just the same. "That would be Wilpurr," he said with a shudder.

She laughed in unbounded joy as the fluffy puss scurried wildly about, attacking the folds of her soft mauve shift. "But where did she come from?" she asked, delighting as the new cat pounced.

"*He*," Orion corrected, picking up an apple from a decorative plate and crunching into it. "Wilpurr of Herstmonceux. An orphan from the raid, so Duncan has said. After he and Ruark rounded up your pusses in a sack, not coming away without a few scratches—" he waved the apple—"they came upon this little orphan near the gates of the village. Duncan could not resist the furry pussy." He cleared his throat. "Said you'd . . . ah, love him."

"I do!" Juel exclaimed, in love at first sight, unaware of Orion's flushed face.

Furry pussy. Orion cleared his throat. *"Ahem . . ."*

She clucked her tongue as Owl hissed at the smaller puss. "Be good, Owl, else I won't feed you your favorite bits of delicious beef."

Orion was watching Hemmingway and could not resist a smile as the puss sniffed a wolf pelt spread on the floor and hissed, hunching his back. Orion tossed the apple core aside and it struck him then, what she'd said.

"Beef!" he exclaimed, hands on hips. "You give those furry beasts meat?"

Juel looked at her handsome lord towering over the chamber. "Of course. Cats not only love fish, they love meat, too." She patted Hemmingway on her orangey head. "Now, Hemmie here, she loves chicken. Not greasy, mind you, but boiled into soft, delicious chunks of white meat—with a little gravy."

"Horns of old Scratch . . . gravy! The pusses are treated better than the king!"

Juel's eyes twinkled as Orion looked over the tray of fruits, selecting an orange. "Hush up and come over here." Invitingly, she reclined on the plush Turkish carpet. "Come here, Orion." She laughed at his furrowed brow as he dropped the orange back onto the plate. "The cats won't bite."

Orion backed up a step. "Sorry. Cats don't like me

256

4 FREE BOOKS

TO GET YOUR 4 FREE BOOKS WORTH $18.00 — MAIL IN THE FREE BOOK CERTIFICATE T O D A Y

Fill in the Free Book Certificate below, and we'll send your FREE BOOKS to you as soon as we receive it.

If the certificate is missing below, write to: Zebra Home Subscription Service, Inc., P.O. Box 5214, 120 Brighton Road, Clifton, New Jersey 07015-5214.

FREE BOOK CERTIFICATE

4 FREE BOOKS

ZEBRA HOME SUBSCRIPTION SERVICE, INC.

YES! Please start my subscription to Zebra Historical Romances and send me my first 4 books absolutely FREE. I understand that each month I may preview four new Zebra Historical Romances free for 10 days. If I'm not satisfied with them, I may return the four books within 10 days and owe nothing. Otherwise, I will pay the low preferred subscriber's price of just $3.75 each; a total of $15.00, *a savings off the publisher's price of $3.00.* I may return any shipment and I may cancel this subscription at any time. There is no obligation to buy any shipment and there are no shipping, handling or other hidden charges. Regardless of what I decide, the four free books are mine to keep.

NAME		
ADDRESS		APT
CITY	STATE	ZIP
TELEPHONE		
( )		
SIGNATURE	(if under 18, parent or guardian must sign)	

Terms, offer and prices subject to change without notice. Subscription subject to acceptance by Zebra Books. Zebra Books reserves the right to reject any order or cancel any subscription.

GET
FOUR
FREE
BOOKS
(AN $18.00 VALUE)

and the feeling is mutual. I don't take easily to pets." He looked around for Shadow, then realized the monkey would not be around with so many new cats in residence; that would take some getting used to!

"What is the difference? You've a monkey, who, by the way, has taken to trailing me all about the manor."

"I am jealous. Shadow no longer accompanies me out on my midnight rides to the border, not since he discovered the tasty fruit dishes you flaunt at bed-time!"

Juel gasped. "Midnight? Border? You go that far? With a monkey on your back?" She clucked her tongue when he nodded. "Poor Shadow. All the way to the border and back."

"Would you like to come—" Orion shook his head. What was wrong with him? He'd almost invited a woman to go with him to spy on the movements of the French. "Ah, come for a walk?"

"Walk? Now?" She shot to her feet, toppling the new kitten onto the carpet. "Oh. Sorry, Wilpurr." She laughed and picked up an apple, rolling it for the kitten to play with. "Who named the big kitten that?"

Orion pulled a sour frown. "Duncan, who else."

"Ah." He had already forgotten about the walk, she noted.

"He fancies himself in love with you, thinks you must be a lost princess." Orion sauntered to the arched window set with imported glass. He kept his back to Juel. "I set him straight, though."

Juel frowned as Orion kept his distance. "What? About being a lost princess?"

"No."

She walked up behind him and wrapped her arms

about his waist. "Then what did you say, my dark dragon?"

"I let him know you've become my mistress this past week."

"What?" She blew on his neck and he leaned away.

"So, are you not my mistress?" Then he revised. "Soon, perhaps?" He looked out over the gardens below, seeing Dawn picking some pretty flowers. There was a hidden figure in the bushes and he strained to see who it was; it looked like Jay Reynaude to him. Orion smiled.

Juel was puzzled. He still did not turn to take her in his arms as he had the last several days. She wanted him to fondle the area between her thighs as he had the night before, parting her curls and plunging one finger deep within until the shudders had come, then his two fingers moving faster and faster . . . Now she began to heat up with a sweet fire winding tortuously within. *What's this?*

Juel's nose twitched and her face fell in disappointment. "Orion—no wonder you avoid me. You have been drinking!"

Orion pressed his lips together. She can detect by her dainty nose very well, he thought.

She moaned sadly and turned away, hating the sour smell. "You promised you would not."

His shoulders lifted, then fell abruptly. "Now you will not come to my bed this night." He was daydreaming about the attic room and the bed that hung by chains; he'd never forget it!

"That is true, Orion. I will not come to you unless you stop the inebriants. For good!"

He had to have her, else he'd go stark staring mad!

Orion turned, desire burning dangerously in his eyes like hot stones. "Ho, Juel. You have been driving me to . . . drink. Do you not realize this? I have fondled you, made you catch the stars. Why won't you lie with me? Must I . . . ravish you like the dragon you once thought me?"

She said nothing, only looked aside to the frolicking cats. *Once* thought? What about now? What was he now?

He shook his head and made a strangled sound at the wide look of her eyes as she looked into his face. "I want you. Badly. See for yourself."

She made a mistake and looked down, seeing his urgent arousal in bold evidence against his taut green hose. She yanked her gaze upward.

"I am no meek and mild maid to spread my thighs so that you can boast to your men," Juel said softly. "And I am not your mistress in sin. You can tell Duncan that!"

"You let me kiss you here and there and caress you intimately with my hand," he said angrily. "Is that not as sinful as letting me put myself in you and make love?"

"No. That is true lovemaking."

"We have already done that. What could be different about once, twice—or a hundred times?" He chuckled, adding, "I'd like that. Again and again. Inch by slow inch. Every day. Every way. Hundreds of times."

"What? A hundred times?" Juel blanched. "I'd be worn out by then."

"Never." He shook his head, his eyes laughing in hers.

"What?" she snapped.

"We could do it forever and you'd still be tight as a fist." He held up his hand thus.

"Orion!"

He shrugged. "You are made that way, I can tell. After several birthings, you would still be—"

Again, "Orion!"

Juel was as red as the new window drapings. "Say no more." She turned her back on him to hide a spreading grin. In a muffled voice, she said, "You are terrible."

"I know," he said.

She bent to scoop up a cat beneath each arm. "Go back to your drink. Or your wayward wife. I will go to work in the kitchen. Come, Flaxen!"

He took a deep breath. "I will rape you!"

"You will not!"

"You reject me?"

"Yes!"

The tawny cat tossed Orion an arrogant look and trotted after Juel as she led the way like a regal cat princess.

"Aha!" Orion bent to snatch Wilpurr by the scruff, brought the half-grown cat to his face, wrinkled his long, handsome nose . . . and Wilpurr yowled and leapt from Orion's hands.

"Ow!" Orion put his finger to his nose and came away with a streak of blood. "Wild cats, that's what they are. I shall never like the pusses."

She was gone. He was alone.

He went to a low cupboard beneath the windowseat to yank out a gigantic green jug. He stared at the red wine that had grown mold on the rim. He used to drink it like that when he was half gone.

"Ugh!" He tossed the disgusting jug into the corner

where it smashed to smithereens; then he strode violently from the room—

He'd rather have Juel than that moldy garbage!

Later that afternoon Orion sent a letter to the king. In it, he asked for an annulment and carefully printed out the words: WE DO NOT LIE TOGETHER. He added that he wished to declare his abhorrence of Ranice and his desire to find Clytie de Monteforte. As it should be. He ended that he could not come to make this formal statement of affirmation in person, since matters with the French were getting difficult on the border.

There, he thought. Now he was free. At least until he found Clytie de Monteforte. But did he really want to?

Juel and Orion met each other halfway in a dimly lighted passageway. The night was beautiful, the moon moving among the clouds like a queen to her throne. It was quiet in the manor and the dark corridors but for a distant chuckle of a knight, perhaps down in the hall or outside in their quarters.

Orion was not feeling so sure about himself as he went down to Juel's room. When he saw her on the stairs, looking up at him, pausing there, just as surprised as he, he blinked wide. "What are you doing here?" he asked in a low voice.

With luminous eyes widened in astonishment, Juel answered, "I? What about you?"

The cat was out of the gunny sack now. "I was coming to your chamber belowstairs," he said.

Juel felt warm and trembly all over. "And I . . . I was coming to yours. I didn't know if you would want me to come." She waved her hand. "I mean, after the way I'd told you . . . you know, that I didn't want to because of—" She gulped. "You know, don't you?" She turned red and ran her hand along the cold stone wall.

Orion's eyebrow shot up. "Should I?"

"Yes. I was c-coming."

"Well, then," he said nothing about her stammering, "what shall we do now?"

She bit her lip and splayed herself against the wall, both hands behind her buttocks. "Should we go outside for a walk?"

"I have not imbibed all evening."

"I know." She grinned happily. "I can smell."

Orion moved closer, one foot planted on the stair she was on, his other below that one. "We will go outside, as you say. But not near the round tower." He watched her eyes widen. "And not yet." Closer yet, he bent to brush his mouth against her cheek. "I would like to go to the place we first made love."

She pretended she hadn't heard his last enticing words. "I was thinking more like down by the river."

He nibbled on her earlobe, then moved to the slim cords of her throat. "We'll go there later." His hand was moving up along the curve of her waist, hugging, pressing. "Now we will go upstairs."

She gazed up into his smoldering eyes. "Are the cobwebs gone?" The heat was moving up her legs and coiling about her body.

"Of course." He took her hand and placed it on himself, where he'd grown hard and ready. "I had them removed days ago."

Joy bubbled in her laugh and shone in her eyes. "Then I will come."

Up in the attic room, Orion lay down beside Juel. She gazed up at his handsome face in the soft candle glow. He'd lighted two fat candles, then come to join her where he'd laid her gently upon the bed moments before.

They wanted each other so much that their clothes were removed in a hurry, not even caring that some seams had been rent in their haste. They had waited long enough!

Orion could see the heat flooding her cheeks, a scarlet stain in the darkness. He came back down over her, his lips hard and searching. He felt her writhe beneath him.

"Easy, my Juel. Soon."

"Orion . . . hurry, love . . . oh, do hurry. I want you so!" Juel gasped in delight when she looked down to see his mouth fastening onto her budding nipple. "Oh . . . that's wonderful, Orion. Oh yes!" He had opened his mouth wide over the rosy areola and was licking, sucking, lapping like stormy sea waves, while below she could feel his palm cupping her, his finger entering her.

The noise of love words drowned out the thudding of her heart.

Grabbing hold of his dark heavy hair, she bucked up to meet his every hard thrust. His finger was large, square at the tip and gave her much pleasure, and before long she couldn't meet him any longer.

He was moving too fast.

"Am I hurting you?" he asked.

"No," she gasped, her head bumping the thick chains. "No."

Orion felt his manhood become engorged as he made love to her with his hand, his middle finger driving hard and fast. When she cried for release, he removed his finger and replaced it with his slick organ.

He moved quickly to hook her legs over his shoulders. Juel cried out at this new position, bringing her so close to him.

Folds of hot velvet caressed the swollen, throbbing length of him. He pushed higher into her, curving himself into the pleasure points of her center. The bed rocked and swayed with his forceful thrusts.

Juel felt he was burning her up inside as he thrust in . . . out, in . . . out. The pressure built with leaps and bounds. His hardness almost hurt. But she was ready, for he had prepared her well.

The explosion burst upon her, and then he followed with a loud cry and his own release.

Afer a while, as they lay spent in each other's arms, Orion sighed, his lips close to her ear. She sighed also. However, she had no idea his sigh was not only of contentment but something else besides.

Later, as they strolled hand in hand down by the river, glinting silver in the moonlight, Orion sighed again. They had made love for the third time, and Juel sighed, too, thinking these were mutual sighs of pleasure and contentment.

Juel began to believe otherwise when Orion held his golden silence as they walked leisurely, enjoying the night sights and sounds. Something was wrong. He was keeping secrets again. What was he holding from her?

It was time she asked him an important question.

"Orion . . . why did you come to me in the night the way you did, shrouded in mystery?"

He looked down at her moonlit face. "I've already told you. I thought you wouldn't have me if you knew my identity."

"No. That does not sound true. You are hiding something."

"I hide nothing from you, woman!" He lifted her up and swung her about, her head whirling among the stars and the moon. "You think too much."

"You've already told me." She gripped his wide shoulders. "Put me down, Orion. I wish to talk."

"And I—" he growled, "wish to make love!"

"Again!" she gasped, screeching when he lowered her to the ground, with her on top of him.

"Take your clothes off and move. I have made love to you and now I would have you make love to me."

To his utter surprise, Juel began to untie his linen hose. He'd left his undergarment, his brief braies, upstairs. All he had on was his hose, and she helped pull them down for the second time outside. He watched as she moved above him, ordering him, removing his clothes as he shifted, lifted, then lay down again.

"And now, m'lord."

"Yes, m'lady."

"Lady?" she giggled, then wondered why he looked suddenly perplexed.

"On with it, wench!" he chuckled.

Now she laughed, a fully deep belly laugh.

When he was naked, she became naked, too. Now atop him, she rubbed herself against him, and Orion sucked in his breath. She took him into her hands and he looked up at her as if he'd never seen a woman before. Her hips were centering over his shaft—

There was an excitement like a storm due to arrive. He knew it was coming and, though prepared, there was still a great thrill of anticipation over how wild it would really become.

He was now inside her, and she began to move, hot velvet, up and down, and it came to Orion to wonder if she'd ever ridden a wild horse. She must know how, he thought, if she could ride him like this!

When her movements began to slow, Orion thought he could stand the torment no longer. He bucked his hips and went higher inside her. Grasping her waist with his hands, he gave one last hard thrust that made their release come at the very same time.

They lay together afterward, Orion stroking her midnight-dark hair. His own hair was wet from the lovemaking, and he thought as long as they were covered with sweat already, they might as well take a swim.

"Come!" Orion pulled her to her feet just as she would have fallen asleep on his shoulder. "Let's go into the water."

"It's cold," she said with a shiver, but he continued to pull her to the river's edge, then out into the water where it was not so deep. "Oh, now it does feel wonderfully warm." There was a gentle current here, not strong enough to pull one along.

Orion was quiet, strangely still.

She heard the night silence broken by a lone songbird's melody; it had a lulling quality. "I have missed swimming outside. I used to swim and bathe in the pond in back of our house at the edge of the forest," she said.

"I used to do that also." He frowned as his feet touched the sandy bottom; it felt too good to be true. "That was a very long time ago."

Juel sucked in a breath. "You have not gone swimming since you were a child?"

"Yes, I have gone. But I've not enjoyed it until this time. It's like I was a boy again. It's good to enjoy things from the past once again. Like eating."

"Eating?" Juel's black eyebrow rose. "What do you mean?"

"For many years now I've eaten only for nourishment, and sometimes not much food at all. Only drink. For days I would drink myself into a stupor." He stroked the gentle line of her chin. "Now you have come, and I enjoy once again."

Deeply he gazed into her eyes, saying, "You are my healer, Juel, my savior. For this I love you. And for so many other reasons."

"Yes, Orion. And I love you." She laid a cool, wet palm along his cheek. "But I need to know what you hide from me?"

When he gave no answer, she rested a cheek on his chest. "You will not tell me?"

Orion swallowed another one of his deep manly sighs.

Should he tell her she was heiress to the Hunter Castle and lands? But could he? She might leave him to go claim her own inheritance. She might never return. He would lose her just as he'd lost his other loved ones. Where would that leave him?

Without her. Desolate. That's where.

Juel looked up at him again. "Orion? What is there that you must not speak to me of?"

"Nothing, Juel. There is nothing." He kissed her full on the mouth, a lovely, wet kiss. "Only us."

And fear.

Chapter Twenty-Six

Ranice was drinking alone in her apartment. In the orangey glow of candles dripping hot wax, she sat before a polished steel mirror. She had ripped off her hennin and veil and her blond hair had been punished into a gigantic puff that surrounded her face, making her look otherworldly. She slammed her brush down onto the marble top and glared at herself. She sat still, staring, her expression so furious that she resembled a fearsome sorceress. She saw only Orion's face as he told her for the fourth time that night to leave his room.

Rising from the dressing table somewhat unsteadily, she mumbled, "I shall fix him. By morning he and everyone else will see what a mistake it was to send Ranice away. Yes, I will begin with Jay Reynaude and work myself through the knights." She giggled as she weaved toward the door, knocking over a salver of olives.

In a drunken sideways two-step and a running forward three-step, she went down the passageways, giggling and looking for Jay. Her full nightdress flowed

269

about her in a haze of white and she felt her way in the darkness along the cold stone walls.

"I know where you are. I'll find you, Jay. Ranice knows how to do ever'thing. I even got rid of my little sister, long time ago. Sent her to that band of thieves. Doan care what they did to her, either." She giggled. "For all I know, she could be a spy for the Frenchies. The English will kill 'er, sure enough if she's come to that."

Ranice hiccoughed as she came to the kitchen and she blinked, wondering how she had walked so far already. It was as if she had stepped out from a dream. She told herself she would remember the passageways in the morning. She had a vague feeling that she had passed through the gardens; she must have, she told herself.

Going back through the buttery and pantry, she came out in the withdrawing room, then whirled around dizzily, hearing something in the passageway she'd just come from. But there was someone there now. She could make out his tall . . . form! It must be!

"Jay . . . oh, Jay," Ranice called in a singsong voice.

Jay had seen her turning to come back toward the narrow passageway to the kitchens. He wanted nothing more than to be free of this woman who had been hounding him for days to meet her. Instead of greeting her in the dark and letting her sink her claws into him, Jay turned away.

Pivoting toward the kitchen, Jay began to hurry. He had been about to plant himself outside Dawn's door to listen to her hum as she readied herself for bed; she did this every night. And he tarried outside her door every night. She would not speak with him during the day, so he contented himself with hearing her angelic voice just before going to bed.

Jay shook his head. He was not going to let Ranice get to him with her grasping lust. He didn't need that anymore. In fact, the only one he lusted after was Dawn. Before her, there had been a hollow chamber deep inside him. He knew it would be different when they made love. It would be for love and not merely physical release with Dawn. So far, all he'd done with her was to steal a little kiss when he'd first met her. He had pressed close, true, but had little memory of that, since he'd drowned in her nut-brown eyes.

Snatching a glance over his shoulder, Jay kept hurrying until he was out in the night. As usual, night or day, his thoughts fled back to Dawn Peyton. She disliked him, that was obvious. His reputation with the women did not sit well with her; other women had found the idea not only appealing but quite exciting. He was a lover, and did not all the world love a lover? He was now of the opinion that they did not. Dawn and Juel at least, found it about as exciting as a loud belch in church.

Jay looked up at the starry summer night sky. This was the most beautiful time of year, he thought, his heart turning romantic. Everything was green and lush. He had walked alone in the forest today, dreaming of Dawn beside him. The forest flowers had drawn him and he had picked a lovely bouquet, but it was quite a walk back to The Keep, and by the time he got there they were drooping from the heat. He had tossed them into the kitchen trash and blushed furiously when Dawn had caught his actions. When she had frowned at the pitiful pile of colorful wood flowers, he had

271

grinned and shrugged. What else could he have done? His heart had pounded so violently, he'd thought he'd die on the spot.

With a deep sigh, Jay leaned against the heavy oak door after he'd stepped inside and closed it. He tried to recapture his breath. This always happened when he thought of Dawn; he was as breathless as a buck after a pretty doe. What was he to do? Always before he'd let his lust lead him . . . or that mighty thing in his hose. It was throbbing now. He was weary of taking matters in hand every night. At times, even that did not work. It just was not the same and it made him lonely just thinking of Dawn and her beautiful brown eyes. Eyes like pussywillows. Velvet.

Pushing himself violently away from the door, Jay yanked at his leather laces and snatched his shirt over his head. Walking over to a crudely hewn bedside table, he leaned to light a candle. This took some time and doing, since his hands were shaking badly. "By the rood! Look at me," he grunted. "I'm like some young pup with his first stirring for a girl."

When the smoky warmth circled the area of the bed with gentle radiance, Jay stood looking down at the feather mattress he had purchased just the week before. All the expensive furniture he'd brought from abroad had perished in the fire. He had even created some of the fine pieces himself. He fancied himself even more of a carpenter than a woodcutter.

Jay continued to just stare at the bed. The light from the single candle lay across his strong, wide chest, the dark hairs there, feathering beneath the waistband of his hose. As he stood there desiring Dawn, the candlelight outlined him boldly, illuminating his most profound thoughts. This was Ranice's profile view of Jay as she slipped quietly into his quarters outside the manor itself.

Her voice was so low, at first Jay dreamed he was hearing Dawn, his thoughts for the delicate blonde so deep and achingly full of love and lust.

As he turned slowly, his heart in his eyes, his lust visible in his tan hose, Ranice gulped and sobered just a little. "I see you have been waiting for me," she said in a voice doubly breathless from the wine and her sudden desire.

Jay had to shake his head. Something was wrong, he thought as he narrowed his gaze into the dark area beyond the candlelight. "I wait only for the woman of my heart. Come into the light so I can see you fully."

Ranice had a wicked idea. "I am Dawn," she purred in a soft, feminine voice.

"Then show yourself, Dawn."

"First put out the candle."

He did not move to do as she said and Ranice continued to gaze in wonder at his physique. He was lean, hard, with long legs, long torso . . . she licked her lips . . . with long *everything*. Even in her inebriated state, Ranice remembered how good a lover he had been. How huge and hard and fast. He had not been gentle with her; and she had loved every second. She swayed. Suddenly she wished she had not imbibed so heavily. She wanted to feel everything. But it was too late.

Coming out of shadow, Ranice walked over to him and placed her cool hand on his leg. He shuddered, feeling intense heat pulsate through him. He looked away from her hand and up into her flushed face.

"What are you doing here? Are you insane?" His eyes narrowed as his nose twitched. "You are drunk then. That is why you are here."

"No," Ranice whispered. "I am just lonely."

Jay stood taller, squaring his shoulders. "I can't have anything to do with you." He took in her questioning eyes. "I can't . . . because I love someone else."

Ranice laughed. "Who said anything about love. I just want you in my arms and between my . . ."

"Smelling like *that?*" Jay said.

"You drank with me before." She waved an arm behind her, indicating she could go back to her rooms and return. "I can fetch more. We will both smell bad."

"I am sorry, Ranice, I need to be up early." *To make a study of Dawn in the dawn.* He grinned at his whimsical thought.

"Hmm," Ranice purred, grinning back at him. "You are liking the idea more?"

'I am sorry, Ranice. You must leave. Orion might discover you had been here. The knights have quarters right next door."

"I know that," she muttered scathingly. "I've been there several times."

He looked at her in blinking disgust. "Already?"

"Of course. At night, they believe I am someone else . . . another with hair my shade."

"What do you mean?"

"They believe I am Dawn."

"They *what?!*"

Jay flew at her, his hands circling her throat. He pressed lightly there, his eyes glaring hotly into hers. "You had them believe they had bedded Dawn?" He saw her eyes go round and the awful truth was in them.

"I should kill you for that. No wonder their eyes follow her about with lust burning in them. You are a bitch. Dawn would never spread her thighs for just any man."

Ranice laughed nastily. She raised on tiptoe to reduce the advantage of his height. "Dawn will not spread her thighs at all, you poor man. Think you that, you might as well go after a nun, you might at least get a feel from one of them."

Shoving her away from him Jay said, "Be gone, slut. I have to get to sleep."

"Slut?!" Ranice screeched, flying at him with her fingernails curved like meat hooks. When she had her chest pressed to his, she gazed into his beautiful green eyes. "Oh, Jay, love me. What has happened to your rammish ways? . . . But I don't care what happened to them. You can be any way you wish. Just . . . love me! I will get you on fire!"

"I said, get yourself lost, bitch!"

This time when he shoved her away, she struck her back against the thick hard wall. Dazed for a moment, she stared at Jay, then shook her head. "It's only for a night, my lover."

Jay's eyes were glowering. "Get out, Ranice. And don't call me your lover, ever again."

Ranice narrowed her eyes into angry slits. "I shall scream."

Jay sat on the wooden chair to remove his half-boots. "Do just that. Scream."

"Ah, better yet I will dance on the rooftops!"

All motion stopped then as Jay looked at her. Did he believe her? Would she? Did she mean the battlements? My God!

Ranice flung the door open and raced up the black

stairwell with Jay hot on her heels. She went out onto the parapets which led from one side of the manor to the other. Jay snatched at her skirts, but she pulled herself up with surprising strength, scaling a curtain wall. She climbed ungracefully from one battlement to the next, kicking her feet in the air and dancing.

Jay swallowed, staring at her nightgown furling and unfurling in the night breeze. "Come down, Ranice! You will hurt yourself!"

"Not until you say you will love me," she shouted. "And I mean *love* me!"

"I cannot," Jay told her. He was beginning to sweat profusely. "Please, Ranice, please come down!"

As she became even more daring, getting closer to the edge, he lunged for her, grabbing the hem of her nightdress, and as she whirled and kicked her foot in the air, her hem tore loose from his grasp. She teetered on the edge while Jay pulled back with only a handful of cloth. Then she was gone over the edge as Jay heard the trailing scream of a name: "Clytie-eeeee!"

Ranice disappeared into the darkness. Jay braced himself. Then he heard it; the thud below. "My God . . ." he whispered. "My God." He froze in terror and dismay. "What have I done?" He looked up into the heavens and knew he had to go and see Orion at once. Blinking his eyes and squeezing them as if a great weariness had come over him, he steadied himself and went straightaway to Orion's chamber.

He found Orion asleep. Orion shouted for him to get out. "What in bloody blazes are you doing waking me in the middle of night, man?" He glared up through the

276

bedhangings. "Have France and England gone to war?"

Jay shivered, unaware he wore only his tight hose. "Almost that bad, milord."

"What?" Orion looked at the half-naked man and pushed himself out of bed. Suddenly he felt alarm. "Juel. Has something happened to her?"

"Juel?" Jay wished he could smile but could not. "Nay, not Juel. Ranice."

"Continue," Orion said, thrusting his legs into gray hose.

"Christ save me, I think I killed her."

Orion's eyebrow rose. "That *is* bad. Where is she?" He pulled on a tunic and left the straps undone.

". . . and then she fell off the edge of the battlement," Jay was saying as he led the way. They both ran outside to find her limp and twisted body, lying in the courtyard. She was in a pool of blood, her head cracked wide open. Her blond hair had turned red with blood.

"My God." Even Orion with his strong stomach was feeling turnings in the gut. They both turned away, unable to look any longer.

"How did you say this happened?" Orion led the way into the hall. He was trying to remain calm. He had just lost a wife. Actually he just lost his wife's *sister*. He shook his head, damning the confusion Ranice had wrought. He called for the servants to bring them strong ale.

After they had each had a drink to ease their taut nerves, the servants came and helped take Ranice to a resting place for the nonce. Orion knew he'd have to contact a priest to give her a proper burial. He had to

277

contact Ranice's father, as well, though he knew he would not come, for Orion had learned that de Monteforte could not wait to be rid of the woman. It seemed he hated his own daughter, and the king had said this was because Clytie had disappeared, which led Orion to believe there had been foul play and he might never find his dark-haired wife.

He was free, he thought again. But now he had no French wife of royal blood to aid him in his spying activities. Ranice had not been much help, for no doubt the English and French alike knew of her infidelities by now.

As they slowly walked back into the manor, Jay explained what had happened, that he had been with his wife. Orion did not appear overly upset by this. He only knew that it was over.

"I do not blame you," Orion told Jay. "You did the right thing by saying no." He looked at a new horn of ale, thought of Juel, and pushed the drink aside. He looked at Juel's brother again. "What more can I say. I hold no ill will against you, Jay of Herstmonceux."

Jay could only sigh with relief and look at Orion with new eyes.

There was a burial for Ranice de Monteforte. She had been placed in a lead coffin shaped to the form of the body like the mummy chests of ancient Egypt. She had brought the coffin with her when she'd come to The Keep, and Orion felt again an eerie chill when he looked upon it gape-mouthed as he had the first time she had shown it to him following her arrival. Ranice's father, writing in a dispatch that he was ill, did not attend the solemn occasion.

Jay and Dawn were among the mourners. Dawn's eyes would not meet his in the bleak haze of the hillside, but she had earlier beheld his young face looking haggard and agonized. She had heard the awful story of Ranice's fall from the battlements; this was the gossip of the castlefolk these days.

A woodcock cried overhead and Dawn's eyes lifted for a moment, then fell to the coffin. She had a good idea what had brought Jay and Ranice together that awful night and she wanted to ignore Jay Reynaude even more. Dark images of them lying together crept into her mind. He was just no good. And then she thought: Who was she to judge? She was not God.

Juel was there, and her eyes came to meet Orion's. Feeling sick, she tore her gaze from his. The flowers on the hillside were blowing as the wind wailed a sorry lament and there was the smell of rain coming from a distance. To add to the mournfulness of the moment when Ranice was lowered into the ground, there came the repeated melancholy slamming of a barn shutter in the distance.

Juel looked up at the rain clouds, low, leaden, and full of foreboding. Her stomach growled with hunger; she had only taken bread and cheese the night before. She had been too ill with the thought of Ranice's burial to eat a bite that morning. Unbidden, a thought came to mind. Now that Orion was free of Ranice, would he continue his search for Clytie de Monteforte, his true wife? Was Clytie alive somewhere? The mere thought filled her with hopelessness. Orion now knew he was the true baron, a Sutherland assuredly, as the king had said.

Juel's hands clenched the fabric of her pale-green tunic. She was still his property; he had bedded her. Juel looked again at Orion, his eyes full of gloom. His mobile mouth looked hardened. He was still searching, she thought. When would it be over?

Following Ranice's interment, Juel dragged herself back to her chamber and fell upon the bed. She clutched her waist and cried, and cried, and cried . . .

Much later she sat up, composed herself, and dried her eyes. Oh, Orion, Orion. Her beloved dragon. Juel thought that she would never fall in love. But she had. She looked around the chamber and gazed into the glimmering cresset flame. She recalled the exhilaration when their eyes met for the first time.

Oh, what shall I do? I love you so. Orion. Orion. I should never have kissed you. But it was too late for regrets.

She would search until she found an answer. Like the Book of Scriptures said: Seek and you will find.

She would go back to telling her lovely and improbable stories to the children, too. Yes. She missed that very much, and there were flocks of children belonging to no one who came to work on the castle with the tenants. They appeared so very sad that her heart went out to them. Geoffrey Johns and Autumn Meaux had been waiting for another story, too.

Orion had said he'd like to hear her tell some of her stories. Orion. Would he ever want just her? Why was it so important that he find Clytie de Monteforte? That one couldn't be his wife, for she didn't know he even existed. And did Clytie even exist herself? Where was she? Who was she now? It could be she was already wed herself. Or dead.

Why did it matter to him so much?

Orion. He had to free himself of the sordid past. He was a tormented human being and he had to find himself before he could love her fully. How could she help?

Juel looked into the center of the flame again. She knew instinctively that she must reach into his heart and free his soul from torment or both he and her love would perish.

Chapter Twenty-Seven

Beyond the wet meadows, where ancient oak trees grew, there stood a stone-and-thatch-roofed refuge, an old nunnery. For many years it had not been used as a cloister and was no longer recognized as an ecclesiastical edifice. Briars and weeds grew behind it now, but the buildings had been turned into storage barns, smelling strongly of hay and stored organic plants and root vegetables. In the old courtyard weeds grew up through the cracks of flagstones. A fat gray cat slunk lazily across the flags, found a place to rest in the slanting sun, lay down and stretched contentedly to lick its paws following a satisfying dinner of mouse.

Not a soul stirred about the place in the summer day. Not until a handsome couple, she with hair so fair, he dark of hair and skin, broke into the clearing. She gasped and spun about, knowing now for certain that she had been followed to her secret place.

"Who . . . ?" she began, and then, to her dismay, her voice broke slightly. "Oh, it is you." It could have been worse. This was bad enough, when the man following her was this one.

"Yes," he laughed. "It is I. Who did you expect? Your lover perhaps?"

"I have none, Jay Reynaude. You, of all people, must know this. You are ever in my sight, day and night."

"Sight?" He looked at her with narrowed, smiling eyes. "I did not know you were a poet, Dawn."

"You are not amusing."

"No?"

"No. Now leave, please. This is the only time I have for peace."

He cleared his throat, almost embarrassed for the lustful feelings that surged through him. "Do you mind if I enjoy your peace with you?"

"If it is only this you seek," she said carefully.

He spread his hands. "Of course."

As they walked along, Dawn slowly skirted the ancient cloister, afraid to go within today as she was in the habit of doing.

Dawn had to be entirely truthful. In times past she had been afraid of worse. Like the time when she had come close to being ravished. Yet, who was to say what this young man would do now that he had her alone? He had been trailing her about for weeks and it was no secret that he was a great lover of women. The gossips talked about his conquests all day long and she was sick and tired of Alice boasting of her lusty times with him. And then there was Ranice and her unusual death . . . it was enough to make her want to run and hide from him!

But they were alone now and she knew she must proceed with caution. She felt his magnetism was already getting to her. Now she knew why he was called a sly and cunning lover. But she, for one, would not be added to his list of conquests!

Jay stopped walking. "Let's go within. Have you been up into the high lofts?"

Dawn kept walking, afraid of Jay's allure. "In times past, yes. This day I would rather not—Oh!"

"Come!" He had taken hold of her hand and spun her about, and now he was running with her. He put his hands on her waist and lifted her, setting her down inside the barn that was like a great rough-hewn cathedral. In front of an old, cracked stained-glass window, its prismatic rainbow colors sectioned off with lead, was one place the nuns had said their prayers. Slanting sun passed through the prisms brilliantly and colored the stone-slab floor in various muted hazy hues.

As they walked, she gazed up at him with a worried look on her exquisite face. Stopping suddenly, he turned to look down at her and he thought he had never seen a woman so dainty and pure. She was soft and beautiful, even in her simple drab brown shift and cream linen undertunic, the sleeves of which had been curiously embroidered with delightful white unicorns and stars.

She looked away again, this time over her shoulder, to the wide, arched doors through which they had entered the sanctuary.

He lifted her chin. "What is it, sweeting? What troubles you so?"

Her heart had nearly stopped when he had touched her face. He was still gazing raptly into her eyes, making her feel soft and womanly and . . . tingly all over. She looked back at him, the blood pounding through her body.

"I must tell you truthfully. I . . . I have not been alone with a man since—" She was going to say 'the time my maidenhood had almost been lost to that burly brute'—"well, since—" She shrugged, feeling her face color. "I . . . memory fails me. I cannot seem to remember."

Jay only smiled.

"Come, we will go up into the loft." He walked over with her to the stairs. "You go first," he said, bowing with a gallant flourish.

Dawn was silent for a moment as she stared at him. "Turn around then." She saw his roguishly lifted eyebrows, questioning. "You know why! I would not have you spying beneath my skirts, Jay Reynaude!"

They went up creaky stairs into one of the barn lofts, she first, him following. As she had asked, he did not watch her mounting the stairs. But he *had* peeped, just as she rose to the top and began to turn. The shapely turn of her slim ankles and calves encased in white cotton stockings had set his heart to thumping wild and hard.

They were up there now. Hay that still smelled sweet was piled up high in one corner to the beams. They kicked up a cloud of hay dust and the motes danced wildly in the shafty light. She walked to the high oriel window and stood on tiptoe, trying to see out. All she could decipher were the tops of trees in the forest backdrop.

"This must have been the upper channel at one time . . . long ago," she said to Jay over her shoulder as she lowered to the flat of her feet again.

286

"I think you might be right." He walked around the room that now served as a loft. He touched all the corners and came back to her, hands on lean hips. "It's fourteen feet square."

Dawn opened her mouth and laughed. "How did you do that?"

"I measured. You count it off with your feet—" He walked, showing her. "Like this. Come here. Try it."

She did, and soon they were walking around the room, counting and laughing, touching arms briefly, bumping together. They were laughing with each other, happy faces and sparkling eyes reflecting their great enjoyment of the late afternoon in the old chapel.

Suddenly, his eyes changed.

Dawn felt it immediately. She knew what it was she saw there, burning in the green eyes. She backed away and fled. Jay sighed as he watched her walk away and pause at the stairs, looking down.

"Don't go yet," he said, his voice low. When she said nothing and continued to pause, he said, "Would you like to talk about Ranice's death?"

"I know how it happened," Dawn said in almost a whisper. "The castlefolk are full of the gossip of what you and Lord Orion spoke about. I know the whole of it. You need not repeat it."

He came up behind her, caught her arm, and spun her around. He looked into her eyes. "Yes, you have heard it. But what do you believe?"

She stepped back, breaking contact with him. "I do not wish to discuss what a man does or does not do with his conquests. What becomes of his affairs with his women is none of my business."

His face became a mask of stone. Grabbing her

upper arms, he pulled her closer. She stood before him, her arms pinned at her sides. When she stiffened, he set her away so she was not so close; he could see the fear brimming in her eyes.

Outdoors wild birds sang and tame doves cooed, having flown from the cote. He continued to look down into her face, and then his narrow swordlike glance swept over her, from head to toe.

"What of my conquests—as you call them?" he asked, no expression on his face now.

"I just said, I do not wish to discuss them." Her eyes flashed up at him. "They belong in your world; not mine."

He grabbed her wrist and she looked down; he let go. "I would that you be part of my world, Dawn. Yes, yes!" he said, taking her hand again. "I see your eyes melt when I speak your name. This is what I want, to see you desire me."

She swallowed hard. "What do you wish of me?"

"I want to—" he looked down at the hay, "have you lie down with me, in the hay. Is that asking too much?"

Dawn saw the melancholy frown crossing his features for a moment. "It is not. Not if you keep your hands to yourself." She looked at the inviting pile of hay, where she'd lain by herself oftimes, dreaming of love, wedded bliss, and babies. "I will do it." After all, she *was* feeling a little weary after her morning tasks and the long walk.

He was immobile for several moments. Now his look was one of faint amusement. She was such an innocent that it nearly brought tears to Jay's eyes. He was strong. He could have her and be done with it. Wanting her this badly, he could almost do it. Almost.

As they lay down together in the warm hay, Dawn closed her eyes and pretended to breathe gently, evenly, as in sleep. She wondered what he would do to her now. Strangely, she was not afraid, and there was only the warm, glowing light inside her.

Jay bent over her and admired her pale ivory skin. He studied the tawny, sweetly curved eyebrows, the pink flush in her cheeks, the gentle swell of her small breasts. All the women he had known had had big breasts which he had fondled and suckled to his heart's content. This was different, these tiny, sweet doves. He could almost taste them, lick them. Almost.

Dawn opened her eyes, looked into his deep green ones, and read his desire. She had seen that look before and it frightened her.

He had kissed hundreds of women but none had stirred his soul as this fair maiden. He had to kiss her fully and find out what it was that drew him. Soon.

She had frightening images of a stallion covering a mare. Of Alice in the arms of a lover! Of Ranice falling to her death because of Jay's rejection! Could this awful fate come to be her own? Would she be left panting for want of him one day?

Holding her waist gently, he bent and kissed her cheek lightly. "I feel something happening within you, Dawn. You are finally responding to me."

You devilish oaf! she felt like snapping at him. *What do you expect? You are ever near like a stag in rut!*

He kissed the corner of her mouth next and pressed a little closer with his long, lean frame. *Dawn, Dawn,* he thought, *you look so pretty and naïve in the hay with your dewy lips, your sweet ivory flesh* . . . He gulped a quick breath.

289

"My God, you are so tempting!"

She blushed and swallowed. Hot, she felt so hot!

Dawn was beginning to feel the shame as she thought how she had lain down, just like a peasant girl. Or Alice Becker!

"No!" She stood and he pulled her arm, catching her hand.

He drew her, protesting, down to him and exchanged positions until she was on her back, he above her. "Dawn, Dawn, I feel an emptiness deep inside me when you are not near."

"No, I say, no," she said more firmly and pried herself loose. "You can't do this."

He smiled. "This? I am doing nothing but looking at you. Though I would love to pleasure you."

Dawn gulped. "We have to . . . be serious . . . and talk."

"I am serious." He smiled into her eyes. "I do believe I love you."

Dawn looked away and did not reply. He had entered her life with his beautiful green eyes and disrupted everything she'd ever believed in.

"No, you do not. You love every woman you think of as a conquest."

"You don't know of what you speak, Dawn. You've no idea how a man thinks. You are a woman. I have not loved all these women I have bedded. True, I have lain with many and many have loved me. They call me lover. This may be true. There comes a time in a man's life when he has had enough of all the wenching. I have experienced much in my lifetime. I know all there is to pleasuring a woman. I can make them scream with pleasure, smile with happiness, shout with delight—"

"Enough!" Dawn said. "I have heard all that I wish to hear of your love life, Jay Reynaude."

"I want you to know all this, Dawn, so that when you hear of my conquests, as you put it, you will have heard all from the horse's mouth."

Horse, aye, a *stud* no less!

Glancing down at her small breasts, Jay said, "Now I want only one, yet I would not hurt you. I have no idea how to love a . . . virgin." He brushed his fingers over her forearm. "You would have to teach me, Dawn."

She blushed furiously. "No such thing will I do and well you know it."

He appeared sad as he looked at the top of her fair head, then away as if it pained him too much to gaze upon her purity. Ranice's wicked words came back to him: "Dawn will not spread her thighs at all, you poor man. Think you that, you might as well go after a nun, you might at least get a feel from one of them."

The barn loft was growing dark with purple shadow and the oaks out in the meadow now cast long shadows of deep green on the gold-fuzzed carpet of grass.

Suddenly Dawn pushed herself to a standing position and he followed. "I must go," she said as the tension stretched tightly between them.

"Dawn—" His eyes met hers beseechingly. "Please . . . Dawn."

Her mind reeled with bittersweet confusion. "I don't know what—"

Jay snatched her to his chest and kissed her, a light kiss, a mere brushing of one pair of lips against another. He held her shoulders and looked down into her eyes. Dawn could feel his heat, his hard maleness, and she was feeling weak, trembly in her stomach and shockingly wet in secret places.

Her heart danced with excitement. Now!

"Yes, you know what it is I want," Jay said softly, mockingly. "Yet, I wonder if you will ever yield, fair maiden."

"You speak so strangely, Jay Rey—"

"A kiss." He wore an intense expression. "Only a kiss for now."

The strong hardness of his lips set Dawn's world to spinning madly. Passionately, he kissed her again and again, his hands cupping the nape of her neck. A soft gasp escaped into his mouth. She didn't know what to do with her hands, and he showed her, putting one at his waist, the other behind his neck.

"I feel . . . faint," she murmured.

"Here, Dawn, hold me here. And here. You will not swoon."

She felt a momentary panic. "I'll not touch you . . . anywhere else."

"You need not. Hold me lightly. I'll do the rest."

When he pulled her closer yet and deepened the kiss, thrusting his tongue at the moist cleft of her mouth, her knees slacked and he had to hold her up. She cried out when one hand seared a path down her abdomen, coming much too close to her maiden's mound.

"I am sorry." He kissed the tip of her nose. "I do desire you and honor you, Dawn." He sighed as if in pain. "We'd better go then, before the sun sets altogether."

She looked up at him, her big brown eyes full of wonder. And desire. And fear.

Dawn was caught in his sensuous web, he knew. For the first time in his life, it was the woman who held him captive. He just didn't know what to do about it. He had kissed her. He was lost. Fully and wonderfully. The damage was done and nothing could be done to remedy it.

On the walk back to the castle grounds Dawn was silent, her heart bursting with love and anguish.

She had just experienced her first taste of sensual longing. She was on fire. Would Jay fan the flame? she wondered as her heart gave a perilous leap into the future.

Only if she let him.

That night Jay had a wonderful dream about unicorns. And Dawn. He dreamed about unicorns playing in a summery pasture, their huge bodies arched, their manes flying and splendid muscles working like pistons. The dream unicorns rubbed their long heads together, horns scraping, and reared high on their hind legs. Their hooves flashed as they rushed across the misty, trembling earth. High grass grew in the purple dream meadow, so high it tickled the horses' ribs. They dipped their velvety muzzles into the scented purple stuff, like swans dipping into water. They lashed their sides with long tails. These were unicorns from some heroic time, when civilization first began. *But where,* Jay wondered, *am I in this dream?*

Then she was standing there. Dawn. Like the morning, in all its purest golden glory. She was holding her arms out to him, but it was not him suddenly; it was a big unicorn. The huge beast shadowed him. Detail after detail unfolded itself, his eyes wandering over the feminine figure in the long white gown. She looked at him in a comical, doubting way with her serious brown eyes, as if realizing he was not to be trusted with a single real thought of purest emotion.

For a long time Jay drank his fill of Dawn, happiness and lust warming him all over.

So strong a feeling of bittersweet joy came over Jay that he came awake instantly and stared around the dark carpenter's cottage. He was wet with desire and she had vanished. He quickly shut his eyes so that he might recapture the bright vision, but both the unicorns and Dawn had gone, lost somewhere in a summery meadow region of his deeper dream being.

The dream. It was like a fairy story. He could not hold her. She seemed to belong with the unicorns, something unreachable, like the stars, the moon. When he had first looked into her eyes, seen her hair, her face, he'd felt almost angry that she'd moved beneath the same roof as he had. He had felt excruciating pain that moments before he'd made plans to meet with that grasping bitch Ranice.

He had lain with a whore when there'd been an angel in the same residence!

She was there, all that time Dawn was there, and he had not known she existed! A week before he'd met her in the stores he'd known something wonderful was going to happen.

Dawn happened.

I do believe I love you, Jay had told her in the old nunnery loft. His desire was great for her, and he could read her fear because of this. She must have realized how badly he'd wanted her.

He loved her. All was not lost. She could still surrender willingly. And there was something else, something refreshing. He loved Dawn for her purity, her goodness. If only he could make her see that he'd changed, too, because of his great love for her and his need to protect her.

Yes, he loved her and wanted her for his wife. If she would not have him, he would remain celibate the rest of his life. No other woman would taste his kisses or lie beneath him, not ever again, he vowed. Dawn was the only woman for him. First he must show her that love need not be frightening. She had experienced strong feelings for him, he knew that much because he'd felt her tremble at his touch. She wanted him. Her eyes, if not her words, had told him that much.

Wasn't that enough of a start?

Chapter Twenty-Eight

The day was a gray rainy one when Juel went to visit her father in the village. The rain sifted down endlessly and the roads became mires through which traffic crawled at a snail's pace. Geoffrey and Autumn had gone along and the knights accompanied Juel again. In the village, the rebuilding of the burned-out homes was progressing. There were people walking about and boards and planks everywhere.

The woman named Evelyn cooked for Juel's father in her small kitchen. She invited Juel, Geoffrey, and Autumn to stay for the "big" meal, as Evelyn called it. The heavy, square table took up most of the kitchen space. They ate goose, crisply browned and heavily stuffed with apples and raisins and accompanied by hot dumplings and stewed plums. There was lots of milk and buckets of butter. Evelyn kept two cows out back.

"It's good, huh, Juel m'girl?" Juel's father asked her, wiping his mouth on an old but clean rag.

Juel gave a feeble smile. Her father didn't seem to notice, since his eyes were straying to the next course.

Juel ate very little of the food, but the younger ones gobbled it up just like Peter did. Juel thought her father ate too much. It was no wonder he was having stomach problems. Before the greasy goose was served there was a steamed pudding studded with almonds and doused with heavy cream. Juel had a vision of her father in a flopping house-robe with his fat legs sticking out, eating sowbelly and green cabbage. She shuddered.

The culinary arts of this heavyset woman, Juel had decided, would hardly advance her father's years on earth.

"Papa, why don't you come to The Keep soon?" She smiled, exhibiting her beautiful straight teeth. "You are better now, I can see." *And I can also see you will become fat and ill if you stay here much longer!* she did not add. "What do you say?"

"Soon." He nodded, digging into the cottage pudding next. "My stomach is getting better day by day. I'll be able to get back to work on that castle of Sutherland's. Heard he's a real baron. That's good, I was beginning to wonder about him." Spooning another mouthful of pudding between his smacking lips—Juel had never seen him eat like this—he looked up at her and added, "You seem surprised, daughter. The news has leaked everywhere, about how the young King Harry made Orion Sutherland a real baron."

"He always was a baron. King Henry didn't make him one, as he did some of his relatives and friends. No one knew it until now, that's all." Juel ended with a matter-of-fact shrug.

Why do your eyes look so empty, Papa? Juel wanted to ask. He was eating too much and not getting enough exercise, she could tell. The stomach problem was not going to go away if he did not get away from Evelyn Burton. "Big Eve," her father called the woman as he looked up at her fondly. Still, there was that sad emptiness in his eyes. He was lonely, true, but food was not the answer to achieving happiness.

"Come to Sutherland, Papa. I will cook for you," Juel whispered when Evelyn slipped out for a moment to check on her cows. Probably to see if she could get more milk!

"Yes," Peter said, patting Juel's hand. "I will come there soon."

Evelyn came back in and gave Geoffrey and Autumn a gooey treat to take with them, but Juel waved away the candy-caked fruit, gave her father a smile, and pushed the boy and the older girl out the door.

Juel popped her head back inside once. "Soon, Papa!" She gave him a mock-ferocious look. "I mean it, else I'll come and fetch you." Then she was out the door, her black slops almost coming off her feet in the oozing mud of the streets.

About to mount the tame horse Howell had found for her in the stables, Juel saw something, frowned, then dropped the reins. "Wait . . ." she told the three knights. "I would like to speak with those children. They look so hungry, so poor, I can't leave without speaking to them."

Duncan, the dark knight, leaned down to briefly touch Juel's shoulder. "Leave them. They're orphans. There are many and you can't help them all."

Howell spoke up, bringing his horse around, close to Juel's skirts. "My lady—" he always called her that, since he thought her too beautiful, charming, and intelligent to be a mere villein's daughter—"there are enough mouths to feed at the castle." The blond knight shook his head when she would not listen and shrugged.

"What is your name?" she asked one of the children. Then touched another towhead. "And yours?"

The knights followed behind her, rolling their eyes heavenward as she stopped to talk to the orphans. She treated each and every one as if they were very special.

While she was in Herstmonceux this day, Juel discovered so many children living in squalor: seven of them, ranging from eleven to four years of age. All had banded together to stay alive by stealing food and clothes to keep warm at night. No one could keep them; the people had enough trouble trying to feed their own families.

Her heart touched, Juel loaded them in the wagon and brought them back to the keep. Orion and several of his knights were gone, riding off to Pevensey early that morning.

"Ho! What have we here?" A moon-faced figure emerged from the manor, flapping her apron in excitement as she raced out to the yard.

Lydia, loving the homeless ragamuffins, helped Dawn to clean them up. Juel smiled when her brother Jay offered to help. Amid squeals of laughter, splashes of water, and happy faces, Jay and Dawn's eyes met, and brightened and held. It was like unearthing something, a discovery.

Jay and Dawn had something in common; they both loved children!

It was a fine, happy day.

Juel cleaned and fed the children and found places for them all to sleep. The eleven-year-old boy touched their hearts in a magical way, as much as the youngest, a four-year-old girl with wispy yellow hair. After being tucked in, with fat stomachs and fresh linens, the children in a single row of pallets, Juel settled down to tell the story of the fierce dragon and the beautiful princess.

Geoffrey and Autumn and the orphans were enthralled by her story, and faces were lit up, even Dawn and Jay's.

"I didn't know you could tell these wonderful tales," Jay told his sister as he sat next to Dawn on a hard bench against the wall.

"Of course you did," Juel told him with a laugh. "You just never listened well." Then she became quiet, her eyes solemn. "Now, hush," she said, directing her words to Jay, then looking around at the wide-eyed children.

"There was once a lovely little girl who grew up to be a beautiful princess . . ."

With enchanting whimsy, she went on to tell the story.

Next to her shoulder, Dawn felt the deep, heavy pound of Jay's heart. Once again, a mixture of fear and heady awareness of him made her feel as if she didn't know herself. It was as if some invisible part of her had roused at this man's touch. She was beginning to respond to him in a way that shocked and alarmed her.

Even though Jay sat beside her quietly, Dawn felt the urge to get up and run. It had been fine when they'd had the children to occupy their hands and eyes . . . and then had come the silent magic while alone in the storeroom fetching the pallets. She had felt his power, a driving but controlled energy that intimidated her. She had crossed her arms in a shield, though there had been nothing she could do to hide the heated blush in her cheeks. Jay just smiled warmly, crookedly, glanced down at her arms over her breasts, and walked away carrying the makings of a bed.

"Dawn," Jay said now, nudging her gently. "Look. The children have drawn closer to Juel."

Dawn smiled. "I see," she said, unaware that Jay's eyes roved her profile, caressed her thick braid of yellow hair, and rested on the curve of her jaw, below her pink lips.

The children had gotten up from bed to make a half-curve below Juel. She sighed, nodding to leave them be as Jay and Dawn began to rise to shoo them back to bed.

The flames from the fireplace were in their eyes and they were as bright as Juel's. She was telling about the princess from a faraway land . . . one who had not known she was a princess, for she had been kidnapped while still very young. Now she was a grown woman, an heiress to a castle, and she was very beautiful.

But there was a dragon she loved and meant to tame.

"Her armor was made so well that the dragon's fire could not penetrate the links." She smiled down at the children on the floor and held up a slender finger. "There wasn't a chink in her armor."

"What about the dragon?" one child wanted to know.

"Wait," Juel said, her greenish-hazel eyes moving slowly along the curve of children below her. "I'm not finished. This was a scary dragon who loved a lady. A spell had been cast on a man, turning him into a dragon. He couldn't be turned back into a real man until the lady who had become a princess kissed him."

The children giggled shyly and Juel went on. "Then she had to get close enough, despite his heat, to lay a kiss on his scaly and scary face. In his spell he did not know her and breathed fire on her. But the intricate pieces of her armor were made of small parts carefully fitted and riveted together. Her armor pressed lightly upon her body and the metal joints moved freely. She almost forgot she wore it until she felt a crossbow's arrow strike her. But this her armor turned easily aside."

"What about a lance?" one of the older boys asked.

"A lance glanced harmlessly off her cuirasses because the plates were joined like expensive glass and a dagger couldn't even pierce and enter them."

Eyes, so big, so bright, looked up at her. "What happened then?"

The moment was tense and Juel leaned forward, elbows on her knees. "The princess got near enough to that flaming dragon and planted a kiss on his face."

Seven voices sang out, "And?"

The young woman smiled and her lips were a mysterious curve of sweetness as she said: "We shall have to see . . ."

Jay clucked his tongue, watching Dawn's reaction to his sister's story. "Now, you can't leave them high and dry just like that, Sis. Come on, tell us the rest. We're curious. Are we not?" he asked the children.

"Yes!" they chorused.

Dawn only nodded at Juel and Jay smiled at her

303

crystal-bright eyes.

Juel's shoulders lifted in a shrug, then she grinned. "With one kiss he was turned back into a handsome young man."

Geoffrey Johns popped up from behind an old table against the wall. "He wasn't evil anymore?" The children covered their mouths and giggled at Geoffrey as he emerged with mussed brown hair and smudged nose.

"What are you doing back there, Geoffrey?" Jay asked, waving him forward. "You don't have to hide. You can join the others."

"Yeah!" they all chorused. "Come on, Geoffie!"

"Go on, Sis," said Jay, automatically resting his muscled arm along Dawn's back on the bench. She jumped and he grinned sheepishly, taking his arm back to his side.

"He wasn't evil anymore?" Geoffrey asked again.

Looking serious, Juel shook her head. "He was never evil, Geoffrey. He was just . . . lost."

"Lost?" they chimed. "Where'd he get lost from?"

"That's all for now, children," Juel said.

"Awwwww."

"Go on. Shoo!" Juel flapped her hand. "Back to bed!"

Juel was looking from a high window in the manor house. She missed Orion; he'd been gone for several days. She wondered if he would find what he was looking for and if he'd have Clytie with him when he returned.

She prayed for his safe return and, in fact, had made

many visits to the chapel, which had been restored to its former beauty. There was now a priest in residence, who took morning service in the chapel and later gave lessons to the pages.

There was also a little social activity to pass the evenings, with storytelling, songs, jokes, and some dancing among the servants. Juel and Dawn liked to watch, as neither knew how to dance. They both preferred the storytelling much more, and Juel did most of that now that Orion was gone for the week, since he'd taken up most of her time before.

Once again, the castle was coming to life.

Juel looked below. Construction was being carried out by a large force of skilled masons, smiths, carpenters, and other workers such as hewers, ditchers, and stone-breakers. All day long the sound of hammers, pickaxes, spades, hoists fitted with pulley and tackle, and chains clanking could be heard.

Soon the new solar, Orion's private room, would be completed. Juel had peeked inside, then walked in after the workers had gone to their quarters for the day. It would be the most luxurious room in the manor; there was to be a four-poster bed, with fine hangings and the Sutherland coat-of-arms, which Orion had found in the attic the morning after he'd left an undergarment in the room. Juel had flushed when he'd told her.

Furnishings for the solar would include a couple of chests, one for clothes and one for documents, silver and gold, a tall stand for candles, a ewer, basin, and brand-new tapestries on the walls. The hooded fireplace would provide warmth in winter and the window, looking over the courtyard, was big enough to make the solar light and airy.

She worried about Orion, and paced rooms, wringing her hands together. She avoided her playful cats and had one-word conversations with those in the house.

It was a time of increasing tensions. Lawless bands of marauding knights and archers still spread disorder. Heavy taxes were a constant complaint. The war of England and France begot massive brigandage, as people felt subject to events out of their control. John of Burgundy was the French people's champion, since mad King Louis left a void in their craving for a protector. And King Henry was taking up the old war—with Orion right in the middle of it.

He was a spy. Juel knew it now. Hadn't he said as much?

Juel looked down from the high window. Under the white glow of midday, a puff of wind swept across the earth. The portent of storms to come. Suddenly the branches of the trees flattened and bent, and the tree-crowns twisted and whitened. The bushes darkened under the wind's press, and over meadows and fields ran great folds, pulsing through the silvery green grass and golden grain.

As she continued to look from the chapel window, hens fluttered wildly in the barnyard, sheep huddled together, and horses lay back their ears. She saw the folk at work in the fields pause in their labors, and wipe the sweat from their brows with swollen hands.

Juel watched as they looked up into the cloudless sky.

She was about to resume her prayers when she turned back to the window. All was still again, eerie, more poised and quiet than before. The trees stood motionless, leaves seemingly veined with steel. *Steel.*

She drew an arm across her brow. What had come over her? Why did the word steel show up in her mind so strongly?

Juel sighed. The impact of so much heat had bred a profound tension. Juel saw the hands in the fields bow their backs and resume their toil. But deep in their hearts lurked the consoling thought that soon the storm would come.

Steel.

Did Orion miss her? Juel hoped so, as she made her way down to find Hugh, the armor smith.

Only time would tell.

Chapter Twenty-Nine

Dawn was coming down the steps from the larder, her thick blond braid hanging to her waist, her clothes freshly washed and crisp from the line. Alice Becker snickered to herself when the blond entered the kitchen. Alice was drawing water from the inside well and paused, leaving the bucket resting on the brick ledge. Just as Dawn was passing by, Alice whirled about, snatched up the bucket, and bumped forcefully into Dawn.

Water slopped over onto Dawn, soaking her from waist to hem before she could step away.

"Clumsy wench!" Alice screeched. "Now look what you've gone and made me do!"

"I?" Dawn said, plucking her long white apron and sodden skirts away from herself with both hands. "It's you who was careless and bumped into me."

"You lie!" Alice hissed, eyeing her brother Fat Will at the table cutting up a side of beef. He was not smiling. "You didn't watch where you were goin'. Hah! Daydreaming, you were, huh?"

A serf carrying faggots to the fire stopped to watch the scene unfold, and another plucking fat geese also arrested his movements. The black cook Cimmerian, who was making pastry, halted in rolling out his dough. Even the hounds stopped licking their chops and the cats stopped lapping up milk. And Shadow took himself elsewhere!

"What're you all gawking at!" Alice yelled, giving Dawn a shove that sent her flying into a side of beef hanging over the work table.

Dawn held her hurting ribs, looked up at Alice, and wondered what she'd done to deserve this ill treatment.

"Well?" Alice shouted to all the kitchen folk. "You saw the bumbling bitch yerselves. She can't do nothin' right these days; all she does is moon over that green-eyed lover in tight black hose—with a big crotch to boot!"

Dawn felt her forehead breaking out into a sweat.

Alice's face twisted with ugly rivalry, making her appear older than her actual years. "Humph! He drops me like a hot faggot and now pants after her scrawny body."

"Who?" three kitchen maids chorused. Their eyes were wide with wonder after what Alice had said about the tight black hose and what was inside of them.

Dawn could only stand there and blink in surprise. She would have fought back, but her emotions were running high these days and she felt she would soon cry. In fact, the night before she had cried herself to sleep. Day and night she dreamed of what it would be like to let Jay make love to her. She was terrified and just didn't know what to do. His advances were getting to her and soon she would be as lost as the other women who loved him, who had gone into his arms before her. She didn't want to become a castoff plaything as they had.

Alice leaned closer to Dawn. "Where you been meetin' him, you skinny little tart!"

Spittle flew at Dawn's face and she didn't even wipe it away. She just stood and blinked fast, feeling her heart leaping in her chest. Where was her self-confidence and courage? Why was she taking all this like a coward? He had her beaten, that's what. And soon he would take her, just like all the others.

"Awww, Alice. You're just jealous," Fat Will said, pulling up the side of beef before it slipped to the floor. "Leave off 'er. She ain't done nothing with him. She don't give Jay Reynaude the time of day, even."

"I don't believe it!" Alice screamed as she went at Dawn's throat, her hands reaching out like sharp talons.

"You're insane!" Dawn cried. "You don't know what you're talking about."

"Jay's mine and I ain't going to let the simple likes of you take him away! You don't even know what it's for!"

Alice's knee lifted and smashed into Dawn's hip.

Dawn fell back again, this time onto a hound that growled and nipped at her heels for being stepped upon. Alice was after Dawn at once, flying at the younger woman's soft neck. Dawn wrenched aside, hitting her chin on the low brick wall surrounding the well. Blood trickled from the corner of her soft mouth.

Alice stared at it with blood lust glimmering in her eyes.

"Here now!" Cook Cimmerian boomed. "That's

about enough, Ali. Leave her alone and get back to work." He often had to break up young maids who'd begun a quarrel, but he'd never once had to where Dawn Peyton was concerned. He'd always liked the blond girl and she worked the hardest of all the kitchen maids.

"No!" Dawn screamed as Alice caught her around the throat and began to squeeze. "Enough!" she cried. "You can have Jay Reynaude, he doesn't interest me one bit."

"You lying bitch, I seen you teasing him in the hall, you little vixen. I saw how hot and bothered he was when he slipped into the kitchen for a drink—and it wasn't from the heat 'cause nothing but lust can make a man's body look like that!" Alice bit her tongue, almost telling that his drawers had never been that swelled for her!

Not liking the look in Alice's eyes, Dawn began to back toward the arched doorway leading into the great hall.

Cimmerian dropped his rolling pin. The serf dropped his faggots. Everyone stood still.

And that was their mistake.

Alice was a strong woman, and she would make three of Dawn in girth and brawn. Now she reached for a sharp knife before anyone could stop her. She whipped it from the table and in one swift motion lunged forward and brought it down!

Chapter Thirty

He moved like lightning. One minute there was no one there, the next a hand whipped out and closed about Alice's fleshy wrist like a vise.

Jay had come from the room that wound up from the kitchen, where the clerk worked at his accounts. He had sensed something was wrong, heard a commotion, and paused for only a minuscule second in time. It was dark in the store area where he'd crept from and no one had noticed his stealthy and rapid approach.

"You bastard!" Alice shouted at Jay's head; and again, "You rutting bastard!"

Alice would not give in. Her hand was clutched about the hilt of the blade like it was an extension of her arm.

It all happened fast. One second the blade was slashing down toward Dawn's throat and the next there came the sound of bones snapping.

Alice screamed, a horrible sound like a banshee wailing.

Dawn's fingers lay on her own throat, her brain

whirling with the thought that had Jay not appeared in that moment she'd now be spilling her blood on the floor.

"Oh my God," Dawn gulped, as she tried not to look at Alice's hand flopping from the wrist as she screamed and screamed and screamed.

With a nasty look in his beady eyes, Fat Will rushed over to take Alice against him, leading her to sit on the low brick wall. "There now, Ali, we'll get the surgeon from the village to set it. Don't worry," he crooned. "Will's here, Ali."

Whimpering and whining, Alice looked at Fat Will's soft profile. "Why ain't there no damn surgeon here, Will?"

Tossing the knife aside, Jay stood shaking his head, wondering what he'd ever seen in Alice Becker. To think he had bedded this crazed and jealous wench!

At the slop bucket Dawn was leaning against the wall and holding her head, bent at the waist, her face flushed and perspiring.

"Oh," Dawn groaned. "Oh—"

Jay turned and saw her. He whitened and rushed over to sweep her into his arms. While she squeaked a protest he carried her out the door and into the fresh air.

Dawn took a deep breath and stared up at him. "Oh, Jay," she cried, clutching him about the neck. "It was awful!"

His jaw hardened. "I know, my darling, I know." He pressed a kiss on her forehead and looked at her with loving eyes. "I'll take you away where we can be alone."

Her eyes were trusting. "Where?" she whispered softly.

"You'll see."

He carried her out the back way where no eyes could see, across a golden field, through a thin stand of trees, and into a thick forest. Birds and small creatures called their welcome, for they knew that these two could harm no one. The humans had only one purpose in mind . . . to be together alone in quiet solitude.

"Dawn, how are you now?" Jay asked as he set her down in a beautiful clearing in the woods. He looked at her with worry in his dazzling green eyes.

"I am better," she said, feeling shy all of a sudden. They were alone and it did not frighten her all that much, especially not after what had happened in the kitchen. "You did not tell me. Where have you taken me?"

He spread his arms wide. "This is my home." He laughed deeply, coming back to her. "The carpenter's castle. It's mine now, Orion said so."

Stopping, he looked into her eyes. There was a grin on his happy face.

She blinked, seeing the small house. "Castle?" She laughed then, holding her hand to her breast, knowing he was making fun, for it was hardly a castle. "It is beautiful here and the carpenter's cottage is perfect." All it needed was a white wood fence surrounding it . . . if she lived here . . . Dawn's eyes were suddenly misty bright with the thought.

Jay stood before her, tall as the oaks surrounding the little house. "Come inside. We can watch the forest creatures from the back, if you like. There is a small porch. You will love it."

Side by side they entered the place and the afternoon shadows filtered in, shifting, mesmerizing. "I have some wine," he said. "Would you like some?"

"Oh," she said, her hand to her chest. "I don't know. No . . . no, I haven't eaten all that much and I . . . I am not used to inebriants."

He watched her, his heart aglow as she walked about, looking like a princess in her own castle. All of a sudden she stood still, studying the motes that drifted in the air.

His eyes grew wide as he realized she had streaks of blood on her cheek. "Come here," he said gently. "I'll wash you off."

As he took up a rag and dipped it in a basin of warm water, he snarled, "That bitch, I'll kill her for this!"

"No, Jay, forget it." She moved away, her eyes wide. "One has already perished because of—"

His face hardened. "Because of?" He waited. When she said nothing, he tossed the rag aside. "I know, because of my lust for Ranice. That was true at first, that we lusted for each other. Alice was one of hundreds, too. I cannot lie about that, but they meant nothing to me, all whores, Ranice the worst of them." He shrugged, then grew serious. "Dawn, I did not kill her, you must know that."

She whirled, facing him. "Do all the women who love you find a terrible end?"

He stared at her for several moments, then tenderly pressed his fingertips to her cheek. His words were almost whispered when he spoke. "There is one who would not. She would only find love and beauty the rest of her life. To this one I would make a loving vow forever if only she would give her heart."

Shyly Dawn looked around the stone-walled room. On the far side there stood a high pallet, a bed piled with lovely soft furs, linen-covered pillows, and a bed throw that trailed onto the floor. Everything was clean and neat.

Jay caught where her eyes had rested, and when she looked back at him he breathed in and out with some trouble, his body beginning to shudder with excitement. He swallowed hard, resting his fingers against the curve of her lower lip.

"We will eat something," he said. "Come, I have some bread and cheese in the chest. I'll not have wine if you prefer that I don't."

"You may if you like."

"No. Not if you're not having any. It isn't proper."

Dawn smiled and looked away. "I don't know what is proper in court etiquette." She looked back at him. "Have you known many proper ladies?"

"To be honest, yes."

They ate bread and cheese and he drew water from the well. Jay had only a few bites. He wasn't hungry, but he ate just because he wanted to share with Dawn. She ate very little herself, and when she was done, she brushed the crumbs from her skirt and stood.

Jay came up behind her, placed his hands on her shoulders, and turned her about to face him. He quivered just as she did. "I love you, Dawn. You must know this."

She gazed into his eyes, unable to look away. "I'm afraid." She bit her lip after she'd said it.

"I know." He moved closer, closer, and yet closer. Now her feet were together and between his. "Do you want me, Dawn?"

Shivering from head to foot, feeling a sweet throbbing ache down below, Dawn pushed her chest into him, winding her arms about his waist. She swooned away and he caught her. Jay sucked in his breath. He knew she was weak with desire and he felt the same, but he was still the stronger one, as a man should be.

Grasping her upper arms, he all but lifted her from the floor as he arched into her and felt her soft mound against his hard stomach.

"Jay, put me down." Her voice was breathless and soft.

With a question in his green eyes, he said, "Where, Dawn? Where should I put you down?"

"I—" she gulped. "I don't know." Her eyes flew to the bed and back.

"Yes you do. Tell me, Dawn."

"Cannot . . . I cannot say it."

"We will make love," he said, simply.

Dawn colored. "Yes."

Tears of heat and desire stood in her eyes and Jay knew she wanted him as strongly as he did her.

Burying his face in the area where wispy tendrils of hair brushed her throat, Jay murmured against her soft flesh, "Dawn, Dawn, what you do to me, it's both wonderful and painful. I'm so full I'm afraid of hurting you." He opened his mouth to softly bite her neck. He drew back to look at her.

Her eyes were big and luminous as she looked into his face. "You would not hurt me. I know you could not do that to me."

"Oh," Jay said, dipping his head, his lips close to hers. "You don't know, do you? It could hurt very much, yes." He kissed her lips and made her quiver, then moistly parted them. "I will do other things first. You will be prepared for me then."

"I am wet," Dawn said, rubbing a hand down her thigh.

Jay's eyes flew wide, then narrowed into slits of flickering green flame. He said no more but carried her to the soft fur bed, where he laid her down and very slowly brought his hips to hers. Kissing her lips, thrusting his tongue in and out, he began to make the same movements with his lower half.

Moaning and writhing, she slipped her little tongue into his mouth. He gasped and tangled it with his flesh and his utterance.

"Dawn Dawn Dawn," he cried. "I love you so very much it almost breaks my heart just to look at you. And now you are here with me."

His heart pounding fast and furious, he was as ready as a buck in rut, but still he went very slowly. Dawn panted and whimpered as he undressed her, touching her here and there, above and below.

"Take me, Jay," she gulped. "I know how . . . it's done. I've seen the act . . . I came upon it once . . ." she panted and circled her hips. "It frightened me . . . but this does not. You do not." She swallowed hard and her eyes were huge. "I am ready. Please."

He dipped his tongue between her parted lips. Then he stilled the motion of his hips. "You lie, little love. You are scared to death. I can see it in your eyes, you can't hide it."

On her knees, lifting herself before him, Dawn arched her back and put her small, hard breast into his mouth. He took her and suckled, blowing, nipping, while the tiny buds blossomed into beautiful roses. Her head fell back, the tip of her braid tickling her buttocks. Jay reached around, pulled the green tie from her hair, then

319

slowly spread the glorious length all about like a spun yellow cloud.

"You . . . my God, you are beautiful." His eyes worshipped each and every corner of her face. "Has God sent me an angel?" He kissed her lips and she opened for him at once. "Or a temptress?" he said between kisses.

With hard-won courage Dawn took his hand, pressed hers over it, and ran it down her thigh. There was a wild look in his eyes when she ran it back up and stopped. Then she pushed his hose apart where they tied at the waist and reached inside. She took him in her hand, and while he sucked in his breath, she lowered her head to kiss him there.

"Dawn!" he gasped, taking careful hold of her hair. "Where did you learn to . . . do . . . that?"

Looking up at him, still on her knees, she whispered, "I have seen this not at all, what I do to you. It is only that I wish to love you, every inch of you. You are so big and manly."

With that ringing in his ears, Jay whipped her legs out from beneath her, sending her back to the bed.

She lay on her back, smiling gloriously.

He loomed above, smiling triumphantly.

She laughed sweetly in her throat. "Now it is you who must remove your clothes."

He heard her follow with a giggle as he looked down, realizing he was still fully clothed. "Ah, little love. I can't do much for you like this." He looked down, seeing only the tip of his staff. "You are right. This clothing must come off." Little did Dawn know that he'd not frighten her and move too fast. She was exactly where he wanted her, in mind and body.

When he had removed all his clothes, he turned and stood before her in all his naked glory. Dawn's eyes widened at the size of this man. Why, he was even larger than the giant who had almost taken her maidenhood!

Dawn gave a shy little whimper and began to rise from the bed. Jay put his knee on the bed and hovered over her. "The fear is back, little love. We need see this thing done."

"I . . . I don't know." She swallowed.

His eyes were moist as he said, "I need you, Dawn, I will pleasure you beyond your wildest thoughts."

Lying back among the furs, Dawn looked up at him with round eyes as he pried her thighs apart, knelt between . . . and used his hand!

Put it where she had never been touched before.

His middle finger thrust into her, not all the way, just enough to test the tender tissue. He watched her begin to writhe while his movements began, then moved faster, bending over to blow in her ear, then suckle her flattened breast. He lapped at the nipple, then the other, making them wet and slippery as he slid his tongue to her navel, then up, to her throat, her lips. He thrust his tongue inside just as he pushed his finger into her moist crevice.

Dawn felt his movements create a small play of love. She arched for him, cried out his name over and over. She was hot, on fire, and he was the one who had set her aflame.

"You are narrow and tight," he said, reaching over for a jar on a table, a jar with some sort of cream in it. "Help me put this on you."

She blinked from her daze. "What is it?"

"It is for you." He bent to kiss her lips as he rubbed the cream over her maidenhead. Her fingers joined his and then moved together, spreading the cream and the hot desire all around until her flesh was slick. "Now, you are wetter than before. Move your hand away."

Just when she thought the torment would never end, Jay centered over her and his large swollen organ penetrated the taut tissue. She cried out and his own cry met hers and hovered in the air. At that most crucial moment she almost laughed, for it sounded as if he were in more pain than she.

Over and over, they continued to meet energetically, with him sliding into her narrow sheath, and out, while she arched, demanding noisily that he thrust harder and faster.

At last, Jay thought, *I am loving you at last. Oh, God. Oh, God. OH! GOD!*

"Oh! Oh! Oh!"

Jay howled.

Dawn sang arias.

Their cries mingled as they came together perfectly, beautifully, his seed jetting white-hot into her. Afterward, they lay together, speaking endearments and kissing moistly, tenderly. He was still inside her, hard and ready again, when he began to move. Once again they came together, and a while later, again, again. They ate bread and cheese, washed each other in a big wooden tub, and while they splashed about like happy children, she bent to take him into her mouth. At the same time he tongued her until she exploded, and he followed with a sensation much like thunder and lightning.

"We almost drowned," he said afterward, gasping

for air.

She giggled and coughed. "I know."

"Did you see stars?" he asked her later when they lay limp beside each other on the furry pallet.

"Many," she returned. "And bright suns. Once I thought I had died." She heard his chuckle. "Laugh, but I almost did."

"And I also."

"Can we sleep now?" she asked, snuggling against him as silver stars peeked in the tiny window.

"Most certainly!" he said, holding her next to his heart, one large hand clasped to a small breast.

He brushed a kiss on her hair. Nothing was more important in his life than this woman.

He pressed her little button of a nipple and blew in her ear.

"No more . . . Jay."

He yawned and tucked her head under his chin. "No more," he said. Not this night.

And   they   slept,   just   like   the   dead.

Chapter Thirty-One

From morning till night the forge roared. With mighty hammer, Hugh, the armorer, pounded ingots of spongy, white-hot iron before the fragments of cinder were forced out and pure metal remained. This he wrought with constant reheating on a dozen different anvils and stakes of varying sizes and shapes. Intricately curved, some of them looked like mysteriously reversed parts of a human body.

There worked a woman at the forge. But no one knew that she was a woman. Hugh Kingsley called her Clyde. She was hiding from John Scardon; no one knew this, either. She wore a lightweight, concealing hood, and Hugh had started the rumor that she'd had leprosy at one time.

No one went near "Clyde."

Juel was standing on the other side of the forge. She had just entered and was staring at a suit of chain mail on a clothing tree. Her head was cocked sideways when Hugh rushed over to her, leaving Clyde to do "his" work.

"Ah, Juel Reynaude, you came back." His eyes were a dazzling shade of blue, his hair pitch black, and he was very very handsome.

"Hello, Hugh." Most women could not look him directly in the eyes, but Juel did so. Again, he looked at her as if he could not believe his own eyes; she wondered at this. "How is the sh—"

"No," he said, putting a finger to his lips. "Don't say it. Remember, you want it kept secret. Here, look, the piece is coming along fine." He led the way to a dark and dusty corner of the room, close to where Clyde was working.

Juel looked at the secret piece he was making for her and she nodded. "It looks very good." Her eyes strayed to the slim, hooded figure and Hugh laughed nervously, drawing her attention elsewhere. But not for long. Juel continued to stare at the small man working in the forge. "I have some questions—"

"I have some bread and wine . . ." He looked briefly to the place her eyes were trained. "I've cheese, too. Come, you must be hungry." She didn't move. "Thirsty then?"

Finally, Juel followed him to the table where there was some food and drink left over from a recent meal. She perched on a stool he pulled out for her, her eyes going back to the hooded figure. "That man," Juel said, munching a crust of bread. "Who is he?"

"Boy?" Hugh laughed nervously again. "His name is Clyde. He can work as fast and hard as any armorer to make a suit of chain mail or plate. He has helped me with the secret sh—"

"Shh," Juel said, placing a finger over her lips, her eyes twinkling merrily. "It's a secret, isn't it?"

He looked at her as if he'd like to eat her up. "Ah, of course. I have said so myself."

Juel had visited Hugh several days ago. He was one of the most important people at the castle, she had recently learned. The knights usually had their own equipment, but Hugh had to keep stocks of weapons for the lesser men-at-arms and for the lord's tenants when they came in to do guard duty. It was the first time she had talked with him, only seeing him from afar as she traversed the courtyard. He had stared at her as he was doing now, as if he couldn't believe his eyes.

He had welcomed her and she had watched as the pure virgin metal was transformed under the blows. The white heat dwindled and the iron turned orange and then dull red. To Juel it was as if limbs grew before her eyes or a head was molded on the anvil that was shaped like a pear.

Again, Juel's eyes strayed. The boy swiped an arm across his brow and tucked a long strand of hair back inside his hood. She drew closer and looked down at his work. Hugh had told her earlier that the final dimensions of each piece had to be measured with skilled accuracy to fit the body of the individual knight. An ill-fitted suit of armor could be a source of great fatigue and even danger to the wearer.

Hugh was sweating as Juel walked even closer to the "boy." He was trimming the edges with heavy shears while the piece was still hot. From beneath his hood he smiled at an orphan boy whose chore was to pick up these dangerously hot pieces with a small metal shovel on a long handle, then toss them into huge baskets of scrap.

Juel recognized the orphan boy working with the

shovel as one of the children she had told her story of the dragon to the night before. He grinned and moved away from her.

The three of them were alone now. Juel looked up at Hugh briefly, then back to the hooded figure. "Why does he wear a hood when it's so hot in here?" Juel whispered to Hugh.

A puny sound was heard from beneath the hood.

"He had leprosy at one time," Hugh said.

Juel stepped back, bumping her hip against a table. Then she relaxed and breathed easier, recalling a time when she'd helped a poor leper woman. She had given the woman some coins she'd earned while working at the merchant's house.

Juel pushed away from the table. "I'm not afraid," she said. "Can I watch?"

A muffled sound came from the hood.

"What did he say?" Juel asked Hugh.

Handsome Hugh looked distraught. "He said . . . yes."

Juel looked down at the fine wrought iron, which was capable of being transformed into steel for gauntlets which protected the hands or sollerets which covered the feet and looked like shoes. These intricate pieces of armor were composed of small parts delicately fitted and riveted together.

"Your piece will be done soon," Hugh said, never asking what Juel Reynaude wanted it to be used for. "It will take a little work to complete because it's very fine work that needs to be done."

"I realize that, and thank you, Hugh."

He thought she would leave now, but she stood there

watching Clyde at his work. He stared at her as if she could not be a living and breathing person. She was as beautiful as . . . He could not complete his thoughts, afraid she might read them. He'd never met a woman this charming and intelligent; but for another . . . who was very close by.

"Can he talk?" Juel asked Hugh.

"Ah . . ." Hugh faltered. "Very little."

"Hugh," Juel said. "Can we speak freely, in front of your worker?"

Hugh grinned. "That depends on what you wish to speak of, my lady."

"Oh, I am not . . . you should not call me that. I am—" Juel paused. What was she? A kitchen maid? Just what? She had taken to working on Orion's accounts while he was away, as he had requested should his clerk be called away. And he had. To a family member who was ailing.

"You are—?" Hugh's startling blue eyes twinkled.

It was no secret that Juel Reynaude was Orion's woman. She had started out as kitchen maid and now had run of the place. She was liked by all, told wonderful stories to the orphans, kept accounts, went everywhere, except, of course, where *no one* dared go—to the round tower.

Juel squared her shoulders. "I am Juel Reynaude."

Another sound was heard from beneath the hood. Juel stared curiously and then Hugh drew her away, back to the table where he poured her a glass of watered-down wine.

"Thank you, Hugh, I needed that," Juel said after she had downed the drink. "I usually *don't* take wine—" her eyes strayed to the bent figure of Clyde "—but felt I needed it just now."

"Good God," Hugh said. "I hope you don't get to drinking like m'lord."

"Oh, no. Never." Juel frowned. "Orion hasn't had a drink in a long time."

Hugh smiled. "I believe it's because of you he doesn't get drunk like he used to."

"It isn't because of me," she murmured, then smiled brightly. "However, I would like to think it is."

"You can believe it, lovely lady." Hugh beamed. "Orion used to be a madman." He looked around to see if anyone else had heard, but there was only him and Juel and Clyde in the huge place. "He tore this room apart one night before you came here. It was terrible; you don't know."

Perched on the stool again, Juel sipped at another glass of the wine he poured. "This is very good. What's in it?"

Hugh grinned. "My own brew. Wine with a little bit of whimberry."

"Uhmm, it has the taste of bilberries. I love it. Now, tell me, what do you know about the round tower? Why is it such a secret? No one else will speak of it."

Hugh took a stool across from her, still staring at her as if she was not of this earth. "As you must know, no one goes there. It is haunted, so they say. Once I stood below it at night and shivered so badly I thought I had caught the ague. I was cold from head to foot. Then the guard came out and chased me away." He shrugged. "This is the same story everyone here tells."

"What about Scardon?"

"Oh-ho-ho, that one. My father was here when Scardon took over The Keep. He was the armorer at the time. He is gone now, died one night; a mystery, that. I had no time to question him before he died and I did not care at the time." His eyes became merry. "I, uh, had other things to occupy my time, being a very young man with love and conquests on his mind. Many who worked here when Scardon was in residence have drifted away. These are all new people, most of them anyway. Rajahr and Lydia remain, that is about all who I know of. Orion was here, but he left to meet with Henry, who was a prince at that time. Scardon left not long after."

"Why?" Juel wondered.

Hugh shrugged. "I have no idea, my lady."

"Why do you insist on calling me that?"

"My lady?"

"Yes."

All of a sudden the one named Clyde was standing before Juel. "Elizabeth" was softly heard from beneath the hood.

Juel was startled. "Why does he say that name?" Her hand was pressed to her breast.

"Maybe," Hugh said, with a sigh of capitulation, "it is because that is your first name."

"What?" Juel leaped from the stool, sending it flying to the floor. "What do you mean?"

The hood was whipped from "Clyde's" head and a young woman appeared before Juel!

"Oh . . . my . . . God," Juel gasped, looking at the face. "You . . . are . . . so like—"

Juel couldn't finish. She felt as if she looked into a

331

polished mirror.

"Yes, my cousin, I am Clytie de Monteforte."

"And I'm the king of France," Hugh chuckled, making a nervous jest.

The two women did not look at him.

Then Hugh grew serious, very serious as the two women stared at each other like ghosts from the past.

Chapter Thirty-Two

"He kills everyone."

Staring in a trance at the image of herself, Juel could only ask, "Who does?"

Even though Hugh warned her not to with his bright-blue eyes, Clytie de Monteforte looked back at Juel. "Scardon," Clytie said. "I speak of him, the evil one. He'll come back here one day to The Keep."

Juel put her hands to her head. "I think I should sit down. Suddenly I am light-headed." Her hands fell to her lap. "This is all too much at one time."

Clytie, too, had fallen silent. She was staring at Juel, knowing it was true now, that they looked so much alike. After a time of recovery, Juel began to speak.

"I have so many questions." She shook her head. "Where do we begin?"

While the cousins continued to stare at each other, Hugh went outside to tell the workers they could return home, then stepped back inside to bolt the door. He stood there for a time, letting the women get their fill of studying each other. They spoke softly now and he waited, not wishing to disturb them. He watched at the window, afraid Orion would return at any time and find the shock of his life. He had been gone for a week now; there was no telling when he would return.

The women hugged, with tears in their eyes, then Clytie sat back down on her stool. "Now," she began. "I think your first question would be how we came to be cousins. Am I right?"

"Yes, yes," Juel said, feeling her head whirl from all the excitement.

Clytie sighed. "Sir Guy Hunter is your father. We are actually second cousins. My father, Piers de Monteforte, is Guy's cousin. Your real father died just recently and, prepare for another shock: He left you very wealthy. You, Elizabeth Juel Hunter, are an heiress now."

Juel swallowed hard. "That is a shock. Do you mean to say—" she shook her head again "—that Ranice de Monteforte is . . . *was* my cousin also?"

"Yes, but that is also very confusing. You see, Ranice was my half sister. Scardon told me all about her, how she had me sent away when I was a little girl. She was only in her teens, but she hated me. She wanted our father's love and he favored me over her. This much I can remember."

"Ranice wanted all, to leave you to inherit nothing," Juel figured for herself.

"This is true. My father is still alive, I am told, but he is old and has been out of his head since I disappeared."

"You were intended for Orion, to become his wife." Juel gasped. "You *are* his wife!"

"I don't know anything about that," Clytie said.

As Clytie drew an arm across her perspiring

forehead, Juel's eyes were drawn to her hair. It was as dark as her own, yet it was very wavy, surrounding her face, with shiny swirls that reached to her waist. She'd pulled it out from the cowl and Juel stared at her eyes now. They were darker and deeper than her own, almost an emerald green.

Juel smiled. "I feel like I'm looking into a mirror."

"Me, too."

"What happens now?" Juel wondered aloud. "Orion has been looking for you, has sent the knights out to search for you. He says he loves me but must find you. There's something that drives him to search for you, and it's more than the idea that you should be his wife. I don't even know if Orion *wants* a wife. I wish he'd make up his mind. Although," she added wistfully, "I'd wait for Orion my whole life if need be. There's no one else for me, nor will there ever be."

Clytie's darker green eyes were full of pain. "I cannot be Orion's wife. I must not be. You see, I could never love him. Soon I will return to my father's home to take care of him. It will be a shock to Piers, maybe a pleasant one that might restore his mind."

"Why is it impossible for you to love Orion?" Juel couldn't believe she'd asked that. If Orion were to love another, like Clytie, she would wither away.

"I love another. But Morgan Locklear does not know I exist. He is one of the king's knights. I saw him one day as he rode through the town of Hastings with King Henry. I looked into his eyes and he smiled . . ." Her eyes teared. "As he was also smiling at all the young women in town that day. He is a lover, that is plain to see. Even if he noticed me, our love would be impossible." *He would kill me,* Clytie did not reveal.

Hoping Clytie's sad face would lift, Juel smiled at her. "My brother is a lover, too, but Jay has eyes only for Dawn Peyton. They are very much in love. They will soon wed, he told me recently."

"I know you have a brother. He doesn't inherit the Hunter Castle because Guy strangely wished for a female in his family to take possession of the castle and lands. Jay will get only what you want to give him," Clytie said. "I would like to meet my male cousin one day, but I'm afraid that's impossible. No one else must know I'm here."

"Why *are* you here? What were you doing with Scardon?" Juel breathed deeply. "I have so many questions, I don't know where to begin."

"This is true. I couldn't answer all your questions, not even in one day. I'm here because I have to hide from Scardon. Hugh was in the village one day, looking for boys to work in the armory. I had some knowledge of this work, since I'd worked in the Hastings forge for a man who also helped me hide from Scardon. When Scardon found out I was there, Andrew told me I must leave there, that he didn't want trouble from Scardon. He helped me out the back way one night when Scardon came looking."

"You have been hiding from Scardon half your life?" Juel said, not asking where Clytie had been when she was a child. "How awful," Juel went on after Clytie nodded sadly.

"I've escaped from Scardon many times. He always found me."

"Did he ever . . ." Juel couldn't form the question.

But Clytie knew what she meant. "Almost, many times. There's a man who rides with Scardon. He is very ugly and bloodthirsty, but he saved me every time when Scardon would have had his way with me. I owe my life to Hadwin. As I said, he's terrible to look at, with one white eye and a scar running down his face."

Visualizing this ugly man, Juel shuddered. "You have been through so much, Clytie."

"And you don't know all of it."

"There is more?" Juel asked.

"Yes. Scardon wants me now because he knows how much I resemble Elizabeth Hunter, the heiress." Clytie stared at her meaningfully. *"You,* Juel."

Juel could only gasp. "He knows I'm here?"

"I'm afraid I don't know about that, he just knows we look alike. Scardon fears coming here. The curses he put on this place keep him away. He believes they've turned on him. But he will come, one day, when he has built enough courage. He will come and try to take Sutherland again."

"He took it once before?"

"Scardon is a robber baron. He has taken over many lands and castles, never staying at each more than five years, to do his dirty work. I believe he remained here almost fifteen years, the longest at any one place, so Hugh said. He murdered Orion's parents to get what was once called Sutherland Castle. Now The Keep.

"Hugh talks about the mystery of the round tower. No one goes there. Last night I stood below the tower looking up. It was so dark that no one saw me. There is a curse there. I could feel its evil breath on my face. There was also a cry of distress coming from that place. Someone is up in that tower. Locked there. I know it, I can feel it."

"Someday I will go there," Juel said. "Before, I told

myself it was not of my concern. One day I'll do it. I believe Lydia expects this of me, even though she tells me to stay away. She goes there, but does not tarry long. Only she is free from the curse Scardon put on The Keep."

"I hope you never have to look into Scardon's eyes, as I've done. You would think you were looking into the pit of hell."

"I've seen this look," Juel said. "Orion has had the same look of dark emptiness in his eyes. But not so much of late. He even drinks less than he used to."

"I have heard Hugh say this," Clytie said. She looked Juel straight in the eyes. "There is more I have not told you."

Juel shrugged and shivered. "What more could there be?"

"I am a spy."

"Oh—no."

"Yes. What is worse, I don't spy for King Henry."

Again Juel jumped up from her stool. "My God, you spy for the French!"

"Yes." Clytie also stood.

"You are in danger! Orion will kill you if he finds you here!"

The woman in the brown cloak sighed deeply and sadly. "I know," she said. "But I don't know how to get out of it. There are those indeed who would kill me if I don't deliver." She spread slender hands before her cousin. "I'm in distress, Juel."

The whites of her eyes rolling as she stared about the forge, Juel said, "No! You do not make armor for the French. You cannot. Not here!"

"Clytie, you've said too much!" a voice hissed.

A man stepped out of the shadows and suddenly Juel was shrouded in darkness as a heavy blanket came over her head. Through the blanket she was forced to breathe vapors that were very foul-smelling. She felt stifled and faint. Her heart was pounding furiously.

Then she knew no more.

Chapter Thirty-Three

A big summer moon glided across the sky as Orion rode out from the inn he'd stayed at. The night-shrouded forest closed around him like a blanket when he entered. His medallion rode his chest this night and winked in the moon's intermittent gentle rays. He did not always wear the medallion with the hunter and the three stars; he'd felt it would bring him luck this night and in many days to come.

He believed he'd need more luck; he hadn't had much lately. Everyone was close-mouthed about the movements of the French near Pevensey and East-bourne.

He would ride far and meet with Duncan in the morning. He could ride without anxiety and dread once again. He could even face the day and walk in the sunlight.

Juel, ah, his Juel, she'd helped him through his many fears.

In other times he'd imbibed heavily, stopping often at pubs to lift a horned drinking vessel, and by mid-

341

night would return home or to another inn drunk as a lord.

Ha! Now he almost detested the stuff. Well . . . almost. He'd been tempted to share a bottle the night before with a winsome wench. Then the image of his beautiful heiress had come to mind. He'd grown hard, and it hadn't been because the wench had leaned over his table one too many times. No, he'd hardly seen the curvaceous melons she thrust in his face. They had blurred and in their place had been the most lovely little breasts ever. Juel's!

He was thinking more about John Scardon these days. He thought of all the armor Scardon had taken with him when he'd left. Worth a small fortune, these trappings of knights could hire many a rough mercenary. Aye, John Scardon would have his own mercenaries. Maybe the very same who'd sacked and burned the village and ambushed him and his men, almost ravishing the lovely young maid Autumn Meaux.

His leg still pained him, and he looked down at the long scar, carved by a close brush with death.

Now he felt strong, and it was all because of Juel. He'd not brought Shadow; it was too long a ride for his pet. Ha, that one had taken to trailing Juel about the manor, and she cared for him, fed him when Orion was away. Orion loved Juel, and he could never love any other. She was important to him, as much as breathing air.

He had dreamed of her every night since he'd been gone. They'd been at the river's edge again, this time in his dream. The river was the one he'd remembered from his childhood. How beautifully it ran in the warm summertime. Willow trees drooped into the water. The sky was filled with slowly drifting clouds, enormous, sculpted masses.

As he rode, he remembered the dream. Behind the river there was a hill, on the top of which stood an ancient fortress in ruins. He saw Juel going into the water on tiptoe and letting out a squeal of delight at the coldness of it. He saw himself wading in until the water reached nearly to his hips. He and Juel were naked, making great splashes as they hit the water, playing tricks on each other. They dived underwater. The shock of the cold took Juel's breath away. He beheld her watery nakedness, her breasts, her womanhood when she came up spluttering. And then he entered her. Water was flowing through his hair, and hers. They glistened with wet in the sunlight. They belonged to the stream, were part of the water's progress, its lively splashings, its undulant movements.

Floating along imaginatively, he saw pleasing landscapes. Juel was with him. Everything was on a grander scale, everything seemed deeper, higher, more meaningful, much more beautiful. Their bodies had almost come together when his dream had awakened him.

Now he shook his head, wishing to God Juel were with him so that he could make love to her. He missed her and needed to get this business done with so that he could be with her, forever.

He skirted Ashurst Marsh and crossed the Brighton-Hastings Road. Once again he would ride far this night, but not to Eastbourne; that would be too far for his horse. He intended to head for Arundel when he met up with Duncan and Ruark.

He was alone this night but for his horse. He would head for Pevensey Bay. French knights hid out in the lagoons and he'd heard there were some mercenaries who would "blast their jabbers" while in their cups, telling of their weak points and positions as they gathered to cross the Channel.

He might even find some who'd ridden with Scardon of late, or knew where he could be found.

Juel knew he was keeping a secret. Soon he would tell her she was Elizabeth Hunter. An heiress. He laughed with love in his heart. He was so happy he could howl at the moon.

This beautiful woman loved him! She loved him!

Juel, an heiress!

Orion was dreaming. At first everything was misty and splintered. He was in the water again with Juel, but underlying the gratification was a presage of catastrophe. Suddenly the waters began to move faster. Faster and faster the images flowed past, as if time had fallen out of kilter. He heard the water's roar and rush. His heart cramped with fear. The water now sped heavily, all roiled and torn, through narrow gateways and against high white walls beneath the water. He was being carried to the church where he'd last seen his parents. The church was full of river water, and it flowed over the silver candelabra on the altar table.

Orion gasped in his dream. He couldn't find Juel. The waves mounted higher, the candles went out. Still, it was not completely dark in the church. The water was faintly lit up from within by a greenish-blue light. He was a small boy of five. Then he saw his mother and he screamed for her to come to him. His father was there, too, but he could not reach him. Dead, they went floating past him. Scardon laughed, a sinister, perverted sound, bubbles emerging from his mouth. Like a corpse himself, Orion let his body be carried along by the waves. Utter despair leaded his heart.

"Juel, Juel!" he heard himself call out from the water. "I'm sinking!"

"What are you so afraid of?" she asked as she swam before him. Her black hair twisted and swirled wildly under the water, her body greenish-white. "Have you no faith at all, Orion Sutherland?"

Orion awoke from his nightmare with a horrible start and sat up. His body was ice-cold, as if he really had been immersed in water. He looked around and saw his horse standing nearby asleep. Orion's hands and feet were leaden and had no feeling, yet deep inside him was a sensation of blessing and comfort.

It was as if there glowed within him a source of warmth and light. Looking up into the midnight sky, he saw three huge stars, no more.

Slowly he folded his hands and thanked God on his knees for Juel.

Chapter Thirty-Four

"Where am I?" Juel asked when she came to, blinking her eyes. She had been dreaming about Orion, kneeling before him as he sat in a wide-armed chair. She'd been about to close her mouth over him, but first she'd told him of her love . . . Her eyes flared wide now as she remembered what had happened before the lights were extinguished in her head. "Where—?"

"You are here, the same place," Clytie interjected, patting Juel's arm. "Can you remember?"

"The forge?" Juel glanced around the heavy stone walls. "But I thought I would be taken away." She looked at Clytie. "Didn't you say too much?"

"Yes," Clytie laughed. "I did say too much. I usually do. It gets me into much trouble, my big mouth. I convinced Hugh that you would not report what has been going on here. He believes me. I'm usually right about people and how they think."

Groaning, her hand to her head, Juel sat up. A blanket slipped away from the pallet she'd been reclining upon. "My head feels like it's been in a vise.

347

What was that obnoxious stuff anyway?"

Clytie did not laugh this time. "It was a sleeping drug. Puts the person to sleep instantly."

Feeling her head, Juel said, "That is one thing I do know. I wish I'd had that some nights when I couldn't sleep. Then again, I wouldn't like to wake up with an aching head like this."

"I'm sorry about that. Hugh did it before I could stop him. He's very embarrassed for having done so and promised he won't do it again."

"He had better not!" Juel looked at Clytie's concerned face. "What happens now?" She came to her feet, dropped the blanket, then brushed herself off where straw had clung to her.

Her cousin shrugged. "I think you should return to the manor before someone comes looking for you."

"That would be wise, wouldn't it." As Juel straightened her dress, she noticed that Clytie was staring at her most strangely. "What is it? Do I have a spider on me?"

Clytie pressed her lips together, then asked, "How long have you been with child?"

One of Juel's eyebrows rose and her eyes widened incredulously. "With ch-child?" She shook her head after she'd recovered. "I'm afraid I don't understand."

"I thought so." Clytie nodded toward Juel's stomach. "I helped you onto the pallet and removed the blanket from around you. It was wrapped around your belly."

Juel shrugged. "So, what does that mean?"

Clytie patiently explained. "I used to help a French midwife tend and deliver babies and I know a pregnant woman when I see one. At first I thought your stomach might have just contracted into a tight, hard ball out of fear. But I noticed it did not relax, it remained that way. You must be a few months along."

"What?" Juel gasped. She looked down, felt around with her fingers, and sucked in her breath again when she felt the roundness Clytie spoke of.

"You feel it now?" Clytie said.

Remembering something, Juel rolled her eyes heavenward. "Oh ... my God, I haven't had my monthly flux in two—"

"Months," Clytie furnished for her cousin. "This is another reason I wouldn't allow Hugh to have you taken away somewhere until we could finish our work."

Her eyes immediately filling with tears, Juel began to cry. She sat back down onto the pallet while the tears began to flow rapidly. Clytie sat next to Juel, her arm about her shoulders, and tried to explain that everything would be all right.

"This isn't so unusual, Juel, it happens to women all the time." She smiled tenderly at Juel's wet profile. "Especially when you're in love," she laughed. "That's when it happens the most. Here, drink this, it will make you feel better."

Taking the cup of spicy apple cider, Juel drank thirstily. Then she looked at Clytie with alarm. "That was not—"

"No, it does not have anything in it that will make you sleep again. I promise."

Juel swayed and then righted herself. "I'm glad. I wouldn't like to wake up with that same bad headache again."

With a flushed face, Hugh stepped into the doorway.

"I had no idea," he said, looking at both women. "We have no desire to harm anyone. Please accept my apology, too."

"Yes, yes, I accept both of yours," Juel said a bit impatiently, waving her hand with a nervous laugh.

Wordlessly, Hugh and Clytie looked at her, waiting.

Juel's lips pressed together in a tight line. "What do we do now?" She looked very helpless. "You are making armor for the French and Clytie is a spy against the English. Orion is spying for King Henry against the French . . . what a tangle! Oh, yes, and I am pregnant!"

A swift shadow passed over Clytie's features. She was worried about her cousin.

Juel moaned, staring around the darkening stone room. "Of course there is more: I find I've a cousin, no less my lover's long-lost wife." She shrugged, giving a helpless whimper. "And I learn I'm an heiress."

Clytie tilted her head. "Why are you looking at me like that, Elizabeth?" She bit her lip. "Juel, I mean."

"Elizabeth. Juel. What does it matter." She gave another helpless little whimper. "What does my father, Peter Reynaude, know about this? Or *does* he know? Of course, he had to have known who my mother was—" Juel gulped. "Why didn't he tell me? And is Jay my real brother or not?"

Now it was Clytie's turn to look helpless. "I have none of these answers, Juel. Why don't you go and ask Lydia?"

"Lydia?" Juel spread her hands. "What would she know about any of this?"

Very quietly, Clytie answered, "Lydia said: You're the one."

Juel's brow furrowed. "How would you know that?"

350

"Simple. You shared the same conversation in your drugged sleep that you had in reality with Lydia."

"I said—" Juel's eyes narrowed to hazel-green slits. "What else did I say?"

Now Clytie and Hugh both grinned. Picking up the empty cider cup, Hugh went laughing out of the room and Clytie whispered very intimately, "I love you, Orion, I love you, love you, love—"

Laughing, Juel held up her hand. "That's enough, Clytie. I hope that conversation went no further!"

"Trust me. It did not."

"Now what?" Juel asked as she made to walk out.

Wisely, Clytie looked Juel straight in the eyes and said with eloquent logic, "That depends on you, Elizabeth Juel. You will do what you must because you hold the key in your hands now."

Juel turned back once, asking breathlessly, "What about you and Hugh?"

"We can only pray you do the right thing for everyone involved. Only you hold the key."

Later, Juel paced the walls in her belowstairs chamber, going over her apprehensions. She had willed herself to walk back to her room; Jay and Dawn had both wanted to see her but she needed to be alone.

"Why must I have this great burden on my shoulders? Look," she said to the wall, as if it were a person she spoke to, "I am only one small woman. My shoulders are not very large. And I'm a pregnant woman, too. What can I do?"

—I must remain silent, for Clytie and Hugh's sake. But they make armor for the French! What if they

are caught? Orion and his knights will kill them!

—Orion works so hard at his spying activities, and if I remain silent on what goes on here in the forge, am I not deceiving him also?

Juel had been pacing the chamber, wringing her hands. Only now did she stop to look at the stone wall, thinking how foolish to speak to a blank wall, and thought of God instead.

"Lord, help me, what am I going to do?" Juel demanded softly but fiercely. "Now I have secrets that must be kept."

"Stop worrying." The words came to Juel as if from a mouth of golden fire. "Whatever will be will be."

Her strength and will flowed out.

God help her, she must have gotten the word!

Chapter Thirty-Five

"Look!" Juel exclaimed. "There's another golden mushroom and there's a lovely frog right beside it."

The children rushed to look at it while Juel and Lydia stood back. "Don't get lost!" Juel called to them, then turned to Lydia. "We must talk, Lydia. Seriously."

"I know this," Lydia said, adjusting the kerchief that rounded her head. She released a held breath as she sat upon a log like an old woman. "You want to ask me about the round tower. You will go there soon, I know this, too."

Her eyebrow shot up. "You will not try to stop me?" Juel was surprised. "I thought there was a curse on the tower and no one must go there."

Lydia sighed wearily. "I believe it is almost time for you to go there." She watched the children walking about the mushroom exclaiming over its spherical beauty. "No, I can't stop you. Whatever will be will be."

Juel gasped softly. These were exactly the words that had been answered in her prayer. "Why did you say the

353

words 'You are the one' to me that day?" She smiled as the smallest girl squealed after touching the mushroom and looked to Juel for approval.

All of a sudden, Autumn came through the trees. The girl had been following close behind after learning they'd gone to the woods with the orphans. Now she had caught up with them. She wanted to be with the children; she missed her own beloved sisters so. Her red hair shone brilliantly in the afternoon sun filtering through the trees, and Juel thought she was most beautiful and mature for one so young and prayed the knights would soon find her sisters.

Turning back to Lydia, Juel asked, "Who is in the round tower?"

"You know someone is there."

"Yes, I do. I feel it."

"It is a woman."

"I thought as much." Juel watched the children playing with Autumn for a few moments. "Who is she?"

With a helpless gesture, Lydia said, "I am not sure who she is. I have only seen her through a peephole as I give her food. She doesn't talk much. There is a curse, you know. I believe Scardon murdered my parents and my children and that now he just might come back and kill me, too, for revealing to you that there is a hex on the woman locked away there."

Juel's eyes burned into Lydia's.

"Scardon kills everyone," Lydia said. "If not their body then their soul."

The same words Clytie had spoken!

Juel had never missed Orion as much as she did at this time. Knowing what she did now, she could talk to

354

him and maybe they could go to the round keep together. This was part of his great fear: the round tower and its abominable curse. Clytie had said she held the key. Had there been a double meaning in those words?

"Is there a guard I must go through?" Juel asked.

"Yes . . . Yardley is his name . . . and he is most fierce."

"I'll go there soon." Juel gave a nervous laugh. "When I have built enough nerve."

Before Juel walked over to the children and Autumn, Lydia said, "I did not use my powers of concentration to bring you to Orion as Will told him, you know."

"What?" Juel said, whirling about. "I'm afraid I do not understand."

"Alice and Will, they said I brought you to Orion that night. They lied. Rajahr has dismissed Alice and Will Becker. He sent them away without food or coin. They are bad people and Alice must be punished for what she did to Dawn Peyton." Lydia shook her head. "I did not use my powers, for they seem to have left me in recent years. I rely more upon the teachings of Christ now."

Juel shook her head to clear it. "Orion brought me to him in the attic room just by thinking about it?"

Lydia grinned. "Yes. He must have. It was not I!"

Twirling about in her rust-colored skirts as she went to the children and the golden mushroom, Juel called out, "Isn't love grand!"

Not far away in a lovely wooded copse, Jay and

355

Dawn were lying together in a bed of leaves enjoying the beautiful late-summer day. She was wearing a pretty yellow shift he'd purchased for her just the week before. She wore her hair loose and it flowed over her shoulders, blending with the yellow of the shift and contrasting with the blackness of his hair. They spoke endearments to each other, rolled in the leaves, touched, kissed, stroked.

Jay was in love. He'd never known what it was like to be in love with that one special woman. He'd had plenty of women, but never had he felt the wonderful emotion he was feeling now.

Dawn was in love. She'd never known ecstasy of any sort, nor had a man ever made love to her. Now she couldn't get enough of making love and was very pleased that soon she would become Jay's bride.

Jay gazed into Dawn's sweet nut-brown eyes. "Should we wait until we are wed?"

Her laugh was delightful. "Wait for what?" She read it in his eyes then, the lust, the love. "Wait to make love again?" She grabbed him about the waist, released him, and sat atop him. "Oh, no, you will not get away from me now, my green-eyed man!"

He stared up at her with love and excitement in his eyes. "What will you do to me?" Helplessly his arms fell back among the leaves. "Ravish me if you must." His eyes twinkled up at her. "But be gentle, will you, love?"

In a few minutes they had both removed their clothes. Dawn's yellow shift lay carelessly upon his darker clothing, among the colorful leaves. The sun filtered in and felt warm on their uncovered skin. Jay lay back down and Dawn began to kiss him all over, starting at his brown nipples, then down the long torso to his belly button.

Jay's stomach contracted as she kissed him there and swirled her tongue around the button's rim. "You know what to do quite naturally, don't you." He chuckled, resting his hand on her head. "I guess I've taught you something about love?"

Dawn said nothing. And he forgot he'd asked a question when she began to slide her tongue down his belly, halting tantalizingly over his shaft. Jay groaned deep in his throat as she closed her hand about him, slim fingers clasping and beginning to move over him.

He stopped her once to take her hands and kiss her fingertips adoringly, one by one. Then he let her go down to do her magic.

A wondrous rapture flowed into Jay as Dawn worked her hands and mouth over and around his shining blade, slippery, delicious, like nothing he'd ever felt before. He'd been with whores who'd not been as dexterous and creative as this angel of the morning.

He looked down at her bright-yellow head, loving this woman who'd captured his heart and soul the moment he'd first gazed upon her. She'd trapped him forever. He had run after her—and she'd caught him!

Before she could bring him to climax, Jay took her shoulders, lifted her in the air, and brought her body down upon his glistening manhood. She straddled him, riding up and down until his eyes glazed, his breath quickened. Reaching up, he took hold of her small breasts—and this was his undoing.

"Dawn! Dawn! Oh! God!"

Her head was thrown back as they exploded together in a blinding flash of shivering heat. When it was over they lay close in the lazy afternoon, amid bright leaves, the sun's intermittent rays washing over them like a warm, sweet, silent lullabye.

Soon they slept, her head on his chest.

Chapter Thirty-Six

"Good-bye," Juel said, tearfully hugging her cousin around the neck, their cheeks close. Then she pushed her away to look at her. "I will miss you."

Standing back as she pressed a cool hand on Juel's cheek, Clytie said, "I will return some day, you know. Now that we've met I cannot stay away forever. It would be like throwing away a part of myself, like a beautiful mirror but so much prettier inside and out than I."

"Oh no," Juel disagreed. "*You* are the one who is so pretty." She giggled softly. "Although we do look much alike, do we not?"

"Yes. And I suppose you could not call us ugly as frogs." Clytie laughed, tossing her dark mane. "I will go before Orion Sutherland returns. It didn't take long to fashion the pieces of armor we needed to give to the French. We will meet some of the Duke of Burgundy's men on the border and a ship will take the armor pieces across the Channel."

Juel breathed in quickly. "Oh, you might meet up

with Orion then. He goes that way. Or, I should say, he *comes* that way. Any day now I expect he will arrive. He has been away too long. I pray he has not met with foul play . . . or worse."

Clytie shook her head. "From what I've heard of Orion Sutherland, I believe he's too mean to die that easily." She took in Juel's sudden frown. "At least, for your sake, I hope he's not too mean."

With a wistful look toward the road beyond the gate, Juel sighed. "Deep inside Orion is kind and gentle. When he drinks he's like—" A verse from the Bible came to her "'—A roaring lion seeking whom he may devour.'" Juel smiled softly. "I believe I've tamed the fiery dragon just a little bit. He's much nicer than when first I came here and he doesn't get drunk as often."

"Why did you say dragon after you said lion?"

Juel stared at Clytie. "I've never seen either in real life, only pictures in books and on tapestries. I believe the dragon is the fiercer of the two. After all, the lion only roars and looks hungry. But the dragon, he throws out flames, owns fierce claws and green scales, and looks . . ." Juel searched for a word.

"Hungry, too!" Clytie said with a laugh. She turned away to climb into a wagon with a strange tent built over it. "I must go, Juel, it's getting late."

Lifting her eyes to the sky, Juel saw that the sun was climbing quickly to midday. "Yes, you should go before the knights return from their road inspection. They check to see if any poachers or other strangers crossed the roads at night and went into the forest on the other side."

"If they do stop us," Clytie explained, "we'll just tell them we are taking armor to the English."

"I don't believe the English are going to be so foolish as to wear such armor," Juel said before she thought.

"Oh?" Clytie looked at the back of the hooded driver. "That's interesting. They will be lighter if they fight without all the heavy armor. How do you know this?"

Juel pulled a vague face. "Hmm, I'm not sure if this was only a dream I had."

For a long time Juel stood and watched as the two covered wagons swayed and bumped down the road. She was worried about the knights coming along and stopping the wagons, but soon she saw them returning, Howell Armstrong among them.

By the time Orion's knights reached the castle grounds the wagons were well out of sight, only a faint dust cloud hovering on the hilly horizon.

The blond knight leaned over his saddle to look into Juel's flushed face.

"Couldst thou, fair maiden, give drink to thirsty travelers?" Howell asked with a very handsome grin as the other knights laughed along with Juel.

"Of course, brave knight of old," Juel quipped as she began to turn back to the guard house, her skirts swishing in the dirt.

Juel swayed dizzily for a moment, then righted herself and kept walking.

The knights were laughing and riding alongside Juel when all of a sudden Howell leapt from his horse. He caught her just as she would have crumpled to the stone flooring under the guard house.

"What happened?" one of the younger knights called down.

"She's fainted," Howell said as he carried her toward

361

the courtyard. "Awake, fair maiden," Howell said tenderly to the woman he fervently wished were his own.

Juel's eyelashes fluttered. "I am not a . . . maiden . . . fair knight." The manor's roof whirled in Juel's vision. "I'm a . . . pregnant . . . woman. Orion's . . ."

Then everything went black again.

The young knight ran after Howell. "What did she say?" He was prone to gossip with the others. "Pregnant? Orion's?"

"She doesn't know what she's saying, Alfred," Howell lied, not knowing if Orion had this news yet. "She said she must get that pregnant woman to do the ironing."

Alfred stopped and scratched the top of his head. "That don't make sense."

"I know," Howell called back, then softly to himself, "Not much does since Orion's absence. Gone too long. Well, he better get back soon."

"What was that?" Alfred called as he tried to keep up with the bigger knight's long stride.

"I said, Orion will be back soon."

"He will?" Hope flared in Alfred's eyes as he stood still in the great hall, watching Howell climb the inside stairs. "That's wonderful news!"

He bounded up the stairs, repeating, "That's wonderful news!"

"Yes," Howell snapped, slamming the door in Alfred's curious face as he brought Juel to Orion's bed. "Isn't it."

When Juel opened her eyes she felt something soft, firm, moist—against her mouth.

Someone was kissing her!

Orion! Home! Then she blinked her eyes wide. "Howell! For God's sake, what are you doing?" Juel pushed to her elbows as the blond knight stepped back. She touched her mouth with two fingers. "What was that all about?"

Howell sighed, looking down at Juel like a big, round-eyed puppy. "I just had to do that. Just once. To see how you tasted."

"Howell!" Juel snapped, rising from Orion's bed. "You . . . you shouldn't say things like that. Why didn't you bring me a cup of water instead?"

He shrugged. "Didn't you let Hugh kiss you?"

"What?" Juel asked with an incredulous look. "Hugh, the armorer?"

Oh-oh, Juel thought. *Tread cautiously here.*

Howell nodded. "Yes, Hugh. You've been making visits to the forge at night."

"You should go now," Juel said, smoothing the covers on the bed. "Please go. I'm all right now."

"You're pregnant."

Juel spun about. "And what would you know about that?" Her hand was pressed to her breast. Howell was grinning silently. "Who told you that, Howell?" she asked again.

"You did, pretty lady," he said, one eyebrow raised. "Before I carried you into the manor and up here." His eyes narrowed as he came closer.

"Kiss me, lovely Juel."

"Howell . . ." Juel groaned. "What is wrong with you? Have you not heard that I am Orion's woman?" She wanted to stomp her foot and reveal that she was an heiress, too, and how dare he! But she had to tell Orion first.

363

"Come, pretty heiress, give this besotted simple knight a kiss and I'll not tell of your visits to Hugh."

Heiress! Did he say—? Juel licked her lips. "Howell, did you just call me an heiress?" Her eyes narrowed. "How would you know about that?"

Howell seemed worried. "Didn't Orion tell you that a messenger came from Baron Hunter's barrister?" He gnawed the corner of his lip. "He was going to break the news before he left to go and meet Duncan and Ruark. He didn't . . ."

"No! He did not!" Now Juel did stomp her foot. "And you get out, roguish knight! How dare you steal a kiss from me!"

She backed him to the door and he grinned sheepishly. "I always knew you were something like a princess." His grin fell away, replaced by a black frown. "You would do well to stay away from Hugh, the armorsmith. Orion might get jealous. I know *I* would want a beautiful heiress like you all to myself."

Howell's eyes grew hot for one moment longer, then Juel opened the door and pushed him out. He grinned and shook a finger at her before she slammed the door in his handsome face!

"Men!" Juel said, crossing her arms over her chest as she tapped one slippered foot. "Will I ever begin to figure them out?"

Chapter Thirty-Seven

Day after day milky clouds wandered across a high
blue sky, making long shadows that raced over the
landscape. The beeches, resplendent in full silver-green
foliage, cast a pleasant shade as Orion rode beneath
their branches. It was delightfully cool in the lustrous
verdant twilight that filtered through the leaves even at
midday and he was comfortable in the leather tunic
that clung to his wide shoulders.

He was riding toward Billings Inn, near Schuneman
Marsh, where he would catch up with Duncan and
Ruark to find out what they had learned, if anything.
He himself had learned of the French Constable
d'Albret's movements across the Channel.

Orion was alert to every sound. He knew that French
knights and the men of robber barons hid in these
forests. He had kept a few Frenchmen from reaching
the border with news by dispatching them in haste.
They had been the first to attack and he'd only been
protecting his own life.

He breathed deeply of rich earth. His thoughts rested

on Juel and what his beautiful heiress could be doing at this time of day. Maybe she told her stories to the little children she loved so much. Her cats and Shadow would trail her, anticipating a pat on the head, a loving stroke, or a delectable morsel from her hand.

Within the stands of beeches the earth smelled richly of humus and fungi, and gnats danced a mad and merry dance in shafts of light. Here and there were low, damp places where a brook slowly wound through the woods. Tall rushes grew at the edge of the marsh, near buttercups of varnished yellow and pale forget-me-nots, here in thick clumps and there scattered over the marshy ground.

The fragile bluish flowers made him think of Juel, what she'd look like with a crown of them about her head.

He had become wonderfully aware of the mystery of the natural world. He felt himself, his own large body, young, strong, and hale, alive with vivid motion. Like the big horse under him he flexed his muscles and opened his mouth wide to shout at the forest. His own voice rang in his ears as a strange echo that resounded from tree to tree.

Orion looked about and grinned, patted his horse's mane. "Hope there are no strangers about who heard that, big lad. Just got carried away, I guess. It won't happen again." Orion kept grinning like a boy with his first love. He had been remembering the first time he'd come into Juel's body and wanted to howl and howl and howl.

Billings Inn lay up ahead, suddenly there at the edge of the forest in a tiny clearing. Duncan and Ruark were waiting, already lifting a drinking horn when Orion stepped into the mote-filled room.

The handsome knights greeted one another and sat down to sup and drink. Orion drank a cider containing no alcohol and smiled as the plump maid placed fat sausages, brown tarts, and smoked eels on the rough-hewn table. He ate as if this might be his last meal, falling silent until the last of the sausages and eels had been finished.

Duncan and Ruark watched the plump maid with the hourglass shape in her white peasant blouse embroidered with brown threads, red skirt, several petticoats, and knitted white stockings. Mostly they stared at her great bouncing breasts. Duncan was the first to pull his stare away.

"You've a hearty appetite," said Duncan, the dark, handsome knight. "You'll need all your strength when you return to The Keep." He chuckled. "A jewel awaits your pleasure."

Orion bit into a blueberry tart with heavy brown pastry. "Don't get me any more excited than I already am to return to her, Duncan," he said with his mouth full.

The three of them laughed and joked for a while. Then it was time for business. The information Orion had unearthed of the French movements and the messages he'd dispatched were being sent by cog even as they talked. Now they spoke of their king and what other spies had related to them when they'd returned from across the Channel.

Orion's voice was low. "Henry is raising an army of thousands of archers and men-at-arms, besides some unarmored lancers and knifemen."

Ruark took up. "Aye. They'll be supported by a large

artillery train with sixty-five or more gunners."

"They've been preparing for the last two years, Harry has told me," Orion said, resting his arm over the back of the high bench. "Provisions, munitions, horses, and ships are being assembled on a massive scale."

"I think our work is almost done. Soon the king will fight."

"Soon," Orion said. "Yes. I've ordered fresh meat for Harry and his men from our yards. Cattle and sheep will be driven to the ports on the hoof. Ships will be supplied by the Cinque Ports or else hired or impounded. Eventually a fleet of fifteen hundred vessels will assemble in the Solent."

The three dark knights left early the next morning and rode all day. There were places where the heather grew, and coarse grasses, broom scrub, prickly juniper. Out in the open on high dry ground, the sunlight glowed and glittered and dragonflies came up from the sedges. The knights looked up to see their stiff-veined wings shining and flashing as they hovered and dashed.

"They seem to know a secret," Duncan laughed. "What if we could fly around in machines that acted as they do?"

"Highly unlikely that will ever come to pass," Ruark laughed right back. "Machines that stand still above the ground?" He shook his dark head. "The only fantastic machine I've seen is the trebuchet. About the only thing that flies, or hurls, from that are heavy stones, large arrows, or rotting animal carcasses."

"I've heard of the bodies of captured enemies being discharged as missiles over the battlements. Now, *they* did fly!"

"Or Greek fire," Orion said. Suddenly he held his finger over his lips for silence. He frowned, seeming to listen to something nearby.

"It's only a dove," Duncan said. "A mourning dove."

"Whom does he mourn for?" Ruark said. Orion did not smile at the joke. Ruark had noticed that Orion seemed to have his mind on something and was more serious over the past hour.

Along with the mourning doves cooing from a woody copse nearby, the cuckoo sang his loudly resonant song. Orion breathed in the sweet air spiced with a hundred essences of earth, swamp, wood, field, and pond.

In the woods at dusk the underbrush again was heavy, pathless, and grew almost to the horses' muscled thighs. All of a sudden, Orion held up his hand and halted his horse.

"Listen."

They did. There was a rustling consisting of thousands of unidentifiable stirrings, chirpings of insects, buzzings of beetle wings, the faint bubbling of spring water, animals moving furtively through the undergrowth.

"The same sounds," Ruark said. "I hear nothing—"

Orion had placed his finger across his mouth.

The three dark knights stared around then. "I have to relieve myself," Duncan whispered urgently.

Orion nodded, saying they would catch up. The next sound they heard was not the bubbling of spring water!

"He didn't go very far to piss," Ruark whispered as he watched Orion's narrowed, darting eyes.

"There!" Orion alerted, almost knocking Ruark

from his horse with the shout and an outflung arm.

Suddenly three hooded bandits were upon them, closing in on Orion and Ruark. Where was Duncan? Orion wanted to know. There wasn't time to think now, for the bandits were circling with drawn swords.

"English pigs!" shouted the first one to die as Orion's sword flashed in the new light of the moon.

It was growing dark now, and very fast as Orion slipped from his horse. Something was wrong; he could feel it.

Ruark knocked one of the brigands from his horse and he lay sprawled, unmoving.

Duncan burst from the trees, riding his mount into one of the French brigands, toppling him, then driving the point of his blade into the man's throat.

There was only one left, and that one was sprawled on the ground knocked out cold. "Stay!" Orion yelled when Ruark would have sliced the unconscious man's throat with his blade. "He's moaning, seems to be coming to. Let's have a word with him."

"He's a skinny one," Duncan observed. "I suppose one as frail as he seems to be can't hurt anyone much now, dazed as he is."

"Sure, and is that why he fought like the devil then?" Ruark asked.

Dragging the thin body of the man over to a tree, Orion propped him up, took hold of his chin, and snarled, "Wake up, Frenchie, let's have a look at you. Maybe you can tell us what you and your friends have been up to."

When the last man alive began to struggle against Orion, he yanked the hood down and jerked back as if he'd been burned.

"Jesu!" Ruark and Duncan exclaimed at the same time.

The moon spilled through the trees just then, its silvery beams falling over the soft, young face.

She blinked, fell forward, then back against the trunk of the tree, and black hair, luxurious and thick, spilled from the confines of her hood. Orion blinked back with disbelief, his heart in his throat.

Dear God!

Shock waves raced through his system. They'd almost killed her!

Juel!

Chapter Thirty-Eight

"Dear God, Juel!" Orion angrily echoed his terrifying thought. "I could have killed you!"

Clytie stared up at the handsome knight in the moonlight. Who was he? He had called her Juel. Then he must be . . .

"Orion Sutherland?" Clytie stammered.

"Juel!" he snapped, peering at her face. "Why do you sound so strange? What has happened to you? Ah, you are a spy for the French, aren't you?" He yanked her to her feet. "Wait a minute, something is wrong . . . who are you then?"

She pulled a tight smile. "I am not this Juel you speak of, of course."

"Of course." He glared at her. "Then just who are you?"

Brushing off her boyish clothes, Clytie tossed her head. "You already asked me that, and I'm prepared to tell you."

He looked her up and down, noting she was the same size as Juel, with same color hair . . . and eyes perhaps the same green. But that was hard to tell for sure in the dark of the moon.

"They must be twins," Duncan interjected, staring at the beautiful dark-haired female who looked so like Juel but was not Juel; that was plain to tell by her voice, which was unlike Juel's. "What are we going to do with her?"

Orion was waiting for his answer.

How much should she tell? Clytie was wondering. She sighed, lifting her slim shoulders. "I am Clytie de Monteforte, sir. As you must already know, I am a French spy and—" She would not tell him wagons were hidden close by, soon to be taken away by the Frenchmen they had been about to meet. Hugh had not come along and she was glad for that now, otherwise he would have been among the two dead men.

"And?" Orion's eyes glittered beneath the late-summer moon. "What else do you hide?" He did a double take then. "You said Clytie de Monteforte!"

Clytie made herself look surprised. "Yes. Is something wrong, sir?"

Orion opened his mouth wide to take in a deep breath. "No, it is nothing. I . . . it is just that you look so much like someone I know."

With slack jaws, Duncan and Ruark looked at each other and then at Orion. "Aren't you going to tell her . . . ?"

"There's nothing more to say," Orion said with a glare. "Go, Clytie, but never return to these forests again. If we find you here again it very well might be the end of your life."

"I'm going home, sir." It was true, she was going back to her father. Let the Frenchies come and find the armor, she was done with this life. It was time she settled down. "I don't wish to die."

"Yes, go home, Clytie de Monteforte, it's where you belong." He had no wish to question her further; his life was with the woman of his heart. This female spy interested him no longer. "Good-bye, mademoiselle."

With that, Clytie found her horse and rode away into the moonlit forest.

"Why didn't you take her back to The Keep as prisoner?" Ruark asked Orion after she was gone. "The king would have—"

Orion whirled on Ruark. "Would have *what?*" He looked around the forest as a chill night wind ruffled the leaves. "I am finished with war and spying. The king has what he wants from us. It's time to go home."

Ruark and Duncan agreed, though they had no say in the matter. But they wanted to go home, too.

Not far away, John Scardon and his robber knights were laughing drunkenly, surrounding the wagons. They had killed the Frenchies who had come for the armor, and now Hadwin, the one-eyed scarred knight, looked at Scardon.

"What will we do with it?"

Scardon, his evil eyes forever slanting into his skull, cuffed Hadwin across the face with his glove. "What do you think, you idiot? We've a keep to gain back. The armor will come in handy."

Looking up in fear, Hadwin asked in a shaky voice, "You mean to take Sutherland back? But Orion—"

"The Keep, you fool! How many times do I have to tell you, it is not Sutherland any longer." He spun his horse around. "Come, you drunken fools, we have plans to make."

"This armor was meant for the French," one knight dared.

"That mad king?" Scardon laughed, a hellish sound in the dark forest. "We'll make better use of it. Damn it, get those wagons going before I murder the lot of you drunken bastards!"

The cowardly knights did Scardon's bidding and said no more.

Juel climbed the winding stairs to the tower room of The Keep. Standing at the top of the stairs, trembling from head to foot, she looked over her shoulder and then called softly into the slit in the door, "Is anyone there?" No answer. Again, "H-Hello?" None. Strongly this time, "Hello!"

She stood on tiptoe to look into the dimly lighted room where a candle glowed softly on a high table. A woman! Juel could see a woman seated on a bench before a small dressing table. She was gazing into a polished steel mirror, brushing long auburn hair with light gray streaks among the strands.

Moonlight sifted into the chamber, coming through a stained-glass window positioned high up in the stone wall. The woman turned slowly, but not fully enough so that Juel could make out her face. "You may leave the food," she said, showing only her profile.

"Where is the guard?" Juel asked, glancing over her shoulder, expecting Yardley, the man Lydia had mentioned, at any moment.

"I said you may—"

The woman turned slowly on the bench, seeming to be rather frail and older than she'd thought but still quite

376

beautiful, Juel could see. Her eyes narrowed. "Speak again," she commanded, beginning to rise from the bench.

"My name is—" Juel shrugged. "It doesn't matter. Please, might I speak with you? Could you come closer?"

The woman stood, walking slowly to the door. "You are not Lydia. How did you get in?" She came even closer, and slanted her head as Juel stood back so the woman could see her face. "My, you are lovely. Who are you?"

"I . . ." Juel began. "I tend the manor for the lord baron when he is away." She brushed her hand in the air. "I do many things. I've just begun to take care of the ledgers and—"

"The lord?" the woman asked. "Who might that be?"

Where has this woman been? Juel wondered, looking around. Locked up in this tower . . . for how long? And why?

"I feel no curse," Juel murmured to herself, looking around again, feeling nothing, just bafflement concerning this lovely woman and her strange isolation from everyone else. What had she done to be locked away in this dreary tower room! She did not look like a criminal, Juel thought.

Juel hid her surprise from the woman, but not for long. "You do not know your own lord of The Keep?"

The woman appeared puzzled, then chuckled softly. "Yes, the Lord. I know Him. He watches from above."

"You have been by yourself much, madam? I mean, away in this tower, away from the world?"

The older woman nodded, then studied the beautiful

young woman on the other side of the heavy door. "What might your name be, young woman?"

"My name is Juel Reynaude. Actually I am . . ." Juel left off; it was not time yet to reveal her true identity since she knew so little about that herself. "And yours?" *God, after all this time I hope she knows her own name!*

Reynaude? The woman's features were cast in a thoughtful expression, and then she shook her head. "That name is familiar," almost to herself. Then she clapped her hands in delight, almost like a child. "My name is Julia. How close our names are, do you not think?"

"Oh . . . yes."

Julia. Julia. Where had she heard that name, a name that seemed to be connected with Orion somehow?

"How is it you came to be here, child? And how long have you been here?"

When Juel would have said something the woman lowered her sad eyes. "It has been so long and so lonely, I cannot begin to tell you. Only Lydia comes to see me and bring food. Only she cares for me. I believe—" she laughed softly "—Yardley is afraid to speak with me. The curse, you know—"

Juel rushed forward, but the door kept her from touching this woman named Julia.

"I know no others here," Julia was saying.

"You know me, now," Juel said with a gentle smile.

"Yes, I'm so happy to see someone else. You are very brave to come here. It is dangerous, child. There is a curse." Her eyes were suddenly wide. "Do you know of the curse on this keep?"

"I . . . no. I mean, I've heard about it. Everyone is

very secretive about this . . . this tower, among other things."

"I see."

After peeking at the inside of the round tower, with its high arrow-slit windows and bars high up in the wall, Juel lowered her eyes. "You've not left this tower . . . in years?"

"No. I was brought here by a man . . . he said I must erase my mind of his name and all that had gone before. He came to me every night, this I know, and worked his evil magic on me. I was repulsed by him and would not allow him to touch me. And so—" she sighed deeply "—he locked me in here before he'd let another man have me. He was a very jealous man who coveted everything."

"How awful," Juel said.

Julia went on. "He had a face like . . . well, as I would think Satan's face would look, eyes slanting upward—" She lifted a finger. "I did not forget all, however, but I must not speak of it or my son will suffer. I promised never to say what was in my heart or mind."

"A promise to an evil man who said you must stay here and never come out?" Juel snorted. "Bah! I will help you see the absurdity of this, madam. You are alive, you are not dead. But your thinking is twisted, as is . . ." She'd been about to say "Orion's."

"My food, bring me the food, my dear. All this conversation has made me feel a little weak. I have to eat often, otherwise I become light-headed or I faint. Would you mind?"

On the way to pick up the tray Lydia had prepared, Juel tapped her chin in deep thought. She crossed the stone floor and came to stand before the lovely old woman on the other side of the heavy door . . . maybe not so old, just sad and lonely, Juel thought.

"Here you are," Juel said, handing it through the wide slit meant for the passing of food.

Juel watched while the woman broke brown bread and laid tasty strips of pink ham across it. As she ate most heartily, Juel thought at least her appetite had not suffered. Never had Juel seen so small a woman put food away so eagerly. There was only one other who could eat like that and not get fat, and that was Orion.

"That's not all there is to life, you know."

Julia stopped chewing to look up. "What do you mean?"

Juel gestured to the food. "You eat as if that is all there is to life."

Placing down the platter and the half-eaten fowl she'd been attacking, Julia looked at Juel seriously. "You are so right, young woman. Yes, I do believe you are a woman and not a child as I first called you. You are brave and beautiful."

Pouring Julia a beverage, and passing it through the slit, Juel went on. "Tell me, can you leave here?"

"Oh, no! Do not even suggest such a thing. I will be put to death and so will my son. He's still alive, you know."

Green eyes glittered guilefully before they lifted. "Yes, but how long has it been since you've seen him? How can you know this evil one you speak of has not already done away with your son?"

"Oh, I would know if he was dead. A . . . terrible feeling would come to me. He is most assuredly alive, I feel this."

"What did—? Or what *does* your son look like?"

"That is one thing I do remember. My son has hair the color of a baby raven's wing and eyes the color of wood in the deepest forest."

"Dark brown."

"Yes, brown. Beautiful eyes, kind and gentle. Though—" she again sighed—"I've not seen him since he was a—"

"Child of five, maybe?"

Juel waited.

"Yes, yes, a child of that age or maybe even younger."

Drawing her eyebrows together, Juel said, "You'll not stay here a moment longer. You'll come with me now."

"But how?" Julia wailed. "I dare not! My son or I will be killed should I come out of this tower."

With strength in her voice Juel said, "You'll not be killed and neither will your son. This is a promise. I shall stand with you, Julia."

"I asked you, how will you do that?"

"Where is Yardley now?"

Julia thought for a moment, her graying head low. Then it lifted. "He drinks and wenches on this night. Yes, that's where he is, where the knights go to drink."

"I will be back," Juel called over her shoulder.

Now the older woman seemed desperate. "When?"

"Soon!"

Lydia hovered over Juel as she tore through Ranice's trunks furiously, looking for something provocative to wear.

"Oh, dear!" Lydia cried. "This is not such a good idea. It could be most dangerous to entice such a man."

Juel chuckled as she pulled out a gown of lush black velvet with full sleeves that were gathered at the wrists. It was richly ornamented with braid, passementerie, and fur, was lined with silk of contrasting silver that shimmered through the revealing divided slit in front. It was a gown fit for a princess, but with a little lowering of the bodice it would be suitable for a lady with a little fun in mind.

"Look!" Lydia exclaimed, growing excited now. "It has a false bodice and we won't have to do any altering to make it . . . uhm, for what you've in mind this night. Just don't do anything foolish," Lydia added, helping Juel into the gown.

"It fits perfectly!" Juel cried, whirling about, feeling the lush material against her skin. "Now, what can you do with my hair?" she wondered, slipping on Ranice's dress slippers that were slightly overlarge, though no one would notice it.

Returning with a brush, Lydia drew it through Juel's hair, fluffing the mass and coiling it about Juel's ivory neck. When this was done, Lydia stood back, her eyes very round and amazed. "You look like a princess."

Juel whirled about to face Lydia. "Or maybe an heiress?" She was breathless and her hazel-green eyes sparkled dangerously.

"Oh, yes!" Lydia's eyes twinkled in her sweet, chubby face. "A beautiful heiress with a mission."

Chapter Thirty-Nine

"How did she know my name?" Orion fiercely asked his knights over and over. "How did she know who I am?"

Ruark shook his head. "You think of this all of a sudden? It's too late now. She's away since last night."

"Clytie de Monteforte," Duncan put in. "Yes, how did she know it was you who she and her bandit friends attacked?"

The dark knights had a laugh at his expense. Orion frowned blackly as the chill of another night began to fall. The west wind had sprung up over the marshlands, and the sun sank long ago in a great red-gold glare, making a slanting half-light in which the land now stood out in stark relief.

"She was very beautiful," Duncan declared. "If time would have allowed—"

"Be still!" Orion snapped, his mood bad-tempered. "I must think."

They had ridden far, to Pevensey Bay, close to the sea. They had crossed the Brighton-Hastings Road again and yet again, then followed the Limene River, where the forests were interspersed with many lagoons, estuaries of the larger body of water.

As they rode homeward, broad-backed hills and wide valleys like the waves of a sea transfixed suggested the prehistoric times when the country actually had been part of the ocean's bed. Deposits of salt still lay buried under the moors, some directly beneath the sparse covering of soil.

Autumn was in the wind.

Orion shifted on his destrier. His sleeves lifted beneath his leather tunic in gentle puffs of wind, harbingers of a storm that was rumbling and growling over the dark horizon.

Soon they would be home. Home and Juel, Orion thought to himself with glad heart as they rode onward.

"She's a sweet, shapely one," said Alfred dreamily in his cups. The young knight belched loudly, then covered his mouth, scraping the fuzz growing over his chin. "And she's a whore."

"Who're you yapping about now, squirt?" Yardley said with a belch that almost knocked the other knights off their bench seats. "There's a lot of whores about."

"Talking to myself," Alfred answered, thinking of the lovely, straying Juel of the household.

The huge guard Yardley seemed bored with life as he looked around the great hall, in the corner near the arched garderobe—the lavatory positioned in a side room. This was where the knights were wont to quaff their ale beneath the beamed ceiling. They sat lower down on benches at trestle tables which could be taken down when the hall was needed for games, dancing or meetings.

A few of the buxom maids danced freely among the fresh rushes in the center of the room with male servants while some ignoble minstrels played music especially tuned for the knights while the lord of the manor was away. It was an unrestrained group that frolicked and danced now and the air was fraught with wild revelry.

Tossing a greasy bone to one of the dogs, Yardley leaned back, his eyebrows drawn together, watching the women while drinking deeply from his cup. The women wore plain dark wool tunics, their ankles showing brown stockings as they whirled about, bumping hips together and laughing, snatching ale cups from tables and leaning back wantonly.

After a time several of the maids wandered off with drunken knights or male servants, until there were only the musicians left to play for the few remaining knights.

Suddenly Yardley stood, veering right to enter the garderobe. He meant to return to the tower when he was done with the remainder of his ale, knowing that Lydia would have come and gone with the meal for the woman in The Keep.

When Yardley came down the two steps into the hall after relieving himself, he stopped dead in his tracks.

Alfred, his head spinning from so much ale, was staring at the most beautiful vision he'd ever looked upon. "Juel Reynaude?" He gaped, his eyes wide and bloodshot, believing she'd become a princess overnight.

"I'm looking for Yardley. Where might I find him?"

The few remaining knights and maids knew trouble when they saw it and fled. The music played on in a scratchy tune, and Yardley gulped as he came to stand in the hall.

Yardley swallowed hard. "You be looking for me, miss?"

"Yes, Yardley. I wish to speak to you. And you alone." She looked around as Alfred leered at her, shaken by the sight of her, spilling his cup of strong brew all over the table. "Might I have a word with you in private?"

Now Alfred was angry. She had not chosen him, instead had picked out the oafish Yardley from a small group of handsome knights. He stood, swaying drunkenly. "Why don't you go to Hugh, the armorsmith, pretty bitch!" he snapped angrily. "How many men must you have while yer lord lover is away?"

"Shut up, Alfred," Juel bit out as she brushed past him, going to Yardley. "You're a drunken fool, a gossip, and have no idea what you prattle about."

With mouth wide, Alfred fell back aghast. "Why, you little bitch!" he snarled, flinging back his greasy hair.

"Be careful," one of the knights warned. "She's Orion's woman."

"Huh," Alfred growled, then grinned stupidly when he saw the blond angel pause before coming into the hall. He'd always liked Dawn and hoped someday she'd cast her eyes his way. But it was not to be, for Dawn was in love with Jay Reynaude.

Just then Dawn entered from the kitchens, Jay right behind her.

Dawn rushed over to Juel. "You look so beautiful in that gown, Juel. But what are you doing here this late at night?" she whispered, leaning away from Yardley. "Alfred is angry. What do you want with Yardley?"

"Yes, Juel," Jay said, holding Dawn's elbow, his eyes

full of sleepy love. "What are you doing here?"

"Never mind, you two," Juel hissed urgently. "There is something I must do." She looked them both straight in the eyes and smiled gently. "Trust me."

Glancing over their shoulders once more at Juel, Jay and Dawn left the hall most reluctantly. They had been making plans for their wedding and were eager to get back to that. But they worried as they left, wondering what Juel was up to. She'd said to trust her, and so they did, unlike others in the hall at that late hour. Too, they were not drunk and as brainless as the others were. Juel must have something important she was working on, as usual, they thought.

Yardley could not stop staring at Juel Reynaude. He had no idea she was the Hunter heiress, all he could think was that she'd sought him out. With an adoring look, he gaped at her, pie-eyed. "You wanted me, mistress?" He bit his fat lower lip. "Sorry I called you that, but most seem to think of you as such."

"I have something I would like you to do for me, Yardley."

"Yes, Juel, mistress," he gulped the words. "Anything you say." His eyes roved her beauty and poise in a single look.

Sweetly, most beautiful in bearing and countenance, she whispered as for his ears only. "I seek you out because only you can ease my plight."

"M-me, mistress?" he said like a big lummox, falling over his feet as he stood in one place. "Anything, just ask it."

Touching his arm, she whispered, "I need something very badly."

"J-just say it, I am at your service."

Huskily she murmured, "The key, Yardley. Satisfy

my curiosity. I need the key to the round tower."

He staggered back. "Key?" His eyes were round and full of fear. "You don't mean—"

"Yes," she said in his ear, touching his arm gently but firmly. "The Key."

After Yardley had removed the key from the loose brick in the wall, he stood back, shaking badly after handing it to Juel. He had never looked into the room to see who was locked in there; he'd always been too fearful of Scardon's curse. He only knew it was a woman in there, one who Lydia came and fed, carried out dirty laundry for, and emptied chamber pots. When Lydia came, Yardley always looked aside. He'd only discussed daily events with "her."

"Thank you, Yardley," Juel said after the heavy door swung free with a loud creak of hinges beneath her hand. "You can do as you wish now. You have been very kind."

"Ye'll be in trouble now, mistress. When Scardon—"

"Say no more of that man."

Yardley averted his eyes. "I'll be going now. Back to my old mother in the village."

Yardley fled before he could look upon the woman who was following Juel from the chamber she'd entered moments before. Out in the fresh air, with millions of twinkling stars overhead, Julia walked on shaky limbs. She looked this way and that, as if expecting some evil being to jump out at her from each and every deep shadow or corner. She walked close to Juel, her hand riding lightly on the younger woman's arm.

Once inside the huge manor Julia was shocked to see

everything, the furnishings and items that once had been near and dear to her. Juel studied her face as it beamed with new life.

Lydia came out from a side room, her eyes wide as she wrung her hands together. Julia smiled. "You are the kind woman who has cared for me all these years."

"Yes," Lydia said. She blinked. "I am."

"Help me prepare a room for Lady Julia, Lydia."

"At once, m'lady." Lydia bobbed as if Juel was already mistress of the manor. When she turned away she was smiling from ear to ear, going upstairs to ready the new chamber that opened into the solar. Orion's room was on the other side. And what would he think of this woman moving into the house after all these years? Oh, Lord, what was going to happen when he returned?

Julia turned to Juel. "I do not wish to go upstairs but rather want to remain belowstairs," she laughed softly. "Near the ground level."

When Lydia returned she and Juel found a nice comfortable chamber off the great hall. It had a fireplace and all the furnishings, tapestries, private garderobe, even a daybed. Juel found a long white nightgown for Julia and soon the woman was fast asleep, snuggled in the fresh linens and rich bed coverings.

She is so weary, Juel thought, looking down at the woman in the bed, her graying auburn hair pulled back from her lovely face and braided neatly. *Her face is intelligent, full of life now. She will sleep the night through.*

They had so much to talk about, Juel thought as a crack of thunder filled the silence. Talk, yes, with discoveries and findings, that would come soon enough.

By the time Orion reached The Keep, he was soaked to the skin. Colorful leaves were already blowing across the courtyard and there was a brisk, invigorating chill in the air that was mixed with rain.

Juel ran out to meet Orion. She was carrying an oilskin, and together they raced to the tall doors, laughing like happy children.

"What good will it do! I am already soaked!" he shouted. His arm was about her waist as they stood before the manor.

"I am here to see that you do not become wetter, Orion!" she shouted right back to him as the thunder rumbled overhead.

Before they went inside he took her in his arms and kissed her most thoroughly, holding her fit to crush her bones. His mouth was wet and slick, sliding over her lips, his even wetter tongue licking and thrusting. His big body turned to her as his arms went around her back and yanked her closer.

On tiptoe now, Juel clung to his neck, smelling man, leather, and horse on his skin as her body melded with his and the steam began to rise between them.

My beautiful heiress, Orion thought. Aloud he said, "You warm my blood, woman. My God, you look happy!" He pressed close to her ear and whispered as the stableboy came to take his horse away, "To warm me beyond this delectable moment, I would have you in bed this night. What say you to this, my love?"

Breaking away and running into the hall, Juel laughed over her shoulder, "We shall see, m'lord!"

With heat in his eyes Orion watched her go to a table and return. He was just removing his soaked surcoat when she handed him a missive with King Henry's seal on it.

"Thank you, my love." His eyes twinkled.

She took his arm, led him to the bench, then motioned to Lydia, who'd come up behind, to prepare some food for Orion immediately. Ruark and Duncan entered and went to sit across from Orion, both smiling at the happy Juel, wondering what lay behind her beautiful grin.

Seeing that Juel wanted Orion to herself, Duncan motioned for Ruark to follow him into the kitchen. "We can't wait to eat, can we, Ruark?" The other man said, "Huh?" and Duncan whipped his head in the direction of pungent food smells. "You are starving, remember?" He eyed the loving pair meaningfully and Ruark at last got the message.

While Orion sat in the great hall reading the letter, Juel brought him out a drink of heated and spicy fruit nectar. He lounged in the warm room with the blazing hearth at the end, while Juel peeled his sodden leathers from his feet.

Orion was distracted from the letter as Juel came up behind and placed a cool hand on his neck. He raised his hands and covered hers with them. "How happy I am to be home, my love." He was thinking that soon they would become man and wife. He almost laughed aloud. If, that is, if she would have him!

"The tidiness of the manor is no doubt the work of your hand?" he asked her, his eyes drifting up from Henry's letter.

"I did have something to do with it," she answered, so thrilled with what was to come that she could barely contain her excitement . . . and yet afraid how Orion would take the news about the new woman in his house.

Having read what the king had written, Orion leaned back, his head resting against the stone wall. He was thinking deeply of the king's message:

Message to Orion Sutherland, Baron Herstmonceux, from Henry V:

Sunday 11 August. A bright sunny day, Henry and his armada set sail.

There was only a slight breeze and so, the Voyage across the Channel took Three days. Instead of landing at Calais as expected, our English land in Normandy at Chef-de-Caux on the Seine estuary. This, as you know, just outside the port of Harfleur. I have told only my closest advisers of this carefully chosen Destination—and You, of course, as my Confidante and Distinguished secret agent. Harfleur is to be the Base from which I shall conquer Normandy and strike down the River at Paris. And conquer I shall! Your aid all in all is greatly Appreciated.

Harry.

Juel was quiet while Orion ate his food. Suddenly he stopped chewing the meat she had served him herself. "What is it? Something is different. I can feel it."

So much has happened I don't know where to begin! Juel wanted to shout at him.

"Just eat. You are hungry," Juel said, unable to keep from grinning happily.

Orion sat back and shook his head. "No, I will eat no more until you tell me what it is you hide from me, Juel."

"I did not wish to tell you yet. I mean *show* you—" She faltered. "I thought it better that you—" Again she stopped short.

"Out with it, damn it!" Orion shouted.

"Would you like some more—?"

"Juel . . ." Orion ground his teeth. "What is it? Did you find out about—?"

Now Juel's eyes narrowed. "What could it be that I found out?" she asked Orion. "Just what?" Would he tell her now that she was Elizabeth Juel Hunter? Or was he too much a coward?

"Ah, you've found out that you are the heiress."

"Heiress?" She sashayed about his chair, her skirts rustling in the suddenly quiet hall. "What is this about an heiress?"

Orion's eyes narrowed dangerously. "Either you know or you do not! Which is it?" he ground out angrily. His head swiveled about to see her then. "Why didn't I notice it before? Where did you get that black dress?"

"Do you like it?" She leaned over, giving him a view of her cleavage. "It befits an heiress with lands and a castle of her own, hmm?"

Crossing his arms over his chest, Orion sat with mouth set sternly, stubbornly.

She slapped his shoulder, once, twice.

He winced.

"You are selfish and greedy! You lied to me!" she began her tirade. "You could have married me, but you called me a mere villager with no highborn blood! Oh . . . all the while you knew I was this . . . this Elizabeth Hunter . . . an heiress!"

"Who told you?" he gritted out from clenched jaw, trying to grab hold of her elbow.

Juel bounced out of his reach, swishing her black-and-silver skirts as she walked about the bench he was perched on like a belligerent hawk.

"Where did you get that gown?"

"From Ranice's trunks." Juel tilted her chin. "Do you think she'll mind?"

"Juel, you are being unduly sarcastic. I'd sooner take you over my knee than speak with you in this mood."

She came around to pummel his chest. "I hate you for lying to me!"

He sat while she continued to strike him. Then he'd had enough of her pounding. "Leave off, Juel!" He grabbed her wrists and held them high while he yanked her around to sit down hard in his lap. "I wanted you to love me for myself, not my barony."

"Bah!"

"You would have discovered that you were an heiress, and then you would have left me to go to Hunter Castle."

"Look." Juel spread her hands in front of his face. "I'm not gone yet. I did not run as soon as I discovered I was an heiress." Her lips tightened fiercely. "Can you explain, m'lord?"

"How could I know that you knew?" he asked, one side of his mouth lifting in a very handsome grin.

"When did you find out?" she snapped, then smiled in spite of her frustrating anger.

"Before I left this last time." He nuzzled her throat. "But what does it matter?" Lifting his eyes, he looked over her softening features, seeing her eyes becoming merry again. "Why don't we go upstairs and settle this in bed?"

She tossed her head. "Is that the answer all men give? To settle all disputes in bed?"

His jaw tightened. "How would you know about other men?"

"I do believe all of you are alike. Am I not right in this?"

For a moment she wondered what Yardley had expected from her after she'd gotten the key from him. The big man had looked relieved to be away from his position, and she believed she had freed him from Scardon's curse—the hell he'd locked the man in, not only poor Julia. Yardley had never wanted to keep that woman in there all that time. She had seen how happy—and a little afraid—he'd been to be away.

Swiping the food from the table, Orion placed Juel before him and began to fondle her right there in the hall.

"Orion—no!" she gasped as his hands found her breasts under the soft velvet. "Not here. My God, what are you doing?" she squealed then as he pushed his face beneath her skirts and blew hotly against her womanhood. "No, no, no!"

"Let them all see how the lord of this manor lusts for his woman!" He stood and lifted her high in the air. "My heiress, Elizabeth Juel Hunter!"

"Orion, are you insane?!"

"Entirely," he shouted as he carried her up the stairs and kicked open the door to his apartments. He slammed the door and carried her to the bed. "And now, you will see how much I've missed you."

Juel's eyes flashed wide as Orion tossed off his clothes and fell on her in the middle of his huge bed. But not before she'd seen the staff standing out boldly in readiness.

"Orion," she laughed throatily as he tickled her ribs. "Have you had a bath?" She shoved at him. "I'll not have you if you haven't bathed, you know."

"I jumped in the stream before coming home, to cool

off so that I'd not rape you when I entered the manor."
He ripped her gown as he took it off her like a man
crazed with lust. "Never mind," he said when she
gasped over the ruined expensive material. "You can
have all the gowns in the world."

"And of course," she quipped, looking up at him
sassily, "I've become a wealthy woman and needn't
pick about in Ranice's trunks for something to wear."

"And I'll purchase the most beautiful gowns in
England for you, Elizabeth Juel," he growled, suckling
one breast and then the other.

"No need, I said. I can get my own." She blew in his
ear and bent one leg to the side, eager for that first hard
thrust.

It came. His penetration was so swift that she cried
out at first. Then they were moving together, with his
strength, her softness, a blending of unique powers.
Soon she had him crying out as they exploded together
once, and then she was atop him, riding him vigor-
ously, the power in her grasp this time.

They made love seven times, in various energetic
positions, then lay very still, looking barely alive to
each other as their heads rolled on the linen pillows.

"I love you, princess."

She smiled lazily. *"Heiress,* silly. Don't you men ever
remember anything?"

Pinching her thigh, he snarled, "I remembered to
bring you some very lovely gowns. Among other
treats."

"Where did you get these special items, hmm?"

"There was a traveling merchant we met with on the
way."

Juel's eyes were bright stars. "Surprises for me?" She
thought to herself: *Wait till you see the one in store for*

you, my love.

"Of course. The gowns will be sure to fit, you'll see."

Her eyes fell and she noticed the medallion he was wearing. "I have not seen this before." She traced it with her fingertips. "It bears the form of a warrior carrying a club and sword. Hmm, and wearing a lion's skin and a girdle composed of three very beautiful stars."

"Yes," he said, suddenly in a strange mood as he moved away and swung his bare legs over the bed. "What is this? It looks delicious, whatever it is."

They sat up in bed and shared a sugary comfit that had been placed on the table earlier. Juel would not say it was she herself who had placed it there.

With the bed coverings wrapped about them, they sat in the bed among colorful pillows, also new, like the bedhangings.

Juel's gaze was drawn to the medallion again. Her story! The one she had told the children of Orion, the mighty hunter who was slain and thrown into the sky by the beautiful goddess who loved him.

"Where did you get this?" She fingered it again, making him sit still as she placed it across her palm.

He looked down and snatched it from her. "The medallion has been in my possession ever since I can remember. I just stopped wearing it for a time, is all."

"I have told a story about this sign in the sky, in the constellation."

He laughed and pulled her close again. "What would you, my beauty, know about constellations?"

She told him again of her working for the wealthy merchant, reminding him of the many manuscripts she'd pored over. "I wish I could get my own copy of the Book of Hours."

"I have one you may have."

She licked the sugar from her lips, staring at his mouth all the time as her tongue moved provocatively over her lips. "You do?" she said, mischief in her eyes. "I will be thrilled to own it. Only nuns have that book in their possession, or the wealthy ones like baronesses—" she laughed "—or ladies of high rank."

"Well you have one now, my heiress!"

"I might have two," she shot back. "Perhaps there's one at my personal holdings."

"You grow too bold with your new title, woman." He grabbed her around the waist, yanked her to his chest, and kissed her with languour, while his hands cupped her buttocks. "You've a lovely behind, you know, sized just right to fill my hands."

Juel rolled with him on the bed and they began to kiss each other, all over. When they were ready to make love, Orion picked her up and pulled her down onto his lap. He came inside her and she cried out. Then they moved together until the position became uncomfortable. He shifted himself atop her, pushing into her as she lifted, then drawing away, only to meet again until they at last exploded. His release came slightly after her own.

She giggled as he fondled her globes of flesh. "My baron?"

He was breathing hard. "I would suppose you could say that I am Baron."

Juel grinned. "You are Sutherland."

"Aye, so the king says. But I've yet to find my mother who Harry says is alive. He says one will show me the way." He shrugged. "Whatever that means. He said there is gold right where I dwell. Me . . ." Orion suddenly pointed at himself. "He meant me, not him."

She tilted her head and smiled lopsidedly, tracing his chest with one finger. "I know, I'm not a stupid wench, you know."

"That you are not," he growled, nipping her earlobe. "I never thought for one moment that you were not intelligent or resourceful."

"The Bible says, 'Where your treasure is there will your heart be also.'"

"Yes." Orion looked excited over that short verse. "It's almost the same as gold, isn't it. Right outside my window."

Juel said coyly, "Why must the king make a riddle of it? Oh, sometimes I believe kings are cruel. Warmongers. Always playing their games . . . just as the French kings have done themselves."

For a moment Orion was reminded of Clytie de Monteforte and her likeness to his beloved. Then he brushed the thought away like a pesky fly. "This talk of the French makes me recall something," he said in a change of subject. "The captain-general of the French military is conducting an advance to marshal troops to protect against the coming English invasion."

He studied Juel closely. She must not know of the French and their movements. How could she? He believed she held no more secrets from him, that they would conceal things from each other no longer.

"The English are going to invade France then," she muttered matter-of-factly. "It is true." Her eyes narrowed over him. "And you are a spy for the king, you cannot tell me otherwise." She grinned. "Orion Sutherland."

"You love saying the name Sutherland, don't you?"

"Of course. That is who you are and one day this keep will again be restored to its former beauty and be called Sutherland Castle again."

"Will you stay here with me, love?"

"Only if you make me your wife. We've dwelt in sin too long now, you know."

He kissed her brow while murmuring to her. "I'll make you Baronness Sutherland."

"Will you be invading with King Henry?"

He pulled back to look at her in surprise. "What?"

"Will you wear a suit of armor? I think you and they should not. Armor is too heavy."

"That you must not know, my love. It's a secret of utmost importance."

"A secret," she laughed. "That they'll not don armor but . . . leathers. And bows and arrows!"

He stroked her cheek. "Are you a spy in my castle, love?"

"I have dwelled on English soil for as long as I can remember. My mother was English, you recall I told you, and now I learn I'm not half-French . . . It's sad, but Peter Reynaude is not my real father. My father is dead and . . . and I never met him."

Tears clung to her lashes and one splashed on his hand.

Holding her close to his heart, he said against her temple, "Don't mourn so, love. I've not seen my parents since a child of five."

With tears drying, Juel smiled secretly. "That's true," she said.

And said no more.

Chapter Forty

"Come with me, Orion. Please. Now."

Looking up at Juel from sleep-filled eyes, Orion let his arm fall back to the bed when he would have kept her from rising. She turned about to tug at him.

"Come," she said, yanking his arms. He fell back as she let go. He was too heavy to pull up.

He gave her an affectionate smile. "I can't anymore. You've worn me out."

"Not that, you silly single-minded man. Get up and come with me."

"What is it?" His mouth spread in a wide smile as she stood, baring her buttocks to him as she walked to pick her clothes up near the foot of the bed. "You've worn me out. Where do you want to take me now?" He chuckled. "Oh my God no, not the swaying bed?"

"Orion, none of your humor. Please. This is serious."

She was dressed before he could pull his chausses on and reach for his rough woolen doublet and shirt.

"How serious?" he said with a yawn as he scratched his chest with two lazy fingers. "It better be good enough to keep me awake," he warned as he finished putting on a wide leather belt. "Where are my leathers?" he asked.

"I took them off in the hall, don't you remember?" She waved her hand. "Forget them for now."

"It better be more than good," he said quietly.

"Don't worry." *It will be the biggest shock of your life,* she wanted to add, but dared not; first she had to get him there. "It's a surprise," she announced while he followed tiredly behind. "Now stop that. I know you're ogling me from behind. This is serious, very, very serious."

He spun her about, frowning into her eyes. "How serious?" he asked again. When she would not answer, he tipped her chin upward. "Serious? Or bad?"

She laughed nervously, brushing moist hands over the velvet dress she wore. "If it had been bad I wouldn't have kept it from you this long."

She grimaced as she turned away. *You'll have no need to fear the round tower after this,* she wanted to say. *A little at a time, Juel, give this to him slowly.* "Come this way."

"To the winter parlor? What could you want to show me in there?" He sighed with boredom. "If it's some new decorating scheme you've created, can't it wait till later? If only I could sleep for a day or two . . . You've worn me to a frazzle, woman." And it was all worth it, every inch of her sweet flesh!

Orion stood outside the room listless and slightly annoyed as Juel knocked and awaited the call for entry.

On the other side of the portal a woman's soft voice was heard after a few moments. "Enter, please."

As Juel slowly opened the door and they both

stepped into the room, Orion's eyes narrowed as he peered in curious wonder at the lovely woman.

It was as if something from out of his past looked him in the eyes.

The older but still beautiful woman rose slowly from a cushioned bench and walked to him, her celadon gown rustling softly. She stood before him and gazed up into his handsome face, the deep-brown eyes, up to the dark, almost black, thick hair. *Yes,* she thought, *oh, yes*.

Orion's eyes opened wider and wider as he looked down at the woman. "Don't I know you?" he asked softly.

Juel and Julia exchanged meaningful glances. Orion had looked from one to the other, but now he stared only at the older woman.

"It is I, your mother," Julia told Orion.

The shock registered on Orion's face and the slight hint of anger frightened Julia. "I seem to have forgotten my last name, however."

Defenseless against the emotions surging inside him, Orion snapped angrily, "How can any of this be verified?"

Julia studied Orion. She thought back to the one thing that could bring them together, make him believe. Her eyes grew bright as she looked into his eyes. "Do you have the medallion?"

A chill passed along Orion's spine. He reached inside his tunic, at his throat, and placed his hand there, then followed the chain down to the medallion resting in the center of his chest. "How do you know of the medallion?" he asked her with heavy voice.

She smiled tenderly. "Remember, my son, the

treasure I gave to you when we were last together. I remember more and more as I look upon you. It was right before John Scardon parted us!"

Scardon! The name sent spirals of rage through Orion, and he knew pain, like dagger thrusts.

Orion removed the medallion bearing the three beautiful stars, looked down, then up at the woman. "I do remember . . . your . . . eyes," he said.

Though she was older, had wrinkles around those eyes and lovely mouth, Orion knew it was she. He was a child again envisioning her as she had been all those years ago. His mother!

A single tear ran down his cheek as he could contain his emotion no longer. "But how?" he asked, as he reached to pull her into his tender embrace. "You are alive. How is this so, Mother? And where have you been?" He looked into her misty eyes. "Have you been far away?"

"Actually," she whispered shakily, "not far away at all." She laughed softly, a sound like tinkling water. "I have been up there, in the tower. All these years."

He gulped hard. "You were right here all this time!"

"Yes. All this time. Here. So near and yet so far."

Julia remembered everything now, for seeing her son again had jogged her mind into clear thinking and understanding.

She told Orion, her son, that Scardon had locked her in the tower room and hid the key; only Yardley knew of this. Scardon had wanted Julia, but she was repulsed by him and his evil mind. He had locked her in that tower rather than let another man have her.

"He was a very jealous person who coveted everything," Julia ended, knowing her son must also

404

have suffered in Scardon's clutches.

Orion took Julia's hand. "Now you'll be cared for as you should have been for all these years. I have questions for you, Mother. Why did you name me Orion? And who was my father?"

"On the night you were born we, your father and I, were traveling," she began her answer. "My time came on suddenly because of the rough ride. We stopped on the road by an open field. It was a beautiful night and the stars were out. Your father, Colin, spread a blanket out on the ground and I had you there. I looked up to see a falling star, as it hurtled toward the earth, and turned to Colin and said, 'Where comes the star?'"

"What did he say?" Orion asked, staring raptly at her face, excited at the story.

"From the constellation Orion, he told me," Julia said to Orion now. "And then you were given your name—after the hunter in the night sky. Your father was an astronomer, he predicted for the king."

"Which king?" Orion asked.

"Why," Julia said with a blink, "King Henry IV."

"He is king no longer, Mother."

Julia seemed lost for a moment. "Who *is* king now?"

"His son, Henry of Monmouth." He chuckled. "But that's another story, particularly now at war time." Looking at Juel, his eyes twinkled merrily as he said to Julia, "Someday we'll tell you all about it."

"Colin's copies of the star charts can never be reclaimed," Julia announced somewhat sadly.

"Someday we'll search for them," he promised.

"What, pray tell, is the name of this stronghold now?" Julia asked, noticing Juel's gentle smile as mother and son spoke only to each other.

Orion glared fiercely at the wall. "It's called The Keep."

"Oh? That's it? Such a homely name, this."

Julia remembered that Sutherland Castle had once been very strong and beautiful and was happy to learn that Orion was restoring it to its former beauty, including a moat. "We'll use the chapel as a family once again," she said, "purging the manor and holdings of John Scardon's evil influence."

"As you say, Mother," Orion said respectfully.

"Now, are you going to marry this beautiful Juel or not?"

"Of course. I love her."

"Good."

"Juel is an heiress." He took the younger woman's hand and held it. "She has only just learned this."

"How wonderful!" Julia looked to the beaming Juel. "You may wed? The king will give his blessing?"

Orion laughed heartily. "King Henry is most busy at this time, Mother. He is preparing for war against the French."

"Oh . . ." Julia shook her head. "Not that again. Will the French and English never get along?"

"Maybe," Juel put in. "If only we women could put our heads together and take ovvv—"

"Juel," Orion cut in and warned. "Not now, please."

Juel curtsied with a quick bounce. "As you wish, m'lord!"

The three of them laughed happily, going together to find some fattening and delicious treat in the kitchens.

After Orion had gone back to bed Juel and Julia

wandered about the manor, cats and Shadow trailing behind, talking as if there were no tomorrow. Before long they would know everything there was to know about each other, and Julia seemed to be remembering more and more as time went by.

Rajahr was just walking beneath an arched door. When he saw them he came rushing over. He was so excited he could barely speak correctly, but he took Julia's hand, patted it, and kissed it over and over.

"Orion just told me. What news! How wonderful it is that you have been saved from imprisonment in that awful tower." He looked to Juel, his eyes full of respect. "I did not know how precious this young woman would come to be. I knew there had to be something very special about her. She got Orion to quit his bad habits and I—"

"Bad habits?" Julia said, trying to think if she'd ever seen this strange little man before.

"Ohh, yes. Very bad. He was mean with drink almost every night before Juel Reynaude came here."

Julia nodded. "Scardon's influence again." She looked at Juel. "I don't wish to speak of him anymore this day. There's too much living to do."

"As you wish, madam. Would you like something special for your late meal this day?"

"Oh, yes." She exchanged a smile with Juel. "I would like some very healthy food. Like piles of vegetables, dark bread, and lentil soup!"

"Ah, my specialty—lentil soup. With lots of carrots and herbs, right?"

"Yes, ah . . . ?"

"Rajahr." He took and kissed her hand again, then rushed to do her bidding. He snapped his fingers and

407

the hungry cats and Shadow ran after the Indian.

Juel laughed after Rajahr had gone. "He's such a nice man." Suddenly Juel's eyes twinkled. "But my father is even nicer. Of course, I would think that—"

"But he is not your real father?"

"No. And I must get him here so we can discuss this. It weighs heavily on my mind, that I'm not of his flesh and blood. I have spoken with Jay and of course he is also very interested to learn of his true bloodlines."

"You have a very lovely name," Julia offered. "Elizabeth Juel Hunter. An heiress!" She clapped her hands. "And we may still call you Juel—how clever!"

"Yes. Leave it up to Peter Reynaude to think of that. I'm sure it was his idea."

"Why don't you go fetch your father? Is he very far away?"

"No," Juel said. "Just in the village. He is eating very poorly. The woman who lives with him means well, but she's feeding him terribly fattening food and in amounts that will make him an obese old man in no time."

Julia tapped her chin. "How can you know what is fattening and what is not?"

"I've made my own recipes. You said yourself you wanted to eat some healthy food and you were correct in saying that vegetables, soup, and dark bread with heavy grain are good for us."

"And legumes, the beans!" Julia laughed, holding up a finger. She grimaced then. "I just wish they did not make a person so . . . what do you call it?" She gave a girlish giggle. "Noisy?"

"Yes. And with bloat. But I have a special herb and juice I put into the pot that eliminates such intestinal distress."

"Well then, let's go!" She grabbed Julia's arm. "Let's get Rajahr to add those powerful ingredients so that we'll eliminate the problem!"

Julia smiled with her mouth open. "You are particularly wonderful, Julia Sutherland."

"Yes," Julia said happily. "And one day you'll be a Sutherland, too."

And maybe *you'll* become a Reynaude someday; Juel was thinking of a match between her father and Julia. She said aloud, "One day your prince will come, too, Julia."

"Oh? He better be strong enough to join with a Sutherland woman."

Juel laughed. "You get more of your strength back with every hour. Your backbone gets more unbending all the time, too!"

"Yes, I do stand much straighter, don't I?"

Their joy rang together as they went to the kitchens to find Rajahr and to have him add the special ingredients to the soup.

By the end of two weeks Julia could hardly remember that there had ever been a man named John Scardon.

Chapter Forty-One

Peter Reynaude walked into the manor and fell in love with Julia Sutherland on sight. She was wearing a gorgeous gown that belonged to her. She had pulled it from the trunks in the attic and had one of the maids clean it. The neckline was low, with frilled edging, elbow-length sleeves, and gold-embroidered silk belt. The chemise sleeve showed below, ending in oyster lace ruffles. The color of the cloth was akin to the ashes of roses.

"This is Julia," Juel said to her father. "I mean—" she laughed with embarrassment. "Julia Sutherland."

"Hello, Julia." She looked so grand that he felt poorly dressed beside her in his traditional laborer's smock of coarse homespun linen.

But Julia did not notice his clothes; all she could see was Peter's gentle eyes, strong chin, and youthfully strong physique. He did carry a little extra weight in the belly, but that would not be hard to take off, Julia was thinking as she looked into his adoring eyes.

In the great hall, seated beside his bride-to-be, Orion

smiled to himself, thinking his heiress a skilled matcher of people.

More social activites were taking place in the hall these days. Orion was actually becoming cheerful and lenient, as there was music played by the minstrels, dancing, high jinks from the mummers, games such as chess and "tables," and storytelling, mostly by Juel.

Earlier Orion had met with his chief officials and tenants in the great hall; he would issue orders, if need be, and listen to grievances. Wrongdoers were generally punished by fines, which provided a useful source of income for the lord of the manor. But the fines had grown smaller, since Juel often interceded, convincing Orion in her sweet voice that most crimes were not that heinous after all.

Juel soon learned the true story of her childhood. Peter could have no children, though he had wanted them badly. When he told her this, tears came to her eyes. A man named Guy Hunter, a baronet, loved Dalenna, the woman *he* loved, and Peter allowed her to go to him. She returned home with child twice. She was angry with her lover for taking other women to his bed. She'd loved Peter Reynaude in a quiet way, but the titled English Lord Guy had been her wanton love.

"This makes me a bastard," Juel said to Orion later in his bedchamber as she came away from the window. "And Jay also."

Jay had listened to his "father's" story, too, not in the least bit affronted that Juel was the one to inherit property and a small, lovely castle in southern England.

Orion stood brushing her hair as she sat on the edge of his bed. "You shouldn't think of it that way, love."

He put the brush aside, sitting on the bed behind her. "All that is the past. You are the one who taught me to forget, to forgive."

"Oh?" She kept her back to him. "Have you also forgiven Scardon for what he's done to you and your mother?"

He stood abruptly. "I would rather we didn't discuss John Scardon."

She looked up at him as he began to pace the room. "He will come back, you know. It's destined. You feel this, too, don't you?" She watched as he stopped at the mullioned window, clenching his hands at his sides.

"I'm ready for him," Orion said, unclenching his hands and pressing them along his thighs. "This time I'll kill him, be sure of that." He spun to face her. "My mother must never know of his return. I believe it would kill her."

Juel came to him and put her arms about his waist. "Your mother is falling in love with my stepfather," she announced.

She looked out the window across his shoulder. Heath country billowed outward in all directions to the far horizons, a dun earth dotted with broom in butter-yellow flower, and clumps of juniper. Scattered among the moors were occasional sorry acres of buckwheat, sprouting meager shoots like hairs on an old man's head. Next year the crops would be better, she thought silently, when war and talk of it diminished.

After several moments of silence, Orion's face broke into a smile.

He turned to take her in his arms. "You fix everything, don't you. I'll bet you even brought your brother and Dawn together."

"All I did was to tell her about him. Their paths crossed day in and day out, then at last they came face-to-face." She shrugged. "They did it themselves, fell in love without any help."

He eyed her closely. "You did not even put in a good word for Jay to Dawn?"

She thought for a moment before her eyes lit. "I did warn her that he was a lover of women and would be after her if they met. Dawn is very lovely. I only told her he'd notice her."

Just then their conversation was interrupted by a loud crashing in the corridor below. "What the—?" Orion rushed to the door in quick strides and went down to the floor below. Juel followed, her skirts held aloft. "What goes on here!" Orion thundered as he stood in the old spinning room.

"There!" Alfred shouted as he saw Juel. "She's the cause of contention among the knights!"

Before he could malign her further, Ruark slammed his fist into Alfred's face, pulling the young, wiry man to his feet, then hitting him again for good measure.

"Stop it!" Juel flew into the room. "What is this all about, Ruark?" she asked as the head of the mesnie pinned Alfred against the wall, his feet dangling several feet up from the floor. There was blood all over Alfred's face.

"I'd rather not discuss it right now," Ruark snarled, knowing that Orion was standing there, interested, his arms folded across his chest.

But Orion was not to be put off; he wanted to know, too. Then Juel's eyes flew wide as she remembered Alfred's hateful words to her the night she had sought out Yardley to give her the tower key.

"Ruark is right," Juel said shakily. "Maybe now is not the time to discuss this."

Orion came fully into the room, looking pointedly at her. "And why not, Juel?" He took her arm, and slid his grasp down to her shaking hand. "Is there something you are keeping from me?"

"There most certainly is!" Alfred yelled, then uttered a croak as Ruark slammed him back hard.

"Let Alfred speak," Orion ground out. "I would like to hear what it is that you both are afraid for me to learn. Ruark. Juel. Be still."

Clutching his bruised throat with both hands, Alfred stood on his feet at last, after Ruark had released him. He saw the warning in Ruark's eyes and realized he'd dared much by fighting with the head of the knights.

Ruark had overheard Alfred gossiping with the other young knights. He had heard him call Juel a "whore" and that she'd gone out to meet with Hugh the armorsmith and stayed with him for several hours before coming out, looking "very pleased with herself." Then she'd sought Yardley out, went the gossip, wearing a provocative black gown, whispering in the big man's ear.

Orion was impatient now. "Let's hear what you have to say, Alfred."

"Your woman . . ." Alfred looked to Juel and his heart fell as he took in her look of chilling foreboding. "She . . ." What did he really know about her? Did she really bed down with the armorsmith? Or was it only his imagination working because he wished he could have her for himself? He was in deep trouble now and was pressed to say something.

415

"Yes, Alfred? She . . . ?" Orion waited, his jaw clenched.

Alfred took a deep breath and then let go. "She bedded down with Hugh in the forge many nights and took up with Yardley right before your return!"

There, he'd said it.

Orion didn't look very impressed with what he'd heard, but nor did he dismiss it. He looked to Juel and proceeded to make one of the biggest mistakes of his life.

"Did you dally with Hugh and Yardley?" he asked her.

She fell back against the wall, aghast, her arms splayed wide. "You dare ask me that?" She shook her head slowly from side to side. "How can you even—"

Pushing herself from the wall, Juel whirled from the room. Her steps could be heard running along the halls and down the stairs. Orion frowned deeply and waited until there was nothing but the sound of Alfred's labored breaths.

Orion stepped close to Alfred, his eyes piercing as he looked into the young knight's face. "If what you say holds no truth—" A tick moved in his taut cheek "—I'll have your head before the week is out, by my own sword. Ruark, lock him up."

"Noooo!" Alfred screamed as Ruark led him by the arm. Two more knights pounded along the hall just then, coming to help take him away.

One of the knights explained that they'd come right away after Juel had tearfully told them there was trouble below Orion's apartments.

"Where is she?" Orion bit out.

"She took to horse!" Rajahr rapped out, wringing

his hands together as he came along the corridor. "Very big horse!"

Orion paled. "Does she ride well?" He was already following Ruark out the door.

Ruark said over his shoulder, "As well as any woman who's grown up on a farm."

"A big horse, you say?" A Percheron Norman. "That should slow her down some." Orion hurried downstairs, grabbing a brown cloak along the way out.

An expert at bareback riding, Juel rode the large, fast-trotting draft horse over the countryside hills and down the shadowed valleys. Autumn colors flew by in her tear-filled vision; there was a nip in the air. She'd taken no cloak and night would soon close over her in a dark shroud so that no one could find her. Maybe she should turn back, she thought.

No, she didn't care what happened. Orion had as much as accused her of being with Hugh and Yardley intimately.

She decided that he could not care that much about her or he'd have questioned her further about the night she'd obtained the key to the tower room. He hadn't even asked her how she'd come by it, how she'd gotten his mother out of the tower.

She was just another mistress he could play with for a time and then discard! Was he really planning to make her his wife? Oh, yes, now he wanted her because she'd become an heiress, and then what would he do, once he had her lands and castle in his clasp? Get rid of her? He would arrange an accident such as Ranice had. He had not been the one with her that night, it had been her brother Jay!

He had not meant to tell her that she'd become an heiress. How long was he going to hold out . . . until after they'd married? Of course. He must have known about it the night he used his evil powers to persuade her drowsy mind . . . to make her body come to him in the attic room. As her secret lover he'd said that he would make her with child. Both his mind and his body held power over her. He must have known already that night that she'd inherited the Hunter holdings. It was only a ploy afterwards when he told her that he was afraid she would leave him and go to her own castle, never to return to him.

"Bah!" she called out now. "He lies! He lies!" The wind shifted and whipped the words back into her face like a hard slap. Defiantly she shouted back into the wind, "Now I shall never tell him I carry his child! Never!"

You believed him, fool!

Now you must give birth to a bastard—just as you yourself came to be!

Fool, silly fool!

Juel careened the draft horse from the top of the hill to the valley floor, then disappeared into the forest from whence she'd come.

Orion rode his destrier at a furious pace, thundering over the hills and down into the valleys. The ground was still damp from the recent rain and he followed the big Percheron's hoof marks easily.

He found her asleep cradled between two fallen trees, having covered her lower half with a blanket of leaves. In the gray twilight, as he came down off his horse, he could see that she'd been crying; the tears had made dirty tracks down her cheeks.

Coming down on one knee, Orion brushed his knuckles over her flushed face, his heart turning in his breast at the dejected look of her. She still wore Ranice's warm black gown, but no cloak, and he noticed she shivered every few moments.

"Juel." His voice was soft and low. "Why did you run away?"

Juel felt her body shivering, and when she reached down for more leaves to cover herself, her hand came in contact with warm flesh. She believed she dreamed a shining knight rescued her. Then a mantle was covering her and she was being carried, placed gently upon a horse, and then the warm body joined hers. They were moving through the forest, she thought hazily, but her eyes would not open, her body would not awaken.

Thunder rumbled in the distance, coming slowly but inevitably closer.

With Juel in his arms, across the saddle, Orion rode through the trees, the great Percheron following right after, its nose almost bumping the destrier's behind.

"Juel, wake up. I have found a place for us to stay the night. It's dark and a storm comes." A few drops of rain fell then, the only sound in the forest. Juel did not answer. "You will awaken once I build a fire and warm you."

Carrying her into an old woodsman's cabin, its occupant long departed, Orion placed her upon a dusty pallet, then covered her with the mantle and coverings of rabbit fur. After finding the tools to build a fire, he went out to gather more logs, and soon a blazing

419

warmth filled the old cabin. Then he went back out again to make a sling and locate some stones.

Juel was sitting up when he returned with a few rabbits he'd cleaned for their dinner. He wasn't surprised to find her glaring at him when he turned from the fire where he'd built a spit to roast the rabbits on.

"Why have you brought me here?" Juel looked not at him now but at the bright golden flames licking at the skinned rabbits. The delicious smell of food filled the small cabin, reaching her on the soft fur bed. Her stomach growled. "You haven't answered me yet."

"After we eat, then we'll talk." He went out again, carrying a water skin and cork, then returned with the bag bulging with fresh water from the stream nearby. "Now eat," he ordered after he'd set the cooked rabbit sprinkled with herbs at the foot of the bed.

Her arms crossed over her chest, Juel refused to eat the food or even look at it. "I'm not hungry, thank you."

"You lie. I heard your stomach growling not long ago."

She gave an unladylike snort. "That was thunder, can't you tell the difference." She ended without a question. She didn't care to talk much with him. "Get my horse. I wish to go home."

"Oh?" His black eyebrow lifted. "Where is home, Juel?"

With a huff, she turned her face to the wall. "I have a castle, you know. I needn't stay with you any longer. I'm a titled woman now, remember."

"I recall."

"You should!"

"Go ahead." He snatched the bowl of food from the bed. "Be my guest." He grinned as just then an ominous roll of thunder sounded and great splashes of rain hit the flimsy roof of straw and mud and wood slats. "You'd better get moving if you want to reach Hunter Castle two nights hence."

"Two nights!" She glared at him. "How would you know how to get there? Oh, never mind. No doubt you've already gone to look the place over, intending to add it to your properties once we'd married."

"What!?" Orion gaped at her. "I've no desire to add your holdings to mine. In fact, my castle is not really my own until my mother passes away. *She's* the mistress of Sutherland now."

"But you're the heir."

He came to stand beside her. "I thought I'd move into Hunter Castle with you," he said with a trace of laughter in his voice.

"I don't even know if it's livable. And I thought you said you had no desire to— Oh, you're making fun of—"

"Be quiet," he said as he pulled her head back with a handful of her own hair. "We get along best during lovemaking."

She slapped his hand away. "Don't touch me, Orion Sutherland. You so much as called me a whore—"

"I only asked." His eyebrows quirked above dark eyes. "So, what *were* you doing at the forge with Hugh? I know all about Yardley, that you sought him out to give you the key to release my mother from her tower prison."

She gasped. "Why did you ask and put me through torment then?" She shivered not with cold now, but with anger.

"In the heat of jealousy I forgot. But of your visits to the armor's I knew nothing."

Her nose went in the air. "Think what you will about Hugh. I tell you it was nothing . . . I just wanted to see how the armor was made." She would not tell him the truth, that she'd been having a special piece made for a time when he might need it. "Hugh is still there, why don't you go and speak with him?"

"What do you mean, he's still there?" His eyes searched her face, reaching into her thoughts. "Why wouldn't he be?"

She sat on the bed, her fingers tensed in her lap. "There was nothing between us. Believe this or not."

"What do you hide from me?" His voice was smooth but insistent. "Juel. Answer me."

How much should she tell concerning Clytie de Monteforte? That she met Clytie there in the forge? But what could have been her cousin's reason for being there? She didn't know how to answer. He interrogated her because he wanted her estate, and was trying to twist things for his own ends! her mind screamed. Not so! her heart whispered back.

Seeing her downcast expression, Orion felt a stab of guilt deep inside. He touched her hair with a tenderness he'd rarely felt until this young woman came into his life.

"I'm sorry I mistrusted your intentions in going to the forge. Maybe someday you'll tell me why you went there. For now, I can only say that my jealousy blinded my better judgment and this was the reason I put the question to you so harshly in front of Alfred and Ruark. Can you forgive me?"

Juel's eyes misted over. He, Orion, the forbidding dragon of Herstmonceux, a man who was always mean with drink, bad-tempered to all who got in his way, was now begging her forgiveness?

"I'll forgive you only if you allow all the orphans to stay on at The Keep . . . I mean, Sutherland," she said, smiling sweetly.

"Orphans? What is this?"

Suddenly Juel was all smiles and animation, her face glowing in the warmth of the blazing fire. "They won't be much trouble. I've put them to work already, even the smallest of them, a little girl of four. She can feed the animals and—"

"Whoa!" Orion held up his hand, then caressed the sweet lines of her face. "Who are all these children you speak of? Where do they come from? And how many are there?"

"Seven!" Juel said, bouncing on the bed with a youthful vivacity that made her look like a child herself. "They're all such good children, you'll hardly notice them at all."

Orion thought this over doubtfully. "Children who never laugh or play?" He looked into her eyes, wishing they could have children of their own one day.

"Oh, they laugh and play, but I'll make sure they don't do it to annoy you, when you are out training with your knights or trying to catch up on some sleep."

Orion kissed her throat, murmuring, "I love the sound of children playing." He lifted his head. "But you didn't tell me where they come from."

"The village. They've been orphans for several years,

since the raid before this last one. Some never knew their parents at all, dying from one sort of illness or the other."

"They can stay." He kissed the cord along her throat, then down further to the softness of her breasts. He groaned his delight over something new a little lower down. Suddenly his head lifted. "What is this roundness I feel?"

A warning sounded in her head: *Don't tell him about the child yet. You can't be sure of the pregnancy yourself. Wait until you've missed another monthly, for it might only be tension that's made you late.*

"I've put on some weight," Juel laughed with tenseness. She bit her lip and tried to make herself sound convincing. "I have been eating more food lately. You have just now noticed?"

"I was tired before when we made love."

He began kissing her all over, even her feet, which made her squeal with delight, for that was the most intimate place on her body, she believed. He kissed each and every toe, and when he was finished, he removed the damp black gown and tossed it onto the floor.

Juel helped him undress, too: his surcoat, his belt, his hose . . . everything. Her quick, excited hands moved over him and disrobed him. "Ah," she said when she was done. "England's most handsome knight."

"And England's most beautiful heiress," he whispered into her hair. "Put me inside you, Juel."

Her soft curves molded to the contours of his strong, lean body as she lay back with him atop her. She touched him and boldly guided him, as he'd asked. Her body arched as he came into her with one long, bold

424

thrust. She had forgotten how big he was. She purred with the burning, bladelike thrust that soon felt better, much better. She twined her legs around him. They moved together in a rhythm as old as the ancient fortresses scattered across England. When she met her pinnacle he was not far behind, clutching her hips as their bodies met in a thrilling kiss of ecstasy.

They lay together after they had peaked several times, mutual sighs of fulfillment coming deep from their throats. The fire blazed on as they slept, content, wrapped in each other's love.

Chapter Forty-Two

"It is a delight," Julia was telling Elizabeth Juel, "to watch Peter open an oyster, pry· rosy flesh from a lobster's claw, put just a little bit of honey on his rye cake. When I told him too much would make him fat, he started to sprinkle it lightly with lemon juice. Cabbage and turnips he still turns up his nose at!" She laughed, looking happy and lovely and young.

One night Juel was telling the orphans more stories around the great hearth, and everyone stopped what they were doing to listen. Even the big knights traversing the hall came to a standstill.

Autumn, with her red hair and deep violet eyes, listened just as intently as the younger ones; she was happy but still could not forget that her sisters were still missing. Orion smiled as Elizabeth Juel weaved her stories of enchantment, then turned to watch his mother, looking so happy and serene seated on a cushioned bench beside a much healthier looking Peter Reynaude.

Orion leaned back, trying to visualize himself in the past. At first everything was misty and splintered. He was remembering the corner of the room where he'd sat watching his mother and father. Yes, he could remember those times without consternation now.

He saw his mother, her auburn head bowed as she sewed busily. A basketful of smallclothes was beside her on the floor, the night candles making shadows on her lovely face, over her beautiful gown. She stitched with unbelievable speed. He saw his handsome father Colin, quill in hand, held like a weapon, so excited by his thoughts that he couldn't sit still for very long.

This picture faded and was replaced by another. He penetrated deeper and deeper into the landscape of his childhood. As he watched Juel's lovely mouth move with her story, half-forgotten impressions came to light in quick succession. He let his memory empty itself in a flood of small scenes remembered . . . of faces and happenings. Then something caught his attention . . .

The recollection of being in the woods at twilight. The underbrush was heavy. It was pathless and grew high over his head. Everywhere blue showed through the dark green of the foliage. He knew where he was.

In the forest near Sutherland Castle.

It had happened when he was a small boy. The place he stood was like a small enchanted island in the dark forest. It was friendly enough during daylight, but toward evening it became threatening. Someone, possibly his mother, had warned him not to go into the woods after sundown. She'd talked of wolves, the remnants of a great pack, she'd explained, that had come into the forest a hundred years before, come from the east. Demon creatures. They could be changed,

she'd added mysteriously, if you did not let y[...]
best you . . .

How hushed it was in the woods. He could stil[...]
Juel's voice, like the faint bubbling of spring wate[...]
past mingled with present . . .

He had gradually forgotten his mother's warning[...]
about the wolves. Farther and farther he had wandered
into the green forest depths. The blueberries and
whimberries lured him on, masses of small round fruits
set against a background of deep green. He wandered
from one bush to the next until he was deeper into the
bushy, ferny tangle. Here the wilderness was a primeval
wood and the boy imagined himself as a fairy prince
bravely venturing into a dragon's thicket haunt to
rescue the fairy beauty. He was caught up by a spirit of
adventure. He felt he must conquer the woods. His
tunic was torn by twigs, but still he lunged forward . . .

". . . making dead limbs crackle as he tripped over
them," Juel was telling, watching the children's rapt
gazes. "The woods were swallowing him up. Hours
passed, and to the boy time stood still. Suddenly a wild
dove called to him. There was one long cooing and then
all was deathly still."

Orion listened, to Juel, to his reverie, every nerve at
attention. Then the bird cooed again. Now the boy
looked all around. He saw that the woods had changed
somewhat. Shadows had grown much longer. Golden
flecks of light dappled the leafy earth. He felt that
someone watched him. Fearful now, he ran with all his
might, tripping over his berry basket, and all the blue
treasure spilled out. In the late afternoon everything
took on a threatening and even bewitched appearance.

Juel went on. "The boy felt trapped in a region of

s, and cruel dwarfs who lived under the
v stones seemed to have faces, sneaking
oods would not give him up. He was
yrinth."

w, sitting in the hall surrounded by knights,
n, and loved ones, Orion could vividly recall his
ror. Remembering it took his breath away, even
now. He tried to smile at Elizabeth Juel as her lips
continued to move in her storytelling, but the pangs of
anxiety stalked his memory . . .

"The boy threw himself on the ground and wept
bitterly. That had not held back the night. The doves
had hushed and the owls did not whoo-whoo now.
Shadows crept together and darkness seemed to rise
from the ground. The boy lay down in the soft moss
and wrapped his tunic about him. He closed his eyes
and prayed that God might guide him back home when
it came light again and protect him while he slept."

Even now Orion remembered how a feeling of relief
washed over him, all his fear gone. The night settled
down and he had slept. He awoke out of the very deep
sleep and what he had seen made him weak with
wonder. The woods had looked enchanted. An unreal
light filtered down from above and branches shone like
pure silver . . .

". . . the grass all hung with spiderwebs, was glistening. He raised himself on one elbow and felt the
coolness, smelled the night's fragrance. He got up,
shivered again, looked around and saw two unicorns . . ."

Wolves.

Orion jerked and looked full into Juel's eyes, saw her
mouth move with the word. She had said Unicorns; he

had thought, Wolves.

Looking at her incredulously, he said, "Go on. Please." He sat up straighter now, realizing with awe she was telling his story.

Only the fear was gone. Now that Elizabeth Juel was here, all traces of fear had vanished.

She smiled at him. She continued her story. "A thrill of joy rushed over him at the sight of the . . . unicorns. The world was so peaceful, different from the daylight world. It was just as beautiful as day, but different and lovely in its own way. He followed the beautiful unicorns, and in the moonlight saw his own towers revealed. Home, shimmering under the moon. He was never so relieved to be at home. Never had he ever felt so completely sure that the world was God's world and that he, together with all things, rested in God's hands." She smiled at the children. "The End!"

Juel's and Orion's eyes caught and held.

Gazing romantically at each other, as if they were alone, Jay and Dawn saw all the love they had ever desired from another human being shining in each other's eyes.

"Oh . . . my," muttered Julia, dabbing at her eyes with the square of linen Peter handed to her. She looked down then and saw that Peter was holding her hand, and she knew his eyes were filled with love.

The children were delighted. They all sighed as children do when a story of enchantment has ended. *But was it a story? Or was it true?* The question was in the hearts of them all.

Plans for a huge wedding were being made, and by

the end of this, the ninth month of the year, they'd almost been completed. Orion received word from King Henry that the battle was over with and they'd won against the French.

Orion sat with the messenger who'd come, and the king's man told of the battle of Agincourt.

Harry sent his thanks for the use of Orion's knights and his appreciation of assistance in spying on the enemy, telling of their weak points and positions as they'd gathered to cross the Channel.

Another message was brought to Sutherland Castle, this one from Clytie de Monteforte, now happily reunited with her father. Juel had received the letter in secret, by a person in a dark cloak who came to her in the privacy of the gardens. He—presumably—left as quickly as he'd arrived.

No one else saw Elizabeth Juel read the letter.

She looked up from the paper, teary-eyed, knowing it was time she told Orion of her pregnancy. After all, she couldn't keep telling him she had gained weight, and nothing more than that. They had not made love since the time in the forest. Although she wanted him fiercely, she told him she'd rather wait till after their wedding. She must tell him soon.

What was there to fear? He loved children.

The time for letting go of all secrets had come, she thought as she felt her slightly more rounded stomach.

There was only one other secret she must keep until the time was ripe. The shining piece was ready. Hugh was gone and he'd left it for her, in a private place where she kept it hidden, dry, and polished every day in readiness.

King Henry's war was over, but Elizabeth Juel knew

that theirs, Sutherland's, would soon begin.

She knew Scardon was on his way. As did Orion. They both felt it.

Soon he would come. And she was ready for him.

Think of the devil!

Orion was informed that John Scardon was on his way to him. He also knew that Scardon would try to snatch back the holdings with a large band of knights that rode with him. This would be his brigand company, those who left their smoking tracks of pillage and massacre across the countryside.

The message was brought to Orion from his man-at-arms.

Scardon was a robber baron. He and his men were mired in crime and sin, blaspheming God everywhere they went. They rode in great routs in random parts of England, took possession of manors and lands, ravishing women and damsels, bringing them into strange counties.

Orion's brow was dark as he paced the new solar chamber. "Now I believe the Meaux sisters have come into the hands of Scardon's brigand company."

He said this almost to himself even though he looked back at Juel where she stood by the windows wearing the new gown he had had the seamstress make for her. It was red, with gold trim, contrasting vividly with her black, shining hair. She wore her hair loose, swirling in masses of tendrils to her waist. Some strands covered the front of her where they trailed downward in flowing midnight spirals.

She looked wild and beautiful and elegant.

"How to tell Autumn," Elizabeth Juel was saying thoughtfully to no one in particular.

Later, in the great hall, she paced, walking from hearth to far wall. She stopped, laying her hands on the table, looking up at Ruark and Orion. They had stood and begun to pace themselves, and now stopped beside her.

Sudden anger lit her eyes to deep green. "They beat and maim the people. They slay the men for possession of their wives and their goods. They hold some for ransom, and come before the justices in their sessions in disguise. They go to court with such force that the justices are so afraid, they are even unable to uphold the law."

"Why can't they be caught?" Jay asked, watching thoughtfully as Dawn poured some verjuice. "There must be something to down such a force."

Orion suddenly clapped his hand over the rim of his cup of apple drink. "Our force is greater now that Henry is done with my auxiliary knights. We will crush him. We only wait."

"They must be crushed soon!" Elizabeth Juel cried. "In England the land is inundated by murders and the feet of men are swift to do the shedding of blood. Scardon has made men insane with killing."

"Aye," said Ruark. "And Scardon will come here."

Julia looked up from the crust of brown bread she'd been tearing into small portions. She couldn't steady her erratic pulse. "So many robberies remain unpunished, when in other countries murderers and thieves are commonly hanged," Julia softly interjected. Peter leaned to put his arm about her and she looked at him with love.

"We'll get them ourselves!" Jay shouted, banging his tankard on the table.

Ruark snorted. "Just you try and find them. They are like slugs in the dark of moon. You see how they went from their pillaging in the village of Herst."

Orion nodded. "Yes. But we caught up with them in the forest."

Duncan straddled a plain wooden chair. "The forest, where they ambushed us and gave Orion that wound."

"It still troubles me," Orion said with a grimace. "In times such as these."

Juel looked at him, smiling with love and concern.

"He will come. We won't have to find him," Orion said, seeing his mother's hand tremble slightly.

Scardon can just try to take this keep! Orion thought angrily. Hatred for the man who'd put his mother in isolation, lonely and deprived of friends and family, had taken from him his mind, though his sanity returned day by day, thanks to Elizabeth Juel.

Orion looked around and saw all the familiar faces, his mother, Julia Sutherland . . . then again, he thought as he looked at Peter Reynaude with his mother, should he and Julia wed, she'd become a Reynaude!

The idea made matters most interesting concerning their properties. He would think on this later.

Howell Armstrong entered the hall in a clatter of weapons. He stood stiffly, sheepish to even glance Juel's way after that stolen kiss. But there was something most important to announce.

"Scardon is in the area!"

Suddenly Orion's cup went flying from the table as he lurched to his feet. "Where?" he ground out.

"At the Herst Inn where they carouse even now. They've turned the place into shambles! A messenger, a cowardly being, was here moments ago bringing communication from him."

Orion wiped his face with his hand. "Send this word to him without delay: 'Do not approach this estate. It is no longer yours or in your possession . . .'"

"'. . . You will perish should you come upon it without right,'" read Scardon. He gave a derisive laugh, reached out and pinched a serving girl spitefully as she passed by, shaking in her much-pawed skirts.

"What will we do now?" Hadwin asked, seeing that Scardon's eyes had turned cold as ice.

"Idiot, you don't remember much, do you?" Scardon asked with bitter sarcasm. "I've a woman locked in the tower. We will get to her before he does. I might as well tell you." He sighed tiredly. "She is Julia Sutherland. I locked her in there years and years ago. She's no doubt a wilted hag by now. Lydia, the stupid wench, has been taking care of her needs. Yardley stands by and guards her door." He chuckled nastily. "They all fear me, including that handsome idiot Orion Sutherland. A drunken fool, even years ago. I should have dropped him in the well when he was just a pup as I'd planned to do one day."

"What message would you have me return?" asked the wretched man who'd been forced to deliver the first one to Orion Sutherland's man.

Scardon sneered. "Tell him I fear nothing he says."

His voice was cold. "I hold the key."

Then his laughter filled the rafters of the inn, and all the serving maids, even the innkeeper himself, stopped what they were doing to cross themselves.

Lydia was crying, and she wouldn't stop no matter what Elizabeth Juel did to try to comfort her. She stopped to sniff. "I knew the curse would be upon us. Ohhh, the evil one is back."

Rajahr patted her on the back. "But the curse has been broken," he explained in a gentle voice.

"No," she wailed. "It has only brought him back to us!"

"Not so," Elizabeth Juel said. She turned to Orion and whispered, drawing him aside, "What does Scardon say now?"

"He says he comes and to prepare to do battle."

There was a strange light in Juel's eyes. "He wears heavy armor?"

"He stole much of it from the forge."

This was good, she thought. Clytie also said in her letter that she hid in the forest that night after a surprised Orion Sutherland had let her go, that she had watched as Scardon and his men took the armor away with them.

"Armor will make him and his men too heavy to fight."

"What are you saying, woman?" Howell asked her. "Armor is what England's knights chewed upon while still in their swaddling. Years ago—"

"Enough, Howell."

Orion began to pace again. "We need more men," he

said as he halted in the middle of the room.

Elizabeth Juel blurted without thinking, "Send word to my relative, Piers de Monteforte. He will aid . . . us . . . in . . . this baaa—"

Orion spun about to face her. "Oh? Your uncle, hmm?"

With red face Juel put her back to him. Oh-oh. Now she'd gone and done it.

Orion crashed into the solar just as Elizabeth Juel raced to a chest and pulled out the letter from Clytie. Pressing it to her chest, she whirled to find him standing there. "Here!" She thrust it out at him. "Go ahead, read it if you want to so badly!"

"No. You read it to me."

She fell upon the window seat then, and told him everything. But not the secret about her shining piece. That she would keep until the time came.

"Juel, you were consorting with the enemy."

"Not so. Clytie is my cousin."

His face was dark as thunderclouds. "What about Hugh? Now he is gone, escaped just like Clytie de Monteforte."

Juel gasped. "But you let her go. The letter says it all." She snatched it from him, but before she could read the words, he snatched it back.

"You've kept secrets, Juel."

She lifted one shoulder. "And so have you. What about the messenger from Baron Hunter's barrister?" A corner of her mouth quirked. "What about that? Was that a secret or wasn't it?"

"Juel—"

"No." She picked up her pretty skirts and whirled from the solar. "I'll speak to you when you've regained consciousness."

Orion shook his head. Unconscious, was he? He looked up into the rays of sunlight streaming into the solar. Most likely she was right.

He'd show her. It was time to do away with John Scardon, the evil influence in the lives of them all!

Chapter Forty-Three

"I come to claim what is rightfully mine!" Scardon shouted across the battlefield, squinting as the sun slanted in his cold eyes.

"And I come to keep what is rightfully mine!" Orion shouted back, then added, "You lie! Sutherland belongs to me and—" He bit off, almost mentioning his mother.

Scardon cursed when he saw no fear in Orion's eyes as he had in the past, when Orion had been much younger.

The two approached each other on their horses, Orion sitting high on his destrier. Orion glared at Scardon, laughing at something Elizabeth Juel had said, as he looked at the full suit of heavy armor Scardon wore. Orion himself wore only his leathers and carried nothing but his sword.

The younger man's voice rang out. "For my king, and my country, the land I sit upon is now Sutherland! And for one other, my mother, I shall slay you upon this battlefield this very day. You have taken from my mother her honor and have slain my father and made me something I was not! This day you will pay!"

"Who has removed the curse I put upon The Keep?" Scardon snarled in a loud voice, his head whirling like a mad dog's, looking to Orion's men but seeing no face of secrecy there. Fools, they wore no armor!

Scardon paled as he looked into Orion's determined eyes, knowing that all the black deeds he'd done before were now upon him. He realized this would be a fight to the death as he rode with haste back to his pack of men, circled in readiness for the moment of battle.

Orion prayed he had enough men. There'd been no time to send to Piers de Monteforte for auxiliary knights. Orion had his own back from the king, but he worried about the younger ones now as they steeled themselves courageously for the fight.

Arrows flew from Orion's men as Scardon gave the bloodcurdling cry for combat. They fought from their horses with sword upon sword in violent clashings of battle. Even though Orion's men were outnumbered, they fought valiantly, dispatching men one by one.

Fighting on in bloody combat, the odds were now changing and it was almost an even fight as the horsemen reared their mounts into each other, falling and fighting now on the ground, each in their own pitted battle against the other.

Orion and Scardon battled on until their horses clashed with such violence that both men were knocked to the ground. Orion sprang to his feet and Scardon, the older of the two, fought almost as quickly and agilely. Their swords clanged like bells ringing in a church tower, but harsher, more discordant.

It was the sound of blood and war and evil hatred.

The younger Orion fought with fierce determination and even though his old wound pained him, he pushed on. Orion feared no defeat, though his men were falling left and right, as were several of Scardon's. Orion knew his men would fight to the death.

As the two hilts sang together the men glared at each other, both their hands attached to their swords. Orion was the first to push back away from Scardon.

A horse gone wild with fear suddenly careened, knocking Orion to the ground. As Orion rolled to his back, he looked up to see Scardon standing above him like a towering dark oak, hair like gnarled, dark branches, sword held with both hands raised above his head. Scardon's fingers clutched like the talons of a hawk meaning to rip apart its prey.

Scardon had the upper hand. But only for seconds.

At that moment a brilliant light struck Scardon in the eyes, blinding and bathing him from head to foot in a nimbus of shimmering rays.

Scardon's hand slipped, one inch, two.

In that briefest of moments Orion thrust his sword upward, then straight, driving the blade through Scardon's chest and out the back, full hilt.

As blood trickled down the blade onto Orion's hands, Scardon looked downward, seeing nothing but a spot of relentless light before his eyes.

"Who has removed the curse I put upon The Keep?" he gasped. Then he yelled, more weakly this time. He gnashed his teeth and blood trickled from the corner of his mouth. His breath was caught in a stranglehold in his throat as he looked beyond Orion.

The younger warrior followed where Scardon's deathly stare went, Orion turning slowly, watching the other askance.

Now Orion turned fully, looking in the direction the beam of light had come from. There, a single warrior stood atop the eastern crest of hill, in a suit of light chain mail and a thick skullcap of leather. The knight was shining all over, golden, silver, magenta, with the sinking sun sending up its glory into the sky.

Orion saw the slim figure standing with a shining shield polished to a mirror finish. He made out the spikes of three stars as it was lowered to the ground.

"It is I who have broken the curse! And now," the mellifluous golden voice called, "damn you, damn you, Scardon, you and your pack, all to hell!"

Scardon lifted his blade one last time to cry weakly, "By the rood!" He was silenced then as he toppled like a felled tree.

Orion heard the thud as Scardon hit the ground. It must be so, he thought: Scardon's end.

He looked to the one on the rise again. From behind the glimmering shield, held against the lone knight's waist again, tipping this way and that, blindingly, he could make out the slim outline of a woman.

Ah, a very special woman.

The knight in chain mail shifted with the shield. The sun's rays slanted again to grant a small favor to Orion's once-again outnumbered company and fell full on Scardon's evil brigands.

The sun on the shield had blinded the one who would have ended Orion's life . . . and now Scardon's men were blinded, too, by fear, and fell back, running for their lives, believing there was a curse upon them!

Some stayed to fight, whirling to the back of Orion's men. Then, seeing their fallen leader Scardon, with a sword clear through him, they ran like the true cowards they were, scattering to the four winds with Orion's men in pursuit. They could not allow such murdering thieves to escape. That was the thought in all their minds.

Orion now turned his full attention on the figure moving toward him. As she slowly approached, skirting the men who had fallen in battle, he walked with haste to meet her.

They met amidst the fallen bodies on the battlefield and she stood before him, tears of joy and victory streaming down her face.

Elizabeth Juel hoisted the shield with the three stars struck upon its steel. "For Sutherland!" she cried. Then softly, "Always."

Orion took it from her, clasping it in one hand with pride as he put his other around her waist and pulled her toward him. "So, my beautiful warrior, this is what you were sneaking away to the forge for, to fashion a mighty shield."

Juel's smile was of victory and sweetness. "I meant this for you, Orion. For us, your mother, our friends, all of us at Sutherland."

Howell Armstrong came to them, going down to one knee before Juel. "Forgive me, my lady." He took her hand, pushed up the saggy chain mail, and kissed her hand. Then he arose.

Orion eyed them closely, with some jealousy. "What was that all about?" he asked after Howell had gone back to the men. "I've never seen Howell that red in the face, or that humble."

She looked up at him. "He, too, wondered about Hugh."

"I see" was all Orion said. Pushing back her coif of leather, watching her glorious hair spill free, he gazed at her tenderly and smiled down at the shield. "This piece you've fashioned saved my life, and that of many of my men. You will be with me, as this shield of armor will be, throughout the rest of our days. You will be my bride. We will join our lands. The Baron and Baroness Sutherland!"

Juel and Orion held each other strongly as they stared at the death all around them.

"This," he said proudly, hefting the shining piece. "This will be our son and daughter's shield also. We'll have it stamped with the knightly heraldry of the two rearing unicorns, with twining leaves between."

"Yes, Orion. And the stars are already there. The additions will be most beautiful."

He cleared his throat gruffly. "For our children," he said again.

"Yes—I heard you." She looked up at him quickly. "Then you know?"

"I know." He laid the flat of his hand upon her rounded belly, more pronounced now beneath the chain mail.

They began to walk, arms about each other, the shield before them. They looked toward the manor as they topped the rise. The sun was setting behind Sutherland, outlining it with gold. Smoke rose from the cookfires, spiraling with the autumn wind.

"It's as if a dragon breathes fire and smoke there." Juel watched the sun glisten through a tall, leaded window, sending a bright shaft from one side to the other. "Hmm . . ." she murmured, an idea brewing.

"I heard that," Orion said.

"I was just thinking."

"I know. That could be dangerous." He laughed then, meaning it as a jest to relieve tension.

She sighed as she tilted her head in the direction of Sutherland.

"My bride-to-be, the storyteller."

But he saw it, too. The window, like a dragon's eye, shining like a jewel.

With pride and love in her heart Juel gazed at Sutherland in the dying sun. "A victory for us all, not only in war, but in life as well." Knowing that Orion Sutherland had laid to rest the evil and bitterness and loneliness he'd known for so many years.

He turned to kiss her full on the lips. Then he nibbled her ear. "You, my love, will have such stories to tell now. To our children."

"Yes." She leaned to press into him fully. "Many."

Elizabeth Juel walked ahead of him, and he followed, one eyebrow cocked as he puzzled over that last word.

DISCOVER DEANA JAMES!